BORN OF NIGHT

TITLES BY SHERRILYN KENYON
(listed in correct reading order)

Fantasy Lover
Night Pleasures
Night Embrace
Dance with the Devil
Kiss of the Night
Night Play
Seize the Night
Sins of the Night
Unleash the Night
Dark Side of the Moon
Devil May Cry
Dream-Hunter
Upon the Midnight Clear
Dream Chaser
Acheron
One Silent Night
Dream Warrior
Bad Moon Rising

ANTHOLOGIES

Midnight Pleasures
Stroke of Midnight
My Big Fat Supernatural Wedding
Love at First Bite
Dead After Dark

The Dark-Hunter Companion

BORN OF NIGHT

SHERRILYN KENYON

St. Martin's Paperbacks

This is a work of fiction. All of the characters, organizations, and events portrayed in this novel are either products of the author's imagination or are used fictitiously.

BORN OF NIGHT

For information address St. Martin's Press, 175 Fifth Avenue, New York, NY 10010.

ISBN: 978-1-61523-615-2

Printed in the United States of America

St. Martin's Paperbacks are published by St. Martin's Press, 175 Fifth Avenue, New York, NY 10010.

For Buddy.
Thank you for believing in me.
I miss you, big brother, and I always will.

AUTHOR'S NOTE

Authors will always tell you that every book they write is special; that they all hold a tender place in our hearts. This is very true, but some of them are particularly precious.

For me, this book is one of them. Nykyrian and Syn were actually my childhood playmates. As a latchkey kid, I used to turn the kitchen chairs on their backs and pretend I was flying through space with my best friends by my side. I know it sounds silly, but I was hooked and I adored them.

Over the years, I wrote down many adventures I took with them, and when I was in college and had decided to write my first "real" novel, i.e., one that I was actually going to submit to publishers, there was no one else I wanted to write about.

I spent a year drafting *Born of Night* by hand— yeah, that was entertaining. Anyone who has ever attended a signing knows how illegible my writing is. During Christmas break 1986, I sat down to type it out and decipher my horrible penmanship. Of course, I didn't own a typewriter and was trying to find one I could borrow.

As with so many other times in my life, my older brother came to my rescue by borrowing one from his roommate. I spent every spare minute, when I wasn't working at my jobs, typing the manuscript. When I finished, my brother came for the typewriter, and I can still remember the smile on his face when he said, "I know it's a winner, baby. I can't wait to read it."

My brother died a few weeks later and I didn't have the heart to send the manuscript out. It would be three years before I'd find the courage to pursue my writing again—and to that I owe two very special people in my life. Diana Porter Hillock, my best friend from high school, and my husband, Ken. But for them, I'm not sure I'd have ever written again. I know without Ken buying me a Brother Wordprocessor (we couldn't afford a computer), I would definitely not be writing today. I can never, ever thank the two of them enough for the gift they gave me. For the precious gifts of love, support, and companionship that my husband continues to give to me every day—I definitely don't deserve him. I hope everyone has someone in their life like my Ken, because I don't know how I'd make it through without him.

Born of Night was bought in 1992, but wasn't published until 1996. There's a long story there and maybe one day I'll tell it. It was the last book I published until 1999. Another long story that you can read about on my website.

It is one of only three novels I've ever had to go out of print, and thanks to St. Martin's, all of them will be back in circulation in the next few months. Thank you, SMP, Monique, Matthew, Sally, and Jen for giving me the chance to soar and for all you, and the rest of the team, do day in and day out to get the books to the stores. I couldn't ask for a greater group of people to work with.

Those of you who have read or who own the original *Born of Night* will notice the size difference. In this version, I was able to return the original scenes to the book that were edited out because they were deemed too harsh for the market at the time it was originally published. Because the original League books were all released by different publishers, I also had to break them apart, change character names and such to make the series look like it wasn't related. All that's gone and the books now read like the series they were intended to be.

I hope you enjoy your adventure in the Ichidian Universe. This is the place where I grew up and where I roamed the streets with an assassin, a thief, and a bounty hunter. Yeah, I was a really strange child, LOL. And I hope you'll return here with next month's release of *Born of Fire*.

—Sherrilyn Kenyon

PROLOGUE

"I quit The League tonight."

Dr. Sheridan Belask paused at the deep, thickly accented voice coming out of the darkest corner of his office. He looked up from the electronic medical files he was reviewing on top of his obsidian glass desk, but couldn't see even the smallest trace of the man hidden in the shadows.

He was used to that.

As a trained League assassin, Nykyrian Quiakides was literally one with the blackest night. No one ever saw him coming or going.

They only felt the sting of death as he dealt it to them.

Even though Sheridan was a doctor sworn to save any life he could, this brutal killer was the only man he'd ever trusted at his back and with his family.

Or more to the point, the only man he'd ever trusted with the most deeply held secrets of a past he'd been running from his whole life.

"You can't quit. You can only retire." A euphemism that meant ritual suicide whenever assassin duties became more than a League solider could mentally bear or their bodies became too scarred or too damaged to carry out their missions any longer.

No one voluntarily left The League.

No one.

Nykyrian stepped out of the shadows so that the dim light highlighted the white blond hair that was braided down his back—an assassin's mark of honor. His solid, flat black battle suit hugged every sharp curve of his well-muscled body. The outline of daggers were embroidered in dark blood red down the sleeves—the only external designation an assassin bore. Nykyrian's daggers held a crown above each hilt, letting the universe know he was the most lethal of his kind. A command assassin of the first rank.

As always, Nykyrian was calm and watchful of the shadows as if expecting someone like him to come for him at any moment. Somber. Cold. Lethal. Traits that had been drilled into him as a child. In all the years Sheridan had known him, Nykyrian had never once smiled. Never once broken that staunch military training that had left him emotionally bankrupt.

The most disturbing thing of all was the fact that his eyes were hidden behind a pair of opaque shades, a safeguard used by military assassins to keep those around them on edge, since there was no way of telling where they were looking or what they were thinking.

Or, more precisely, who the assassin was targeting.

Nykyrian's handsome features were as stoic as his rigid stance. "I refuse to complete this mission."

Sheridan frowned in confusion. This wasn't the steadfast, merciless man he knew. The one who didn't hesitate at any brutality.

"Yeah, right. You have to complete it." Harsh though it was, it was the law of the world in which they lived. Once a target was given, it was given. Succeed or die. There was no third option.

The last thing Sheridan wanted was to see the only

brother he'd ever known ruthlessly hunted and executed. Better someone, anyone, else die than Nykyrian.

"They sent me after a child." Nykyrian's tone was flat, deadpan.

Sheridan's blood ran cold as he finally understood the one line neither of them would ever cross no matter the necessity. The one line that had once saved Sheridan's life when Nykyrian would have killed *him*.

Sheridan glanced at the holocube a few inches from his hand where his own infant son smiled out with an untainted innocence neither of them had ever known.

Nykyrian continued, "The League wanted an entire family swabbed."

That was icy cold, but far from unheard of. It should probably bother Sheridan that his best friend killed for a living, but then, given his own brutal past, it didn't affect him at all.

The world was harsh and it was bitter, especially to those who couldn't protect themselves. He had firsthand, intimate knowledge of that fact, and it'd left as many scars on him as it had on Nykyrian.

Besides, he knew the side of Nykyrian that no one else had ever seen. The side of him that wouldn't harm a child no matter the cost to himself.

Nykyrian was nothing like the monsters in their pasts, and neither was he.

"If you don't kill them, The League *will* kill you."

Nykyrian cocked his head at a sudden noise outside. It sounded like the whisper of a patient lift whizzing by. He didn't speak again until it'd passed and he was sure no one was coming into Sheridan's office. "I swabbed the father before I realized there was a child in the house. She was asleep in her mother's arms when I went for her."

"And you refused to kill them?"

Nykyrian gave a subtle nod. "The mother and child are safe in a place where The League and their enemies will never find them."

"Are you . . ." Sheridan didn't bother finishing the sentence. Of course Nykyrian was sure. He didn't make those kinds of mistakes. Sheridan's current life and safety were living proof of that. "What are you going to do?"

"What I've always done. Stand and fight."

Sheridan let out a bitter laugh. How easy Nykyrian made it sound, but he knew what The League was capable of. They both did. "They'll come for you with everything they have."

"And I will fight them with everything they taught me to be."

A chill went down his spine. What they had taught Nykyrian to be was a predator of the first order of insanity. May the gods help them all. This was the one man who wouldn't go down without a costly head count. Nykyrian was the best they'd ever trained and The League had no idea exactly what it had created.

But Sheridan knew. He'd looked into the eyes of Nykyrian's madness and seen the horrors those shades concealed. He knew the rage that they both kept under a tight leash for fear of what it could make them do.

The lengths they would go to, to make sure no one ever hurt them again. They might appear calm on the surface, but inside, their battered souls screamed for vengeance and release.

Most of all they screamed for appeasement.

Nykyrian moved forward and placed a small silver disk on his desk. He pushed it toward Sheridan. "I've erased every trace of our friendship and every part of your past. You won't see me again." *For your protec-*

tion and for the protection of your family. Nykyrian
didn't have to say the words. Sheridan knew the un-
breakable bond they shared.

Brothers to the end, even through the fires of hell
and beyond.

Nykyrian took a step back toward the shadows.

"Wait." Sheridan rose to his feet.

Nykyrian hesitated.

"If you need me, *aridos*," he said, his voice tight with
sincerity as he used the Ritadarion word for brother, "I
will be there for you."

Nykyrian's tone was still deadpan and emotionless.
"If I need you, *aridos,* I'll be dead before I can make
the call."

And then he was gone like a ghostly whisper on a
harried breeze.

Ill with what his friend had done, but understanding
it completely, Sheridan sat down and pulled the disk to
him. He cracked it open to find the small chip that all
assassins had embedded in their bodies. It was what
The League used to keep track of them. Nykyrian must
have dug it out of his flesh and crushed it to keep them
from finding him. The final act of severing himself
from their ties.

An act that in and of itself was a death sentence.

He cringed in sympathetic pain, remembering the
day when he'd dug a similar device out of his own young
body. The blood, the pain . . . There were some memories that never faded over time. They were too brutal to
be forgotten.

And what an eerie memento given the fact that this
chip was what had led to their friendship . . . He would
think his friend sentimental if it wasn't for the laugh-
ableness of that.

Closing his eyes, he held the chip in his fist, wishing

things had been different, that *they* had been different. That they had been born one of those normal people Sheridan treated in the hospital wings every day. People who had no idea of what horrors truly existed in this universe.

Yet he was proud that, given all Nykyrian had been through, he'd still retained his soul.

That through it all, the monsters had never taken his will or his decency. Everything else had been stripped out of him just as it had Sheridan.

Everything.

And because of Nykyrian, he was living a life he'd only dreamed of having. He owed everything to that man.

A man who most likely wouldn't live to see the coming dawn.

He released a long, disgusted breath. Life wasn't fair. It was something he'd learned at the back of his father's fist in early childhood. All he could hope was that Nykyrian would finally find the peace that had always eluded them both.

Even if he had to die to find it.

CHAPTER 1

Nine years later

She'd been kidnapped!

Kiara Zamir came awake with indignant anger riding her hard. Even now, she could feel the cold, rough grip on her arms and mouth, feel the bite of the injector as the drug sped through her bloodstream and quickly rendered her unconscious. Her abductors had moved so fast, she'd had no chance to call for help.

Or better yet, fight.

Crippin' cowards! She hated people who attacked like that. At least be a man and face her. But no . . . they'd resorted to the lowest means of capture. Sneaking around in the dark to take her while she slept.

There was nothing in the world she hated more than those who hid in the shadows, waiting to prey on people. Assassins, kidnappers, muggers, rapists, etcetera, they were all worthless, soulless scum who deserved nothing but pain and death.

Now, her head ached terribly as the last remnants of the drug wore off. An acrid smell filled her senses, choking her with its stench. Her throat was so dry, she could barely swallow as she tried to lick her dry lips to keep them from cracking.

She tried not to breathe deeply as she opened her eyes to confront who or whatever held her prisoner.

To her relief, she was still dressed in her pink nightgown, lying face down on a rotting mattress.

Ew, nasty . . .

There was no one else in the room and no sound warning her there was anyone nearby. Thank God for small favors. It would give her time to plot an escape or at the very least a counterattack.

With a grimace of distaste, she pushed herself up and nearly fell as a wave of nausea and dizziness buzzed through her head. She caught herself against the wall next to her, a roughened spot of rust scraping the palm of her hand.

"Great," she mumbled. "So much for equilibrium. Bloody bastards." At least they hadn't bothered to bind her hands or feet. No doubt they assumed she'd be like other women of her station, too terrified and docile to fight them.

But if they thought she was going to blithely wait around for them to return to kill her at their leisure, they were sorely mistaken. She may have been born a princess, but docility wasn't in her blood and neither was patience. Not to mention, she'd learned many tricks over the years while living with her overprotective military father, including the ability to pick a good lock.

As well as how to beat an attacker into the ground.

A determined grimace settled over her face as she headed toward the door on unsteady feet. True, it'd been years since she'd bypassed the intense security and picked the locks on her house to sneak outside and meet her friends after curfew, but she was sure she would remember how.

She had to.

Besides, the chance that this rusted-out junker had

the latest in security was slim to none. If they couldn't afford a clean mattress and repairs, they surely couldn't pay the exorbitant fees a security company charged to update their systems.

Reaching the door, Kiara ran her hand over the smooth keypad. Very old indeed. How quaint. It reminded her of the locks on her grandfather's house from twenty years ago.

She looked around for anything that might give her a clue about the key code, but there were no numbers listed anywhere. Nothing personal about her attackers other than what they ate and how filthy they were.

Ugh! There was no use in simply guessing random number sequences since that could very well lock her out completely and trap her here. It might even gas her back into unconsciousness.

Or death.

One could never be too sure what tricks a lowlife might use.

"I'll have to rewire you." If she could find a means of unbolting the lock from the wall . . .

With a sigh, Kiara glanced about the room, noting the inordinate amount of garbage strewn across the floor. She wrinkled her nose in distaste of the disgusting odor. The thick, steel walls were covered by huge spots of rust and corrosion. How in the universe had this craft ever passed space inspection? It wasn't fit to carry the stinking garbage offending her, let alone human occupants.

They must have greased a major palm.

"Suck it up, baby," she said under her breath. "You have to find something for that lock and get out of here." Surely there was an escape shuttle or pod she could find and launch.

Heck, at this point, she'd be willing to eject herself

into space and float home—at least if she could find a
suit that would protect her from the vacuum of space.

She curled her lip at the nastiness as she kicked at a
pile near her, looking for something she could use on
the door. *I'd rather be eaten alive than call this place
home . . .*

There was a pile of half-gnawed food under a small
towel. "Ah, gross."

One would think the sheer disgustingness of this
mess would kill them. Where were flesh-eating para-
sites when she needed them?

Suddenly she heard footsteps approaching in the corridor outside. Even more determined than before, she
cast her gaze around, searching for a weapon.

Nothing but the wilted garbage met her sight.

Kiara growled deep in her throat. The only help the
garbage offered was the possibility her kidnappers might
faint from the stench.

If only *she* were so lucky. They probably smelled
worse than the garbage did.

Clenching her teeth, she pressed herself against the
wall by the door and waited to attack them when they
entered.

CHAPTER 2

"I can't wait to get some pleasure out of this," a man said, his voice slowly drawing near her room. "Did you see her? That tight body is the stuff of legends."

Kiara narrowed her gaze as rage and fear consumed her. No one would ever make her feel powerless again.

Ever.

"I don't know, Chenz," another man spoke. "I think we oughta wait till we get further out. I keep thinking about Poll's message that Nemesis is after us. We need to take that seriously. Don't get me wrong, I want a piece of her too, but I'd rather wait until we're safe."

Her vision dimmed with fury. They might kill her, but she intended to take a large piece of them with her on her way out the door.

Chenz's laugh echoed in the hallway. The arrogant sound sent a shiver down her spine. "Nemesis ain't nothing to fear. We done been paid, I say we ought to enjoy every minute of this."

The gears hummed in the door as it slowly slid upward.

Kiara tensed, waiting to pounce.

Two of the nastiest beings she'd ever seen walked inside. Yeah, their stench beat out the garbage and then some. Why did she have to be right on that point? It was enough to make her gag. Had they never taken a bath in their putrid lives?

She conceded they were human, though neither did honor to her race.

Kiara curled her lip at the shorter one, wondering how he could stand to look at his ugly, warted face long enough to shave. But then, by the amount of stubble on his pudgy jowls, she could tell he didn't look too often.

The man at his side was only a few inches taller. His long, sharp, angular features reminded her of one of the beasties her nurse used to frighten her with when she was a child.

Their eyes mirrored a coldness in their souls that chilled her own.

"Well, where is she?" It was Chenz's voice. He was the shorter one.

Before they could react, she launched herself at them. She caught Chenz with a hard kick that knocked him into his accomplice and then ran for the door.

Before she could reach it, someone tripped her. A trained dancer by trade, she was able to flip over and keep going. At least until something solid hit her back and sent her slamming to the floor.

Cursing, she realized it was Chenz's overweight frame holding her down. He turned her over quickly and struck her a vicious blow across the face. Kiara reeled as pain exploded through her cheek and eye and she tasted blood. For a moment, she was completely sense-less.

Only the sound of her nightgown ripping brought her back to the present and her mind away from the pain. With a curse born of desperation, she sent her fist into Chenz's flabby belly. Releasing her, he doubled over in pain, allowing her to roll out from under him.

The other man came at her the instant she was back on her feet.

Kiara scissor-kicked him, catching him in the center of his chest. Her nightgown tore more as she scrambled from them. There was no way they would have her.

Better they kill her first.

She would never submit quietly to an attacker again.

At least that was her thought until something coiled around her throat and lifted her off her feet. She landed on her back, against the floor, so hard it knocked the breath out of her.

"You'll pay for that, bitch," Chenz said through clenched, rotting teeth, coiling the metallic rope even tighter around her neck.

Kiara gasped for air as the rope bit into her flesh, choking it from her. Desperately, she tried to pry or claw the rope free. She kicked her feet and attempted to scream.

Not even a whisper left her bruised lips.

She was dead, she knew it.

"Kill her, Chenz!" The taller man rubbed his chest where she'd kicked him, his eyes burning with smug satisfaction.

The rope tightened even more.

Kiara's sight dimmed as she struggled to stay alive. *I will not die like this. I won't!* The words rolled around her head, becoming her mantra as she fought with everything she had.

She pulled at the rope.

Just as she thought Chenz would finish her off, the noose loosened. Kiara gulped air into her burning lungs as she coughed and sputtered. Her vision dim, her head buzzed loudly. She rubbed her neck, feeling the welts left by the rough texture.

Chenz wrapped his hands in her long, dark reddish

brown hair and reeled her to him. "Your life's nothing to us, girly. But how you treat us in the next few minutes will decide if we kill you quick or make it *real* painful."

She choked at the stench of his breath falling against her cheek. Before she could think of a retort, his wet, scarred lips covered hers.

Kiara gagged.

"Why you . . ." He drew back to hit her again.

A sharp lurch in the ship sent them tumbling.

An instant later, a loud warning siren blared.

"We're being attacked." The tall man ran out of the room at a deadly pace.

Before Kiara could move, Chenz grabbed her by the arm and hauled her to a rusted steel beam in the wall. Still coughing, she tried to fight him as he handcuffed her there, but she was too weak from her beating and from her near strangulation to do the damage to him she wanted to.

"You worthless bastard!" she snarled, an instant before she tried to bite him.

He grabbed her jaw and shoved her back against the wall so hard, it blinded her for a moment. "I'll finish with you when this is over," he promised, his fingers biting fiercely into her face as he twisted her mouth with his hand. Giving her a lecherous sneer, he released her and ran to join his partner.

The door slammed down, jarring the room.

Kiara let out a loud, frustrated scream as she jerked so hard against the steel cuffs that it cut through her skin. Insane with her fear, anger, and determination, she yanked, not caring if she lost a hand in the process. All that mattered was getting free.

"I will not die here!" she shouted as her childhood nightmare tried to weaken her.

Do as they say, Kiara. Don't fight them. Her mother's voice whispered to her from the distant past. *It'll be okay, precious, I promise.*

But it hadn't been. All their compliance had gotten them was a brutal execution. Her mother had died before her eyes—a single shot to her head and Kiara had been shot three times by her father's political enemies before they'd left her for dead, too.

Only eight years old . . .

Her trusting innocence had been shattered that day. And when she'd finally recovered from her physical wounds, she'd made a solemn vow to herself that no one would ever again control her.

No one.

She would never obey anyone except herself and she would never again be a victim.

Yet the cuffs remained. No matter how hard she fought, no matter how hard she tried, they weren't budging.

Unable to deal with it, she slid slowly to the floor and banged her head against the wall so that the pain would override her hysteria. "Don't you dare cry," she growled at herself. "Don't you dare."

Boo-hoo-hoo, their leader had maliciously mocked her while they held her and her mother captive. *Cry all you want to, little girl. Daddy's not coming to save you. I love nothing more than the sound of someone's fear. The sound of someone begging me for their life. Life is pain, bitch. Too bad you won't live long enough to get used to it.*

Never since the day of her mother's funeral had she shed even a single tear. And she wasn't about to let the worthless scum who had her now break her.

She was stronger than that.

The lights dimmed and the ship tumbled hard to

the left as a shot broke through whatever force field they had.

For the briefest moment, she thought it might be her father with a rescue party. But she knew better. He was still at the consulate meeting and thought her safely guarded in the dance company's hotel rooms.

Just like that fateful day when she and her mother had been taken out of the winter palace, her father had no idea she was under attack. He wouldn't know until he was notified of her death.

You can't protect yourself. No matter how safe you think you are. No matter how much precaution you take, the rodents always find a way in . . . She'd written those words in her own diary when she'd been sixteen and an assassin had taken a shot at her while she was eating dinner with friends in a restaurant. Even surrounded by guards and with her father beside her, she'd almost died that night, too.

Her life was nothing but a paycheck to the scum of the universe and they intended to cash it out fully.

Unshed tears choked her as she realized the hopelessness of her situation. She would die out here in space, raped and tortured. Alone. The only hope she had was that whoever was attacking them, destroyed them.

Please let it be painless . . .

Unlike her mother's death.

That had been as slow and painful as the mercenaries could make it. They had tortured her for days before they finally ended her life—and those screams for mercy for her and her daughter had been forever seared into Kiara's mind.

The things they'd done to her mother.

The things they'd done to her . . .

Her throat tightened even more as she listened to the sounds of battle. The old walls of the shuttle creaked ominously. Blast after blast struck the craft and kept it rocking beneath her. This rusted-out ship wouldn't be able to sustain much more damage. It was a miracle it'd taken as much as it had.

Closing her eyes, she prayed for a quick death.

But that relief didn't come either.

Instead, she heard the popping of damaged electrical circuits in the hallway. By now, all the power to the doors had been drained and transferred to the ship's weapons and shields.

The lights went out.

Kiara sat in total darkness as she mentally prepared herself for the inevitable. There were no more sounds of lasers being shot from this ship.

The end was near now.

God, how she was going to miss her father and her dancing. Miss the sensation of the first warm spring breeze on her skin while she sat reading in her garden.

Drawing a deep breath, she took control of her fear. She was a commander's child. Her father had been born in poverty and had climbed by his wits and skills through the ranks of the military to end up as president of their planet. While many might not like him, they all agreed on one thing. Her father was fearless and he'd given that courage to his only child. She would meet death calmly, with dignity. Whatever it took, she would not beg or plead.

"I will do my parents proud."

Suddenly everything was completely still and silent. The odor of burning wires and smoke filtered into her room. Kiara coughed from the smoke until her throat burned again.

Outside there was the sound of approaching feet and then blast shots. She tensed, but whoever it was quickly ran past her room.

She continued to try and work her bloodied hands out of the cuffs.

At least until she heard someone else outside her door.

Her heart pounded in short, staccato beats at the sizzling sound of a laser torch cutting through the steel.

"I'm checking it out now," a man's voice said from the hallway in the Universal language that allowed the Empire to communicate with all sentient species. It was deep and accented, but she couldn't place the muffled tone. "There's some life-form in here about the size of a small human. Might even be another child . . . I just want to make—"

He was silent for a few seconds as he continued to cut through the steel. "Ah, screw you, Hauk. Some of us aren't the same low-bred animal you are . . ." He paused as if listening to something before he barked, "Hell no, I'm not sober. You think I'd be doing this shit if I were? And I notice I don't see your fat ass down here in the trenches so shut it before I forget I'm supposed to actually like you."

What in the known galaxies? He didn't sound like a rescuer. He didn't even sound nice.

Kiara wasn't sure if her situation was about to become better or . . .

A whole lot worse.

There was a loud pop just before a large piece of the door fell in. It landed with a clatter as smoke wafted up from the irregular circle.

Her stomach knotted into a cold lump.

Light from a small hand torch traveled about the room, stopping as it illuminated her.

Despite the pain of her adjusting eyes, she tried to see beyond the light, to whomever held it, but all she saw was a large, black blob.

The blob stepped through the hole and entered her room.

Kiara tucked her legs under her so that she could quickly rise to her feet if she needed to. A trickle of sweat ran down her temple. She tensed, ready to strike out with whatever resistance her battered, tired body could muster.

The overhead lights returned, burning her eyes. She blinked several times and the blob turned into a soldier dressed in a black battle suit that was covered with a padded flight jacket. A dense, black helmet covered his face, preventing her from seeing what race he belonged to. No insignia or flag marked his uniform in any way.

Who was he?

What was he?

Human? Humanoid? Or some other creature she could only guess at?

She stared at him, still uncertain whether he would help her, or harm her more. Until she knew the answer, she would play docile, lulling him into thinking her harmless. And if he did intend to hurt her, she would knee him hard in that part of his anatomy that men prided themselves on most and hope that whatever his species, it had the desired effect.

But he didn't move closer.

To her surprise, he shut off the torch and slid it into a pocket on his right leg. He moved slowly, as if trying to reassure her of his intent. He unstrapped his helmet from the lines securing it to his battle suit and removed it.

Kiara was amazed by the handsomeness of his face. His shoulder-length black hair was pulled into a pony-tail and two small, silver hoops dangled from his left earlobe—the same ear that held an earpiece and mic so that he was still communicating with whomever he'd been talking to earlier. His dark eyes were encircled by thick black eyeliner—something that made him look savage and dangerous. A common habit among thieves and criminals.

His gaze moved slowly over her body, taking in every detail with an accuracy a mecha would envy.

When he looked back at her face, she saw pity and concern. "I'm Syn," he said gently in the Universal language as if coaxing a skittish kitten. "I'm not going to hurt you. I promise."

For some reason she couldn't fathom, she believed him, even though there was an air about him that said he could be lethal if need be.

Relief poured through her.

Syn moved toward her cautiously and the kindness of his actions choked her. "Can you understand me?"

She realized his accent was Ritadarion, an allied planet to her own. "Yes."

He nodded as he removed his jacket and draped it around her shoulders. "Everything's all right, we'll take you home." He knelt down to examine the cuffs and grimaced as he saw how bloodied and bruised her wrists were.

She hissed as one of the cuts rubbed against the steel. Now that she was safe and no longer consumed with terror, the throbbing pain of them was excruciating. "We have a bit of a problem with those."

"So I see. You were definitely determined to get free, weren't you?"

Nodding, she could smell the alcohol on his breath, yet he appeared completely sober to her. There was no hesitancy or unbalance to him at all.

"I have a feeling you would have been equally determined to escape had they locked you in here."

A light of amusement played in his dark eyes as he pulled a pair of cutters out of another pocket. Smiling at her, he twirled them around before positioning them over the chain.

His light air died an instant later.

He tapped at his earpiece to open the channel. "You did what?" he snarled at whomever was on the other end. "Damn it, Cruel, you stupid, son of a . . . I've got a prisoner here who I'm trying to cut loose from a set of cuffs. Couldn't you have given me a little warning first? I swear to the gods . . . If I live through this you're a bad memory . . . And you assholes wonder why I do this shit flagged. How long?"

Kiara swallowed hard as dread washed through her. "How long for what?"

"Three minutes?" Syn growled. "I hate you. I really, really hate you." He let out another curse as he tried frantically to cut through the cuffs.

"They're military grade," she told him. It would take something a lot more powerful than his tool to cut through them. "The ship's about to blow, isn't it?"

He gave her a look that confirmed it as he pulled at the chain that linked the cuffs together. Yeah, right, like he could break it with his bare hands.

She was dead after all.

Her heart sank painfully into her stomach. She couldn't believe she'd come so close to freedom to lose it all again. She covered his hand with hers. "Go on while you can. And thank you for at least trying to save me."

His angry and determined look touched her. "I'm not leaving you here to die."

"You've done your good deed for the day. You shouldn't have to die for it."

He laughed bitterly as he worked at the cuffs. "No good deed goes unpunished. Believe me, I know."

"Please, go." Her voice broke, but she meant it. She

was resigned to her fate. "There's no need in both of us dying tonight."

His feral look cut through her. "I took an oath to save every life I could. I'm not about to back out on it now. I might be a lot of things, but a coward has never been one of them."

Kiara started to argue with him, but before she could a dark shadow fell over them.

Cringing, she looked up, expecting it to be Chenz.

But it was something far more sinister and a thousand times deadlier.

It was also the last thing she ever expected to see . . .

Nemesis.

For a moment, she thought she might faint after all. Nemesis was the most feared assassin to ever live. Every known government, including her own, wanted him dead, and the price on his head was staggering. No one had ever borne a higher one.

No one.

Maybe it's not him . . .

She knew better. Everyone above the age of three knew the stories of the creature who wore a black battle suit with a jacket that held a metal skull with a steel halo and crossed League swords on the back of it. It was a trademark he left on all the bodies of his victims. He took pride in his brutal trade, especially when he killed others of his kind.

To her knowledge, no one had ever survived an encounter with him.

Expecting him to kill them both, she was stunned when Syn stepped back and Nemesis broke the cuffs apart without using anything except his gloved hands. He scooped her up in his arms as if she weighed nothing at all and wrapped the jacket around her.

"What are you waiting on, Syn?" he growled in an electronically distorted voice. "Get your ass moving."

Syn snorted as he retrieved his helmet from the floor. "I'm waiting on you now."

"Fifty-five seconds and counting. You bastards better start running. You're about to fry."

CHAPTER 3

Syn ran ahead of them.

Kiara couldn't breathe as she held on for dear life while Nemesis ran toward the air lock that they'd drilled into the side of the ship.

The instant they were aboard their ship, Syn threw the lever and sealed them in while removing the temporary bridge to the other craft. "Clear!"

But they weren't clear and she knew it. The explosion of Chenz's ship would hit them hard. The debris could still kill them.

Someone threw their ship into hyperdrive. The sensation of it was enough to knock Nemesis into the wall and make him grunt from it. Yet he didn't loosen his grip on her. Even more surprising, he kept her from getting hurt as he slammed against the steel.

His face a mirror of disgust, Syn threw his helmet down so hard on the floor that it bounced almost three feet before rolling down the hall. He glared at them. "I *really* hate this shit." He started down the corridor.

Nemesis's grip on her tightened. "Where are you going?"

"To get a drink and kill Cruel . . . not necessarily in that order."

She felt the muscles in Nemesis's arm twitch in

response. But he didn't say anything more as he started down another corridor away from Syn. She shivered at the reality of him holding her.

I'm in the arms of the most lethal being ever born . . . Or spawned.

A creature who was currently being hunted by every known government. He was everything she hated in the universe. Violent. Ruthless. Relentless. Yet she couldn't make herself hate *him* and that made no sense whatsoever.

Maybe it was because she'd never thought of someone like him being capable of kindness . . . or of having someone as kind and altruistic as Syn in his company.

To her knowledge, Nemesis had never saved anyone. Until her.

"Why did you save me?"

He didn't answer. Instead, he took her into a room that served as some sort of infirmary. Medical tools and bottles of medicine were carefully placed in a glass cabinet not far from a large bed. The odor of antiseptic stung her nose. Everything was pristine white and orderly, a welcome contrast to her kidnappers' filth.

Kiara glanced up at Nemesis, afraid he might still kill her. But he seemed to be ignoring her, at least as much as he could given the fact that she was in his arms.

He placed her gently on the bed, then moved to retrieve a warmed blanket from a drawer at the bottom of the cabinet. With a gentleness she'd never have attributed to a ruthless killer, he wrapped it around her.

Kiara was minutely attuned to him, even right down to the way the light gleaned off his strangely shaped helmet with an eerie sheen. He seemed larger than a human, taller, stronger. Massive. She had no idea what species he belonged to, yet he had to be at least humanoid.

She watched the play of well-defined muscles under his battle suit as he pressed a panel next to the door and opened the closet.

Who was he?

That was the trillion credit question and if she knew the answer, she'd either be the richest person alive . . .

Or dead before she could draw another breath.

No one guarded their identity more closely than this creature.

And she had to admit there was nothing hotter than a man with that kind of honed physique whose face was totally hidden. Whose past was a complete mystery to the entire universe. A total renegade who answered to no one's law but his own.

This was the deadliest creature ever born and he silently removed her cuffs from her bruised wrists with a tenderness that was unfathomable.

Her fantasies ran wild with the possibilities. Surely his face would have to match the rest of him.

Don't bet on it. For all you know, he's a Pigarian with three eyes and buck teeth. Or one of the upright reptilian species.

Ew. What a waste of a gorgeous body that would be . . .

Stop it, Kiara. You hate *assassins. You hate everything he is and everything he stands for.*

He's the same kind of cowardly filth who killed your mother while she tried to protect you . . . The same filth who cold-bloodedly shot a helpless eight-year-old girl and left her for dead.

It was true. There was no telling what atrocities this man had committed for nothing more than a paycheck. *Every life has a price tag . . .*

He turned around, holding a black battlesuit like the ones he and Syn wore.

Kiara could feel his gaze on her, it was almost as tangible as a touch. He hesitated by her side as if unsure of himself.

Oh please, girl. He's not hesitating. The idea of so lethal a killer being bashful . . .

Ludicrous.

Her best bet was that he was sizing her up for a burial pod.

She thought he was about to speak, but the door opened to reveal Syn, who held a half empty bottle of Tondarian alcohol. Something so potent, it was banned on most planets.

Unaware of what he'd interrupted, Syn took the battlesuit from Nemesis's hands. "Hauk wanted me to tell you that the next time he says run, we should leave the vics on board and get the hell out. I tend to agree."

Kiara still sensed Nemesis watching her.

"You were the one who didn't run," Nemesis reminded him.

"Oh yeah, that was me, wasn't it?" He took a swig right out of the bottle. "Since when do you listen to me anyway? I'm an idiot."

Nemesis didn't respond to that particular comment. "Is Cruel still alive?"

"For the moment. But only because the little bastard moves faster than I do when I'm flagged."

A sharp lunge told her their ship was coming out of hyperspace. "Are you taking me home?" she asked them.

A dreadful pause greeted her.

Finally, Nemesis spoke. "Soon."

Before she could even blink, he grabbed the alcohol from Syn's grasp and was gone.

"Hey! You crippin' bastard asshole . . ." Syn glared at the closed door before he rebelliously pulled a small flask out of his pocket and took another nip. Something she admired since she was sure Nemesis would have killed him for it had he seen it.

This man was either braver then any soul alive.

Or dumber.

Nykyrian locked the door behind him before he leaned against the wall and let out a long breath of relief at being away from Kiara. He knew Sheridan's doctoring abilities well enough to guess the dancer would be sedated so there would be no chance of her nosing around where they didn't want her.

Still, an image of her lithe body outlined by her sheer, torn nightgown scorched him. Though her breasts were small, they were as beautiful and inviting as her lips. Even now he could feel her pressed against his chest. Feel her thin, supple arms wrapped around him as he'd carried her.

What he wouldn't give to have her do that while they were both naked . . .

His body was so hard it was all he could do not to limp. And to think, he'd mistakenly believed he'd survived real torture in his past.

That had nothing on this.

Get a grip . . .

Honestly, he'd rather she get a grip on a certain piece of his anatomy that was draining all the blood from his brain before he lost what little reasoning he had left.

You are in control.

Yeah, tell that to his cock. It wasn't exactly listening to him at the moment.

Forcing his mind to other thoughts, he removed the

hot helmet so that he could breathe in and try to relax. He freed his damp, blond hair from the tie holding it at the nape of his neck and let it fall over his shoulders.

With a tired sigh, he chucked the alcohol into a garbage chute, then pulled his dark shades from his pocket and moved to join the rest of his crew in the control room at the front of the ship.

Dancer Hauk and Darling Cruel—and yes, those were their real names, which showed that even loving parents could be sick and twisted—were joking with each other when he entered.

"Hey, Cruel," Hauk said snidely. "Check it . . . the man is without his guise. You think he wants to be found out or is he looking for a reason to kill the woman? What odds are you taking?"

Darling snorted. "I'm not betting shit, troll. I already owe you two weeks' pay. Anymore and I'll be working only to pay *you*."

Hauk let out an evil laugh. But then, at almost seven feet in height, he could be obnoxious to most people and get away with it. Especially those like Darling, who only came up to just past his waist.

A typical Andarion male, Hauk belonged to the most brutal of all known races. One that valued physical beauty only second to physical strength. With long black hair that he wore in tiny braids, his features were perfect and sharp. His white irises were ringed by a band of blood red. But Nykyrian didn't care what he looked like. Hauk was raw, savage strength and a brilliant techspert.

Darling, on the other hand, looked almost frail in comparison. Where Hauk was built solid and huge like a tree, Darling was lean and finely boned. His straight red hair fell across the left side of his face, covering a vicious scar that they never talked about.

Ignoring them while they exchanged barbs, Nykyrian dropped his helmet on the floor and took the pilot's chair. He ran over their settings, knowing there'd be no corrections. Hauk and Darling were the best. Otherwise they wouldn't be here.

They'd be dead.

"Did you bathe in Chenz's and Petiri's blood?" Darling asked him.

Nykyrian gave Darling a condemning stare. "I would have, had *someone* not detonated their charges prematurely."

"Yeah, Cruel. You have to watch that premature detonation problem of yours."

Darling tossed a throwing knife at Hauk's head.

Hauk caught it and laughed before he tossed it back at Darling who caught it just as easily. "You keep doing that, human, and you're going to hurt my feelings."

"You don't have feelings, Andarion."

"Not true. Compared to Nykyrian, I'm as sensitive as a woman."

"God knows you're beginning to whine like one." Nykyrian rubbed at his right eye under his shades as his thoughts returned to the mission they'd just completed.

Justice had been served swiftly and coldly. Tomorrow Syn would inform their client about Chenz's death. Granted it wouldn't bring back the senator's son, but it would ensure that Chenz never decapitated another child and delivered his head to his mother.

That alone made him wish he'd had more time with the bastard.

But there was nothing more to be done. Chenz was dead and they would be paid.

Aching for the poor senator and a grief he couldn't even begin to comprehend, Nykyrian stared out the window at the blackness swirling around them. The senator's pain over the loss still haunted him as he tried to imagine a parent who cared so much for her son. The gods knew none of his parents, either real or adoptive, had ever given two shits about him.

It comforted him on some level to know that not everyone was as cold and unfeeling as he'd learned to be. That there were people like Sheridan and the senator who could love and who could cry over the loss of the child they'd brought into the world.

In the lightless void he was staring at, an image of Kiara dancing in her last ballet floated before his eyes, which didn't help him calm his arousal at all.

Damn it, why did he feel like this?

But then she'd always been able to stir his senses. Every time he'd seen her dance, she'd touched a part of his soul—a part of him he preferred to think was long dead and damned. She, alone, had made him see beauty in a universe he normally despised. Had made him feel something other than cold, corrupt emptiness.

She was beauty and gentleness personified.

Nykyrian scoffed at his own stupidity. He knew better. No one was good and no one over the age of ten was unscarred. Life was brutal and it made victims of everyone.

And thoughts of her weren't helping his foul mood in the least.

Hauk turned in his chair. "Speaking of women . . . who's the trim you guys almost died over?"

Nykyrian ground his teeth as anger whipped through him. He'd always hated that demeaning term for women. The bizarre thing was he didn't even know why. It just seemed wrong to dismiss a person so. Something that made no sense when one considered the fact that he killed people for a paycheck.

Yeah, he was definitely a head case.

Clearing his throat, he kept his tone even and flat. "Kiara Zamir, the dancer."

Hauk gave a low, appreciative whistle. "What was *she* doing with those scabs?"

Nykyrian cut a droll stare at the Andarion and a question that was so stupid there was no reason to even bother answering it.

"Yo, dumbass," Darling said sarcastically. "What do you think she'd be doing with them? Giving them ballet lessons?"

Hauk narrowed his gaze at Nykyrian. "Tell me again why I can't kill him?"

"You're afraid of handling explosives."

Hauk cursed. "One day I'm going to get over that and when I do . . ."

"I'll wisely stop annoying you." Darling winked at him.

Nykyrian rolled his eyes at their incessant swipes. The two of them were like recalcitrant siblings. But for all their bluster, they were loyal to each other as much as they were loyal to him.

That alone made them invaluable.

Ignoring them, Nykyrian rechecked their headings, then pulled up an e-ledger and started making notes for his next mission.

Within an hour, they began docking at their secure station, one Nykyrian had built nine years ago when he'd left The League. It was only in the last four years that it'd grown into a monstrosity of workers who proudly followed his new code.

Protect the innocent and kill the vermin.

Simple and elegant—it was finally a code he could live, or die, by.

Sheridan, or rather Syn, had been the one to name their operation. The Sentella. A word that meant a quorum of sentinels in Syn's native tongue. And that's what they were. Guardians for a better world.

The League checked the united galaxies and kept their governments in line. The Sentella kept The League and the independent assassins others employed in check.

At last, the innocent had their own paladins. And it was a calling none of them took lightly. Whenever an assassin or politician crossed the line, they answered to The Sentella.

More to the point, they answered to him.

Nemesis.

Syn joined them on the bridge, reporting that Kiara was in a sedated sleep. Nykyrian replaced his helmet before heading back to their patient.

After the landing, Nykyrian carried her from the ship. He took her to the upper floor of their command center where he charged Mira, one of their nurses, to care for her until she woke.

Mira was thrilled to be assigned watch duty over such a famous personality. Her gaze nervous as she watched "Nemesis," she ran to their supply room to find sleeping attire for the tiny dancer in his arms.

Shaking his head at Mira's undue haste to flee his presence, Nykyrian took his precious bundle into one of the observation rooms and carefully placed her on the large bed. He covered her with an extra blanket.

As he stepped away from the bed, he heard her whispering in her sleep. Entranced by her melodic voice which he'd only ever heard on programmed interviews, he turned back to take a final look at her peacefully resting form.

How could anyone be so beautiful and tiny?

He stood over her, intoxicated by the smoothness of

her features, her pert nose, the high cheekbones, her finely arched brows. Her long, dark mahogany hair fell in soft ringlets about her beautiful face and shoulders.

She was exquisite.

He traced the line of her bruised cheek, wanting to kill Chenz again for hurting her. But most of all, he was tempted to remove his glove and feel the softness he knew her flawless skin would hold.

You don't need softness.

It was true. Sex came with a severe risk and since intimacy was an alien concept to him, he tended to avoid it. He didn't like being naked and unarmed around anyone. The few minutes of release weren't worth his life.

At least they hadn't been until now . . .

Kiara might make a shot to his head worth it.

He sensed Mira's presence as she returned. Looking up, he saw her questioning brown eyes.

With a curt nod to Mira, he left the room and headed to their meeting. That was what he needed to focus on. Not tiny dancers who'd almost gotten them killed.

Nykyrian met up with Syn, Darling, and Hauk downstairs, anxious to finish his business and return her home. He didn't like the unfamiliar feelings she evoked. He was used to being numb and untouched. It was comfortable to him.

Hauk arched one cynical brow. "What kept you?"

Nykyrian didn't answer as he led them to their council chambers where Jayne was already seated and waiting for them.

He could tell Hauk wanted to press the issue, but fear for his life kept him silent as he moved to sit down across from Jayne.

The room was covered with a myriad of star charts and maps as well as whispers from some of their monitoring equipment. Everything was neat, tidy, and efficient, just the way he liked his life.

Nykyrian walked to the monitor on his left and called up their assignments. He sent them to the table which was a large interactive monitor for their files where all of them could review their schedules.

As he waited for his friends to remove their helmets and take their chairs, Nykyrian perused the listed items. It was a heavy load they were carrying, but that was nothing new, since The League and others seemed to think they were above the very laws they'd put into place.

Nykyrian removed his own helmet and took his place at the head of the table. He gave the small group a cursory glance before he spoke to Syn. "Send a message to Kiefer Zamir that I'll return his daughter. I want him to know The Sentella had nothing to do with her abduction."

Syn snorted as he made a note with his stylus on the terminal that glowed through the glass of the table. "No good deed goes unpunished." That was Syn's mantra that he repeated constantly, not that Nykyrian blamed him for it. It seemed to be ever true.

He glanced up at Nykyrian. "Your luck, they'll shoot you down when you take her back." He made another quick note on his tablet. "By the way, I got the news from one of our spies that the Gouran Consulate fell apart two days ago when the Probekeins threatened to assassinate the councilors' kids. Eight contracts were drawn up for the terminations. Six children have been found mutilated, including Councilor Serela's boy we saw last night. I'll make sure word gets around that Chenz's death was because of his brutal murder of the kid."

Nykyrian mentally flashed on Serela's tormented face and the sight of her son's remains. He'd killed

Chenz too mercifully for his tastes. If only they'd had more time . . .

"Other than Chenz, who were the others who accepted the Probekeins' contracts?"

"Don't know," Syn answered.

Nykyrian rubbed his jaw. "What were the negotiations between the Probekeins and Gourans over?"

At Syn's shrug, Nykyrian folded his arms over his chest. "Sher, you're supposed to stay informed of all contracts for assassinations. Get off the bottle and find out the definite reasons for the killings as well as the name on the last contract and who holds it. My guess, the murders are over the new weapon the Probekeins are building. Either way, we need to know."

"I'm on it." Syn quickly jotted it down.

Nykyrian waited until he was finished. "You'd best inform Zamir immediately that his daughter's safe. I'm sure he's about bended over her disappearance."

Syn stood, moving to comply with Nykyrian's last directive.

"I think we should target Emperor Abenbi," Hauk said, watching Syn leave. Abenbi was the Probekeins' leader and head asshole. "It's time we showed the Probekeins they can't continue to bully other governments. Give them a taste of their own feces."

Nykyrian shook his head. "That's not our decision. We'd best attend to our contracted hits. Our backlog is already too long. It'll be several weeks before we can take on any new assignments. At this point, it'd have to be a major emergency for new hire."

Jayne sighed irritably as she leaned forward to read the table monitor where she'd maximized her schedule for viewing. "Why don't we expand our number? Surely out of the multitude we employ, there are a few suitable to doing the physical executions of contracts."

Nykyrian gave her a dry stare. "Would you trust them at your back? The five of us are friends, have been so for years. Our loyalty to one another is without question. Are you willing to put your life into the hands of a stranger?"

Jayne snorted. "Not with the price on my head . . . I suppose you're right."

No shit. Jayne was one of the best, but sometimes she didn't think things through. Then again, he had a bad habit of thinking things over to the point of exhaustion. Between the two of them, they formed an almost normal balance.

Syn returned a few minutes later and took his seat. He met Nykyrian's gaze. "Zamir will be expecting you. He also wants a meeting with me. Funny how we're wanted criminals until they need us." His gaze was as bitter as his tone. "I think Zamir's going to propose a contract for Kiara's protection."

Nykyrian's heart quickened, but he hid all signs of it. "Did you schedule a meeting?"

"This evening."

Hauk turned in his chair, a smirk twisting his lips. "I thought we were too backlogged to take on anything new."

Nykyrian shot him a venomous glare.

Hauk held his hands up apologetically.

Satisfied Hauk knew better than to question him further, Nykyrian pointed to the table where their schedules were displayed.

As was typical, Hauk complained immediately about his. "Why am I always the backup for Darling and Jayne? Especially Darling. I wish you would teach him how to breach access codes. That dick's dangerous."

"Me, dangerous? Last time we went out together, you set off two alarms. For a techspert, you're seriously lacking."

"Careful, human," Hauk warned, showing Darling his fangs. "I might get hungry one of these nights and decide we no longer need a weaptech."

Nykyrian shook his head at their bluster, knowing they were good friends. However, they continually harassed one another about their racial differences.

Darling was from Caron, a human system. Hauk was Andarion—an advanced predatorial race that sometimes fed on humans. A hybrid of the two races, Nykyrian didn't really like listening to their bullshit.

Hauk had the traditional Andarion features which made for an exceptionally handsome face. The long canine teeth flashed as Hauk smiled.

Nykyrian was grateful his own teeth were smaller versions of Hauk's. Still, they were long enough to mark him as a bastard half-breed, especially when combined with his eyes, which he never showed to the world.

Unlike Hauk, he couldn't stand his.

But that was neither here nor there.

"Jayne," Nykyrian said, facing the Hyshian assassin. "If you need help with your hits, I'll back you. That will free up some of Hauk's time."

Jayne gave him a seductive smile. She loved the thrill of hunting and killing the corrupt. Nykyrian remembered a time past when he'd shared her enthusiasm, but those days had long fled. Now, he just wanted peace and solitude.

"The number is low this week." Jayne scanned her list. Dragging her finger over a picture of the Probekein Emperor she'd called up, she electronically shot the photo across the desk to Hauk's seat. "I think I could schedule an opportunity to take out Abenbi." She winked at Hauk.

Nykyrian shook his head as he closed Abenbi's file at Hauk's end. "Stick with the assigned political assassinations. I want no messages of the Probekein Emperor's murder."

Hauk curled his lip. "That bastard deserves to die."

Nykyrian tensed at the direct confrontation. "We have enough warrants out for our arrests. Let's not give them a reason to execute us, shall we? We need solid proof before we act. When I have it, I'll gladly allow you and Jayne to have him. Hell, I'll even help," he compromised, unwilling to fight with one of his few true friends. He had enough enemies for that.

Hauk retreated back into his chair.

Nykyrian glanced around at each of them. "We haven't any missions in the near future that require the entire group. There are some overlaps. Note them and plan accordingly. Keep your links open in case of an emergency. Our next meeting is in eight days, the time is noted on your schedule. Good luck," Nykyrian finished more out of habit than necessity.

The members downloaded their assignments into their various portables, then grabbed their helmets and took their leave with Hauk donning the guise of Nemesis—a safeguard in case someone was watching the room.

Syn remained seated with Nykyrian, waiting for the room to clear.

As soon as the door closed, Syn turned to face him. "I don't know if you should accept Zamir's contract. We can't afford liabilities."

Nykyrian hated the way Syn was able to read him. Though he kept his expressions and moods carefully guarded, Syn had always possessed an uncanny ability to see past his facade and he was the only creature alive Nykyrian allowed to question his actions. "I really wish you'd stop second-guessing my thoughts. Like I told

Hauk, we're too backlogged to take on any more. You'll have to apologize to her father. Tell him to call out his Gourish troops to protect her."

He moved to the right wall and pushed the buttons for his change of clothes. "We're killers, not babysitters," he finished, stripping his battlesuit off.

Syn turned his back to Nykyrian and continued talking, "You're attracted to her." It was a statement, not a question.

"No shit," he said drily. "I'm not blind or dead . . . yet. Can you tell me she holds no appeal for you?"

Syn laughed. "Oh hell yeah—I'd definitely love to get a piece of that. But I also know how many times you've gone to see her dance. Face it, Kip, you're infatuated with her, and that's not like you."

"She's a beautiful woman. I lust for her, nothing more." Nykyrian replaced the wall, unwilling to let anyone, even Sheridan, know about his real feelings. Picking up his boots from the floor, he sat in his chair.

"Nothing more?" Syn swung his chair around to face him with a cocked eyebrow.

Nykyrian glowered at him as he jerked his boots on. "This discussion is terminated." He retrieved his shades from the table and put them on to hide his odd, green, human eyes.

With one last grimace at Syn, he quit the room.

He shoved Syn's words out of his mind as he walked down the corridor while people scurried away from him as if they feared he'd kill them just for being there.

Like he would bother with any of them.

Nykyrian rolled his eyes at their actions and Syn's stupid fears. He was a soldier, not some lovesick idiot. All too well, he knew his duties and obligations, nothing would ever distract him from them. Especially not a dancer whose father ruled a government and an army that wanted him dead.

He was and had been many things in his life, but stupid had never been one of them.

Making his way toward Mira and her post, he was glad to shed his Nemesis disguise. The birth of Nemesis had been a necessity—it left him free to roam without too many snipers taking shots at him. And with his unique hybrid features, if the authorities were to ever learn the identity of Nemesis, it wouldn't take them long to run him into the ground.

Not that they weren't already trying, but he didn't need to give them another reason to come for him.

For now, people assumed Nykyrian Quiakides to be another minion of Nemesis; a role that suited him well. So long as his identity was secret, he could maintain a quasi-normal existence.

But his identity was only one of many reasons he could never involve himself with someone. If he'd learned anything in his life, it was that no one could ever be trusted.

People were his friends until he looked the other way.

Even as much as he trusted Syn and the others, he still wouldn't be surprised if one of them went for his back someday. It was, after all, inherent to all their species. The entire histories of their worlds had been written in the blood of friendships and alliances gone bad.

But Kiara . . .

Nykyrian stifled the emotions that filled him as he thought of her, and reverted to the soothing emptiness he relied upon.

She was nothing to him and she would never be anything more than a leftover memory.

At least that's what he thought until he entered the room and came face to face with her and those haunting amber eyes . . .

CHAPTER 4

Once again, Kiara came awake to unfamiliar surroundings, but these didn't seem quite as ominous as before. For one thing, she wasn't lying on a pile of filthy garbage, and for another, her wrists had been cleaned and bandaged. They no longer hurt her at all.

But as she recalled Nemesis, she jolted up, her heart lodged in her throat.

Where am I? This wasn't the ship where she'd fallen asleep. There was no movement. No gentle hum of engines . . .

She was on the ground somewhere.

What had they done with her? It was extremely disconcerting to wake up with no idea of her location or how she'd come to be here. She was alive, but for all she knew, she was still being held captive.

Angry and scared, she searched the room, looking for some clue about her fate.

Suddenly, the dim lights brightened. The door faded to transparency to show Kiara a heavy-set, elderwoman in a nurse's uniform looking into the room. The woman hesitated as if uncertain whether or not she should enter. A kind smile like that of a doting grandmother curled her lips as the door finally slid open to admit her.

"You're safe." She moved to stand next to the bed.

The door returned to being an opaque dark gray. "No one here will hurt you. I promise." The woman's dark brown eyes glowed with honesty and warmth. Kiara trusted her.

With the lights brightened, she noticed the richness of the furnishings. The bed she sat on was made of dark, carved wood, a rarity few could afford. White gossamer sheers hung over the tall posts, shielding the bed from a stray draft. Yet there was an armoire of medical equipment next to it. The room looked like a strange cross between a hospital and a hotel.

Confused, Kiara looked back at the woman. "Where am I?"

"The where isn't important. You'll be home soon now that you're awake." She beamed with a face Kiara recognized as one belonging to a fan. "Are you hungry or thirsty, Your Highness?"

At Kiara's declination, she moved toward the door. "My name's Mira. You stay here and I'll retrieve your battlesuit for you. If you need anything, just press the call button and either I or another nurse will come immediately." With one last smile, she left.

Kiara let out a slow breath, hoping the woman wasn't lying to her. Mira seemed harmless enough, but one could never be too sure.

In the still quietness of the room, she heard the fierce wind outside and an insistent thumping. Her gaze was drawn to the brightly colored windows on the far wall. An oddly shaped, knobby tree blew in the strong wind, knocking branches against the window.

Frowning, she wished she could identify the tree. That might help her figure out where she was.

But then she'd never been the most attentive of students even on her best day, and while she knew the basics about the planets that made up the United Systems of the Ichidian Universe, she didn't know anything as advanced as their different vegetation.

Scrap, her father had been right. That trivial garbage they'd tried so hard to teach her could have come in handy after all . . .

Kiara sighed, her thoughts turning to her father. By now someone had most likely discovered her absence and reported it. No doubt he was frantically gathering forces to search every fraction of space for her. Given what had happened the last time she'd been kidnapped, she could only imagine the terror, fear and anger he was going through.

Her throat tightened as she prayed these people really intended to return her to Gouran. She wasn't sure her father could mentally handle losing her like this.

Not after what had happened last time . . .

The door slid open, startling her from her thoughts. Expecting Mira, she turned, then froze as her breath caught at the last thing she expected to see.

Whoa . . .

This wasn't Mira.

Tall and lean, he was the sexiest thing she'd ever seen in her entire life, and given the hot pieces of cheese employed by her dance company, that said a lot. But none of them compared to the dangerous stranger in her room. While the men she was used to were hotter than hell, what they lacked was the fierce aura of power that emanated from this man and his stern, steely features.

It was as if he were the deadliest of predators.

Feral. That was the only word to do him justice. Surely there wasn't another soldier in the entire universe who could match him in terms of raw beauty or lethal demeanor.

His blond hair was snow white and his features sharp and icy. He wore a pair of black shades that annoyed her since she couldn't see the upper part of his face or the color of his eyes. Not that it mattered. She saw enough to know that in the land of gorgeous men, he had no competition.

As a stark contrast to his white hair, his clothes were a black so deep they seemed to absorb all light, and they were trimmed in silver . . .

No, not silver. Those were weapons tucked into the sleeves and lapels of his ankle-length coat. The left side of it was pulled back, exposing a holstered blaster that was strapped to his left hip. The tall flight boots had silver buckles going up the sides that were fashioned into the image of skulls. At least that's what she saw at first glance, but as he moved closer she realized those could come off and double as weapons, too.

Wow, he was either extremely paranoid or more lethal than a team of League assassins.

And that said something.

The collar of his shirt was high, but opened enough at the neck to show her a glimpse of a vicious scar along his throat. It looked as if someone had tried to behead him.

And as he came closer, she realized he had more scars just above and below his ears, along with fainter scars that cut across his cheeks to his nose. They didn't mar his attractiveness, but were obvious nonetheless. Like something had clawed him . . . only they were more precise—as if his face had once been inside a vice or some sort of contraption.

Had he been tortured?

As he turned his head to the side as if listening for something outside, she saw the silver and black comlink in his ear and the long braid down his back—the mark of a trained assassin. And since he wasn't in a military uniform, it meant he was freelance. The lowest of the low.

No, he wasn't dangerous.

He was a coward and a bully.

Her blood ran cold as her anger snapped.

Nykyrian paused as he caught the look of hatred in Kiara's amber eyes. He'd assumed, or maybe hoped, she'd still be asleep—that he'd be able to return her to her father before she awoke.

He should have known better.

She was awake and by the look in her eyes it was obvious she hated his guts . . . and that was without knowing he was Nemesis. Damn, how much worse would her lips curl if she knew the truth of him?

Not that it mattered. She was just a momentary blip in the stream of his life.

Yet even with her obvious disdain for him, his body reacted to her as if she caressed him with her hands. He was so hard and aching, it was all he could do not to curse. Every part of him was attuned to her.

Every part craved her . . .

Syn's right. I am an asshole.

Kiara was the only woman he'd ever really wanted and damned if he knew why. There was just something about her that reached out to him. The way she moved like a dream. So graceful. So tranquil.

Something about her seemed pure and untouched. Innocent. And it made him forget, even for a moment, how sullied he was.

You're such an idiot.

He was Nemesis. Alone. Lethal. Cold. That was all the comfort he'd ever need. Yet a part of him he hated wanted to know, just once, what it would feel like to be held by a woman like her.

Gah, you're nauseating. If he kept this crap up, he was going to make himself sick.

Narrowing his eyes in aggravation at himself, he finally spoke. "I assume Mira has gone for clothing."

Kiara scooted back on the bed as she eyed him warily. "You're *Andarion*."

Wow, he'd stupidly thought her disdain couldn't increase. There was more venom in that one word than in the poison capsule he kept tucked in his pocket for the seriously off chance he might be in a no-win situation one day.

He ran his tongue over his long, canine teeth. Ah, hell, who was he kidding? They were fangs, pure and simple. And by now, he should be used to humans despising him for them. "Don't worry, I've eaten already."

That only seemed to anger her more. "Are you the one who will take me home?"

"If you prefer, I could float you back."

He expected her to cut loose with profanity all over him. But she surprised him. "You know, your sarcasm isn't appreciated right now. I've been drugged, beaten, nearly raped, saved, drugged again, hijacked, and now threatened by you. Tell me, what else should I look forward to? Torture, or just a good maiming?"

Nykyrian did something he'd never done before. He backed off. She was right. She'd been through one hell of an ordeal and all things considered, she'd come out of it with her spirit intact.

He cut a slight bow to her. "Forgive me, *mu Tara*. I'm not trained for manners."

Kiara would have asked him what he was trained for, but the answer was obvious.

To kill.

Their exchange was curtailed as Mira returned with the battlesuit Syn had given Kiara earlier. "Oh, Nykyrian," she said in startled alarm. "I didn't know you were here."

Kiara noted Mira's instant discomfort. The woman literally cringed as if terrified he'd lash out and hit her.

Just how many times had he beaten her for her to react that way?

"I'll wait outside." He moved to the door.

Mira's frown followed him.

As soon as he was gone and the door solid again, Kiara drew the bed veil to one side and stepped from the bed. Her toes curled away from the chilly floor. "You don't like him?"

Mira jumped as if she'd stepped on her foot. "No," she said in a rush. "It's not that. It's just . . . He's just . . . a little frightening, I guess." Mira handed her the suit.

No, he was a *lot* frightening.

"Who is he?"

"Nykyrian . . ." Mira paused, her brows knitted. "I don't know his last name. It's never used."

"Really? Why?"

"They don't say."

Now that *was* odd.

Mira leaned closer and whispered, "The rumors that run around here claim he's a renegade League assassin."

Kiara's jaw went slack before disbelief filled her. No, it wasn't possible. "The League doesn't allow their assassins to leave."

"Exactly. Nykyrian's the only one who's ever left who managed to live beyond a few hours. I've heard it whispered he was some kind of decorated hero, too. A commander even. They say he dug out his tracer with his own bare hands, threw it in their faces and walked away."

Kiara found that even harder to believe. There was no way he could have done that and lived. Most likely it was a story the man made up to make himself appear even more fierce.

Cowards tended to do that. They lived off reputations they didn't deserve.

"Why did he leave?"

Mira shook her head. "No one knows. It's not something he ever talks about. Then again, he seldom speaks even when spoken to. Most people around here tend to avoid him because he's a hybrid."

Kiara's frown deepened. "Hybrid what?"

"Half human, half Andarion."

That too surprised her. "I didn't think we could breed with them."

"Neither did I, but have you ever seen a blond Andarion before?"

No, she hadn't. "How odd."

"Hmmm," Mira mumbled. "But don't worry. I'm sure you'll be fine alone with him. He's one of the best The Sentella has." She held her hand out to Kiara. "Enough gossip. It's been a great pleasure meeting you, Princess. I wish you success with your new show. I've heard it's one of the best out right now."

Smiling, Kiara took Mira's warm, velvety hand and gave a short, smart shake. "It's been an honor to meet you, Mira. Thank you for your kindness. If you ever want to come to the new show, just give my company a call and I'll leave you a pass at the door."

Mira's eyes were bright with friendship. "Thank you, Princess. I just might do that." With one last smile, she quit the room.

Quickly, Kiara exchanged her gown for the black battlesuit. After she finished lacing the front, she opened the door and entered the corridor to meet her hostile escort.

Once again, she was stunned by the fierce sight of

him. Even though he leaned nonchalantly against the wall with his arms crossed over his chest, she had a feeling he could launch himself at an enemy faster than she could blink.

He could probably kill her just as quickly. The lethal power of him was absolutely compelling and mesmerizing. Like staring at a beautiful wild animal you knew could rip you to shreds before you could even call for help.

He pushed himself away from the far wall, his jacket moving like water that flowed gracefully around him. "Are you ready?"

Kiara nodded as she tried to discern the truth of his past and character. She'd heard many tales about The League's most prized soldiers. They were a fierce lot, trained to kill political targets and jealously protected as The League's most valuable commodity. Most were bioengineered. Others were taken into The League's academies at a young age and trained to be ruthless.

Even intentionally psychotic.

If they were accepted into The League after a harsh battery of tests that included killing another trained assassin, they were allowed no spouses. No friends, family, or social relations of any kind. No physical comforts.

Isolated to the point of insanity.

It was kill or be killed.

Once trained, they were The League's eternal property. The only way out was to die.

Kiara wondered what kind of man could defy the nefarious League that protected and intimidated all governments with its military power. Even her own father, who had more courage than most, refused to disobey a League directive.

"Were you really in The League?" Granted it was a

blunt question, but she wasn't one for timidity, and her curiosity was killing her.

Nykyrian showed no emotion whatsoever. Nor did he answer her question. "You need to tel-ass," a slang term that came from teleporting one's posterior quickly. "Your father's worried about you."

"You called him?" Kiara was shocked he would be so considerate.

"One of our people did." Again, no emotion whatsoever as he continued on his way without even looking back at her to make sure she wasn't getting lost.

Kiara was miffed by his rude dismissal. She had to struggle to keep up with his long strides which rapidly took him down the corridor to a large landing bay thrumming with activity.

Whoa . . .

She'd never seen a more impressive collection of ships and fighters. They had things here her father's army would kill to possess. Very high tech and cutting edge.

Except for one that looked really out of place.

Nykyrian led her toward the antique black fighter in the far left corner of the bay. They passed several people, but no one spoke a greeting to him. In fact, a number of them purposefully moved out of his way or hid behind something as soon as they saw his approach.

Just what kind of bully was he that everyone feared him so?

He stopped next to the antique fighter and released the cockpit hatch by splaying his hand over the lock on the side. The controls moved as fluidly as he did, but not nearly as silently. Turning, he waited until she was next to him. Since she was a full head and shoulders shorter than him, she couldn't reach the boarding ladder.

"Should I jump for it?" she asked sarcastically.

That seemed to amuse him, but his features didn't change at all as he placed his hands around her waist and effortlessly lifted her up to the ladder. The heat of his strong hands through the material of her suit seared her. Not to mention that the scent of him hit her hard.

He was delectable even for a psycho killer.

Unwilling to go there, Kiara climbed to the top, then paused in confusion as she glanced inside his fighter. There was only one seat . . .

She looked down to where Nykyrian stood on the ground, oblivious to her.

Uncertainty filled her as she glanced back inside the cockpit. Was this the correct ship? Where was she supposed to sit?

His lap?

As if . . .

"Sit forward on the seat," Nykyrian instructed from below as he finally noticed her hesitation.

Still unsure about that, she did as he said. It was actually a lot roomier inside than it'd appeared at first. But there was no place for him to sit except behind her.

Touching her.

That wasn't exactly what she wanted and if he tried anything, assassin or not, he'd be limping.

From her seated position, Kiara saw someone come forward with two helmets and a computer log. Without a single comment to the worker, Nykyrian quickly signed the log, grabbed the helmets, and joined her in a fluid jump that the dancer in her envied. Very few men possessed that degree of agility and grace.

Who are you fooling, girl? There aren't many women who could do it either.

Trying to distract herself from the warm body sliding in behind her, she studied the ship's controls. The main panel reminded her of a museum piece. But even so, it was in prime condition and more than well kept.

Nykyrian must have noticed her interest. "It's a Bertraud Trebuchet Fighter."

A chill went down her spine as she recognized the model. Expensive and fast, they were the preferred ships of the top scum and elite outlaws the universe over. "Doesn't Nemesis fly one of these?" She turned to look at him over her shoulder. "Are you he?"

His features were impassive. "We're really *good* friends."

She arched her brow at the way he said that. There seemed to be a note that told her they were closer than just friends. "Like lovers?"

He handed her the helmet. "I fuck him all the time." Again his tone was completely devoid of emotion.

Kiara curled her lip at his unnecessary crudity. She didn't know why, but her heart sank at the thought of his being gay.

Figured. Men who looked that yummy were never straight. What a wasteful tragedy for all of womankind . . .

"Have you any idea how much money you could make by turning your lover in?"

"Yes, I do."

"Then why haven't you?"

"It's not worth my life. Besides, some days I actually like him."

What an odd thing to say. "I would think you should always like your lover."

"Do you always like yours?"

Kiara blushed at such a personal question. Then it dawned on her just how nosy she was being with him. He placed the black helmet over her head and fastened it for her.

She could feel his arms moving behind her and realized he was removing his shades.

Curious, she tried to turn around.

"Don't!" he snapped, finally breaking through that facade of ice.

Kiara stiffened. What about his eyes made him so angry? Was he deformed?

He's an assassin, girl. You know they're not right in the head. None of them.

It was true. Normal people didn't kill for a living and normal people didn't sleep with the most notorious assassin to ever live and not turn him in.

His strong arms came around her to press and flip the switches in front of her. As he did so, his sleeve pulled back enough that she could catch a glimpse of The League tattoo on his wrist in the gap between the sleeve and his black gloves. Her breath left her with an inaudible gasp.

It was true.

He really had been in The League.

Holy . . .

With a deafening roar, the engines fired, then settled down to a soft whir. In the crackling distortion filling her ears, she heard the controller's voice through the intercom in her helmet as he gave them launch instructions.

She leaned back as Nykyrian reached across her. The moment she did, his body jerked at the unexpected contact and she brushed against a part of him that was swollen and hard.

A wicked smile curved Kiara's lips. He was so not gay.

At least not entirely . . .

Nykyrian was instantly inflamed by her body pressed against his. Her hip was right against his cock which only made him harder. The sweet scent of her body filled his heightened senses, making him want to bury his face against her throat and inhale her as he cupped one of those perfect breasts in his hand.

God, he was an idiot. Why hadn't he thought to borrow Jayne or Syn's double-seated fighter?

But then he knew. If he had to dogfight, there was no ship out there faster or better than this one. And it was one he was so intimate with that it was like an extension of his own body.

In his world, he needed every advantage.

What he'd really underestimated was how Kiara's presence would affect him. Could he make it to Gouran without his hormones taking over?

Of course you can. You're a soldier.

Fully trained.

Sex equaled exposure. Exposure equaled death.

Never let anyone at your back. Never let anyone see you. Those lessons had been hardwired into his psyche and he wasn't about to forget them now.

Not even for her.

He forced his thoughts from the soft body molded against his and gave full attention to the directive for launch.

The g-forces brought her body solidly against his, increasing his discomfort. And his arousal. His hand trembled as he clutched the throttle.

But he ignored the heat he felt, just as he ignored her. Besides, a woman like her would never willingly touch something as unclean as he was. And it wasn't only the blood on his hands that would offend her. Nothing about him was decent or right. He was an abomination.

Never forget what you are . . . what I've made you. His adoptive father's words echoed harshly in his ears. How could he ever forget?

He remembered, even when he didn't want to.

You're a disgusting animal.

And that was all he'd ever be. Hell, he was lucky his adoptive father had even allowed him into his house—for that matter that *anyone* had ever allowed him into their home.

He flinched as old memories came back to bite him.

There was no use in reliving a past that had been excruciating enough the first time. So he did what he always did and shoved those memories aside and focused on his mission.

Getting her home to the people who loved her.

Within a few minutes, they cleared orbit.

Kiara watched as the murky gray planet shrank out of sight. She still had no idea which one it was. Shifting in the seat, she heard his sharp intake of breath.

"Sit still," he ordered, his voice hard. Not that it was by any means the only part of him hard . . .

His tone irked her. "What do you expect with me crammed in front of you?"

"I expect you to sit still."

"And I expect you to be a little less acerbic. You know, I didn't want to be here. You're the one who put me in your lap. If anyone should be bitching over it, it should be me. Not like I'm getting any kind of thrill from this, especially not with your attitude, buddy."

Nykyrian cursed under his breath. He knew he should apologize for his curtness. But apologies weren't something he'd ever concerned himself with. Honestly, he was amazed that he'd barked at her since he could count on one hand the number of times in his adulthood that anyone had elicited that much emotion from him.

She crossed her arms over her chest and slammed back against his chest so hard that he felt his breath leave him. Grinding his teeth, he fought the urge to take her head off again.

Or kill her.

But that was what she expected him to do and God forbid he ever do something that was expected of him. Not to mention, she'd been right earlier. She hadn't asked for any of this to happen to her. She'd been through a lot. The bruises on her face and neck and the deep cuts on her wrists testified to the severity of what she'd suffered.

At least she hadn't been raped. Her earlier tirade had told him that much. She'd been spared that particular humiliation, but by the looks of her, they'd more than intended to do it. Better than anyone, he knew what it was like to be held down while other people took their anger out on him.

To feel powerless and lost . . .

Violated against his best fight.

So he gave her space and silence for the rest of the long journey.

Kiara sat as still as she could, but she couldn't keep her anger up. She was too tired for that. And as Nykyrian relaxed behind her, she found herself following suit as the deep thump of his heart and the warm scent of his skin lulled her. It was actually kind of nice to be held in someone's arms after all she'd been through. She wanted comfort.

No, she needed it, and she hated herself for that weakness. She'd always prided herself on being strong. But right now, she felt like that scared little girl who'd begged for her mother's life. Like the little girl who wanted someone to hold her close and to reassure her everything was all right and that she'd be home soon where no one could touch her.

Unfortunately, she knew that even there she wasn't really safe. She would never in her life have safety . . .

But at least Nykyrian wasn't mocking her while he held a blaster to her head.

Yet.

She blinked her eyes, trying to stay awake, but the engines were so lulling and she was so tired . . .

Nykyrian barely caught her before she slumped into his controls. He could hear her even, slow breaths in his helmet.

How can you be asleep with a trained assassin sitting behind you?

And yet she was completely unconscious in his lap while her soft little snore came through the link in his helmet.

The woman was nuts. She had to be.

Or suicidal.

Damn, this had to be a first. He made most people so nervous that they practically wet themselves in his presence. No one had ever been this relaxed around him before.

Not even Syn.

Pulling her back, he cradled her with his body so that she could be as comfortable as possible. She turned in his arms and laid her head on his chest with one hand resting just above his cock. His body erupted with heat as he imagined her like this while they were both naked.

This is going to be a long ride . . .

The worst part was that on some unknown level, he actually liked the feeling of her like this. The warmth of her body against his.

You are out of your friggin' mind.

He picked her hand up to look at her long, graceful fingers that were perfectly manicured. Like the rest of her, they were dainty and beautiful.

Before he could stop himself, he removed one of his

gloves so that he could hold her hand in his and feel her flesh against his. He'd been right. Her skin was softer than velvet. And the sensation of it played havoc with his mind as he imagined her touching him.

Don't be stupid. She would never voluntarily touch you.

It was true and he knew it. But still he couldn't stop wanting to take his helmet off and lay those fingers against his face. To nibble the pads of each one . . .

What would it be like to have a loving hand touch him?

Just once?

Grinding his teeth, he saw the ugliness of his scarred, damaged hand covering the beauty of hers. *You are revolting. Every part of you an eyesore to humanity . . .*

His stomach twisting at the insults that were en-graved in his soul, he put her hand down and replaced his glove. *You are such a pathetic fool. There's no such thing as a loving hand for anyone. How many times has a wife tried to hire you to kill off her husband for his money or just for the hell of it?*

Yeah, people were treacherous to the bitter end and only an idiot ever trusted one.

Kiara jerked awake at the small beep that pulsed on Nykyrian's control panel. Her heart hammering, she tried to get her bearings.

"What's that? Are we under attack?"

Nykyrian pointed to the left . . .

She sat up quickly, half expecting to find an enemy ship there. But that wasn't what she saw.

She laughed as her home planet came into view. Never had she been so happy to see Gouran. She splayed her hand on the cold glass, staring at it, afraid that if she so much as blinked this would be a dream and her planet would vanish. The green and blue that was mixed with the red soil of the desert regions . . . It was so beautiful.

She was home . . .

They'd kept their word and not harmed her.

In that moment, she could have hugged Nykyrian for it.

Are you insane?

No, she was just that grateful.

Before she knew it, they were in the planet's atmosphere and blue skies were once again above her while the green undisturbed countryside sped by below. Nykyrian's deep voice spoke her native Gourish flawlessly as he talked to the controller. "I'm here on a diplomatic mission to return the Princess Kiara Zamir to her father. I need the coordinates to land in or near his palace."

The controller's voice cracked as he gave them instructions to land in her father's private bay.

But before he finished giving the proper coordinates, a squadron of eight fighters surrounded them. The ships were not a welcoming party.

They were military fighters, fully armed and ready to fire.

A warning alarm sounded in Nykyrian's fighter, letting them know they were in the lock zone for a missile or laser strike.

Nykyrian's arms tightened in expectation as he activated his own weapons and moved his left hand toward the trigger. "I'm here on a peaceful mission. Deactivate the lock. Now." She admired his even, nonaggressive tone, especially given the fact that one of the fighters rolled in front of them, forcing him to slow down abruptly.

"You disengage first," the command pilot demanded.

Nykyrian's thumb rested on the trigger. "Not until you drop target on me."

Her heart pounded as all of them refused to back down. What if one of her father's soldiers panicked and fired for no reason? Though pilots were carefully trained, mistakes happened and she didn't want to be included in a statistics report under "uh-oh, my bad."

"Release the fighters," she snapped into her mic.

"Kiara?" Her father's relieved voice burst through her headset. "Is that really you, angel? Are you all right?" His voice broke on the last word. He must have thought Nykyrian was returning her body . . .

She rubbed her arm against the chills that thought caused. "Yes, Papa. I'm fine. Please have them stand down. He's here only to return me and has caused me no harm whatsoever. Call your troops off."

Silence greeted her for a few seconds.

Finally, her father recalled his soldiers to base.

Nykyrian's arms relaxed around her as the fighters dropped away and the ship's alarms subsided.

He deactivated his weapons.

She let out her own relieved breath, grateful she was almost home. It took several more long minutes to reach the main landing bay.

Made of glass and concrete, she'd never thought the building particularly attractive. But today, it was the most beautiful place in the universe. Never had she been happier to see it. The capitol city hummed with activity as they lowered their altitude and prepared for landing.

Nykyrian slid the ship inside the bay with barely more than a whisper of a bump before they came to rest in the center of the dock.

After releasing the canopy, he unbuckled Kiara from

her seat. She removed her helmet and turned to face him. She raised a questioning eyebrow as she noted he made no moves to remove his own gear. "You're not going to greet my father?" Most people considered it the greatest honor to meet the legendary commander.

Looking over the side of his fighter, Nykyrian shook his head at the large number of soldiers gathered. "They look nervous."

Kiara handed him the helmet. "I can never thank you enough for what you've done."

"Just do yourself a favor and stay out of trouble."

His words sparked anger in her, but not at him. At the sad reality of her life. "All I did was go to sleep. There shouldn't be anything safer than that."

When he spoke, she heard the bitterness underneath his tone. "Spoken like a true civilian. Trust me, princess, that's the most dangerous thing anyone does . . . Well that, and go to the can."

Those words made her wonder how many times he'd killed someone that way.

It sent another cold chill over her.

"Thank you again," she whispered, wanting to get away from him as quickly as possible.

She dropped over the side of his ship.

Once her feet touched the ground, she ran to her father's outstretched arms. Her heart was light now that she was safe and returned.

With short, gray hair and a well-trimmed beard, Kiefer Zamir was a distinguished-looking man. But right now, he had dark circles under his eyes from lack of sleep. He frowned at the marks on her face as he cupped her bruised cheek in his hand.

Kiara gave him a tight hug. "It doesn't hurt."

She saw the doubt in his brown eyes. "The Sentella told me they killed the ones responsible."

Kiara trembled at the reminder of her captors and their fate—not that they didn't deserve it. "They did."

Kiefer squeezed her to the point she feared her ribs would crack. "You shall have an armed guard in the future no matter where you go. I don't know what possessed The Sentella to return you unharmed. But I thank God you're safe."

Safe. Kiara gave a nervous laugh. She found it difficult to believe she'd been inside the fabled Sentella Command Center, seen Nemesis, and none of the mercenaries had even threatened her life.

Much.

Just the same, she wouldn't tell her father about them, or what little she'd been privy to. She owed them that much and more.

Turning around, she watched as Nykyrian secured his canopy. She didn't know anything about him really, but for some reason, she wondered if she'd ever see him or Syn again.

Nykyrian paused as he saw Kiara watching him. Her father continued to hold her in his arms as if afraid of letting her go—not that he blamed the man. He'd do the same with his kid if he'd had one he'd almost lost. Then again, he would never take that kind of chance with a kid of his.

His child would never be allowed out of his sight.

And still she watched him . . .

Damn, she was the most beautiful woman he'd ever seen. Even in a battlesuit that didn't fit her and with her face bruised and her hair mussed, she still took his breath away. And for a moment, he couldn't help wondering what it would feel like to hold her . . .

Stop being stupid. You're an assassin, dumbass. Act like it.

Pushing her out of his thoughts, he prepared to launch and get out of this place before they made him a memory and proved Syn's adage. He didn't belong here with decent people.

He was an animal and he knew it.

As soon as he could, he launched.

But as the tiny planet faded, he couldn't get the image of her and her father out of his mind. What did that kind of love feel like? He had no concept of it. Although sometimes when he dreamed, he saw an Andarion woman he liked to think was his mother holding him as a child. She sang to him and brushed his hair back from his face while he smiled at her.

But that was only a dream.

No one had ever hugged him or sang to him. Very few had even been kind to him. Scorn. Disdain. Brutality. That was all he'd ever known after his mother had abandoned him to a human orphanage. His mother hadn't even thought enough of him to dump him there herself.

She'd sent her staff to do it.

Not even your own mother wanted you, freak. He flinched at the sound of Commander Quiakides's cruel voice in his head.

His adoptive father . . .

The man hadn't wanted a son anymore than his mother had. The commander had only wanted a legacy.

And that was what had been beaten into him for the whole of his childhood. *You are my gift to The League and you will be legend.*

A legend that had turned into their curse . . .

Nykyrian scoffed at his maudlin thoughts. What did he need with kindness anyway? It only made a soldier weak, vulnerable.

Things that would get him killed. And he had no intention of dying.

He shrugged off the melancholy thoughts, turned his ship around and made his way to his own isolated home. That was the only place where he felt safe. The only place where he felt even the slightest bit like he belonged.

It didn't take long to reach the orange and yellow planet that wasn't on most maps. It had a peculiar orbit that system engineers had deemed impossible for development. But it worked well for his needs. Besides, his home wasn't on the planet itself. It hovered in the upper atmosphere where the outside was coated with reflekakor—a mineral that would keep it from showing up on any scanners.

And with fifteen thousand square feet, the house was more than large enough to fulfill his needs as a lair, home, and isolation chamber.

The only person who knew it existed was Syn.

Which worked well for him since he hated interacting with other people. And at this point, he'd been around them too long for one day. He needed time to himself.

Buzzing past the house, he docked in the hangar adjacent to it.

He pressed the button on his control panel that closed the portal behind his ship and waited for the artificial air to replace the deadly, natural one. When the light came on notifying him it was safe to leave, he exited his fighter.

As soon as he entered his house, his four pets assailed him with happy leaps and licks.

The lorinas were feline creatures many assumed could never be domesticated. It'd taken Nykyrian a long time to make them docile, but as with most beings once they learned he could be trusted not to hurt or neglect them, they settled into an easy camaraderie.

They were the only balm against loneliness he would allow himself. Fiercely loyal, they couldn't be bribed or turned against him for any reason, unlike humans or other so-called civilized beings. Hell, every day he lived without Syn or one of the others in their organization taking a shot at his back he considered it a miracle.

Rubbing the soft fur of the lorinas' heads, Nykyrian dropped his helmet by the door. He was grateful it was still night on his part of the planet. With any luck he might be able to get some sleep.

The stars twinkled brightly through the clear ceiling while his home floated placidly above the gaseous world below. It was a peaceful, soothing place that never failed to ease the tension in his muscles or relax his troubled thoughts.

He'd purchased the planet several years earlier after deciding he was tired of living in cramped flats inside noisy, crime-ridden cities. There was no chance here of anyone finding him. Of an assassin or officer throwing themselves into his line of fire.

For the first time in his life, he could sleep in peace and not have to bolt awake at every sound.

Wearily, Nykyrian made his way up the stairs to his left. His large, soft bed welcomed him. He pulled the tie from his braid, shook his hair loose, then fell on top of the black fur covers.

Oh yeah . . . This was what he needed in the worst sort of way. Not a dancer who'd hate him. Not the comfort of a friend.

Just his bed and a few hours of sleep.

He rolled onto his back and lay for hours watching the sky above him as that precious sleep eluded him for some reason. It was all he could do not to curse in frustration. Despite the tranquility of the heavens, there was none for his mind. The lorinas draped across him, offering him what solace they could, but it didn't keep his thoughts out of places he didn't want them to go.

Stroking their fur, he thought of bouncing, dark mahogany curls as the trim dancer ran to her father. Imagined what it would be like to make love to her until they were both sore for days . . .

Gah, it was sheer torture.

As the sky began to lighten, he saw a ship zoom overhead. He knew the markings as soon as he saw the sleek fighter.

Syn.

How weird that he hadn't called. But then Syn was probably drunk and not thinking. It happened more than he liked.

Nykyrian didn't move while he waited for Syn to dock and enter.

The lorinas heard the loud crackle of Syn's engines and jumped from the bed, anxious to greet their other friend. Nykyrian grunted as they used his stomach for a launching pad.

"Kip!" Syn yelled below, bombarded by the lorinas. "When are you going to chain these mongrels up?"

Running his hand through his unbound hair, Nykyrian sat up. The lorinas bounded up the stairs, followed by Syn.

Nykyrian stacked his pillows up along the wall and reclined against them. "Well?" he asked as Syn sprawled across the foot of his bed.

"I told Zamir we were booked. Ignoring what he didn't want to hear, he offered us a chunk of money which I told him changed nothing. He made another huge counteroffer which I was tempted to take and guard her myself. I could use a planet of my own, you know? Not to mention, it'd be worth guarding her just for the eye candy alone—sheez, can you imagine being around *that* day in and day out . . ."

He paused to look at Nykyrian. "Wonder if she sleeps naked . . . Bet she showers that way. Every day even. Think about it. I'll even bet she's naked underneath her clothes."

Nykyrian rolled his eyes. As always, Syn's brief was efficient, short, and comical. He drew his leg up and draped his arm over his knee. "What are the Probekeins up to?"

"They want the Gourans to relinquish all rights to Miremba IV to them. You were right about it pertaining to the weapon. Seems the Probekeins have need of the resources on that outpost to complete the explosive."

Nykyrian frowned. "I wasn't aware there was any surata on Miremba." His mind ran through all the chemicals the weapon needed; surata was the only one the Probekeins didn't have in their own territories.

Syn didn't comment. He rolled over and propped himself up on his elbows, staring at the rose- and amber-streaked sky. "This is really a great view. You should try looking at it when you're good and flagged."

"You should try it sober."

"Ouch. That hurt." Syn laughed. "I'm sober now and I must say it's not nearly as interesting." He shifted his gaze to Nykyrian. "I haven't had a drink in over three hours. I'm doing good."

"You could do better."

Syn snorted. "I'll quit *my* drinking on *your* wedding day."

Nykyrian stood, unamused. "I need to eat." He headed toward the stairs.

"Wait," Syn called, stopping him. "I thought you might want to know. The Probekeins have upgraded their contract on Kiara's life. Both Pitala and Aksel Bredeh have signed on to track her."

Nykyrian went cold. Pitala was a putz, but he was lethal and cruel. As for Bredeh . . . that bastard was insane. Brutal.

More than that, he was trained by the best of The League and, while he'd failed to be admitted as an assassin, he was dangerous to the extreme. "When did you find that out?"

"On my way over here."

Thoughts tumbled through Nykyrian's mind. Pitala could most likely be stopped.

Bredeh on the other hand . . .

He could bypass any system and he wouldn't stop until his target was mutilated and dead. Nykyrian knew firsthand just how vicious and unfeeling Bredeh was. How much joy he would take in making Kiara beg for a mercy the man completely lacked.

An image of Kiara lying dead twisted his gut. He'd spent the first half of his life killing for The League and he knew only too well what an assassin, especially Pitala or Bredeh, would do to her before he ended her life. Part of an assassin's job was to make the kill as gruesome as possible to intimidate the victim's relatives and allies.

He hated himself for that past even though it'd been forced on him.

Now Nykyrian was an avenger, not a murderer. When he'd left The League, he'd sworn he would protect the innocent victims chosen by The League and other assassins . . .

He couldn't let her die.

You're not the law anymore, Syn's voice echoed in his head from an argument they'd had years ago. *You left that behind the moment you dug out your tracer.*

Syn had been right. He wasn't the law. Now he was retribution and justice. Retribution usually came too late and justice would never allow Kiara to die over something that didn't even concern her.

Nykyrian stared at Syn in indecision. It wasn't his job or his responsibility to guard Kiara. He'd done his sentence in hell when he belonged to The League. To be alone with her and not touch her would be an even worse torture for him than the missions he'd been forced to execute against his will.

Kiara's battered face drifted through his mind. Had they been a few minutes later, she'd have been raped and murdered . . .

In that instant, Nykyrian made his decision.

"Call Zamir."

CHAPTER 5

Kiara stretched her tense joints. She hoped she could give a decent performance tonight, but she doubted it. She hadn't slept for the last four nights with any kind of peace. Every time she tried to rest, nightmares of her mother's death plagued her, along with the memory of the lasers cutting into her own body.

Kill them both.

Would she *ever* get those cold, soulless words out of her head? It'd taken her years of therapy after that attack to be able to sleep through a full night. Years of therapy to dull the memories of blood and fear.

Two years to be able to go to the restroom alone.

A year after that before she could close the door to a room or stall while she was inside it.

Even though her father had hunted down and killed the ones responsible and paid a fortune in plastic surgery to remove her scars from the attack, it hadn't been enough.

That day lived forever inside her.

But on the day when she'd turned sixteen and had narrowly missed being shot in her favorite restaurant while she celebrated another year of her life, she'd decided that she was tired of living in terror.

No, she couldn't stop the animals from trying to kill her. She had no control over their greed or actions.

All she could do was control her own.

She would *not* live in fear another day, under lock and key. They may have taken her mother from her, but they wouldn't take her sanity or her freedom. She refused to give them that power over her. While the inner scars remained, she would stand strong against those demons.

Always.

No one would make her feel weak and powerless again. No one. She wasn't going to be like her mother or other aristocratic children who could only leave their protected rooms under heavy security. She was going to be normal and to live her life the way she wanted to. Animals be damned.

Yet words were easy. Living by them was what was hard, and it'd been a battle every day since.

Today was harder than most. Every sound made her jump. Every shadow made her flinch. She hated being like this. But for all her bravado, she knew the truth. There was no sanctuary safe enough. No place secure enough that they couldn't get to her if they wanted to . . .

Make the most of it all. That was her mantra since any second she breathed could be her last.

With a tired sigh, she went to stare at her reflection, checking her costume for any telltale flaws. The tight, red, sequined bodysuit clung to her figure, making her regret the large amount of sweets she'd eaten that afternoon in an effort to cheer her mood.

She was still miserable, only now she had a fat butt to go with it.

But at least her bruises were almost gone. She was a bit surprised the media hadn't questioned her about her battered face. Most likely it was hidden by the heavy amount of red and gold makeup her costume required. They probably hadn't even noticed.

Kiara made a face at herself and returned to her nervous pacing.

Loneliness filled her as she glanced around the tiny, empty room. Her father thought his absence comforted her. Everyone seemed to think she preferred solitude before a performance, but the truth was very different. She needed company most in the minutes prior to a dance. Just the sound of another voice would alleviate some of the anxiety tearing at her.

What if I trip? Forget a move?

What if my costume rips?

Just don't let me embarrass myself . . .

Those doubts and fears never went away. "You would think by now I'd be used to this."

But no. It never seemed to get any easier. Every show was hard and her fear of screwing up and being laughed at never abated. The worst part was the knowledge of all the other dancers in the company who wanted her to fail. Those who would laugh if she made a mistake or who would revel in her humiliation.

For that matter, half of them would hire an assassin to kill her if they could get away with it.

Why did people have to be so cruel? She'd never once in her life taken pleasure at someone else's pain, let alone their torture.

Chewing her thumbnail, she continued to pace the room. As she neared the door, she heard the muffled voices of her father's guards outside in the hallway.

"You know, I didn't enlist for this kind of bullshit. I'm a soldier, not a babysitter for some rich bitch who can't keep her whiny ass at home. Hell, I wish someone would try to kill her just to get rid of the boredom."

The other guard laughed. "I can think of a better way to end my boredom."

"What do you mean?"

"Imagine having overnight duty at her place. I envy Yanas and Briqs."

"Yeah, I'd like to show that little dumpling my nightstick."

Repulsed by their bantering, Kiara crossed the room and rifled through her bag on the table. Pulling out the small blaster, she made sure it contained a full charge.

"You pigs," she said under her breath, appalled by their words. She wasn't whiny and while she could be a bitch if the occasion warranted it, she'd been nothing but courteous and respectful to them.

Why would they be so hurtful toward her?

At the moment, she didn't know whom she trusted less, the Probekeins or her father's uncouth soldiers. Either way, she wasn't taking any more chances with her safety.

After she replaced the weapon, she returned to pacing. It was almost time to start the show. The director's assistant would be here any second to lead her out. She could hear the orchestra warming up, making a loud cacophony that echoed all the way to her room.

There was something muffled out in the hallway, but the music covered it. Assuming it was the assistant trying to get past her guards, she headed for the door.

As she moved closer, a tall shadow fell across her.

Her breath caught as she froze in terror. No . . . she was safe here. Not only did the show have its regular security, her father's men were all over the place. No one could get in. She was just imagining the fact that the shadow looked like a giant man.

It was just her paranoia making her scared. Nothing more. Nothing less.

No one was here.

Still, unreasoning dread filled her. She didn't want to turn around, but she did anyway, then wished she'd listened to herself.

Cold, black eyes stared at her from a handsome human face that lacked all compassion. A maniacal smile twisted his lips letting her know he enjoyed the thought of hurting her.

She looked to her bag on the table next to him. Could she get to her blaster?

As if he could read her thoughts, he glanced to the bag. With a swipe of his arm, he knocked it to the floor. She took a step, then froze as her blaster landed at his feet with a heavy, soul-wrenching thud.

He laughed cruelly and retrieved it in his large paw of a hand.

Kiara ran to the door, only to have him grab her and sling her away from it. She rolled across the floor, then came to her feet—the beauty of being a dancer. She could catch her balance and bend with the best of them.

"Guards!" she screamed, knowing the soldiers outside would come to her rescue.

Clucking his tongue, the assassin shook his head. "They can't hear you, sweetmeat. They're dead."

Those words rang in her ears as old memories flashed . . . Her mother's guards being blown to pieces as she and her mother were dragged into a waiting transport. The smell of blood and her first taste of real terror.

Her breathing became labored and rapid. She wasn't dead yet . . . Glancing to the door, she knew it was the only chance she had.

She tossed a chair at the assassin and ran.

Her hand touched the icy knob. She grasped it like a lifeline, but before she could twist it open, a blow struck her across the back, knocking her away.

Dazed, she hit the floor.

Desperately she wanted to scream again, but her lungs were incapable of anything save the cold rasping breaths rattling in her chest. She scooted along the floor in an effort to put more distance between them as she tried to think of another way out of the room.

But there wasn't one. Panic twined through her, blinding her eyes. There was no way out.

There's no . . .

No, wait . . .

The window. That must have been how he got into the room.

She looked up at it.

It was still open.

You can reach it. It was her only hope. Rising up fast, she ran, intending to jump for it.

Before she could make it, the assassin grabbed her by the throat and shoved her across her dressing table. Her bottles of perfume and makeup rattled, biting into her back, tearing at her flesh while he tightened his grip. Tears of frustrated pain welled in her eyes as she stared into the assassin's unfeeling face.

Kiara kicked and punched as she fought against him with everything she had. It just wasn't enough.

The assassin held his blaster to her cheek, his twisted laughter filling her ears as she waited for the final explosive sound that would end her life.

CHAPTER 6

The door burst open with a resounding crash.

"Drop it, Pitala."

Kiara went cold in relief at the deep accent she remembered so well. It was him . . .

Nykyrian.

Opening her eyes, she turned her head to see Nykyrian standing calmly in the doorway, his arms braced on either side of the frame as if he was leisurely chatting with a friend.

His long coat was pulled back on both sides to show two holstered blasters and an assortment of weapons she could only guess at. As before, his long, blond hair was braided down his back and a pair of dark shades covered his face.

"I'll kill her, freak," Pitala snarled in warning as he clicked off the blaster's release.

Nykyrian appeared unaffected by the insult and threat—and why wouldn't he be? It wasn't like the blaster was pressing against *his* temple.

He released a bored sigh. "Then I'll kill you and laugh while I do it. Either way it's no real sweat off my balls. Release her and you can at least walk away alive. But that's not a standing offer. Make your mind up quick before I kill you just for getting me out on a night when I'd rather be at home doing needlework."

Kiara swallowed at the ambivalence of his tone. She would appreciate his ability to remain calm had it not been her life they were negotiating over.

Pitala glared at her in indecision.

His blaster moved away from her head. She took a shaky breath, offering a prayer of thanks. "Do you think I fear you, half-breed?" Pitala sneered, refusing to release his grip on her throat.

Nykyrian shifted to one side of the door frame. "Stop stalling, asshole. Do you honestly think I'd be stupid enough to stand here until your partner comes up behind me?" He snapped his fingers.

An unconscious man was shoved through the door. Pitala cursed.

"I really hate taking out the trash." Syn joined Nykyrian as he wiped his hands together.

Pitala released her.

Kiara rubbed her bruised throat and slid from the table. She jumped in reflex as Pitala moved his weapon toward the pair standing in the doorway.

Before he could aim it at either man, two blasters came out of nowhere to balance their sights on his body. Two red targeting lasers hovered without shaking—one between his eyes and one over his grain.

"Think," Nykyrian said ominously, clicking back the release of his blaster with his thumb.

Pitala gave a nervous laugh, and held up his hands. "I wouldn't actually try to shoot you. I just wanted to see if you were as good as they say."

"Better." Syn moved forward to pull Pitala's blaster from his hand. "And that's with me drunk off my ass. Imagine what I'd do to you sober."

It was only after he was disarmed and Syn stood

between her and Pitala that Nykyrian's red light vanished from Pitala's forehead.

With an amazing nonchalance, Nykyrian holstered his weapon. "Apologize to *Tara* Zamir for ruining her night and you can leave."

Angry black eyes focused on Kiara with an unspoken promise he would be back. "My apologies, princess," he rasped. "It was nothing personal."

Cold sweat beaded on her body as Pitala bent and slapped his partner awake. Within seconds, the pair of assassins were gone.

Her relief at their departure gave way to suspicion over the two of them and *their* intentions. "What are *you* doing here?"

"Saving you," Nykyrian said absently, looking down the corridor with his back to them.

Still, Kiara wasn't sure the danger had passed. The Sentella had turned down the contract to protect her. Maybe they'd only saved her from Pitala so they could collect the bounty on her life themselves.

Syn stared at her. "She's not quite in shock, but I bet she faints before you get her home."

Kiara opened her mouth to remind him she didn't faint, but was silenced by Nykyrian returning into the room.

"Here." Syn handed her a piece of candy.

"I'm not hungry."

He put it in her hand. "Eat it. You need it. The sugar will help with the shock."

Kiara took it even though her stomach knotted in protest.

Syn looked back at Nykyrian. "Did they go out the back?"

"Yes. Fifty *dorcas* they're setting up an ambush near my ship."

Syn snorted. "No bet. I know they are. They're too stupid to not be obvious and predictable. Gah, I hate abiding by the law. Too bad you can't slaughter them where they stand."

Nykyrian inclined his head to Syn. "Stop bitching. You know what to do. I'll meet you at rendezvous point and time."

Syn returned his nod. "Smoke and burn," he said to Nykyrian on his way out the door.

Nykyrian turned his attention to Kiara, whose makeup had been ruined by her tears, as she opened the candy with shaking hands and placed it on her tongue. He wanted desperately to comfort her, but didn't know how. The handful of times he'd ever cried, he'd been beaten for it. Since tender words and touches were all but alien to him, he had no idea how to offer them to someone else.

He didn't even understand why he had the urge.

Compassion for others had been drilled out of him and yet she breached the sanctity of all that training. The League Academy would be horrified to find out that one woman's tears could undo all their expensive programs. No wonder they kept their assassins locked down.

Her tears still glistened on her cheeks where they'd washed away streaks of her makeup.

His hand tightened around the grip of his blaster as anger over that burned him. He should have killed Pitala for the grief he caused her.

I hate this legal shit.

But so long as Syn was with him, he had to stay on the right side of the law or see his friend executed. So the scum was able to live even though he wanted to gut him.

Pushing his emotions back into restraint, Nykyrian

retrieved her cloak from a peg inside the door. He handed it to her. "Here. We need to go."

Kiara swallowed the piece of candy. For a moment, she was unable to understand the words through the fog clouding her mind. "You mean leave?"

"Yes."

She shook her head. "I have a show to perform." Her voice sounded hollow even to herself. She had to dance. People had paid too much money. Her promoters would never forgive her if she disappointed the audience for any reason.

The show must go on . . .

It was the one code that she'd lived her entire life by. The one her own father had drilled into her. No matter what happened or how she felt, her performances came first.

Yet inside she heard someone screaming and couldn't place the source. She felt strangely numb. Like walking in a dream. Everything seemed to have slowed down.

All she could think of was getting to the stage . . .

Nykyrian grabbed her arm as she tried to walk past him. Her lucidity worried him. Had she suffered a breakdown from the attack? "You have to leave the theater."

"I can't. It's not allowed."

Her voice, haunting in its emptiness, worried him. While that tone was normal for him, it wasn't normal for others. Not for people who weren't used to seeing death and fighting for their lives.

He wanted to shake her. Her amber eyes were glassy, devoid of any emotion. Syn was right, she was in shock.

"Listen," he said, trying to break through the mild sedation her mind had provided for her. "Pitala didn't go far. You go out on that stage and he can take you out from anywhere in the audience. Every minute we delay, he's looking for a place to take a snipe at you. We *must* leave. Now."

Kiara laughed, not really understanding his words. Pulling away from his grip, she walked into the hallway.

Her toe struck something solid.

She looked down.

Her numbness left her in a wake of consuming terror. On the ground were the bodies of her guards. Their eyes opened and glazed, red blood seeped through their uniforms and spread across the tiled floor in a sickening mess. And in that moment, her past tore through her with serrated brutality. She could feel her mother falling against her as she was shot down. See their blood mingling.

Her mother's weight . . . It had been crushing . . .

Her hysterical screams echoed in the hallway as she saw the barrel of the blaster that had shot her as a child. Saw the cold eyes of the assassin who'd meant to kill her.

Over and over, she felt the sting of her wounds and heard her mother's screams for mercy . . .

"Make it stop! Please, make it stop!"

Nykyrian winced at the sound that seemed to come from some dark place inside her soul. It was bone-chilling.

Without thinking, he drew her into his arms and cradled her head against his chest to block the sight of the dead soldiers. "Don't look."

He held her quietly while she sobbed inconsolably. He'd long ceased being horrified by bodies. The only emotion the grisly sight evoked in him was anger over the waste.

Her hot tears soaked through his shirt, forming chills on his skin. The soft scent of flowers drifted from her hair that had been sprayed with glitter and braided with pieces of ribbon and lace. Her slender arms clutched at him in desperation as her body was wracked with sobs.

Why the hell wasn't Syn here to deal with this? He'd know what to do and say. He'd actually had a wife at one time. Nykyrian felt completely lost and unprepared—two feelings he despised.

"Everything will be fine," he said, hoping that was what he should be saying. He started to pat her back, then stopped since he didn't want to hurt her. She was so frail and tiny. The last thing he wanted was to inadvertently damage her with his Andarion strength.

How did humans comfort each other?

Telling her to stop and let it go just didn't seem right.

What else was there?

Unsure, he let her weep while he held her.

Kiara clutched Nykyrian like a lifeline. She needed the safety he offered, the protection. She found a strange comfort in his arms. His heart beat a steady, soothing rhythm under her cheek. He was as calm on the inside as he appeared. A faint smell of leather and musk came from his skin, soothing her in spite of the terror of this night and her past.

She didn't want to die. Not like this. Not like those poor men on the floor . . .

Someone help me!

Nykyrian clenched his teeth as her embrace tightened. Never in his life had anyone held him in such a manner. He knew it was only her emotional state that prompted her to touch him at all.

You're wasting valuable time.

He had to get her to safety.

Pulling away, he held her shoulders and forced her to look up at him. "We must leave."

With a ragged breath to steady her frayed nerves,

Kiara took her cloak from his hand and wrapped it around her shoulders. She shielded her eyes from the bodies. For now, she had no choice but to trust this stranger to get her past Pitala. Nykyrian had saved her life, obviously he knew what he was doing.

They had to get out of here.

Nykyrian checked both ways before he stepped into the hallway. Keeping one hand on her and the other on his blaster, he led her to the caterer's entrance, then to the back door and out onto the curb.

He hailed a transport from the line of them across the street.

Kiara stepped inside the car, pushing herself as far over in the seat as she could. She just wanted to fade into obscurity and never be bothered or hunted again.

Nykyrian gave her address to the computer.

She went cold with dread. "How do you know where I live?"

"All good mercenaries know it. The Probekeins have been listing your name and address for the last week on their bounty sheets."

She shook even more. All this time, she'd deluded herself into thinking she was quasi safe. She should have known better.

Her stomach churned as she thought about her father's soldiers. It was all her fault they were dead. Even though they'd said such unkind things about her, they didn't deserve what Pitala had done to them. No doubt they had families and would have had a future had she . . .

Kiara couldn't go there.

The Probekeins wanted her dead and anyone near her could be the next victim. "Aren't you afraid to be with me?"

"Afraid?" For the first time she heard emotion in his tone. It was full of disbelief.

"The next assassin could kill you by accident."

"Let me to assure you, if anyone kills me, it won't be by accident. The price The League has on my head makes a mockery of the one on yours. Not to mention the instant prestige killing me would give a mercenary should one of them ever succeed."

Kiara nodded, unable to speak around the clump of tears in her throat. Here she sat, next to a true mercenary, a brutal killer if the truth were spoken.

Why was he helping her?

"Are you going to kill me?" Her voice shook from the strain and fear of her words.

He didn't react to the question at all. "If I had that intention, you'd have been dead before you ever saw me."

Those emotionless words sent a cold chill over her. "But why are you protecting me? I thought mercenary assassins were only motivated by money."

Nykyrian rubbed his right hand over his left bicep—the place where his full League tattoo would be located. "You haven't met enough of us to know what motivates us."

Kiara conceded he was right, but it didn't change her suspicions. "You avoided my question. Why are you helping me?"

His hand stopped. He looked away from her. "Maybe I'm a fan."

"Are you?"

"Yes."

Kiara stared at him too shocked and confused to feel anything. Nykyrian sat so still next to her, he seemed ethereal. Like an angel of death, only in her case he was protecting her—or at least that's what he claimed. His blond hair was so pale and smooth. As before, the dark shades obscured his face, giving her no real idea what he looked like.

He was a complete enigma. If she was to trust in him to keep her safe when it seemed to go against his nature, she wanted to know something about him. Something that would make him seem . . .

Human.

"Who are you? Really."

Nykyrian shrugged. "Never figured it out. Takes too much time to think about myself, and time is one luxury I don't own."

Kiara fell silent, thinking, remembering. She couldn't get the image of the dead soldiers out of her mind no matter how hard she tried. "I killed those guards you know."

Her words seemed to soften some of his rigidness. "The Probekeins killed them."

Kiara shook her head, unwilling to see reason right now. "No, they were protecting *me*. They should have been home with their families, not in the Probekeins' line of fire."

Nykyrian looked in her direction. "They were soldiers, *mu Tara*. Death is nothing more than the hazard of the business. They knew the risk and accepted it the moment they donned their uniforms."

"Could you accept it?"

"I have."

She frowned at his disclosure. "You were brought back?"

He didn't respond to her question. "Death is the final blow we're all dealt sooner or later. No one is immune, believe me on that, and tonight the mistress took them home. Don't cry for them, princess. I assure you, they wouldn't cry for you."

His words cut through her. "How can you be so cold?"

"I'm a soldier, *mu Tara*. Emotions are hazardous for us so we dump them."

Kiara scoffed. "You're a mercenary. There is a difference."

"True. Mercenaries are better paid."

Frustration welled up inside her. He was of the same caliber as Pitala. Would he hold a blaster to her head if given the right amount of money?

The thought chilled her.

She couldn't trust him. She knew it. Trust belonged to the past. She'd trusted the dance company's security to protect her in the hotel and she'd been abducted. She'd trusted her father's soldiers and she'd almost been killed. Never again would she be so foolish.

Nykyrian would have to be watched until she knew exactly where his loyalties lay.

"Why are we in a transport anyway? Isn't this dangerous?"

He shook his head. "Random is safer than habit. Since they don't know this transport, they couldn't have it marked or traced."

Marked . . . a military euphemism for armed with a bomb. God, how she hated being in this situation.

The transport stopped outside her building. Nykyrian exited first and scanned the street before he stepped out enough to let her leave.

He shielded her with his body as they crossed the sidewalk and she inserted her key card into the door's lock. When the door opened, he grabbed her arm to keep her from entering the building before he scanned the hallway, then the street.

"You're making me nervous," she snapped as her shaking hands almost caused her to drop her key.

"You should be nervous."

Kiara let out a frustrated breath. So much for having a guard reassure her . . . She stepped into the corridor and headed for the lift. "My flat is on the top floor."

"I know."

He infuriated her. If he knew so much, why didn't he lead the way? Oh, what she wouldn't give to knock some of his cockiness out of him. "It must thrill you to always be right." She pushed the number for her floor.

As the doors closed, he faced her. "You can attack me all you wish. I don't give a *minsid* damn whether or not you like me. But you *will* respect me, listen to me, and *obey* me. Do you understand?"

Anger stung her cheeks at his rapid, even-toned dictation for her behavior. "I'm not yours, you have no ownership papers. My God, I haven't even hired you."

"You haven't. Your father has."

Kiara stiffened in confusion. "What's that supposed to mean? I was there when Syn turned my father's proposal down."

"We reconsidered."

The knot in her stomach loosened. "Why?"

He stepped back from her. "Pitala and Aksel Bredeh."

Kiara frowned. Pitala she knew only too well, especially since she could still feel his slimy hands on her. "What is Aksel Bredeh?"

"He's another rancid mercenary assassin, *mu Tara*."

She clenched her teeth. "Why do you keep calling me *Tara*? Is it an insult?"

Nykyrian tensed for a moment. "It's Andarion for lady."

"Oh." His explanation caught her off guard. Why would he choose to call her that after his rough treatment of her? It didn't make sense and it went a long way in softening her anger at him.

"Who's Aksel Bredeh?" she asked in a softer tone, wondering what there was to the new mercenary that would motivate Nykyrian to help her after they'd turned her father down. Could Bredeh be any worse than Pitala? She shivered at the thought.

Silence answered her question.

She glared at Nykyrian, waiting for a response. Before she could ask again, the doors opened on her floor.

With one hand braced on the door of the lift to keep it from closing, he stepped out and scanned the corridor.

Tempted to shove him and say boo, Kiara bet herself he'd jump twelve feet.

Or shoot her. As an ex-League assassin, he would be very dangerous if startled.

He tapped the comlink in his right ear to activate it. "We're in the hall. Any alerts?" He paused before allowing her to lead the way to her flat.

She reached her door and stopped. There was some kind of strange device hooked into her card slot. "This has been tampered with."

Someone was inside her flat. She could hear them.

Cold fear washed over her.

Not again . . .

CHAPTER 7

Nykyrian pulled Kiara behind him, then knocked twice on the door to her flat. It was all she could do not to hold on to him for support. She was so scared, she was amazed that her legs were still holding her upright.

"Who is it?" a deep voice growled from inside.

Nykyrian answered in what had to be the most sarcastic tone she'd ever heard. "Definitely not your mother, but I am willing to beat your ass if you don't stop playing games. Open the damn door before I get shot in the hallway."

"Geez, what a temper," the man said, even though Nykyrian's tone had been anything but angry. The door slid open to reveal a large Andarion male.

And she meant *l-a-r-g-e* . . .

Kiara's heart slid into her stomach at the massive form. She'd thought Nykyrian to be tall. This man stood a full head taller and was twice as wide. His long teeth flashed at her as he offered her an evil grin.

Was he considering her for dinner?

Nykyrian grabbed her arm and pulled her past the man.

Her eyes widened as she accidentally brushed up against the Andarion's hard chest. The crimson ringed white eyes sent a chill down her spine. No wonder

Nykyrian wore dark glasses. Eyes like those were terrifying.

The Andarion grimaced as he came back into her flat and shut the door.

"Where's Syn?"

Nykyrian released her. "On his way."

Kiara stared at the human male who'd asked about Syn. He reclined on her couch with his feet propped up on her table. His red hair, almost as long as Nykyrian's, was worn loose and concealed the side of his face. He seemed completely comfortable in her home.

The sight angered her.

How dare they invade her privacy in such a manner and disrespect her things . . . Her agitation increased when the Andarion returned to her favorite armchair, picked up her bag of friggles from the low table, and began munching them.

Seizing the bag, she narrowed her eyes. "This is my home, not some free-house."

The Andarion looked at Nykyrian, his eyes wide. "She's got spunk," he rasped with a dark laugh. "I bet her meat is equally as spicy."

His gaze returned to her as if he was sizing her up for a kettle. Kiara took a step back, clutching the bag to her chest.

"You might want to return the food to him," Nykyrian said from behind her. "It's unwise to starve an Andarion. If Hauk decided to nibble on you, there's not much we could do to stop him."

Hauk raked her with a calculating grin.

Her anger vanished. Handing the bag back to Hauk, she quickly put distance between them. What had her father gotten her into? How could he have turned her over to these people?

The redheaded man flashed her a dazzling smile. He

really was gorgeous. "They're only teasing you." He stood and extended his hand to her. "I'm Darling Cruel and yes, my parents really were nasty enough to name me that."

Kiara shook his gloved hand as she realized this was the man Syn had wanted to kill when they rescued her. Something in Darling's manner reminded her of an aristocrat. He seemed easy enough to get along with, unlike the two Andarions.

He indicated the Andarion eating her food as he retook his seat. "The glutton is Dancer Hauk."

"Dancer?" Kiara was amused by the revelation.

Hauk stiffened. "It means 'killer' in Andarion."

Darling laughed, a deep throaty sound as he draped his arms over the back of the couch in a decidedly masculine pose. "You wish. Nykyrian told me it meant 'of beautiful cheeks.'"

Hauk gave Nykyrian a glare that bordered on murder.

Nykyrian shrugged, apparently unconcerned by the unspoken threat. "Don't waste that look on me, *chiran*. I didn't name you and I can't help it if your adoring mother was as sick as Darling's."

Kiara was relieved by their play, which took some of the coldness out of them and the awkward nervousness out of her. Surely they couldn't be all bad if they shared this kind of friendship. It made them seem almost normal.

Then again, normal wasn't exactly a term someone could ever apply to this group.

Darling smiled again. "I'm sorry if we overstepped our bounds. Being the only one here with Hauk, I encouraged him to scrounge for another source of food."

At least Darling had manners. "It's all right," she assured him. "I'm just upset over everything that's happened and I'm taking some of it out on you guys."

"I completely understand. Having someone try to kill you can ruin even your best day. It seriously sucks on a bad one."

Turning around, she faced Nykyrian. He leaned against her bar with his arms folded over his chest. His head was angled toward Darling, but she was sure he was watching her. She could feel his eyes on her. If only he wasn't wearing those blasted shades.

Did he ever remove them?

"I need to change. I suppose I don't need to tell the three of you to make yourselves comfortable, as you've already done so."

Nykyrian didn't so much as twitch.

She really hated those shades. She would love to be able to read his emotions and moods.

Kiara paused at the entrance to her hall and glanced back at the three men. She was extremely uncomfortable about removing her clothes with strangers in her house.

It just seemed . . . dangerous.

She looked at Nykyrian's stoic face.

"You don't have to worry about us," he said as if he knew her thoughts. "Hauk isn't attracted to humans. Darling isn't attracted to women, and I'm . . ."

Nykyrian paused. What could he say? All too well, he remembered the sight of her in that torn, skimpy night-gown she'd been wearing when he carried her off Chenz's ship. Her body was lithe and honed from her years of dancing. And even as disheveled as she was right now, she was still the sexiest thing he'd ever seen and all he could think about was stripping her clothes off and nib-bling every part of her. He wanted her more than any-thing.

But that would probably scare her senseless.

"I'm not interested," he finished.

Kiara felt the sting of those words much more deeply than she should have. In fact, she couldn't believe how much they hurt.

Why do you even care what he thinks?

Yet she did. Narrowing her eyes, she seethed in her embarrassed humiliation. How dare he set her down like that in front of his friends when she'd done nothing to cause it! Talk about rude. Did he possess no manners whatsoever?

Without a word, she lifted her chin so that he couldn't see how much that stung and went to her room.

What had she been thinking when she considered him handsome? He wasn't even human!

Kiara paused. That *must* be his problem.

No, he'd said Hauk didn't like humans and *he* wasn't interested.

Jerking her costume off, she tossed it on the bed. Never had she been so embarrassed by a put-down. And it wasn't that she was vain. Far from it . . .

It was just rude and it hurt.

Remember, Kiara, he doesn't like women. He sleeps with Nemesis.

But that wasn't what he'd said.

Trying to let it go, she belted her robe around her waist and entered the hallway. She stopped and looked back to where Nykyrian still leaned against her bar. Her body trembled in rage as she wished she were large enough to make him feel the bite of her mood.

Nykyrian's skin tingled. He knew he was being watched. Turning his head, he saw Kiara's blazing amber eyes. Good, she hated him. Hatred was one thing he could easily deal with. But then, why did he ache with the knowledge that she despised him? He should be happy.

Refusing to think about *that,* he returned his attention

to Hauk. He heard Kiara enter the bathroom. When the water came on a few seconds later, an image of her naked body caressed by the water's spray haunted him.

Damn, if Syn wasn't right. She probably did shower naked.

Against his will, his body responded to that thought with a hammering need.

What he wouldn't give to strip his clothes off and join her . . .

Darling scowled at him. "You all right, bud?"

"Tired." Nykyrian returned to their briefing on the beefed-up security they'd installed in her flat. "You were saying you placed scanners outside in the corridor."

Darling nodded. "Right. We have the scanners in place with your DNA, hers, and ours already programed in along with Syn's and Jayne's. Hauk reworked the communications system to prevent anyone from accessing it. The channels will be clear should you need to contact us."

Nykyrian shifted his weight to keep his muscles from stiffening. "I still intend to use the link."

"Probably for the best," Hauk said. "Once Bredeh learns you're guarding her, he's going to come after you full arsenal."

"I'm ready."

Hauk snorted. "I wouldn't be so arrogant. He won't stick by League rules and attack you openly. He wants your life more than he wants Kiara's."

Nykyrian shrugged nonchalantly. Aksel was the least of his present concerns. Besides, dealing with that punk had once been a daily occurrence for him.

At least this time, he wouldn't have someone pulling him off the bastard.

He heard Kiara leaving the bathroom. Squelching the desire to look at her, he focused his thoughts on their discussion. "So what? Bredeh's been trying to kill me since I was ten."

Hauk scratched his chin. "True, but—"

Kiara's scream echoed in the flat.

Nykyrian went cold. Drawing his blaster, he ran down the corridor to the back room where her scream had originated. Carefully, he entered the studio, then froze.

With a stern frown, he looked at Kiara's rage-flushed face. She stood in the center of the room, hands on hips. There didn't appear to be any kind of threat in here at all.

Well, nothing more than her anger.

Irritated over her unwarranted shriek, he holstered his blaster. "What's going on?"

"What have you done?" she demanded. "Look at my room." She gestured toward the black blast shields over her floor-length windows. "How dare you people come into *my* home and rearrange *my* furnishings. And what is *that* thing?"

Nykyrian stared at the opaque window coverings. "It's a blast shield."

Darling and Hauk exchanged wary looks.

"I forgot to mention that," Darling said. "We covered all the windows to keep snipers from seeing a target."

Kiara fumed. "I want you to leave. All of you. Out!"

Nykyrian nodded to Hauk and Darling, excusing them. Without a word, they left.

She continued to glare at him. "I meant you as well."

"I know you did. Get used to me. I'm not leaving."

She walked right up to him, her fists clenched tightly at her sides. "You're fired. Now get out!"

Her audacity almost made him smile. It'd been a long time since someone dared stand up to him in anger without a weapon pointed at his head. "You didn't hire me."

Kiara's eyes widened. Never in her life had she been so angry. In fact, it was rare she ever lost her temper. She stared at Nykyrian wishing she were Trisani and could splatter him against her walls with just her thoughts.

"I want you out of my home."

For a brief moment, she thought he winced, but his face quickly turned emotionless. He left the studio.

Satisfaction washed over her as she surveyed the empty room. Tomorrow she'd have the building's maintenance crew remove the shields. Tonight she would enjoy the peacefulness of being alone and alive.

She wanted her life back and she intended to claim it!

A movement in one of her mirrors caught her attention. Stepping closer to the glass, she recognized Nykyrian in her front room.

She narrowed her eyes dangerously. He hadn't left. In a heated daze, she went to expel him from her life. She was tired of having no control over anything that happened to her. Yes, they might kill her, but at this point she was willing to risk it for a moment of sanity.

Reaching the kitchen, Kiara paused by her counter, shocked by the sight before her.

What was he doing?

Preparing dinner?

Her anger dissolved as she watched his fluid, confident moves. Never had she expected an assassin to cook. "Why are you doing that?"

"I thought you might be hungry. I know I am."

Kiara watched him rinse assorted brenna vegetables in her sink. Pulling her cutting board off the wall, he pulled one of her knives out of its block and tested the edge with his thumb. "Do you ever cook?"

"All the time."

He held the knife up for her inspection, his features bland. "With this?" Finally there was emotion in his tone. It was mocking and snarly, but at least it was emotion.

"Yes. Why?"

He scoffed. "I've used sharper spoons." He pulled a knife out from the folds of his coat.

Her eyes widened at the way the light glinted against the black titanium blade. "Is that sanitary?"

"I'm sure it's cleaner than yours. I wash mine with alcohol and sterilize them, then put them in airtight sheaths, not a porous wood block that can hold bacteria." He struck the knife several times against the spike on his right vambrace in silent, short, quick strokes before he started slicing the vegetables with a shocking ease.

No . . .

That couldn't be what she thought it was . . .

Could it?

"You travel with a whetstone on your arm?"

He paused before he returned to chopping. "You don't ever want to kill someone with a dull knife. It takes too long to sever their arteries, or puncture organs, and it makes it even messier than normal."

"Is that a joke?"

He didn't answer and the way he handled that knife put a painful knot in her stomach. Yes, it was graceful and impressive, but it showed an expertise and precision that made her blood run cold. He chopped fast, the blade slicing like a diamond-tipped razor through everything.

It was actually a wonder he didn't cut his own fingers,

as fast as he moved. Yet he never missed a beat. He pulled out a stockpot and added herbs and seasoning to the water.

Kiara frowned. "You actually look like you know what you're doing."

He stopped chopping and looked up at her. "Why does it surprise you? Even killers need food."

She ignored his obvious barb. "Food yes, but Cretoria? That is what you're making?"

"Yes." He finished chopping the vegetables, then placed them on the counter.

"So, you're a killer and a gourmet."

Nykyrian shrugged while he walked to her cooling unit and pulled out her defrosted trona meat. He returned to her counter. "You could say I'm a gourmet killer. Being Andarion, I like my human meat cooked well."

"You told me you don't eat humans." She was sure the look under his glasses was a sharp glare.

Without a word, he began slicing the meat—this time with an even larger knife that he pulled out of his sleeve.

Just how many weapons did he have concealed on him?

Kiara wasn't sure she wanted an answer to that.

Her eyes wide, she watched as he twirled the blade while he sliced. How weird that he inadvertently made a show out of it and, by the way he moved, she could tell he was doing it subconsciously—unaware of how out of the norm his movements were.

Was she safe alone with him?

Surely her father wouldn't have hired him if he thought there would be any danger to her. Right?

"Do you ever remove your gloves?" she asked, trying to distract herself from that disturbing thought.

"No."

"Why not?"

He didn't answer.

Kiara hated when he did that. So she moved on to her next question. "What about your shades? Do they ever come off?"

"No."

She pursed her lips at his curt response, trying to figure out why he wanted to wear them inside. "Don't they make it too dark?"

"They adjust automatically to accommodate various light levels."

Fascinating tidbit . . . but it still didn't tell her why he wore them all the time. "Are you embarrassed over your Andarion eyes?"

"Nothing about me bothers me. But my eyes seem to make everyone else uncomfortable."

"Even Hauk?"

He added seasoning to the meat. "Especially Hauk."

Kiara wondered at his words. How could an Andarion be made uncomfortable by another of his kind?

She glanced about for Hauk and Darling who were nowhere in her home. "Where did the others go?"

"As per your highness's demands, they left."

She was a bit surprised by that. "You mean someone actually listened to me?"

"Don't get used to it."

His clipped words silenced the conversation. She felt rather ridiculous over her outburst and as she stood there, she realized she was wearing nothing except a bathrobe while confronting a complete stranger in her kitchen. "I need to dress."

Nykyrian let out a long breath as she left him. *Thank you.* The low dip in the front of her robe had caused him quite a bit of discomfort. Since she'd called his attention to the studio, the only thing he'd really noticed had been the tiny droplets of water clinging to the deep cleft of her breasts.

Water he wanted to lick off that skin in the worst sort of way.

Stop it!

He vowed to keep his mind on business and not Kiara's body. To help achieve his goal, he switched on the music player located on the kitchen wall. As he finished placing the meat and vegetables into the pot, he heard Syn in his ear telling him he was outside in the hallway.

The door buzzer sounded.

Kiara came running from her room, fastening the last three buttons of her blouse. He groaned inwardly, regretting he'd ever told her he wasn't interested in her body. No doubt, she figured she could run around naked and not stir him.

This was going to be a long mission.

Reining his body back under his rigid control, Nykyrian moved to the door, ready just in case.

Kiara opened it, admitting Syn and her father.

"Thank God." The commander pulled her into his arms and held her close. "When I saw the bodies, I was terrified you were hurt."

Her face paled before she glanced at Syn, then Nykyrian. "Luckily Nykyrian and Syn were there to save me."

Kiefer released her and faced Nykyrian. "I thought you people were going to wait until tomorrow before starting your protection."

You people . . . Could there be any more loathing in the way he said those words?

Nykyrian had to bite back a sarcastic reminder that they were both housebroken—though to be fair, given their pasts, that was a miracle. "Had we waited, she'd be dead now."

The president tensed before returning his attention to Kiara. "I wanted to tell you about this, but I was waiting until after your performance. I didn't want to upset you."

"I'm not upset."

Nykyrian rolled his eyes, grateful they couldn't see the action behind his shades. Not upset . . . yeah, right. She was more than ready to kill them all.

Kiefer gave her a grim smile. He looked back at Nykyrian with a stern scowl. "I have misgivings about this. I warned Nemesis, now I warn you. Should anything happen to her, I won't rest until I have destroyed every member of The Sentella."

Nykyrian had to stifle the urge to make an obscene gesture over a threat that was as preposterous as it was unneeded. If The League couldn't kill him, a Gourish president damn sure couldn't. "We're trained professionals. Kiara is safer with us than she'd ever be with you."

Kiefer narrowed his eyes in a way that made Nykyrian want to punch him. "She'd better be. I intend to keep in constant contact." He gave his daughter another fierce hug. "I hate to leave, but I need to get back to the base and deal with the reporters and paperwork over what happened tonight. If you need me, call."

"I will," she promised, kissing his cheek.

"I'll check on you when I get home." He released her and headed for the door. "I love you, baby."

"I love you, too, Daddy."

He kissed her brow before he took his leave.

Kiara ached as her father left her alone with the two men she wasn't so sure about. Her heart heavy, she locked the door, then frowned at the mocking expression on Syn's face as he walked over to Nykyrian.

"What the hell was that action?" Syn asked him.

"I think it's something called 'paternal concern.'"

Syn scowled at his bland explanation. "What . . . ? You sure? I thought that crap was a myth."

Nykyrian shrugged. "No, really. I watched it once in a documentary. It was fascinating. Believe it or not, there are people out there who actually have feelings for their progeny."

"Get the fuck out. No way. You're screwing with my head again, aren't you?"

"No. I swear. You just saw it with your own eyes. I did not make that shit up."

Syn shivered. "Yeah but it's really messing with my concept of the natural order of the universe. Paternal love? What's next? Limb regrowth? Genetic splicing reversals?"

Kiara gave Syn an irritated grimace. "Don't your parents ever worry about either of you?"

Syn arched a brow. "What parents?"

A ripple of apprehension went through Kiara that she might have been insensitive to them. "Are they dead?"

"Careful," Nykyrian said, returning to the kitchen. "You might not want an answer to that question."

She tried to understand his cryptic response. "What do you mean?"

Syn laughed evilly. "Kip wasn't born, he was spawned."

Now she was completely confused. "Who's Kip?"

Syn indicated Nykyrian with his thumb.

"You were a tubie?"

Nykyrian glanced up from his dinner preparations. "Syn has a brain disorder that causes him to lie most of the time. Ignore him."

Syn snorted. "I don't lie. I merely tell the truth creatively."

So Nykyrian wasn't a test-tube baby. This really didn't make a bit of sense to her. "But neither of you has parents?"

Nykyrian put a lid on the pot. "They're dead."

"Isn't that what I asked to begin with?"

They ignored her as Syn took a seat on one of the tall stools in front of her kitchen bar.

Nykyrian handed him a glass of spara juice. "Are you staying for dinner?"

Syn looked at her. "Do you mind?"

Wow, Syn had manners. Who knew?

"No," she said, surprised by the honesty of the statement. For some reason, she liked Syn despite his unorthodox looks. His black hair was pulled back into a short ponytail. His deep brown eyes were ringed in black eyeliner, giving him the look of a feral hunting beast. Not to mention he had a small stud in his left nostril that matched the two small hoops in his left ear.

He was definitely not the type of man who attracted her, but she had to admit, he was oddly handsome.

He took a drink of the juice and cursed. "What is this shit? Poison?"

Nykyrian took his acerbic tone in stride. "You can't live on alcohol."

"Wanna bet?"

"Wanna die?" Nykyrian pushed the juice back toward Syn. "Drink it and quit bitching."

Syn mouthed those words back mockingly and added an extremely obscene insult to it. "You know, you're a little hairy to be my mother." He pulled out a small flask and added it to the juice.

Nykyrian let out a deep, fierce growl that actually scared her.

Syn ignored it as he drank the alcohol-laced juice. "Much better."

Nykyrian went back to cooking, but there was a tic in his jaw that betrayed the anger he was doing an amazing job at hiding.

Kiara shifted her gaze to Nykyrian as he talked with Syn. He seemed far more at ease with Syn than he had with his other two friends.

As Syn made another joke, she realized Nykyrian never smiled or laughed. She couldn't remember ever seeing him do either.

What could take away someone's laughter?

Severe military training. Like her father. He seldom smiled either.

But unlike Nykyrian, he did on occasion.

Her chest tightened as she considered the life Nykyrian must have lived. No parents, no laughter, a League assassin. In truth, it was a miracle he was still alive. The normal life expectancy of an assassin on the job was five to six years. Tops. Seldom did they make it to age thirty.

Never did they make it to thirty-three.

Yet he appeared to be a year or two older than that.

She sat down on the stool next to Syn. "Out of curiosity, why are you keeping me here?" It was against military protocol. In the past, whenever her father had "protected" her, she'd been moved to a safe location.

Nykyrian took a drink of his juice before he answered. "When you're being hunted to the extent you are, there's no real safe place. You're famous, which makes it all the harder to hide you. Better to keep you here where you have the advantage of knowing the terrain and are most comfortable."

"Not to mention, we're using you for bait."

Nykyrian cocked his head at Syn. "Are you *that* drunk?"

Syn's eyes widened. "What? I wasn't supposed to tell her that?"

Kiara was horrified. "I'm bait?"

"No, you're not bait. Ignore the alcoholic whose view of reality is distorted by his brain-damaged hallucinations. What the psychologists have found is that people in your position cope best when there's as little interruption as possible in their routine."

Kiara swallowed. "Not to mention we both know the one truth neither of you is talking about."

"And that is?"

"That I'm really nothing more than a waco." It was an assassin's term that meant walking corpse. "I'm not going to live through the night, am I?"

CHAPTER 8

Nykyrian went still at the cold fear in her voice. It touched a part of him that he'd forgotten existed.

His heart.

And, for some reason he couldn't name, he wanted to comfort her. "You'll survive, *mu Tara*. We'll make sure of it."

She shook her head, her eyes shiny with unspent tears, which was one thing he admired most about her. Most of the time she had the best control of her emotions of any civilian he'd ever been around.

"You can't guarantee that. You said it yourself. Even you're living on borrowed time, waiting for one of them to kill *you*."

Syn added more alcohol to his glass. "And you said *I* was scaring her? Damn, bud. You're socially awkward to the extreme."

"Syn . . ."

He ignored Nykyrian's warning. "Don't worry, princess. We've been living that way our entire lives. There's nothing they got that'll touch us. If they did, we'd already be dead."

Nykyrian inclined his head to Syn. "I was born fighting and we've wired your place to such an extent that we'll know if an uninvited cockroach visits a flat ten stories down. Not to mention we have exit strategies for any and all scenarios. They won't get you without getting us and believe me, we're not about to make our enemies happy and die here."

Syn laughed. "Damn straight. We have too many people to continue pissing off."

She frowned at him. "You're really not afraid?"

"No," Nykyrian answered honestly.

Syn inclined his head to Nykyrian. "Death is just a new beginning . . . at least in my religion. And extreme inebriation seriously helps."

Kiara wasn't amused by his quip. "Mine, too, well, the religion part, not the alcohol, but I'm in no hurry to meet my maker." She let out a tired breath. "I don't see how you guys live the life you do."

Syn shrugged. "There's an old Ritadarion saying. You're never more alive than when you walk hand in hand with death."

"Or crawl inside a bottle and stay there."

He met Nykyrian's gaze. "Yeah, well, it's not my death that bothers me."

Nykyrian clenched his teeth as he felt his friend's pain. No, it was the brutal loss of his family that haunted him and for that Nykyrian couldn't fault him at all. Syn had been put through a meat grinder by life. The fact that man could still get up and make it through a day without blowing his brains out amazed him. It was a call he waited daily to receive and he had more respect for Syn's continued survival than he'd ever had for anything else.

He glanced to Kiara and by her face he could tell she understood Syn's tone and had the decency not to question him about it.

She swallowed as she fidgeted with the ring on her finger. "I'm really sorry about the way I overreacted to

voice, which was punctuated by occasional light laughs, drifting from her room. Her silken, dulcet tones pierced him. Used to the deadpan voices of assassins or the deep baritones of men, he'd never realized until this moment what a typical female voice sounded like in conversation.

No, not entirely true. There had been a handful of females he'd listened to when he was younger. And Jayne, but her voice was unnaturally deep like a man's. It'd been decades since he'd heard a typical woman talk to someone. It was different than the rehearsed conversations on vid broadcasts or even interviews. This was natural. A voice filled with true, spontaneous emotion.

And she was just in the next room . . .

Like that matters to you.

Get your head in the game, chiran.

Because if he didn't, she would die. They both would.

With that thought foremost in his mind, he retrieved his laptop from the bag Hauk had left for him on the floor.

Nykyrian took a seat on the couch. Kiara's laugh rippled again, distracting him. She had the most amazing laugh. Light and soft.

Get to work, dick.

Shaking his head, he turned his computer on and focused on what he was supposed to be doing. His thoughts back on his job, he pulled his glove off to scan his fingerprints and allow it to boot up.

And again, her soft voice caught his attention and made him instantly hard.

Shoot me . . .

Maybe he should have assigned Syn watch duty tonight. If only Syn hadn't made plans with Caillan. But since he seldom took time off, Nykyrian had given him the night. Not to mention, Syn was using the night for his "other" company.

Damn, this mission.

He'd spent the entire dinner wanting her, feeling her presence next to him. If only he hadn't allowed her to touch him at the theater, he might have been able to focus better. Having felt her touch, it was hard to get it out of his mind.

No one hugged him. Ever. And it was now seared in his memory like a stinging brand.

Nykyrian scoffed at himself. Who was he trying to fool? It didn't matter that she'd touched him. Since the first performance he'd seen her in three years ago, she'd haunted his dreams like a stalking phantom out to steal his rotting soul.

No matter where he was, she was never too far from his thoughts.

The logistics of this just sucked more than normal since he really couldn't escape seeing and hearing her.

Smelling the sweet scent of her body.

He sighed heavily, wishing he could think of some way to clear his head that didn't involve removing body parts.

After a few minutes she finished her call and entered the front room with a warm smile on her face as she looked in his direction.

Kill me . . .

Nykyrian's blood heated in response to her gentle expression. No one had ever looked at him like that.

Like she was glad to see him.

She glanced around the room with a frown. "Is Syn gone?"

"Yes."

That didn't seem to please her. "I thought there'd be more than one of you to guard me. Isn't that standard protocol?"

Yeah, for a *normal* person.

He wasn't normal in any sense of the word. "Believe me, I'm more than enough to keep you safe." There was no arrogance in those words. It was just a simple statement of fact.

Kiara paused at her favorite chair, across from Nykyrian and his rigid pose. He'd finally removed his long coat and draped it right where she'd planned to sit. How strange that he seemed even more formidable without it.

Not an easy thing to do . . .

Maybe he was right about not needing anyone else. He looked more than capable of single-handedly bringing down an entire army.

Now she could finally see the full, ripped outline of his body . . . and the presence of more weapons.

Daggers and knives were cradled in sheaths from hipbone to hipbone around his back. More sheaths were attached to his wrists and biceps, front and back, along with the two blasters. No doubt there were more weapons in his pants and boots. And he seemed oblivious to all of them.

A shiver went over her.

As she tried to pick up his coat, she frowned at the unbelievable weight of it. How did he manage to wear it so flawlessly? She could barely lift one sleeve. It had to be lined with armor, and the flash of silver said there were even more weapons hidden within its folds.

Nykyrian stood up and took it from her with one hand before he laid it down beside him on the couch. That, too, was impressive.

She arched a brow at the clinking sound the coat had made. "Just out of curiosity, how many weapons are in that thing?"

"Enough to make me happy."

Kiara was unamused by his curt reply. "So is there any part of you that's not a lethal weapon?"

He sat back down before he answered. "No. Even my wits are sharpened."

Rolling her eyes at his dry sarcasm, Kiara was a little more respectful of him and his strength as she took her chair. Her father's dire words echoed in her ears. He'd warned her of The Sentella's ferocity, telling her to stay alert and call for him if she had any suspicions toward them at all. While he knew they were the best at protecting her, he still didn't fully trust them and he'd left his own guards all over the street outside and patrolling the inside of her building.

Just in case.

And who could really blame him for being paranoid? In spite of what Nykyrian had said earlier, they were all mercenaries whose only loyalty was to currency.

Watching Nykyrian closely, she tried to read his thoughts. Would he sell her out? Or kill her himself? Could he be that cold-blooded?

Of course he could.

And yet she wanted to believe he was better than that. That he had some form of moral fiber hidden underneath that icy facade and mountain of weapons.

Nykyrian's own words drifted through her mind. *Emotions are bred out of us during training.* Still, she refused to believe he was completely without feelings. Were that true, he wouldn't have comforted her while she cried. He wouldn't have cared enough to even bother.

His gloved fingers flew over the touch keypads while he worked with only a whisper of light tapping.

A wicked smile curved her lips as she studied the gorgeous body and profile of the man who seemed oblivious to her presence. She'd been around many men who constantly worked to improve their physical appearance, but none of them had ever appealed to her as much as he did.

A man who should repulse her.

Yet there was something about him that called out to her like a hurt child needing comfort. Kiara almost laughed aloud at the thought. She studied Nykyrian, his jaw tense, his features blank. The epitome of fierce soldier and lethal killer.

No, there didn't appear to be anything about him even close to hurting or needy.

So why did she feel this way?

"What are you working on?" she finally asked.

He growled a low warning in his throat that made her a bit uneasy. "I have a lot of work to finish. I'm not here to be sociable. I'm here only to protect you. Ignore me and go about your business as if I'm not even in the room."

She arched a brow at that ridiculous comment. "Have you any idea how much space you take up? In case it's escaped your notice, you're not exactly small or easy to ignore."

She could have sworn she saw one corner of his mouth twitch as if he'd almost smiled. But he said nothing in response.

Kiara folded her arms around her leg and rested her chin on her knee. She watched his flying fingers, amazed he could type and talk at the same time. "But since you're here . . ."

His fingers stopped moving, the sudden silence echoed around her, increasing her discomfort.

"I just thought you might as well tell me something

about yourself. We could end up spending days together, weeks even, and I for—"

"Fine," he snapped, cutting her off.

Kiara hid her triumphant smile behind her knee, but she was sure her eyes glowed in mischief.

Nykyrian sat back and defensively crossed his arms over his chest. "If it will solace your mind, I will allow you to ask me eight questions. After that, you'll never again ask me another thing about my past, or my colleagues, and you'll remain quiet and let me finish what I'm doing."

The sharp, clipped words irked her. She stared at him, trying to think of things that would give her a working knowledge of what kind of person he was. "Okay," she said as she thought of the first one. "What's your surname?"

"One, Quiakides."

She choked in surprise over the last name she'd expected to hear. She wouldn't have been more surprised to find out he was a royal prince. "As in the universally famed and acclaimed Commander Huwin Quiakides?" In The League, that name carried more prestige than all the presidents and royal families of all the United Systems combined. The late commander was a legend revered by all.

"Two, yes."

"Was he your father?"

She thought she noticed his teeth clench before he answered, "Three, yes."

Kiara gave an unladylike snort. "That doesn't count. You should have said that when I asked the second question."

He shrugged in an aggravating manner of disinterest. "Be specific. Anything counts."

Oh, that little booger . . .

But arguing with him was pointless. The one thing she did know about him—he was stubborn to a fault.

Kiara sat for a minute, thinking over what little information Mira had given her while she'd been in The Sentella's base. "If he was your father, why did you leave The League?"

This time, she definitely saw the angry tic in his jaw as his features hardened. "What makes you so sure I was in The League?"

Kiara gulped at the harsh, deadly tone. At that moment, she could easily imagine him tearing someone into pieces and she had no desire for that someone to be either her or Mira. "I saw part of the tattoo on your wrist. It is true, isn't it? You were a League assassin?"

Some of the tenseness left his lips, and she wondered why. "Four, yes."

Kiara was getting tired of him numbering his answers. "You know, you could try and be a little friendlier."

"I'm not paid to be nice. I'm paid to kill."

A lump of dread closed her throat at the thought. "Do you like to kill?" she asked, her throat growing tighter by the heartbeat.

Kiara witnessed the first truly visible, emotional response from him—he went completely rigid and tense. There was no mistaking the anger, even though he held it in well. He closed the computer with a sharp snap and tossed it aside.

Without a word, he left the room.

Kiara sat in her chair for several minutes, wondering about his reaction. Since he brought the subject of his killings up so often, why would her question bother him?

She went to find out.

He stood in front of the blast shields in her studio.

She watched him from the doorway as he slid his hand over the plastic panels as if looking for a hole. He appeared ambivalent again.

"You said you would answer my questions."

He dropped his hand. "I didn't expect you to ask that one."

"Why not?"

Nykyrian crossed the room with that powerful, commanding gait to stand before her. For a moment, she thought he might actually touch her, but he remained less than a foot from her—just close enough to warm her with his body heat, with an intangible wall so thick around him, she didn't dare reach out and touch him or even step closer.

"Why would you care how anything makes me feel?" His low tone seemed somehow searching.

"I don't know, I just do."

He turned around and changed the topic. "Do you practice in here?"

Kiara frowned at the unexpected question, curious about what had prompted it. "Yes."

He walked over to the mirrors and touched her favorite spot on the stretching bar. She'd used it so much there was a slight dip in the wood from her ankle and a permanent stain there from the oils in her skin. "Do you enjoy what you do?"

"Of course."

He shook his head. "That was a well rehearsed response. Tell me, honestly, do you enjoy the grind of what you do? The discipline, the hours and hours of rehearsal, the promoters who make demands, the fittings, the other dancers who envy you, the media who criticizes every move you make, and all the bullshit that goes along with each performance? Do you *really* enjoy what you do?"

Kiara looked away. No, she hated all of that. She couldn't even eat what she wanted to for fear of gaining any weight . . . or just as bad, losing it. Once the costumes had been created, they were fined heavily if they gained or lost more than two pounds.

And she was weighed every single day.

Everything she did out in public was scrutinized. Everything that happened in private was fodder for the public gristmill.

Then there were all the blisters and sore muscles. The cramps and pulls. The doubts and fears. Worst of all, the backbiting and two-faced friends.

She hated every bit of that. But she wasn't about to let this stranger know about her private hell. So she answered with the truth. "Dancing was all I ever wanted to do."

His grip tightened on the bar. "Really? Or do you do it because someone expected you to? Because it's what they trained you for?"

A chill crept up her back. "What makes you think that?"

Nykyrian turned around and faced her. "The pictures and awards you have in the main room on your shelves. Most of them are of you as a child, dressed for dance recitals with people applauding you or of you holding the awards that you so proudly display. You don't look old enough in any of them to make a life-shaping decision. And from the amount of them, I doubt you ever had time to try and do anything else."

He moved close to her again. "I would say you dance because you were told it was what you *should* do with your talents."

She froze. "Why would you say that?"

"Again, the pictures you have. When you're in practice clothes, there's a look of nervous fear in your eyes.

Like you're afraid of disappointing someone. And in the ones where you've won an award, there's no real joy. Only relief."

The truth in his words cut through her consciousness. How could he see something about her that she'd never admitted to anyone? Not even herself.

Yet he was right about all of that.

Why had no one, especially her, ever noticed that before?

"Are you always this astute?"

He shrugged. "In my business, it pays to read and understand people, especially what motivates them. It keeps me alive."

Kiara ran his words through her mind. And in that moment she had her first insight into him. "Is that why you do what you do? Because someone told you, you should be an assassin?"

Silence answered her.

"You still owe me six answers."

"Four answers," he corrected, folding his arms over his chest. "And I've answered enough for tonight."

He walked past her and Kiara knew the subject was closed as firmly as if it were held in trust by League Protectors. With a weary sigh, she realized she didn't know much more about him now than she had in the beginning.

But she did know that he was the son of one of the most feared commanders in the universe. The burning question now was how did Huwin Quiakides father a son with an Andarion?

Who *was* Nykyrian's mother?

Most importantly, given his pedigree, why would he leave The League? Why would anyone risk their life and disappoint their father so?

Curious, she returned to the main room where he was once again occupied with his computer.

"Will it disturb you if I turn on the viewer?"

"No."

Returning to her chair, Kiara picked up the remote and began flipping through the channels. She listened more to Nykyrian than to her programs. Even though he appeared oblivious to her, she sensed the rigid wall of defense he'd closed around himself. Somewhere, there had to be a chink.

But did she really want to find it?

Given his past, there was no telling what secrets and ghosts haunted him. What had he seen in his life?

What all had he done?

That thought made her stomach shrink as she re-membered her own brutal past. Could he have tortured her mother the way her kidnappers had? Would he abuse a child and laugh at her tears as he threatened her?

Was he capable of killing a child?

How many women had *he* raped before killing them?

She glanced askance to see the tiny bit of colored flesh showing on his wrist from between his glove and sleeve.

The mark of a brutal killer . . .

Terrified of that past, she switched off the viewer. "I'm going to bed." Standing up, she paused in the small area between the couch and chair until he looked up at her. Embarrassed, she cleared her throat before she ad-mitted to the one thing she hated most about herself. The one thing she'd never been able to let go of no matter how hard she tried. "Please, don't turn off the lowlights in my flat when you go to sleep. I-I don't do well in darkness."

He didn't respond at all.

Retrieving what little dignity she had left, she quit the room.

Nykyrian stopped working and listened to Kiara as she prepared for bed. He closed the computer to ease some of the ache from his eyes and allowed the rigidness to leave his body as he relaxed against the couch.

The sounds of Kiara moving around her room formed a strange comfort to his soul. It was such a normal thing to do and normality had always been the one thing missing from his life.

He removed his shades, balanced them on his knee, then pressed the heel of his hand to his right eye that burned like fire. He'd had a bad injury on his right eye years ago that had damaged the tear duct. As a result, that eye tended to dry out and ache. Most of the time, he could ignore it, but whenever he stared too long at a viewer or computer, it would really bother him.

And as he sat there, an image of Kiara taking off her clothes flashed through his mind. Because of Chenz, he already knew what her breasts looked like. Pert, pale, and just the right size to fill his palm . . .

Enough! he roared at his treacherous thoughts. *Put her out of your thoughts.*

Yeah, right. He'd have to gouge out his eyes and even then the memory was seared into his brain.

You're an idiot.

She's a just a client. No more. No less.

Forcing himself to remember that, Nykyrian placed his shades on the low table and stretched out on the couch, listening to the soothing, empty silence surrounding him. He drew strength from it and swore to keep his thoughts on the men tracking Kiara, and not on her naked body.

* * *

Nykyrian never really slept away from his home. The League had trained him to go days without sleeping and to take only small combat naps whenever he absolutely had to rest.

Lying on the couch and staring at nothing, he kept his attention on the sounds in the hallway outside the flat and on their monitoring equipment. He was aware of everything on a heightened level.

All of a sudden, he heard Kiara leave her bed, something that wouldn't normally alert him except for the way she was breathing. Her breaths were sharp and short, like she was about to hyperventilate.

She opened her bedroom door and headed for her practice room.

Glancing at his chronometer, he frowned before he picked up his shades and put them on. It was the middle of the night. Surely she wasn't going there to practice . . .

He got up and headed after her.

She'd turned the lights on full strength and was in the room with her arms wrapped around herself. Her amber eyes were filled with terror as she mumbled under her breath in a tight, strained tone. She walked in a frantic circle. "Oh God, stop it, please. Please. Please. I can't breathe. I can't think. I can't . . . oh God . . . I don't want to die. I don't want . . ."

He knew exactly what this was.

A severe panic attack.

"Princess?"

She glanced at him, shook her head and clutched even tighter at herself. "Please, leave me alone. I can't breathe."

His heart went out to her and her fear. He closed the distance between them and placed his hands on her arms to help steady her. "Kiara? Hauk wears women's underwear."

Kiara froze at his words, not quite sure she'd heard what he said. "Come again?"

"Hauk wears women's underwear. Pink and really girly. You know, one of those skimpy things that tucks into the crack of his fat ass."

In spite of her terror, she laughed at the image of the huge, fierce Andarion in a tiny pink G-string. "Hauk wears women's underwear?"

Nykyrian's grip loosed on her arms. "Better?"

Surprisingly enough, she was. Somehow that unexpected image had managed to break through her panic and center her back in the real world. No one had ever been able to do that before.

Her father, for all his love of her, would yell at her for doing it even though she couldn't control herself. It was why she didn't like anyone seeing them. Not to mention, it was extremely embarrassing at her age to act like a lunatic for no reason, especially in the middle of the night while others were sleeping.

She didn't even know what caused them. Only that every so often she'd wake up in the middle of the night, terrified and unable to calm herself.

Who would have ever dreamed a man like Nykyrian would know how to help her?

"Yeah, I think I am. Thank you."

He inclined his head to her and dropped his hands away. "C'mon, I'll make you some warm milk. It'll help you sleep."

She tightened the belt on her robe, then turned down the lights in her exercise room and followed him to the kitchen. "How did you know what to do?"

He shrugged. "Anxiety attacks hit everyone eventually."

"Even you?"

"No. But I've been around others who have them. Random stupidity has a way of breaking through the panic and helping the sufferer to focus on something else."

She still couldn't believe how easily it'd worked. She'd been suffering from them most of her life. Her father and therapists had never come up with a better coping mechanism for them.

"So does Hauk really wear female underwear?"

"No, but it's a good image, isn't it?" He opened her cooling unit and pulled out the milk.

How could he deliver lines like that and not even smile?

She laughed as she took a seat on her barstool in front of her counter. "It is indeed. Does he know you use him in such a manner?"

"I doubt it. I'm still breathing." He poured milk into a glass and then heated it in her warmer.

In a few seconds, he put it down in front of her along with a napkin.

Kiara sighed as she reached for the hot mug and cupped it in her cold hands. "I'm really sorry you had to see that."

As he put the milk away, she realized he was still fully clothed and armed. He even had the gloves on his hands. Did he always sleep like that?

"Don't apologize. You've been through a lot this week."

That was certainly true and she hoped tomorrow was much calmer for her. "How do you cope with this life?"

"Death doesn't scare me."

"Honestly? You have no fear whatsoever of what's on the other side?"

"Not at all."

How could he feel that way, especially given the way he lived? Given all the things he must have done in The League? "No fear of being judged and condemned for what you've done in your life?"

Nykyrian didn't respond. The truth was, people already did that to him. He didn't see it being any different than the life he currently lived and the saddest part of it all was that his life now was infinitely better than his past.

He'd already lived through hell.

"Nothing scares me, *mu Tara*. Really."

"I admire you. I wish I could live that way."

"No, you don't. Trust me. Your life is much better than mine."

She sipped at her milk. "Yes, but you don't have to worry about anyone making a victim of *you*."

"Princess, in the end, life makes victims of us all."

CHAPTER 9

Kiara woke from troubled sleep. She couldn't get Nykyrian's harsh words out of her mind. But more than the harshness of them was the fact that he was right. Life did make victims of them all and there was nothing anyone could do to safeguard themselves from that reality.

Life was the one predator no one could defeat and death would eventually claim everyone.

It was something she was trying really hard not to think about. Taking a deep breath, she pulled her robe on and went to the kitchen to grab her ritual glass of morning juice.

At the opening of the kitchen, she paused in shock. On the kitchen table placed before her chair was a warmer with a full breakfast waiting for her.

Whoa . . .

She hadn't seen the like since she'd left her father's palace. Amazed at the fare, she looked over to Nykyrian who sat on a barstool reading from a small portable, and as usual, completely oblivious to her. Once again, he was dressed in full black regalia complete with the long coat that weighed more than she did.

"Impressive." She retrieved a piece of toast from the warmer. Her taste buds reeled at the strange, sharp spices he'd added to the bread. "Very impressive. Thank you so much for being so thoughtful."

He ignored her compliments. "What do you have to do today?"

Kiara swallowed a sip of juice. "I have rehearsal this afternoon, then my performance—"

"No. No performances or rehearsals until this is resolved." His tone was clipped, but emotionless.

She set the juice down on the table and narrowed her gaze on his rigid frame. "You're insane if you think you can keep me from dancing."

He stood up and moved to stand by her side. Looking down at her, he dwarfed her much smaller size. "There are too many random variables to keep you safe during a live performance. You'll be on stage for hours, completely exposed and in a bright red costume that will make targeting you way too easy, and it will hide a targeting beam. Meanwhile, the crowd will help camouflage the assassin from even the best spotter. And an open auditorium with hundreds of people screaming and panicking after you've been killed is the best place to escape from. So let me repeat, there will be no more performances until this situation is closed."

Kiara swallowed the lump burning in her throat as she realized for the first time just how lucky she'd always been in the past. It was a thousand wonders she hadn't already been killed there. "Why didn't Pitala do that?"

"He was paid to torture and mutilate you before he killed you and that requires hands-on participation which he couldn't do from the stands. You've been downgraded from a thrill-kill to a simple bill-kill."

A thrill-kill she knew, but the other . . . "Bill-kill?"

"Kill you any way possible and send the bill in for payment."

She pushed her plate back as a wave of nausea consumed her. "I can't believe that someone's life can be bartered and sold so easily. That it's so common that there are even names for the different ways to take a person's life. For torturing them? My God, what is wrong with you people?"

"We're not the ones who are sick, *mu Tara*. With us—the predators—you know what we'll do and why we do it. What we're capable of. We make no bones about it and we wear the uniform so that you can see us coming. The ones who are sickening are the cowards who masquerade as sheep. The ones who lull you into trusting them and smile at your face while they plot your downfall behind your back for any number of psychotic reasons. The friends who turn on you out of jealousy or greed. Who try to ruin you for no reason at all. They are the ones who should be put down." For once, she heard the hatred underlying those words. "And they're the ones who are truly sickening."

She didn't agree with that statement. Killing was wrong no matter who did it. "Why do the Probekeins want me dead so badly? I've never done anything to them."

"To hurt your father and to scare the rest of their enemies. You're just a means to them. Nothing personal."

For a moment, Kiara really did think she was going to be sick.

Nothing personal.

They wanted her raped, tortured, and killed and there was nothing personal in it? What kind of world did they live in? But then she knew that answer all too well. The kind of world where a beautiful, gentle woman was beaten and then executed while she tried to protect her daughter. The world where an eight-year-old child was shot while she begged her mother to wake up.

Kiara rubbed her head as she ached over the harsh reality he was making her face. Again. A reality she'd tried so hard to escape from and deny.

But it wouldn't let her.

"What am I supposed to do?" she asked bitterly. "Stay imprisoned here, waiting for the next assassin to come in and kill me? Why not just bomb this building and have done with it?"

Nykyrian didn't so much as twitch a muscle as he responded in his low, unwavering voice, "League rules."

Kiara stiffened in confusion. "What?"

"The League forbids a free-assassin to destroy a housing building to get to one, single target."

She laughed at the absurdity of the idea of paid killers adhering to something so simplistic. "You mean assassins actually have rules to follow? Why should someone who kills for a living give a sneeze about some League ordinance?"

Still no visible reaction from Nykyrian. "If you'd ever disobeyed The League, you wouldn't ask that question."

"What's that supposed to mean?"

He moved away from her. "Very few free-assassins have the ability to outwit League Assassins or Protectors. Despite the corruption inherent in their own system, The League does try to keep some type of law over the free-assassins to make sure they don't become more powerful than the fat bureaucrats. So they will hunt them down and make them pay in ways that give even the stoutest soul nightmares."

That gave her even more pause as she stared at him. He'd thrown all their rules in their faces and had managed to live when he shouldn't have. "So what would they do to you if they ever found you?"

"They would make an example out of me."

How could he be so calm and lackadaisical as he said that? She envied him that ability until it occurred to her how horrific his past must be if not even that threat could make him flinch.

What had they put *him* through?

"And do you abide by their laws?"

"When it suits me to."

Kiara clutched her robe closed. The underlining threat of his words wasn't lost on her. She'd been right. He respected no man's rules except his own.

He turned his reader off and changed the subject. "So what other things were on your schedule for today?"

"I'd planned to take a few things to a charity drop and go shopping for my best friend's birthday present. But I guess I'll be sitting here, staring at the walls instead."

Nykyrian wanted to be immune to the hurt bitterness in her voice, but the sad truth was he felt for her pain. She was trying hard to be strong. Even so, he saw the way her hands trembled and he'd seen the fear in her eyes.

Her entire life had been taken from her over something that didn't even concern her.

Has severe phobic reaction to cramped spaces and darkness. Doesn't like feeling trapped or confined. Almost suicidal need to maintain normal schedule even in the face of danger.

Her file had been explicit about the trauma of her past and its effects on her present state of mind. He remembered how much damage she'd done to her own wrists in an effort to get free from Chenz—she'd almost severed one hand.

For that, he respected her. She'd been willing to do anything to save herself. It was primal and courageous.

And so he did for her what he'd seldom done for anyone else. He showed her mercy. "We can go out for a bit so long as you don't stick to a routine or go to a favorite store."

"Really?" The hopeful look on her face hit him like a blow to his gut. Damn, she was beautiful when she smiled.

He nodded.

Her face fell an instant later. "But I can't make my charity drop?"

Why did he even give a shit that she sounded so disappointed?

But he did. "As long as you're quick about it."

The light returned to those amber eyes as she smiled once more. "I will be. I promise."

"Then get dressed and we'll leave as soon as the stores open."

She got up and started to leave, then paused. She turned to give him a look that tugged even more at the heart he'd thought was dead. "Thank you, Nykyrian."

He'd never heard anything more wonderful than the sound of his name rolling off her tongue with her lilting accent. Inclining his head to her, he stepped back so that she could leave.

His gaze went to the table and her barely touched food. Hauk always said he had a way of ruining even the stoutest appetite. It looked like he was right.

With a heavy sigh, Nykyrian set about cleaning it up.

Kiara paused in her dressing as she heard Syn talking with Nykyrian in the main room. He must have come in while she was showering.

Tilting her head, she tried to hear what they were discussing, but it did her no good. They spoke a strange language she couldn't understand even though she listened very carefully for her name or any other word she might recognize.

Whatever they discussed, they sounded very serious about it.

She sighed. Well at least Nykyrian's harshness seemed to fade a tad around Syn. She liked seeing some reaction from her bodyguard other than shrugs and clipped retorts.

As she entered the main room, Syn turned around in his chair and almost fell out of it as he scanned her body. He cleared his throat and cut an appreciative look to Nykryrian. "Dayum . . . woman be hot."

Nykyrian didn't react at all.

Kiara's cheeks scalded over both their reactions. Syn's for being so overt. Nykyrian's for being nonexistent. "Thank you," she said to Syn.

Nykyrian came to his feet with a grace she admired given how heavy his coat was. He looked lethal and gorgeous. "We've already loaded your drop in the transport. Are you ready?"

She nodded and thought Nykyrian would at least take her arm to keep her near him, but all he did was open the door and scan the corridor before waving her out of the flat.

She glanced back at Syn who hadn't moved a muscle. "Is Syn staying here?"

Syn's laugh answered her. "Yeah, Kip gets to guard you and I get to house-sit. Life bites the big *tee-tawa*."

She frowned. "The big what?"

"We won't be gone long," Nykyrian cut in before Syn could answer. He shut and locked her door.

"That was rude," she chastised.

He took her tone in stride. "Rude would be my

translating what he said. Never ask Syn what half his vocabulary means. He was raised by animals and most of it's too obscene to be translated even for hardcore soldiers and prostitutes."

She smiled at his humorous warning, but curiosity was riding her hard. "*Tee-tawa*?"

He pressed the button for the lift. "Unless you want your face as red as the shirt you're wearing, don't go there."

The doors opened with a soft whir. "So what's your favorite Synism?" she asked, stepping into the lift.

A corner of his mouth twitched. For a moment, Kiara thought he might actually smile, but he just tucked his hands inside the pockets of his long, black coat and the doors closed with a ping. "*Duwad*," he said at last.

She smiled. "Which means?"

"You're not old enough for me to answer that. Hell, I'm not even old enough to say it."

Kiara shook her head at his dry wit that he delivered in a perfect deadpan monotone. He was strangely entertaining in a lethal, 'I'll rip out your heart and eat it' kind of way. "Why did he call you Kip? Is that an insult, too?"

"The answer to that is another of your allotted questions about me, *mu Tara*. Is that really what you want to waste it on?" He led her from the lift, through the lobby, and outside to the curb.

Kiara walked up to him, deliberately invading his personal space. To her surprise, he didn't back away. "I still would like to know."

Their transport, which was driven by a beautiful woman dressed in blood red, pulled up to the curb, its brakes squealing.

He opened the door for her. "It's a Ritadarion term for a brother in war, blood, spirit, and fire."

She slid inside and waited for him to join her. "And are you?"

"In many ways." He jerked his chin toward their driver as he shut the door. "Kiara, meet Jayne."

There was an air around Jayne every bit as dangerous as the one that clung to Nykyrian. Kiara held her hand out toward her, not quite sure how the woman would react. "Nice to meet you."

Jayne smiled warmly as she shook her hand. "Same here. So where to, princess?"

Kiara didn't know why, but she had an instant liking for Jayne. "I'd like to do the drop first, if that's all right with you two."

Jayne pulled out into traffic with such force, Kiara was thrown against Nykyrian's hard body. He gently put her back on her side of the seat.

"Sorry."

He ignored her apology. "Jayne? For once, could you drive like you didn't just knock over a bank?"

Jayne laughed. "Sorry, boss. Old habits die hard."

Kiara arched a brow. "She was a bank robber?"

Jayne signaled her next turn. "I prefer the term 'wealth redistributor.' After all, a woman has needs, and I have more than most."

Kiara was aghast and impressed, and a little scared. "You really robbed banks?"

Jayne winked at her in the rearview mirror. "My father was Egarious Toole. He had me on the job with him from the time I was four, and he taught me well."

Definitely impressed, Kiara grinned. Egarious Toole was one of the most renowned thieves ever born. But unlike most of his ilk, he was also known as the Gentleman Bandit because he was always so polite to those he robbed.

The only thief more notorious was . . .

C.I. Syn.

And unlike Toole, he was known for being brutal and nasty. The most accomplished and the most lethal.

Her stomach flip-flopped as a bad feeling went through her. "Syn . . . is he . . ." she couldn't even bring herself to say it.

"He doesn't do that anymore," Nykyrian said. "But yes, he's an old colleague of Jayne's father, who was in the same line of work."

She let out a long breath in fearful respect. "He doesn't look old enough to have his reputation."

Jayne glanced behind before she changed lanes. "Expertise doesn't have an age requirement."

No, she supposed it didn't. "So are all of you wanted criminals?"

Jayne laughed at her bluntness. "Basically, yeah. It's why we're so good at what we do. We know how criminals think because . . . we are they."

And Kiara was amazed her father had hired them. "Does my father know?"

"As long as we keep you safe, he doesn't care." Jayne glanced back at Nykyrian. "Amazing how that happens, isn't it, boss?"

"Never ceases to amaze me. Everyone's dearest held morals and values have a price on them. It's just a question of how much."

Kiara didn't miss the low-key venom in that statement. "Do you really believe that?"

"I know it for fact." He glanced askance at her. "But some are a little more noble in their reasoning than others."

Such as her father being willing to contract with outlaws and thieves to keep her safe. "What would you sacrifice your morals for?"

"I have no morals to sacrifice."

"I don't believe that."

Jayne snorted. "Believe it, little sister. You are sitting next to the most lethal creature ever born. Don't make him angry. You won't live long enough to regret it."

Kiara arched a brow at that. "Is it even possible to make him angry?"

Nykyrian answered. "Oh, it's more than possible and as Jayne said, you definitely don't want to be there when it happens."

"Why?"

"Because, the last person who made him mad, Nykyrian ripped his heart out with his bare hands and fed it to him."

Kiara shrank back from him. "You're both messing with me."

Jayne shook her head slowly and seriously. Nykyrian didn't respond at all.

Suddenly scared of them both, she sat back in her seat and focused her attention on the people and buildings outside the window.

Nykyrian smelled Kiara's exotic perfume and yearned to bury his lips in the sweet, scented flesh of her neck. *What is wrong with me?* He'd briefly been around more than his share of beautiful women, not the least of which was Jayne, who was extremely attractive, but none of them had ever appealed to him the way Kiara did.

He found it difficult to breathe with her so close to him. Steeling himself, he dared a glance at her.

His breath caught in his throat. Her arms were crossed over her chest as she stared out the window, and displayed to his casual glance was the top swell of her breasts covered by the black lace of her undergarment. From his vantage point, he could practically see all the way to her lap, and that did nothing to alleviate his erection.

C'mon, Nykyrian. Stop it. It wasn't like wanting a woman was anything new for him.

True, but being this close to one for any length of time was.

Finally, the car stopped in front of the shelter where Kiara had wanted to go. Nykyrian got out first and checked the street before he helped her out.

Jayne grabbed the bags of clothes and followed them into the small shop where a handful of people were shopping. The manager smiled when she saw Kiara and then it faded as her gaze went past the dancer to Nykyrian.

The moment the woman saw him, fear darkened her eyes and she literally recoiled.

"Should we ask him to leave?" one of the cashiers asked her.

Hortense gulped. "Are you going to ask him? 'Cause I don't want to die."

"Maybe he'll leave on his own."

"I hate Andarions. They smell funny."

Hortense nodded. "I don't like them either, but I don't want to anger him. He might eat one of us if we do."

Kiara froze as she saw and heard Hortense's reaction and that of the other shoppers who mumbled similar comments. She'd grown so used to Nykyrian that, while she knew he looked lethal, she wasn't afraid of him anymore. Even before she'd really known him, she hadn't been *that* afraid.

And she'd never criticized his race.

What was wrong with people?

Nykyrian took it in stride. "I'll wait by the door," he told Jayne. He went to stand post so that he could watch the store and the street.

Kiara saw the anger on Jayne's face as she took the donated clothes to the counter and all but threw them at Hortense and her staff. *"Chratna po kah."*

Kiara had no idea what Jayne had said to them. The tone, however, told her it wasn't complimentary.

Hortense scowled at her. "That was rude."

Kiara lifted her chin. "But not nearly as rude as what you just did to my escort. In the future, I'll take my charity work to someone a little less close-minded."

"Princess, wait."

Kiara didn't. She walked back outside without even waiting for Jayne.

Nykyrian brushed past her to open the transport door and then waited until she was in before he joined her. "Sorry."

Kiara scowled. "Why are you apologizing?"

"I should have sent Syn with you."

Jayne got in and started the engine. "Never thought I'd have respect for an aristo, but good girl, Kiara. I think I could learn to like *you*."

Kiara ignored her praise. "Why do people act like that?"

Nykyrian shrugged. "People judge. It's what they do. You get used to it."

Do you? She couldn't imagine ever getting used to people reacting that way to her. Judging her for something she couldn't help. How offensive. "I'm sure not everyone is like that."

"Want to see the playback of the look on your face the first time you met me?"

Her stomach hit the floor at his question. She had recoiled from him. The horror of that memory made her ill. "I'm sorry I was stupid."

Nykyrian was shocked by her apology. Most of all, he was shocked by her sincerity. It was completely unexpected. Unsure of how to deal with it, he turned his attention to the street outside.

They remained silent until they reached the small shopping complex.

Nykyrian hung back. "You two go on ahead. I'll be scoping the back."

Kiara wasn't sure about that, but she did as he said. Jayne, who was unbelievably tall for a woman, cut through the crowd in a way Kiara envied.

"Wow, you're good," Kiara said with a hint of laughter in her voice.

Jayne smiled. "I hate crowds. I hate shopping and I think shoppers know that so they give me space lest I break out into a killing spree."

"I think it's because you're *really* tall." She had to be at least six foot four.

"That might have something to do with it, too."

Kiara paused outside of a gift store to window-shop for her gift.

"Cannibal!"

"Killer."

"What's he doing here?"

"Should we notify the authorities?"

"C'mon. Let's leave."

Kiara glanced through the crowd to see them eyeing Nykyrian. Mothers literally picked up their children and fled.

One woman even spat at his feet as he walked by. "Filthy animal. Andarions sicken me."

He ignored the other shoppers as he kept his attention on them and any threat to Kiara.

The hostility appalled her.

"We should go," she said to Jayne.

She saw the sympathy and pain in Jayne's eyes as she watched his stoic acceptance of people's behavior.

"Honestly, princess, he's used to it. Believe me, he's not thinking anything about it right now. You and I are the only ones feeling the pain."

Kiara didn't believe that for a nanosecond. "There's no way this doesn't affect him." And yet as she watched him, she realized that Jayne might be right. He didn't react to any of the insults or actions.

Just like in The Sentella headquarters, he appeared immune. But how could he be?

Grab a present and get out of here.

Trying her best to ignore the imbeciles and their prejudice, she made her way to the women's store next door and found a jacket that was on a display right up front.

Nykyrian hung back in the crowd, but not quite enough to keep her from hearing and seeing how he was mistreated. She felt so bad for him, and yet, true to Jayne's words, he seemed completely oblivious to it all.

It took several minutes before Kiara could find a clerk who would wait on her. "Excuse me," she finally said, cornering one before the woman could escape to another department. "Do you have this in a size thirty?"

The clerk's eyes drifted over her shoulder to where Nykyrian was eyeing the crowd and Kiara wanted to shake the woman for the unwarranted fear. The clerk's gaze returned to Kiara and the jacket. "I think so."

She took it from Kiara's hand and disappeared into the back. Kiara's eyes narrowed in anger.

After a minute, the clerk returned with the right size. "Will this be all, ma'am?"

Kiara nodded, her teeth clenched. Jayne said nothing as she remained by her side.

After ringing the order, the clerk leaned over the counter and whispered, "Where did you find an

Andarion? I've never seen one on Gouran before. Aren't you afraid to be with him?"

Kiara tossed a strand of hair over her shoulder as if she were completely vacuous. "Why no, I'm not afraid. He's already had his daily feeding."

"What do you feed him?" the clerk asked with an audible gulp.

Kiara narrowed her gaze on the idiot. "Babies. Lots and lots of babies."

The clerk shrank back.

Jayne laughed.

Kiara glared, unable to believe the nerve. Snatching up her package, she left the store with Jayne, who was still laughing, in tow.

"Babies," Jayne repeated. "I have *got* to remember that one. Oh, I definitely like you, princess."

Kiara was glad someone was amused. She, on the other hand, wasn't. "I'm ready to go home now."

Nykyrian inclined his head to her as Jayne led the way back to the transport. What amazed her most was the fact that he didn't make a single comment about what had happened.

"Do people always act this way around you?" She got into the transport first.

Joining her, he shrugged as if it were just a normal occurrence to be overlooked. "You should have seen the reactions when I wore a League uniform. Those were actually comical. Except for the ones who lost control of their bowels. Then it was just messy."

She ignored his sarcasm, even though a part of her wondered if he was being honest. "Do Andarions react the same way to you?"

He paused before he answered. "I should live long enough to see them be so kind."

"Why?"

He shrugged. "Humans fear me because they think I'm going to feed on them at any minute, Andarions look at me like a pitiful, weak *giakon*."

"Which means what?"

Jayne answered as she pulled away from the curb. "A castrated coward."

Her mouth formed a small o. No wonder he'd closed himself off from people. He was caught in the middle of all the hatred and fear of both races. "Has anyone ever attacked you for your mixed blood?"

"You can deduce that without my help."

She sighed at his emotionless tone. "I just don't understand why people behave this way."

Nykyrian folded his arms over his chest. "They fear for themselves. I'm a reminder humans and Andarions aren't two separate species, as they like to pretend they are, but derived from the same genetic makeup. Unfortunately, neither race wants to admit it could possibly be anything like the other, so they see me and I'm an easy target to attack. I quit blaming them for it years ago. As Syn would say, it is what it is."

Coldness consumed her as she thought about what it would have been like for him growing up anathema to everyone. "What about your parents?" she asked. "How did they cope?"

He took a deep breath. "They didn't. My mother abandoned me when I was five."

"And the commander?"

"I wasn't his natural son."

Kiara smiled as she considered Huwin's kindness in adopting him. She remembered Nykyrian's father from a few of the political trips he'd made to Gouran when she was a child to meet with her father. Though stern, he'd always brought her presents and had been very cordial and kind. "He must have loved you dearly."

"Never assume anything."

This time, there was no mistaking the emotion in his voice. Hatred, cold and simple.

Kiara wanted to reach out and soothe away Nykyrian's pain. She couldn't imagine what it must have been like for him. Her parents would have torn apart anyone who looked at her the way people did Nykyrian. She couldn't believe a mother would give up her child for any reason.

She sat in silence the rest of the way home, her mind mulling over her lessons for the day.

Jayne left them outside her building and went home.

When they returned to her flat, Syn looked up from where he lay on the couch watching the viewer, shock etched on his face. "That didn't take long. I've never known a woman not to take at least half a day to shop for anything."

"I can't imagine why the trip was so short," Nykyrian said in a sarcastic voice that made Kiara take a second look at him.

Laughing, Syn switched off the viewer and sat up. "You should try smiling. I think it would take the edge off people."

Nykyrian doffed his long, black coat and draped it over her chair. "Actually, they mistake it for an attempt to bite and then it only gets worse."

Syn laughed even harder.

Kiara didn't find it amusing in the least. She set her bag by her chair and moved to the closet to get wrapping paper and tape.

As she listened to them talk, all the stories of C.I. Syn and his legendary skills went through her. The man who seemed, well, normal was a bit of stretch, but not too extreme, was hard to reconcile in her mind with the notorious outlaw.

She would have never guessed his reputation by his almost playful demeanor.

"Do you want me to relieve you tonight?"

Kiara paused at Syn's question. Biting her lip, she looked at Nykyrian.

He continued to face Syn. "No," he said to her immediate relief. "I got it."

Syn looked suspicious. "How long has it been since you last slept?"

"I'm not tired." There was a warning in Nykyrian's tone that Syn seemed to pick up on.

What a strange conversation.

"Fine." Syn glanced at her. "By the way, if he ever looks like he's sleeping, don't touch him or make any sudden moves. He's been known to bite."

She pulled the tape off the top shelf. "I'm not worried."

Syn lifted a questioning brow. "What, no fear?"

She shrugged and plopped her bundle of wrapping supplies on the floor. "I'm the daughter of a soldier. My father comes awake with a blaster aimed at your head if you disturb him from his sleep."

Syn gave Nykyrian a knowing smile. "And I thought it was just you and your idiosyncrasies."

Nykyrian shrugged and sat in the other chair across from the couch. "I've told you not to think. It's just a waste of your time."

Kiara was startled by the barb. There was a tiny lifting of the corners of Nykyrian's mouth that might actually have been a smile. She glanced at Syn who took the words in stride.

"Well, I guess I should be going. I've got a shipment to take care of." Syn hesitated for a moment, casting her a sheepish glance before looking back at Nykyrian. "Are we still planning on tomorrow?"

"We can't. Everyone's scheduled tomorrow."

Syn crossed his arms over his chest. "Then when are we going to do it?"

Kiara glanced up, wishing she knew what they were talking about.

"Hauk's free the next day. He can watch Kiara."

Syn nodded. "I'll have Hauk come over first thing." He gave Kiara an encouraging smile. "You two be careful and don't let the *diras* get you."

Kiara waited until Syn had left before questioning Nykyrian. "What are you two planning?"

"I've got a few things to take care of."

She unrolled the wrapping paper and cut a square large enough for the box. "Can't Darling stay with me instead of Hauk?"

He arched a questioning brow.

She realized too late what he must be thinking. "It's not because he's Andarion," she snapped irritably, wrapping the paper around the box. "Even you have to admit Hauk's not the nicest person."

He relaxed. "I guess not." He paused before he spoke again. "Darling has his own things to do. Hauk just likes to intimidate people. Stand up to him and he'll back down."

"Or have me fricasseed by the time you return."

"There's always that possibility."

With a grimace, Kiara finished wrapping her present, then put her things away.

Hours passed excruciatingly slowly while Nykyrian worked and Kiara tried to find some way to occupy her time. Because of her career, she'd never spent much time at home. She was either rehearsing or performing. Doing interviews or PR or charity work. She ran from minute to minute at a record pace. So lying here on her bed, staring at the ceiling, was irritating her.

What did people do when they stayed home all day? It was mind-numbing.

After awhile, she got up and went to the studio to practice. She might not be able to perform for the next few weeks, but she couldn't afford to let her muscles stiffen.

In spite of Nykyrian's best efforts to concentrate on the boring reports he was reviewing, the sound of Kiara's dance music lured him. Without conscious thought, he found himself walking down the corridor to her studio.

His breath caught as he saw her in all her lithe glory twirling about the room. Her body glistened from her perspiration, and tendrils of her mahogany hair had come free from her tight bun. Every single move she made was a study in grace and beauty. She moved like water.

Chills ran down the length of his body as she jumped and gyrated. God, what he wouldn't give or do for the right to peel the tight exercise suit off her body and make love to her for the rest of the night.

He gripped the wood of the door frame until his knuckles turned white.

Kiara spun about and caught a sudden flash of black and silver. She almost stumbled as she realized Nykyrian was watching her.

She froze in place. "I'm sorry." She took deep, calming breaths, unsure of what made her more breathless, her exercise or his obvious interest. "I didn't realize you were there."

She reached to turn off the player.

"Don't stop," he said with an odd note she couldn't quite place. "I love to watch you dance."

Kiara let the next song begin. She walked up to him on her toes. Intending to awe him with her pirouette, she gasped as her foot gave way under her weight.

Nykyrian caught her before she fell. The sudden impact of strong muscles surrounding her stole her breath.

"Are you okay?"

She smiled at the warm concern in his voice. "It's my ankle. I think I might have hurt it."

He eased her to the floor.

Kiara wished she could think of some way to keep his arms around her, but his warmth vacated her and left her longing.

With deft movements, he unlaced her shoe and pulled it free. A hiss escaped his lips. Her eyes widened at the unexpected emotional display. "What happened to your foot?"

Kiara wiggled her toes and looked down at the member expecting to see it broken or swollen. Instead, it looked quite normal to her. "There's nothing wrong with it."

He brushed his fingers over the ball of her foot as if he held a holy relic. Chills crept up her legs despite the burning sensation she felt where his hands touched her.

"You've got more blisters on your foot than I've got . . ." his voice trailed off.

Kiara gave a half laugh as she dismissed his concern. "It's the hazards of *my* business. I'm used to them. They only hurt when they bleed."

His grip tightened as he locked gazes with her. "You shouldn't do this to yourself. I'm sure it hurts like hell."

She studied his face, wishing she could see what he looked like without those dark shades. "Why would you care how anything makes me feel?"

"I don't know. I just do."

Warmth flooded her body as he used the same words for her that she'd used on him. Thinking only of how gorgeous he looked, she leaned over to kiss him.

For a moment, she thought she'd succeed, then he pulled away and released her foot.

"You should take a few days and let those blisters heal. At the rate you're going, you'll end up crippled by the time you're thirty."

Disgruntled, Kiara unlaced her other shoe before she snatched it off. "Why is it I have a feeling someone has said that to you?"

"In my case, it wasn't crippled, it was dead." The cold words hovered like a pall. As soon as he spoke them, he vanished like a silent specter.

Dread gnawed at her stomach as she stared after him. The blase delivery chilled her. It had sounded almost as if he wanted to die.

Why do you care?

You are a dancer. He's a paid killer.

Yes, but she'd seen the kindness in him that he hid from the world, and she'd glimpsed some of the pain that he kept to himself. While she knew she should hate him, every day they were together, she discovered another part of his soul, and it wasn't frightening.

It was strangely beautiful.

Nykyrian heard the shower come on after Kiara had entered the bathroom. He walked to the door and leaned his head against the panel, wanting, craving the courage to enter the room, to feel her arms wrapped around him.

He wanted her so badly that he ached from it.

But he knew better. Softness didn't belong in his world and neither did beauty.

What kind of life could he offer her? A shot in the back one day because some asshole wanted vengeance on him?

He had no choice but to remain alone. There was no room in his life for anyone.

Nykyrian sighed. He refused to think about what he wanted. His wants were unimportant. He had a job to do and that's exactly what he was going to do.

Protect her, nothing more.

He pushed himself away from the door and returned to the main room so that he could work on his reports.

After a few minutes, Kiara came out and bid him good night in that wonderfully gentle voice, then she took herself to bed.

With a curse, Nykyrian snatched his boots off. In morbid retaliation to remind himself of what he was, he checked the retractable blades hidden in his boots. The cold steel shot out, glinting in the light. He fingered the blades, feeling the razor-sharp edge scrape against his skin. He was a killer, that was the only destiny he had.

Satisfied that he had controlled himself where Kiara was concerned, Nykyrian pushed the blades back into their hidden compartment and set the boots on the floor next to the couch.

With a sigh, he tossed his shades to the table and rubbed the bridge of his nose where they'd made an indentation. He should be used to wearing them, but, honestly, he hated the necessity.

He'd learned a long time ago that his eyes disturbed anyone who saw them. It was just easier for everyone to keep them covered.

Kiara's bed squeaked under her weight as she shifted position. His cock twitched in response. Too easily, he could imagine himself in there with her, brushing his hands over her body while she—

Stop!

He had to get her out of his thoughts. Pulling his shirt off, he gathered up his things for his own shower. Yeah, a cold shower would do wonders for his body.

Bullshit. But at least it would distract him. Steeling his willpower, he entered the bathroom and turned on the water, making sure he added no hot water at all.

I hate cold showers. And he took a sick pleasure in the pain of the icy water stabbing his body.

This was something he could handle. Pain had always been his best friend and, after a few minutes, he felt much better. Grateful he was in control again, he went to the kitchen to get something to drink.

Kiara's door opened.

Nykyrian froze. He glanced to the low table in the main room and realized too late he was too far from his shades to get them on before she saw him.

Shit.

Having no choice but to wait for her to discover him, Nykyrian gripped the glass tightly.

Kiara yawned as she plodded down the hallway, belting her robe closed. She stopped as she reached the opening to the kitchen, her eyes riveted on Nykyrian's bare back.

Wide, muscled shoulders tapered down to slim hips. More deep, white scars crisscrossed his tanned, well-muscled flesh than she could count. It looked as if he'd been beaten to the brink of death. Her heart twisted at the sight. She'd never in her life seen anything like it.

His left arm and shoulder were covered with brightly colored League markings—as they were for all assassins. The one on his bicep was the usual human skull with its jaw resting on a dagger's hilt. The blade of the dagger came out of the top of the skull, where pieces of bone were flying in a macabrely beautiful image. But what made his tattoo special was the crown surrounding the skull and the red colors used to highlight it.

He was a Command Assassin of the First Order.

Holy saints . . . That was the hardest rank to achieve and only the most lethal of them, less than one percent, ever held it.

Yet against all common sense, she wasn't afraid of him.

Her gaze returning to his scars, she crossed the room, longing to touch him and to soothe the skin puckered by welts. Her hand reached out, but she stopped it before she made contact with his flesh. He wouldn't like that and he was too old for her to coddle.

"I was thirsty," she whispered in an awkward apology.

Without facing her or making a single comment, Nykyrian pulled a glass down and handed it to her over his shoulder.

As she poured her juice, Kiara realized he was missing his shades. She was so surprised by that fact, she forgot what she was doing. Juice spilled over the rim of her glass, soaking the sleeve of her robe and splashing up against her feet and legs. Gasping, she plopped the glass and juice down on the counter and reached for a towel.

"I'll clean it up," he growled.

Kiara's hand trembled as she tossed the towel back to the counter. She tried to see his face, but he turned away.

She took the hint. Despite the overwhelming curiosity, she grabbed her juice and left.

Racing to her room, she shook with emotions she couldn't quite name and she wasn't even sure if she wanted to know what they were or what they signified.

She wasn't sure why she felt like she'd narrowly escaped death and yet . . .

Who was this man in her home?

*   *   *

Nykyrian wiped up the sticky juice, his thoughts and emotions churning. He wished for the strength it would take to trust Kiara. But experience had taught him that no one could be trusted.

He would have her assassins tracked down soon and hand them over to her father. With Bredeh and Pitala out of action, no one else would dare accept a contract on her life knowing The Sentella protected her. Then he would be free to return to his life.

Alone.

An ache twisted through him worse than any physical pain he'd ever experienced. Clenching his teeth, he vowed to himself to see Bredeh and Pitala caught soon before he made the worst mistake of his life.

You already did that when you left The League.

No. That had been easy. The worst mistake would be kissing a dancer whose touch he craved to the point of suicide.

CHAPTER 10

Kiara peeked around the corner of her hallway to watch Nykyrian tapping away at his computer. How could he sit there like that, hour after hour, without cramping or going out of his mind? She'd never seen anyone work so hard or for so long.

He looked up while his fingers never missed a beat. "Something wrong?"

"I'm so bored, I'm bended." She flounced forward to throw herself into the chair across from him. Sighing, she propped her chin in her hand and stared at him. "What do you do all day to keep from losing your mind?"

"Work."

She'd figured that one out, but there had to be more than just working all the time. "Yeah, me too. Any idea what we're supposed to do with free time?"

"No."

"You're not being very helpful. Can't we do something?"

"Like?"

"I don't know. You could start by laying off the monosyllabic answers—in case no one ever told you, that's really annoying." She sighed. "What do normal people . . . Um, never mind."

He tilted his head back like she'd slapped him. "Are you suggesting I'm not normal?"

She held her hands up in mock surrender. "Oh yeah, baby, you ooze normality. From the top of that assassin's braid to the tip of those boots that I'm pretty sure conceal retractable blades. You're just an average joe. No doubt about it. Cause, you know, everyone sits for hours doing nothing but typing . . ."

Nykyrian felt another peculiar urge to smile at her sarcasm. He had no idea why she charmed him, especially given the implied insult. But . . .

He set the computer aside and stood up. "C'mon."

Kiara frowned as he headed for her studio. "I've already practiced until I'm bored with that, too."

"You haven't practiced what I'm about to show you."

She arched a brow at that as she followed after him. "You gonna show me your moves, baby?"

He snorted. "Get that cheesy line a lot, do you?"

"Oh yeah. It's one of the drawbacks of being a dancer. Every guy seems to think he's the first one to think of it. Scary really."

Nykyrian didn't comment as he pulled his outer shirt off. If she accidentally hit the armor in it, she'd bruise her hand at best, break it at worst. And the last thing he wanted was to see her hurt.

Kiara had to force herself not to bite her knuckle at the sight of that ripped body as he tossed his shirt aside. He had on a sleeveless black undershirt that clung to every sharp dip of a body she'd love to explore with her tongue.

The scars on his left arm blended in with The League artwork. There were more scars on his right arm. They curled around like he'd grabbed a laser whip at some point.

Everything about him screamed danger. Power.

Sex.

It was actually hard to look at him, he was so gorgeous. She glanced toward the shirt that had made a heavy thump on her floor when he'd dropped it. No doubt it was as armored as his coat. "You really wouldn't feel it if I shot you, would you?"

"Depends on where you shot me."

"Hmmm."

He came up behind her so close that it gave her chills. His body heat warmed her. He was so tall that she barely came up to his shoulder. She trembled at his fierce nearness and had to fight the urge to lean back against him.

Completely unaffected by her, he put his hands on her shoulders as she faced the mirrored wall. "Vulnerable spots." He pointed to each one on her as he listed them. "Eyes, nose, throat—" He paused before he added, "Groin."

"I know all of this. My father had me adequately trained."

"Had you been adequately trained, Pitala would never have been able to pin you down."

"He surprised me."

"And those are the three magic words to always remember. Surprise is your best friend." He turned her to face him. "Attack me."

Kiara hesitated. He was a huge man with a lot of scary skills. "I don't know about this . . ."

"Yes, you do. I come at you, you fight me with everything you have. You don't stop no matter what. It's me or you and for you, it better be me." His voice was deadpan and yet she didn't miss the underlying ferocity of those words.

"You sure?"

He nodded. "Don't worry. You can't hurt me."

"All right." She scissor-kicked him.

Before she could make contact, he backed up quicker than she could blink and slid fluidly to her side, then caught her around the throat in a gentle grip designed to make her aware, but not hurt or scare her. "Too easy."

He let go and stepped back.

She tried to strike him with her hands, but again, he dodged and came up with a mock blow that would have sent her flying had he made contact with her.

Frustrated, she attempted to kick his groin. He moved away.

Kiara growled at him. "What are you made of? Rubber?"

"Calm down. Not every blow will make contact." He gestured to the scars on his right arm. "Even I miss from time to time. No matter what happens, you have to maintain control of your emotions. Frustration and anger are your enemies. The goal is to piss off and kill others."

He stepped away from her and called out to her media player, "System, find and cue 'Bodies' by Drowning Pool."

Kiara cringed as a loud obnoxious song started playing over her intercom and the lead singer screamed out in rage. "What is that ungodly noise?"

"It'll help, trust me. You're a dancer. Listen to the beat of the song. One, two, three, four. One, hit the eyes." He demonstrated each punch without making contact. "Two, hit the nose. Three, hit the throat. Four, hit the groin. Don't let up. Don't stop the attack. One, two, three, four," he repeated several more times until she had the sequence.

Kiara nodded to the rapid tempo he counted off in time to the song.

"Now attack me to the beat of the song. In the exact order I gave you."

She did and this time, she saw how much more effective the hits were. Even though he dodged her blows, she felt the flow and the power of each strike.

"Now, the next secret is to do the unexpected. When I attack you, I expect you to run or pull away. Come at me with everything you have. If I grab you, go completely limp."

"Limp?"

He nodded. "Ever tried to pick up a pissed-off toddler? Even though they don't weigh much, they go completely limp and unbalance you. What happens when you're off balance?"

This one she knew all too well from her dancing. "You hit the floor."

"That's right, and when an attacker is down, you have the advantage. Remember, one, two, three, four. No mercy. No leniency. Attack until they're down for the count. Don't pull away to run. It only gives them a chance to recover and come at you again and by then, they're really pissed off and wanting blood. You beat them down until they can't get up. Mercilessly. Coldly. Them or you." There was no mistaking the deadly earnestness of his emotions on this point and she never wanted to be on the receiving end of *that* venom.

"You are one scary man."

"And I'm alive even though I should be dead."

He did have a point with that.

"Now attack."

Kiara threw herself against him. The instant her body slammed into his, he stepped back instead of staggering, but it was still impressive.

"Sweep the legs, gouge the eyes, hit the nose. You can crush the average windpipe with only five pounds of pressure. Three pounds to tear off an ear. Even less to blind someone completely."

"You *are* gory."

"Yes, but you will survive if you listen to me. Human bodies are frail and some aliens are even more so."

"What about the ones who aren't?"

"Everyone is vulnerable in the eyes and throat. If they can't see you, they can't attack. If they can't breathe, they can't attack. If they bleed, they *can* die. Never met a species yet that didn't breathe or bleed. Eyes are tricky. Not all races have them, but most of those who come at you do."

Kiara nodded and they went over and over the moves until she was hot and sweaty, and most importantly had them programmed into her muscle memory.

Winded from the exertion, she realized he hadn't even broken a sweat. How did he do that?

She leaned back against her bar, panting, as she watched him retrieve his shirt from the floor. She ground her teeth at the sight of his well-rounded butt cupped by his leather pants. Damn, he was hot.

"Do you ever dance?" she asked, trying to imagine how good he'd look.

"No."

"Never?"

He shook his head.

"Everyone should dance, Nykyrian." She took his hand intending to show him, but the moment she did, he hissed at her and jerked away.

Shocked by his unexpected reaction, she stepped back.

"Don't *ever* touch me."

The hostility caught her completely off guard. "I'm sorry. I didn't mean to offend you."

He didn't respond as he left her alone in the room.

"System, stop," she said, ending the music he'd trained her to.

Curious about his reaction, she went to the main room where he was retrieving his computer. "Nykyrian—"

"You need to get ready for your party tonight."

His order stunned her. "You're going to allow me to attend?"

"For an hour, per your father's request. He said it was something you couldn't afford to miss."

"Okay." She paused to look back at him and his emotionless form. She was still worried that she'd over-stepped some unknown, invisible line with him. "Are we good?"

"Fine."

She sighed, realizing he was back to his monosyl-labic self. So much for reaching out to him. Obviously, he wanted to keep his distance and she would respect that.

But there for a minute, she'd thought they shared something more than client and protector.

Don't be stupid. It wasn't like there could ever be anything between them. He was an outlaw and she was a princess.

Then why did the fact that she'd hurt him hurt her? Why did she feel like this? Shaking her head, she went to her room to lay out her clothes before bathing.

Nykyrian touched his hand where her fingers had brushed against his. His flesh still burned from that brief contact. But that wasn't what bothered him. It was the fact that he wanted to feel her hand on his face. The fact that he wanted to dance with her . . .

Don't go there.

Bitter, harsh memories surged strong enough to take his breath.

You are an animal.

And she was beauty and grace.

He would keep his hands to himself and make sure they extracted him out of her life as soon as possible.

CHAPTER 11

Kiara smoothed her dress with her hands, double-checking to make sure she looked fine for the party. Tiyana had warned her a group of promoters would be there, and a disillusioned promoter could damage her career as much as death. In the dancing business, image was everything.

Opening the door to her room, she went down the hall to find the most lethal group ever imagined assembled in her main room. All in black, all armed, and all looking like they were hunting for blood.

Jayne, Hauk, Darling, Syn, and Nykyrian.

She frowned at their collective fierceness. "What's going on?"

Nykyrian shrugged his coat on. "Protection detail. But don't worry. We won't cramp you at the party. We know how to blend."

Syn snorted at that. "Yeah, baby, you blend."

Nykyrian shoved at him.

Kiara bit her lip to keep from smiling at their good-natured ribbing. Though to be honest, Syn, Darling, and Jayne did all look like sophisticated socialites. Especially Syn.

His eyeliner and piercings gone, he looked better than human. He looked absolutely stunning, and with his hair pulled back into a sleek ponytail, he had an air of refinement to him she would have never guessed he possessed. Nor would she ever suspect him of being one of the most notorious thieves in the United Systems.

He stepped forward to offer her his arm. "I'm your escort for the party. Anyone asks, we met at an art show."

She arched a brow at that. A notorious outlaw with facial piercings at a hoity-toity gallery? The image was preposterous. "An art show?"

He nodded. "Klasen opened a new one two weeks ago, here in Wecsiz on Fifth. It's featuring his bronze period. Not as impressive as his gold, but worth visiting anyway. You can really see how his talents progressed from the early work to what he does now. It's the finely patterned brushstrokes, though, that really mark the bronze. You can see him developing his technique."

"Oh, gah," Jayne moaned, pulling out her blaster and aiming it at Syn's head. "Can I shoot him now before he bores us all to death with his friggin' art shit?"

Syn disarmed her. "You're such an uneducated pleb."

"And happy that way. Not to mention much less boring." She grabbed her blaster from his hand and holstered it underneath her dress.

Kiara took Syn's arm. "You really do know your art. I'm impressed."

"Please don't encourage him," Darling begged. "He really will bore you with it all night if you let him."

"Shut up, all of you. Uncultured baboons."

Nykyrian led the way to the door. "All right, children. We're going out into public now. Let's all play nice and try to stay out of trouble."

Jayne made a kiss at him. "Yes, Dad."

sophisticated, not to mention strong. "How could I miss it? It's not every day you turn twenty-six."

Tiyana shuddered and put her finger to her perfectly rouged lips. "Don't say that so loud," she whispered, looking around to make sure no one heard them. "I've told all the promoters I'm twenty-two. If they ever found out how close to thirty I am . . ." She held her hand up to her head like a blaster and pretended to pull the trigger.

Kiara laughed at the gesture. "Do me the same favor and we'll call it even."

"Done." Tiyana pulled her into another hug.

At least until she realized Kiara wasn't alone. Tiyana stiffened as she swept a curious glance over Syn. "Who's your . . . friend?"

Syn oozed charm as he took Tiyana's hand into his and placed a debonair kiss on her knuckles that made Tiyana visibly shiver. "Sheridan Belask, *miratoi*. It's an honor to meet you. I've been an admirer of yours since that brilliant interpretation of Terigov that you did three years ago. It was stunning, as are you."

Tiyana preened under the praise. "Oh, thank you . . . um, Mister . . . or Lord Belask?"

"Please, call me Sheridan."

"Sheridan." Tiyana's gaze went to Nykyrian and widened in trepidation.

Syn waved a dismissive hand in a way any nobleman would envy. "My bodyguard and servant. I hope you don't mind? I find that in my position in life there are those who are always looking to take a shot at me. I'm sure you understand."

"Absolutely. Please, come in." She stepped back so that they could enter.

Tiyana grabbed Kiara close as soon as they were inside and whispered in her ear. "Oh my God, girl! He is the hottest thing on two legs."

"Sy-S-Sheridan?"

"Who else! You have been holding out on me."

Kiara glanced over to Nykyrian, who scanned the crowd with precision. True to his word, he stood back, but not so much that he couldn't get to her in a heartbeat if need be. Then she looked at Syn who was pulling two glasses of wine off a passing tray.

Yeah, he was choice, but compared to Nykyrian . . .

He just didn't compete, in her mind.

Kiara smiled as he offered her a glass. She handed the present to Tiyana before she took the proffered drink. "Thank you."

Tiyana shook the box. "Let me guess, clothes?"

Kiara rolled her eyes. "I hate when you do that."

Tiyana laughed. "That's what friends are for. Let me go toss it on my loot pile. I know I'm going to love it. You always have the best taste." She looked around the huge crowd. "I think you know everyone here. If not, just give me a wink and I'll introduce you." She then pulled Kiara to her and whispered in her ear, "Paulus is here and he's drunk off his arse, so be warned." Tiyana wandered off in the crowd.

Syn gave her a wicked grin. "He's not the only one flagged off his ass." He downed the wine in one gulp before he grabbed another glass.

"Why do you do that?"

"Cause it's easier to keep a buzz going when it's in place than to have to start from scratch once you're sober. Not to mention, if you keep drinking, you don't have to contend with a hangover."

Kiara shook her head at his reasoning.

Syn scanned the crowd with the same precision Nykyrian used, except she noticed the way his gaze would pause on particularly nice jewelry as if mentally calculating its value. As well as pause on any attractive woman and her 'assets.' "So who is this Paulus dick?"

Kiara cringed in distaste. "He's a walking nightmare. His father made a fortune with their media company before becoming an art sponsor and, as a result, Paulus thinks he should have the privilege of sleeping with any dancer who catches his eye."

"I can tell you love him."

"Yeah, like a boil in my nether regions."

Syn laughed out loud. "Nether regions, huh? I'm going to have to remember that one."

Kiara searched the huge gathering for friendly faces. So much for Tiyana's comment that she'd only invited a "few" friends and associates. It looked like everyone Tiyana had ever spoken with was here.

She glanced back at Nykyrian. At least he was a friendly face.

Well, given his lethal glower as he watched everyone around him, maybe *friendly* was stretching it a bit. But he was familiar to her. She sipped at her wine while Syn downed another glass, then moved on to something harder.

"Kiara!"

Kiara spun around to face Elfa Dicuta, her understudy and worst enemy. Ugh, did *she* have to be here?

I should have stayed home. Had she known Elfa was invited, she would have.

And even though she wanted to snatch every strand of dark hair out of the woman's head, she had to be nice to the little toad. "Hi Elfie," she said, using the nickname she knew the backbiting woman hated, "how are you?"

Elfa gave her one of her notorious fake smiles. "Just fine, sweetie. I can't tell you how sorry I am you had to pull out of the show. I feel just terrible about it."

I'll bet. "So how's the show going?"

This time, Kiara suspected the smile might be real. "Great. Absolutely great. They say that it's making even more money now than when you were the star."

Probably because they weren't having to pay Elfa the same amount of money . . .

She hoped.

Elfa's eyes drifted to where Nykyrian stood with his back to a wall. "Didn't you come in with that Andarion over there?"

Kiara tightened her grip on her glass, wanting to toss it in Elfa's face. "Yes, I did."

A scheming look crossed Elfa's face. "The promoters might not like that. Andarions are a controversial thing." Kiara detected a hopeful note under the girl's tone. "Have you been hooked up with him long?"

Syn stepped forward with a snide grin. "She's not hooked up with him, love. He's my bodyguard. I, on the other hand, am the one she's here with."

A calculating look darkened her eyes as she took in the expensive shoes and suit Syn wore. Her smile turned flirtatious. "And you are?"

"One of the reviewers who wrote that you were a piss-poor substitute for Kiara and that the entire system is saddened by the loss of her from the show. I was just telling her that if she doesn't return soon and they leave your clumsy ass in, the show'll be closing prematurely for sure."

Elfa's nostrils widened. "You're a pig!"

"Oink, oink."

Furious, she stalked off.

Kiara tsked at Syn, even though she was grateful for what he'd done. "You are *so* wrong."

"Always, my love. Always. I hate conniving, insincere people. My father used to say you have friends for a reason and friends for a season. That bitch there is definitely the kind you have for a reason and that is only if it's serving her."

Kiara saluted him with her wineglass. "It amazes me how quickly and accurately you and Nykyrian sum people up. Terrifies me what you must think of me."

"There's only one word for you."

She cringed at the thought. "And that is?"

"Naive."

This time, she scoffed at the preposterousness of that. "Hardly."

"Trust me, princess. You are what we affectionately call a snap."

"Snap?"

"Easy to fool and to lead astray. But don't worry. It's not an insult by any means. I envy you that ability to look at people and not see the ugliness inside their souls."

"I'm not as blind as you think."

He downed his glass of whisky. "Yes, you are. Otherwise you wouldn't be talking to me. You'd know better."

She swept an appreciative gaze over his tall, handsome body. It was so hard sometimes to reconcile these people with the reputations she knew they carried. "You're not as bad as you think you are."

"Trust me, this suit hides a lot."

"Perhaps, but I still remember the man who refused to leave me for dead on that ship. You could have saved yourself, but you didn't."

"I was too drunk to know better."

She shook her head. "Keep lying to yourself, Syn. I know the truth."

"No, love, that you most definitely don't. The truth would horrify you. The gods know, it horrifies me most days and I'm the poor sap who lived it." He knocked back another drink.

She opened her mouth to speak, but her words were cut off by the sound of another dear friend.

"Ooo honey, leave it to you to show up with the two finest pieces of ass at the party!"

Her face heating up exponentially, Kiara cringed at Shera's words as Syn laughed, then moved to a more discreet distance so that they could talk.

"Shera! Finally a friendly face in these shark-infested waters."

"Girl, you know it." Shera pulled her into her arms for a quick hug. Her dark skin was a stark contrast to Kiara's paleness. Beautiful and sweet, Shera was the first friend she'd made at her dance company. The head costume designer, she was always good for a laugh and quick pick-me-up. "Now don't wrinkle me." Shera pulled away. "Some of us have to work at looking good."

Kiara laughed. "Please. I've seen you in the morning. You always look gorgeous." She squeezed Shera's hand. "I'm so glad you're here."

Shera popped a piece of shrimp in her mouth as she surveyed the crowd. "Like I had a choice. Tiyana threatened my life if I missed this." Turning serious, Shera pulled Kiara off to the side, away from Syn and the nearest group of people. "Please tell me you're making a sandwich in your bed at night with those two men."

Kiara shook her head at her friend. "No."

"Are you insane? If I had *that,* I'd be at home doing a serious sheet dance." Shera looked over at Nykyrian and made a purring noise. "You think he wants a drink . . . and a little me in his lap?"

"I don't think he's interested."

Shera's look turned serious and predatory. "Oh,

honey, I'm willing to find a way to make him interested."

For some reason the idea of Shera coming on to Nykyrian seriously irked her.

Kiara narrowed her eyes at Shera. "You are incorrigible and he told me he has a *boy*friend."

Shera made a noise of supreme aggravation. "Figures, and I always say incorrigibility is good for the soul, but sex is infinitely better." She glanced back at Nykyrian. "Any chance he might be a switch-hitter?"

Kiara rolled her eyes as she refused to comment. The last thing she needed to do was encourage her near-nympho girlfriend.

"Seriously though—" Shera looked back in the direction Elfa had disappeared. "I wanted to warn you about your understudy."

Kiara's laughter died instantly. "What?"

"Little crab-butt got a fantastic review last night and since then, she's been going around telling all the promoters and directors that a certain dancer is past her prime. That your fears of being replaced are what led you to a mental breakdown and that, *that* is why you had to pull out of the show."

"I'll kill her!" Kiara slammed her glass down on the table and started toward Elfa.

Shera grabbed her arm. "Not now. There are too many promoters here for you to cause a scene. If you start something, she'll tell them you're too temperamental and impossible to work with. You'll prove her points."

Kiara clenched her fists at her sides, wanting to jerk every strand of hair out of Elfa's head.

Shera patted her arm. "Let it go, little sister. Beat her where it counts most. On the street and at the box office. I promise you her paltry review was nothing compared to the ones you get." Shera's laugh returned. "Besides, think of this, I had to let your costume out two sizes to accommodate her fat ass."

In spite of herself and her anger, Kiara laughed. "Did you really?"

Shera nodded. "She's shaped like a pineapple, lumps and all. And red isn't that girl's color. Looks ghastly on her."

She shouldn't take comfort in that, but it did make her feel better. Calmer now, Kiara retrieved her glass from the table and reluctantly allowed Shera to drift off.

Syn had vanished and she no longer saw him in the crowd.

Looking over to Nykyrian, who stood a full head taller than anyone else there, she smiled at him as she recalled Shera's words. He was definitely the best-looking man at the party even with those shades obscuring the majority of his face. And she would like very much to do a sheet dance with him, if he would only cooperate.

"Aw, there you are. Tiyana told me you were here."

Kiara cringed. It wasn't Paulus, it was worse. Wicmon—her own show's promoter, the one man she couldn't afford to be rude to no matter what.

"Hi." She smiled her prettiest smile for him.

Wicmon took her hand and placed a sloppy kiss over her knuckles. "I was so disappointed you pulled out of the show." She wondered if he thought that lecherous look on his face was becoming. "I'd so hoped to become better acquainted with you."

For the first time, she was grateful for her kidnapping that had kept her away from him. She tried to tactfully withdraw her hand, but his grip tightened. She admitted he was handsome, if he just didn't have that cold, calculating look behind his clear blue eyes. And at the moment, she felt like cornered prey.

How was she going to extract herself from him without offending him?

Fretting, she looked up to see Nykyrian moving toward them. A smile curved her lips as he stopped next to them. "Princess, Tiyana was looking for you. She said it was extremely urgent."

Anger clouded Wicmon's eyes at the interruption. He turned around, then took a step back as he realized the size and width of Nykyrian.

He gulped audibly.

Kiara stifled her laughter at his reaction. No doubt he'd assumed Nykyrian would be another dancer he could intimidate and send on his way.

Kiara sidestepped him. "If you'll excuse me, Wicmon, I better go see what she needs."

She didn't wait on his response. Instead, she led Nykyrian away through the crowd. "Thank you for that. How did you know to come over?"

"The look on your face said it all. Not to mention I read lips and I didn't like what he was saying to you."

Grateful for his intervention, she ached to kiss him. "I owe you."

Now, he looked uncomfortable. Without a word and to her great dismay, he moved away from her to drift back into the crowd. Kiara wanted to stamp her foot in frustration. How could he be so kind one moment, then aloof the next?

Needing a moment alone to regroup with herself, she started toward the balcony. Just as she reached it, a rough hand gripped her elbow. Kiara was tempted to cry out, but assumed it was just another promoter.

Until she heard a voice that made her blood run cold. "I knew we'd meet again."

Her heart pounded.

Pitala.

And he was here to kill her.

CHAPTER 12

Two thoughts went through Kiara's mind at the same time. One was the fear that Pitala would kill her, the other was the fear she would live and this episode would end her career.

She felt a sharp jab in her ribs. Without looking, she knew it was the barrel of a small blaster.

His grip tightened on her arm. "Walk outside to the hallway like you want to talk to me. No sudden moves or warnings to the others or I pull the trigger and spray your guts all over your friend's apartment. Then I open fire on everyone here and they can join you in hell."

Kiara nodded, her heart lodged in her throat as she shook all over. She looked about for Nykyrian, Jayne, and Syn, but they seemed to have vanished. There was absolutely no sign of any of them.

What kind of protectors were they?

Sweat beaded on her body as she moved to do what she'd been told to even though it galled her. Nykyrian's instructions went through her mind, but he hadn't covered what to do in this kind of situation. As Pitala had warned, he could open fire and kill half the people here, including Shera and Tiyana.

No, she couldn't be responsible for innocent deaths.

She was the target. Not them. This was her destiny.

Kiara prayed her legs didn't buckle and that no one approached them.

Glancing sideways, she noticed Pitala was dressed in an expensive suit, his hair slicked back. To the casual observer, he would pass for either an aristocrat or a wealthy promoter. No one would think anything of her leaving here with him.

Help me!

Fear choked her as tears gathered in her eyes. Fiercely, she bit her bottom lip to keep from screaming or begging for help. She wouldn't embarrass herself or hurt anyone else.

Kiara neared the door.

A trickle of sweat ran down her temple.

If she crossed that threshold, she knew Pitala would kill her. If she struggled inside Tiyana's apartment, everyone would see—the promoters, the directors, everyone. And they would be next on his hit list.

She heard Tiyana's laughter above the chattering crowd.

It was her best friend's birthday. She wouldn't let it be the last time Tiyana drew her breath.

With that final thought, she opened the door.

Pitala shoved her into the hallway, then slammed the door shut behind him and threw her to the ground. Her entire body trembling, she looked back to see Nykyrian grabbing Pitala's blaster from his hand.

He slammed Pitala back so hard, it dented the wall.

He brought his own blaster up and held it under Pitala's jaw. "Listen to me, you bastard. I'm only going to say this once and I will speak slowly so that even you can understand. Kiara is under the protection of The Sentella and I'm getting really tired of seeing your face around her. If you harm her, threaten her, even look at her again . . . even a fucking picture of her, you're going to have a visit from Nemesis. And when he gets through with you, your own mother will have to run what's left of you through a DNA sift to identify your remains."

Even Kiara cringed at the threat.

Nykyrian's lips curled into a ferocious snarl. "You'll find your partner down the hall locked in a storage closet. Take him and leave. And if you value all the pieces of your body remaining in their current positions, you'll revoke your contract on her life tomorrow and never hunt her again." He clicked back the release of his blaster. "Do you understand?"

Sweat covered Pitala's face. "My retraction will be posted tomorrow. I swear it."

Nykyrian replaced the latch on his blaster. "Good." He shoved Pitala away from him.

Kiara watched the assassin hurry down the hall away from them. She looked up at her savior, her breathing labored, her head light in panic.

Nykyrian holstered his blaster, then held his hand out to her. She grasped it with her shaking hands, and he gently pulled her off the floor. "I'm sorry we didn't help you sooner. But I didn't think you wanted your friends to know what was going on. Darling warned us Pitala was coming in so we thought it best to let him make his move to extract you from the party and then deal with it out of sight of your colleagues."

Before he could move away and before she could stop herself, she put her arms around him and hugged his lean waist with all the relief coursing through her body.

She was alive and, once again, he was the reason.

Kiara leaned her cheek against his chest, listening to the soothing sound of his strong, calm heartbeat. Though his body was rigid, he made no moves to push her away or to even hold her.

He just stood there awkwardly while she trembled, knowing Nykyrian would never let anyone hurt her. She was safe with him.

Nykyrian reveled in the feel of her arms holding him close. He put his arms around her, trying not to hurt her in any way. Since the only person he'd ever hugged had been her, he had no real knowledge of how much pressure to apply or exactly where to put his arms.

So he loosely enclosed her as her scent stirred his body to a level of desire he'd never before tasted.

Her arms tightened around him and she leaned her head back to look up at him, her eyes bright with gratitude. Unconsciously, he moved to kiss her, then caught himself just before he complied. *That* would be disastrous.

Her breath fell against his lips and it took all of his self-control not to complete the one thing he wanted to do most.

"We have to get you home," he said, pulling away.

Kiara nodded as she tried to calm herself.

Without a word, he led her down the hall, checking every few steps to make sure Pitala wasn't still hovering. Syn joined them at the lift that Jayne had secured and was holding for them.

Kiara was strangely numb as she followed, her thoughts drifting over the entire party and the assault.

Maybe she was just getting older. Maybe it was the fear of what had happened with Pitala happening during the party for all the promoters to see. That must be why she didn't enjoy herself today when she normally would have had a good time. Maybe it was why Elfa's biting comments cut her more this afternoon than they had last year when her understudy had said the same thing.

She studied Nykyrian's back as he led her out of the building. At least there was now one less assassin after her. With any luck, Nemesis would be able to bully the rest of her pursuers into leaving her alone, then she could return to her old life.

Couldn't she?

Kiara swallowed the clump of tears. She was just tired. A little sleep and everything would be fine. She'd be fine.

But inside, she knew instinctively that she'd been altered by all this and that nothing would ever be the same again.

Two hours later, after she'd bathed and tried to sleep to no avail, Kiara sat curled in her favorite chair, watching Nykyrian check the spring loaders for his weapons. Death had become a morbid fascination to her as she wondered how many people had lost their lives to the weapons he carried.

"I didn't think experienced soldiers broke apart their weapons and cleaned them."

"Some don't. I do. These are highly sensitive devices and one speck of dust can interfere with their timing mechanisms. Since my life and now yours depends on them working in synch with me, I'm a little anal about making sure they're oiled and reliable." He picked up his blaster. "There was a slight tug in the release today and I wanted to double-check it."

That made sense to her. She didn't want a weapon malfunction either.

He changed the battery pack on his blaster. The sharp click raised the hair on the back of her neck.

She closed the small gap in her robe that exposed her bare feet. "Why didn't you kill Pitala today or at the theater?"

He screwed another piece back into the blaster. "Would you rather I had?"

A chill stole up her arms at the blandness of his tone. "No, I guess not. But it seems strange to me that you allowed him to live given your . . ."

"Brutality?"

"I was going to say past."

He pulled his other blaster out and ran through its settings. "You can call me an animal. You won't hurt my feelings."

How many people had insulted him with that word that he was immune to it? "You're not an animal."

He didn't respond to that. "Since Pitala didn't draw blood, I couldn't officially kill him."

"But he was there to kill *me*."

"And had you killed him, you could go before the Grand Justices and explain that you were trying to protect yourself. For you, they would be lenient and forgiving and let you go. I'm a trained assassin, a lethal weapon, and therefore have another set of standards to live by. Unless I was bleeding and could prove he was coming at me with grave intent and that I really did have to use deadly force as the only means to protect myself, I would be executed immediately for his death, which would be fine by me, except I wasn't there alone today."

She frowned. "I don't understand."

"I'm an outlaw, princess, with a staggering price on my head and a death sentence waiting should I ever be taken. So while I can kill anyone who pisses me off and it won't effect the outcome of what The League will do to me if they catch me, Syn and the others don't have my death sentence hanging over their heads. Had I killed Pitala without blood being drawn, they would be considered accomplices to his murder, committed by me, and a death warrant would be issued for them. As it is right now, they only have jail sentences if they're caught. No offense, I'd like to keep it that way."

"And if one of them had killed him?"

"They are licensed tracers and assassins. As such, the first blood law governs them, too—because they're trained. Unless they have a death warrant for the person, they'd better be bleeding when they kill them or they're screwed."

She let out a tired breath. "I didn't realize how complicated the laws were."

"You're a civilian. There's no need for you to know."

Perhaps, but what a way to find out. "I can't believe that a government can take out a contract on me and have me killed with immunity while my protectors could be executed for keeping me safe. It just doesn't make sense."

"Welcome to The League, princess. The bureaucrats are idiots and so long as a government pays a high enough fee, they make the laws that govern all of you dumb enough to subject yourselves to them."

"But not you?"

"I only follow the law when it impacts those around me."

She watched him put the blaster back together, his hands running through the procedure with practiced ease. It was a strange ballet, mesmerizing. "When you decided to quit The League, how did you do it? Did you just tell them no thanks, or what?"

He grimaced, slamming a piece of the grip back into its firing position. "Why do you want to know?"

She shrugged, an image of the promoters running through her mind and how they'd react if she told them to go roast their parts like she'd wanted to many times in the past.

"Because of the courage it took for you to do so. Most people would rather suffer through a bad situation than take the steps needed to free themselves, especially if they knew that by freeing themselves, it would make them hunted. I just want to know how you did it. Did you walk up to your boss and tell him to stuff it or did you go quietly?"

He set the blaster down on the table between them. "I'm not completely suicidal and it wasn't something I'd ever planned to do. One night I came face to face with what I was, what I'd become. I didn't want to be that mindless dog anymore, so I took my targets to a safe zone, deposited them there with enough money to make sure they would be cared for for the rest of their lives, and then dug out my tracer and never looked back."

She frowned. For some reason, she hadn't imagined it would be that easy to leave The League. "Why?"

Nykyrian paused as he remembered the sight of the little girl screaming as she saw him coming out of the shadows to kill her and her mother. Her mother had been terrified as she'd clung to her child.

Please, not my baby. Please, let her live. She's only five. She's done nothing wrong. For the love of the gods, don't hurt her. Kill me, but spare her. I'll do anything you ask. She'd jerked her expensive necklace off and held it out to him. *Take it. Just spare my baby.*

The mother was just as innocent as the child, but she'd never uttered a single word to spare her own life. Only her daughter's.

Nykyrian had held his knife in his fist as all the years of League training ripped through him. *Kill or be killed. If you fail, you will die.*

No exceptions.

A part of him had wanted to end their lives simply because they had something he'd never known.

Maternal love.

A mother willing to die for her child. One who would suffer anything to spare it. Rage and jealousy had torn through him as he remembered his own mother sending him into hell when he'd been the same age as the little girl. There had been no compassion on his mother's face. No tears for him. She'd handed him off to her guards and told them to take him away.

You sicken me, you ugly, worthless bastard. The cold look on his mother's face still haunted him. *Make sure he never returns here.*

He could still feel the wrenching sobs he'd cried as he begged his mother to let him stay with her, as he'd cried and promised to be good. To stay out of sight of the rest of the world so that he couldn't shame her.

She hadn't listened or cared. Instead, she'd pried his desperate fingers from her wrist and turned her back on him.

But the mother he'd been sent to kill had been different. She'd held her daughter close and shielded her daughter from him with her body.

How could he kill someone whose love was so pure?

He'd given them their lives at the expense of his own. He didn't even know if it'd been worth it. There really wasn't much difference in his life. The only thing that had changed was the person telling him to kill and the number of people trying to kill him.

Everything else was the same. The loneliness. The mistrust. The empty place in his soul. All that seemed to be eternal.

And now he looked at Kiara who'd asked him a question he'd asked himself many times over the years.

Why?

There was one truth above all others.

"Because some things are more important than our own lives." Such as the love of a mother willing to die to save her child. To him that was so rare that, having found it, he hadn't been willing to destroy it.

Kiara tilted her head to stare at him. "I don't understand. If you're an assassin—"

"I was tired of blindly following orders, princess, and in one night it all came to a head. All my life, everything I wore, ate, or did had been dictated to me by someone else. In that one moment, I decided that I would rather be dead than live one more second enslaved to people I couldn't stand or respect. It was just that simple."

And it had been just that hard.

She shook her head. "Do you regret it?"

"No. It was the best day of my life."

"Even though it made you hunted?"

"Yes."

Kiara nodded, her heart hanging heavy with just one more thing she needed to ask. Finally, she found the courage to bring it up. "Do you ever think of dying? Really?"

Nykyrian rubbed his hand across his jaw. "No. I really don't care one way or the other."

He had nothing to live for.

Tears welled up in her eyes. "I want to be like you. But I'm so scared of death. Of what's on the other side. What if it's nothing? Or cold and dark? What if we're there alone without our friends or families? Oh God, I'm so scared." Covering her trembling lips with her hand, she ran down the hallway to the safety of her room.

Nykyrian sat on the couch, looking down at his weapons on the table. "That is my life now, princess," he whispered. And she was right. It was hell.

He heard her sobs through the wall. They were the same soul-wrenching ones he'd cried when his mother had abandoned him. The kind that came from the darkest part of the soul where all the pain of the heart lived.

Leave her alone. She's nothing to you.

But unlike him, she wasn't used to hurting alone. To knowing no comfort.

His gaze went to the photos of her with her parents and friends. The happy smiles and the hugs.

She was a creature of the light. One used to comfort and warmth.

Damning himself for the weakness, he got up and went to her room. She lay curled into a ball, her sobs wracking her body. She held a pillow to her stomach as she let out all the fear this day had laid at her feet.

Nykyrian remained silent as he pulled her against him and offered a comfort he didn't really understand. He brushed her hair from her wet cheeks, rocking her gently in his arms as he'd seen people do in shows, or mothers with their young.

Kiara held him close as she tried to put her fears behind her. But she didn't want to die. There was so much she still wanted to do with her life.

She wanted to be a mother. She wanted to travel more.

Why did they have to hunt her? Why?

She didn't want to be raped and killed . . .

And yet in the arms of a killer, she had never felt so protected. Or safer.

She didn't know how long she cried, but when she finally pulled away, the material of his shirt clung to his chest where her tears had fallen.

"I'm sorry." She sniffed and wiped the back of her hand over her cheeks.

He moved her hand and wiped the moisture away for her. "Feeling better?"

Kiara nodded. "This isn't like me." She reveled in the feel of his warm, strong hands moving over her icy cheeks. "I know you don't believe me since I burst into tears every other minute. But I swear I'm stronger than this and I hate that you've seen me so weak and emotional. I swore I'd never cry again. That no one would make me do this. Ugh! I am pathetic."

"Don't apologize. Everyone cries sometime."

Kiara couldn't imagine him doing that no matter how much pain he was in. "Do you?"

"Inside I do."

"I don't believe you."

"Yeah, well, I am lying, but I was trying to make you feel better."

Kiara laughed through her tears. "You did. Thank you." She stared at him, wishing she could see his whole face. In so many ways he was a complete stranger, yet they sat now like old friends or even lovers, and she'd shared things with him that she'd never shared with another living soul.

In spite of his ferocity, he was amazingly easy to talk to. He didn't appear to judge her. Rather, he accepted her with all the evil emotional baggage that came along with her, and that was rare enough that she fully appreciated it.

And right now, she ached to kiss his lips. But she knew if she tried, he'd push her away again and end this peaceful moment.

She desperately didn't want it to end.

"What do you think is on the other side?" she asked, wondering what he believed in.

"I hope nothing. No voices, no sound. Just me and the darkness forever."

That would be hell to her. She couldn't stand darkness and silence. "Doesn't that thought scare you?"

"No. It would be peaceful, I think."

"But don't you want to see your loved ones again?"

Nykyrian looked away from her innocent face. How naive she was, thinking such a childish thought. In his world, things like that didn't exist. Loved ones were just the first to betray—the ones whose treachery hurt the most. "I don't have any."

By the scowl on her face, he could tell she couldn't accept what he was saying.

"No one? What about your friends?"

"They wouldn't miss me long." He knew that for a fact. All of them were used to loss and while they might have an occasional twinge whenever he crossed their thoughts, they would never really mourn him. They'd move on with their lives as they'd always done. He wasn't angry or bitter about that.

It was just the way of things. It was the way of them.

Kiara shook her head in denial. "Not even Nemesis? Surely your boyfriend would miss you?"

He snorted bitterly at her question. Like he'd ever given a shit about himself. "I assure you, he'd care least of all if I died tomorrow."

"You don't really believe that, do you?"

"There's not a lot to miss, princess. Trust me."

Kiara still couldn't accept what he was telling her. How could no one mourn him? Surely someone loved him. They had to. There wasn't a day that went by that she didn't want to cry over her mother. To have one more moment to hold her. To feel her mother's gentle touch . . .

And he had no one who would hold that painful place in their hearts for him? Not out of selfishness, but out of love. Out of respect and care and the knowledge that the universe would be missing a vital part if he were no longer in it.

"Don't you ever socialize with your friends? Drink? Have dinners?"

"Sure, when we're working."

That wasn't the same. Gah, what a horribly lonely life.

Aching for him, Kiara reached up to touch his face. The moment she did, he set her aside and stepped away.

"No one's going to harm you, princess. On my life, I'll keep you safe." Then he was gone faster than she could blink.

Kiara's heart pounded at the audible sincerity behind his words. Her cheek burned from the memory of his gloved fingers touching her skin. There was so much more she wanted to say to him, to ask him, but she didn't know how.

He was such a dichotomy. In one minute he pulled away and snapped if she dared to even touch him, then the next he held her like a treasured love and comforted her tears.

How could such a man not be missed by anyone? It made her want to hold him close and show him that not everyone was callous.

Kiara drew a trembling breath, wishing for the nerve it would take to strip her clothes from her body and go out to the main room where Nykyrian stayed. Shera had done that to gain her last lover and had told Kiara it was a never-fail ploy to be used when she really wanted someone.

But she could never do anything so bold.

She was a coward.

Sighing, she leaned back on her bed, imagining what it would be like to have Nykyrian by her side, making love to her, soothing her fears all night long while he kept her safe.

He was still on her mind when she finally drifted off into a fitful sleep.

* * *

When Kiara awoke, she knew instantly something had changed, but she wasn't sure what. She grabbed her robe and belted it before she went to see what made her feel so strange.

As soon as she entered her main room, she understood. Nykyrian was gone and Hauk sat on her couch munching what was left of her friggles.

He gave her the most menacing glare she'd ever received. "Something wrong?" he barked.

How could anyone look so fierce while relaxing? Was there some course they all had taken to tell them how to do that?

Or did it just come naturally?

"No." She gave him a shy smile, then lots of space as she went to dress.

Kiara took her time, wishing she'd stayed in bed and slept through the hulking Andarion's guardianship. The last thing she wanted was to spend a day with his threats and taunts.

Oh well. She'd suffered worse.

Maybe.

When she returned to the main room, Hauk had a plate of muffins waiting for her. She lifted a questioning brow, shocked by the gesture.

"They're not as good as Nykyrian's, but they won't kill you either," he said gruffly as if being friendly with her embarrassed him.

She picked one up. "I thought you hated me."

He shrugged and flipped stations on her viewer. "I hate over-privileged people in general. You just happen to fall into that category. No offense. But Nykyrian said you weren't a total bitch so I'll trust him until you make him out a liar."

Kiara shook her head. "You seriously lack social skills, don't you?"

"Basically. Kind of pride myself on that, too."

Because it weeded out those who didn't care about him. Kiara paused as she remembered her therapist telling her that when she'd gone through a nasty period of repelling anyone who came near her.

You're so afraid of being hurt that you attack first. Only those who really care about you will weather the assault of your verbal attacks and stay. The rest will fall away.

After a time, Kiara had put her anger aside and realized that her loved ones deserved something more from her than her anger and hostility.

Knowing what she did about Nykyrian and his crew, she understood their need to deploy all defense systems. It wasn't personal.

It was a grudge they all carried against the entire universe and she just happened to be a part of that outer group.

She smiled at Hauk. "Nykyrian doesn't strike me as being exactly poor. As the son of a wealthy, respected commander I would think he falls into your despised category as well."

A harumph was all that answered her.

After a moment, he tossed the remote aside in anger. "I don't suppose you have a better way of occupying our time? There's nothing on that's even good enough to rot my brain with."

Kiara laughed as she remembered her own tantrum over that very fact. "Other than eat friggles and humans, what do you like to do?"

Hauk stood and towered over her. "Anything beats talking."

"I have some games." She pulled the console out of her media armoire and blew the dust off the keyboard and controllers. The console had been a gift, but she didn't really play games so it'd never been used.

Without a word, Hauk moved to the closet and began rummaging through her small collection of discs. He emerged with a wide smile, his long fangs flashing. "Tareba. Now there's a game I haven't seen in years." He pulled out the classic strategy game. "Would you mind playing? It sucks to be solo."

Kiara smiled in disbelief at his unexpected exuberance. "I'm probably not very good at it, but sure."

He reminded her of a kid as he attached the console to her viewer and set up the program. She was actually beginning to warm up to him.

"Where'd Nykyrian go?"

He looked up from the keyboard with a stern frown. "Did you ask him?"

"Didn't have time."

The frown lessened. "He went to get information about the people after you."

She finished off her muffin, trying to bolster her courage enough to ask the next question. "Why is Aksel Bredeh so important to Nykyrian?"

"What do you care?"

The hostility in that tone was biting. How in the world could the answer to that threaten any of them? "You guys have to be the most defensive group alive. *Mia kitana,* can't I ever get a simple answer out of any of you?"

Hauk laughed deep in his throat, a sound that she found far from comforting. "You're right. We live for evasiveness. You should play Questions with them sometime. I've never seen anyone hedge better than Nykyrian or Syn." It was magical the way his personality changed from coarse to friendly as he set up the controllers for them. "As for Aksel. I don't really know. Bad blood from the beginning I think."

"Why do you say that?"

He shrugged. "They were always at each other's throats. I think most of it stemmed from Aksel not being able to pass the League Academy tests while Nykyrian was always the high scorer on anything he did."

She should have figured that. Nykyrian didn't strike her as someone who'd accept second best on anything.

"So how long have you known Nykyrian?"

Hauk gave her a cold stare before he answered. "I was thirteen when we met."

"How old was he?"

"No idea."

She stared at him. "You don't know Nykyrian's age?"

"Nope. No one does."

"I'm sure Nykyrian does."

"Nah, I don't think so. The rumors in school said that he was sent to a human orphanage when he was a toddler or infant and raised there. Hell, he didn't even have a name when we met."

She had to force herself not to roll her eyes. "You're joking now."

He shook his head, his eyes burning with deadly earnest. "No. He didn't have a name until he'd been commissioned as an officer into The League—they require a name for all officers and so he picked one then. His academy records only held an approximate age range and his name was listed as Unknown Andarion Hybrid."

Kiara felt sick. "Are you serious?"

"I saw the file myself. Everything in it was listed as unknown. Parents. Planet of origin. Name. Age. It was pathetic, really."

She was ill with the thought of not knowing anything about herself or her parents. No wonder Nykyrian was so cold. "You met him after he joined the academy?"

He nodded.

"What did you call him if he had no name?"

"We didn't. None of us interacted with him at all . . . well, not entirely true. There were a lot of kids who picked on him because he came to the academy with a training collar already in place. But what they called him isn't fit for mixed company and doesn't bear repeating. Stupid fuckheads."

If that was his idea of an acceptable insult for mixed company, she had to hear what they'd called Nykyrian that he wouldn't repeat.

But it said a lot for Hauk that he'd broken from the pack and become friends with someone the others had alienated. Most kids, herself included, didn't have that strength of character at that age when peer acceptance was so important. She'd like to think better of herself, but it would be a lie.

She was better now, but as a kid . . .

"How did you two become friends?"

There was shame in his eyes before he answered. "The rotten bastard saved my life. One of the pods we were practicing in malfunctioned. It crashed and caught fire. I was trapped inside and my leg was pinned by the wreckage. No one would help me—they were too afraid of getting hurt. Even the instructors. They were too busy keeping everyone back while I baked and burned. Nykyrian shoved past them and broke me out, then carried me to safety just before the pod exploded. He still has scars from where the glass tore into his back and the gash he took to his right forearm when he pulled me out."

She knew that scar. "And you were friends after that?"

"Not really. Nykyrian refused to speak to anyone in those days. I tried to thank him, but he just ignored me."

"Then how did you become friends?"

He untangled the controllers. "Syn. Nykyrian got into The League. I washed out. So I ended up in private sector IT. There was this one hacker son of a bitch who kept breaching my security no matter how good I made it and I had to meet him. It turned out to be Syn. And Syn, for a human, is a hard man not to like, especially back then when he was sober. His humor was infectious and it wasn't until I'd known him for about two years that I found out Nykyrian was his best friend."

She wondered why Nykyrian had let Syn into his life when he seemed so determined to keep everyone else out. "So he talked to Syn?"

"Like I said, Syn is a hard man not to like."

There had to be a lot more to this story, especially given how reclusive Nykyrian was. "How did they meet?"

"I have no idea. They're not real big on sharing."

He definitely wasn't kidding about that. She was actually stunned that Hauk was being so chatty.

Which made her wonder what other personal tidbits he might give her and there was one in particular she was dying to know about . . .

"So, have you ever seen Nykyrian's eyes?"

"Yes."

"Do they look like yours?"

He froze, then shook his head. "Look, I've already spoken too much. Nykyrian is an extremely private person and I owe my life to him. He's saved it more than that one time so I'd rather we play the game and pass the time with only meaningless bullshit until they get back."

Kiara nodded even though her mind spun at what she'd learned. Nykyrian had been abandoned without even a name to call his own.

What kind of parents could have done that to him? No wonder he didn't like being touched. What was that called? Disassociation? She'd have to look it up later to make sure. It was something about infants who were refused by their mothers. Infants who weren't held and nurtured. They never felt connected to anyone else and it left a lifetime of scars on them.

She couldn't imagine the horror of what Nykyrian had been through. And her heart ached at the past Hauk described. She wondered if Nykyrian knew answers about his past that he preferred not to share.

Hauk held the controller out to her. She took it and remembered what Nykyrian had told her about himself the night before.

No family.

No friends.

Nothing.

Even though she suspected Hauk would die for him, Nykyrian still felt alone in the world. Isolated. Abandoned by everyone. And that broke her heart.

What do you care? He's just a bodyguard . . .

But it wasn't that simple. She'd seen inside his heart and knew Nykyrian to be so much more. Like Hauk, she owed her life to him. And somehow she was going to give him a life, too.

One filled with trust and kindness. Surely he deserved that after all he'd done for them?

Nemesis might not care about him, but she was

learning to and somehow she wanted to give him the friend he deserved to have. Any man who could accept a callous lover could surely accept a well-meaning friend who only wanted to help him.

But the real question was, would Nykyrian ever allow someone that close to him?

CHAPTER 13

Kiara and Hauk were watching a comedy when Nykyrian returned. She looked up at him with a welcoming smile, but he didn't even bother to glance in her direction. He dropped his backpack by the door and just stood there like he was dazed or thinking heavily about something.

Disappointed, she shifted her gaze to Hauk, who offered her an apologetic shrug before standing.

"Well, I guess it's time for this babysitter to evaporate." He picked up his own bag and slung it over his shoulder. "Beware of her roast. It's killer." He gave Nykyrian a mocking salute before he took his leave.

Nykyrian finally looked at her. "What was that about?"

Kiara shrugged in confusion. "He told me he liked it. Would you care for any? I left a warmer on the stove." She tossed the pillow from her lap and uncurled her legs so that she could get up from the couch.

"I'll get it." He headed down the hallway.

Kiara frowned. He was acting strange, even for him. His movements were missing their usual grace and fluidity, and his tone had seemed odd.

Several minutes went by as she waited for him to

rejoin her, but he stayed in the kitchen, out of her sight. Worried and curious, she went to check on him.

He sat at the table, his food untouched. His head was propped against one gloved hand and he appeared to be staring at the table as if he were concentrating on an invisible spot.

Something definitely wasn't right.

She took two steps into the room. "What's wrong?"

Immediately, he straightened up and retrieved a fork. "I'm tired."

Kiara sat down across from him. Drawing her legs up in the chair, she propped her chin on her knees. "Hauk and I spent the afternoon playing games. Do you play any?"

His grip tightened on the fork. "No," he growled from between clenched teeth.

She glared at him for that. "You don't have to bark at me. I was just—"

"Look," Nykyrian interrupted her, making her jump in surprise at the sharpness of his tone. "I'm in no mood to be sociable right now. Just leave me in peace."

Her worry tripled. It wasn't like him to lose control of himself like this. He *never* lost his temper.

Rising to her feet, she rounded the table to stand beside him. "Something's wrong. I know it is." She reached out to touch his forehead to see if he had a fever.

He caught her wrist in a tight grip. "I told you to leave me alone. Can't you accept the fact that a man can be in your presence and not want to sleep with you?"

She sputtered at his insult as fury singed her. Where had *that* come from? All she'd been trying to do was help him. How dare he insult her so. "You arrogant bastard! Why would I *ever* want to sleep with you?"

His features turned brittle as he rose slowly to his

feet to tower over her. This time, there was no mistaking his rage. "Get the fuck out of here before I kill you."

A sharp knock sounded on the door. Nykyrian pushed past her to answer it.

Kiara stayed in the kitchen, gripping the counter as a multitude of emotions tore through her. Rage, indignation, but most of all hurt.

Did he really think her a whore? *Why* would he think such a thing?

That one undeserved and wholly unjustified insult made her wish she were big enough to give him the beating he deserved. So much for trying to be nice to him. What an asshole!

A lump in her throat, she moved toward the front room to see who was here and what was going on. Why Nykyrian hadn't returned for his food.

Syn was on his knees in front of him. That unexpected sight gave her serious pause as she watched Syn slowly unbutton Nykyrian's pants and peel his shirt back.

Ooookay . . .

Maybe she was intruding on something very private and should leave them to whatever it was Syn was about to do with Nykyrian. Not that she was clueless about what it looked like they were going to do, but wouldn't two such private people do *that* someplace other than her front room?

Her feet seemed to be riveted to the spot as she watched them. Nykyrian didn't protest Syn's groping in the least. Not even when Syn skimmed his hand over Nykyrian's stomach. Instead of snapping at Syn, he just looked down at him while Syn lifted his shirt up to expose more flesh.

Syn cursed before moving away to pull his pack closer to him.

Kiara went cold as she realized Syn's hands were covered in blood.

"How'd you reopen the damn thing?" he barked at Nykyrian. "I told you to be careful, you idiot. You're lucky you haven't bled out."

"Stand down, asshole. You keep making commentary like an old woman and I'll put your rank ass in a dress."

Syn glared up at him. "You better take a different tone, too, dick. Remember, I'm the one about to have my hands on that wound. You snap at me and I'll have you crying on the floor like a little girl."

"And I'll have you lying dead at my feet."

Kiara stepped forward.

At her movement, Nykyrian looked at her over his shoulder and bared his fangs. "Get out. Now!"

Kiara narrowed her gaze in anger at so much hostility when all she'd wanted to do was help. "Fine. Just keep your blood off my carpet." She turned and went to her room.

Syn sucked his breath in sharply between his teeth. "That was a harsh thing to say to you. And here I thought I was the only one you pissed off to that extreme." Rising to his feet, he pushed Nykyrian toward the couch.

Nykyrian didn't say anything as he lay down and tried to hide how much the wound was hurting him. It took all of his concentration to remain conscious through the throbbing, heated agony splitting his side. Breathing was getting harder by the heartbeat. God, how he hated being shot like this. He felt like his guts were boiling. Like his skin was crawling over sandpaper, off his body.

He tensed as Syn struck a tender spot while trying to stop the bleeding again, but didn't comment. He thought about what he'd said to Kiara and wished he could take it back. Truthfully, he hadn't meant to insult her.

She'd only been trying to comfort him. But he wasn't used to kindness and he'd never known how to deal with it.

Syn was right. I am an asshole.

He could use the pain as an excuse, but that was all it would be—an excuse. He clenched his teeth at his stupidity. What did it matter? It was better if she hated him.

And yet the thought of her hatred shredded his soul.

Syn rummaged through his bag. "I'm going to give you some Synethol."

Nykyrian hissed at him.

"Don't even waste that sound on me, you shit. I know you hate it, but it'll help you heal a lot faster and this is one time I can't afford for you to be nursing a wound and neither can you."

"You got guts taking that tone with me."

Syn scoffed. "What you gonna do, oh great wounded one? I'm the one with the injector." He clicked the trigger to prove his point.

It was now Nykyrian's turn to scoff. "I could have that in my hand and shoved up your ass before you could even blink."

Instead of being angry, Syn grinned. "Probably. Just make sure you put me totally out of my misery. I don't need anything else to cripple me. Now shut up and take it like a man."

"I fucking hate you."

Syn laughed as he screwed the vial of medicine into its chamber. "Of course you do. That's why you're the one lying shot and I'm doing the tending. If you really hated me, I'd be dead right now and you'd be healthy."

Nykyrian looked away as that one simple truth hung between them.

Syn rolled back the sleeve of his shirt. Exposing the crook of Nykyrian's elbow, he positioned the injector over the skin. "I'll stay over tonight so that you can try to sleep in peace. Don't worry. If anything happens, I'll pump your ass full of adrenaline cause I'm not going to fight alone while you sleep in a chemically induced coma."

Nykyrian snorted at that as Syn pressed the trigger and the needle bit into his flesh. Like Syn was afraid of fighting. He could scrap with the best of them and come out on top. Hell, he was better at fighting and surviving than half the assassins Nykyrian had worked with.

He felt the thick syrup moving like fire through his bloodstream. When the capsule was empty, Syn pulled back and tossed the injector back into his bag. He pulled out a small green container and held it toward him. "Here, I'll swap you."

Taking it, Nykyrian opened the case to grab his retainer and put it in his mouth before he handed Syn his shades. He hated wearing that damned retainer whenever he slept.

Another thing the humans had done to him . . .

Images and memories sifted through him as he felt himself involuntarily relaxing. That was what he hated most about meds. They lowered the barriers he kept around himself and made him feel all the things he kept buried deep inside.

He had no resistance.

Most of all, they made him think about things he didn't want to.

He looked at Syn who now had two heads and eight eyes. "Tell me something, *aridos*. What was it like being married?"

Syn paused at a question Nykyrian had never asked him before. Damn, the drug was taking effect fast. But then that was part of his friend's human-Andarion metabolism and it was why Nykyrian couldn't be left alone tonight. Both human and Andarion drugs could have unexpected complications with his unique genetic makeup.

One simple shot of an antibiotic could kill him and painkillers could burn out his insides. *That* memory made him wince.

Syn started not to respond, but the look in Nykyrian's eyes was too sincere and too raw. His friend wanted an honest answer and he owed him too much to brush it aside snidely. "It was good." He swallowed against the painful knot in his stomach as he admitted something he'd tried his best to bury. "Even on the days when it was bad, it was good . . . At least until the end."

He pulled out his flask and uncorked it as he remembered the last days of his marriage. The anger. The fights. The accusations and insults.

But it was his wife's hatred that he couldn't escape from. To have gone from being her entire world to her nightmare in a matter of minutes . . .

I wish to the gods you'd been killed. Why are you alive, you lying, filthy bastard?

The worst part . . . he couldn't agree more with her.

Why couldn't he purge that misery from his memory? In a life marked by harsh brutality, those last few days of his marriage stood out as the ultimate in suffering.

And they wonder why I drink . . .

"You still miss them?"

Syn took a deep drink and tried not to feel the stab of pain that continually hammered his soul and the truth that haunted him constantly. "Every fucking day." Yes, Mara had been shallow at times, and pretentious.

But she'd given him the things he'd never known in his life.

Tenderness and respectability. She'd given him normality and, there for a time, he'd known what the word home meant.

Most of all, she'd given him a beautiful son, and together they'd made a family.

Until his past had come home to roost with a vengeance.

He cursed silently over that vicious stab.

Disgusted, Syn looked back at Nykyrian. "Actually that's not true. I don't miss what she became when she found out about my past. I miss the woman I married, the one I had Paden with. Gods, she used to look at me like she could eat me up. And hold me at night until I forgot about my past. Best of all, she made me feel safe. No matter how bad the day had kicked me, her touch made it all better. She was the only shelter I've ever known."

And to have had it so brutally ripped away . . .

There were times even now when his soul screamed from the pain of it all.

Nykyrian pinned him with that harsh stare of his that seemed to be able to penetrate all the way to his bloodied soul. "I'm sorry about what happened."

"It wasn't your fault, *aridos*. The gods know you did more than your part to protect me from it. Life just is and the gods have their plans for us. We're powerless against them. In the end, we are what our pasts have made us and we live the lives the gods have chosen for us."

Nykyrian scowled at him. "You never deserved what happened to you. How can you still believe in your gods after all you've been through?"

That was the question of his life and yet he'd never

allowed his faith to waver. "We all have to believe in something, sometime."

Nykyrian scoffed. "I only believe in me."

Syn took another swig. "I know. Go ahead and call me a fool. I've been called a lot worse."

"You're not a fool, Syn. We're both just seriously fucked up." Nykyrian closed his eyes. "Tell Kiara I'm sorry for what I said to her." His speech was extremely slurred as the drug finally took him under.

Syn frowned as he checked Nykyrian's vitals to make sure he was all right. It was the first time he'd ever known Nykyrian to apologize to anyone, for anything.

Damn, what had he said?

Shaking his head, he rechecked Nykyrian's bandage. A red stain was already creeping back through the white cloth. Again. That thing was going to be messy.

Just as he pulled back, Nykyrian's nose started hemorrhaging like a slashed carotid artery. Syn cursed as he tilted Nykyrian's head back and did what he could to staunch the flow of blood. He quickly retook the vitals. They were still relatively strong. The drug didn't seem to be eating anything, but something was causing his nose to bleed like this.

He just didn't know what.

Damn it! He hated giving Nykyrian anything. No one ever knew how his body would react to it and it was a gamble every single time.

After a few minutes, Syn stopped the bleeding and had Nykyrian resting quietly. Grateful Nykyrian was all right for the moment and pissed over the needless injury, he shook his head. Syn and that little dancer had almost cost Nykyrian his life tonight.

That knowledge ate at him. In all his life, Nykyrian had been the only person he could rely on. The only one who'd ever tried to help him.

Yes, he had other friends, such as Caillen Dagan, who made him laugh and were good drinking buddies. Caillen, who would be with him, locked up in jail, laughing over whatever antics had landed them there. But Nykyrian was the one who'd get them out and make sure no one touched them for the deed.

More to the point, Nykyrian was the only one who knew about his entire past and didn't condemn him for it.

And Syn had damn near gotten him killed. He ground his teeth as he cleaned the blood from his hands and clothes.

With short, angry strides, he walked down the hall to Kiara's room. He pounded on the door, using the wood as a good scapegoat for his mood.

"Come in."

Syn heard the pain in her voice and hesitated, all the anger instantly draining out of him. He'd always been a fool for an upset woman. It reminded him too much of his sister and the courage she used to show.

You have to learn to smile through your pain, little brother. Sometimes it's all we got.

But what cut him deepest was the day when his sister had refused to smile another smile through her pain . . .

Clenching his teeth and violently pushing that thought away, he opened the door.

Curled up into a small ball on the bed, Kiara looked about as pitiful as anything he'd ever seen, and given the daily misery he'd experienced growing up on the streets, that said something. "I need to get some blankets or a sleeping bag or something."

She drew a ragged breath before she spoke. "Are you staying over tonight?"

He nodded.

She went to a closet across the room from him. Despite his normal code to enter no one's threshold without an invitation, Syn joined her.

Kiara handed him a pile of blankets and two pillows. "Nykyrian never asked for any."

"Yeah, well, he doesn't ask for much and he probably hasn't slept since he's been here anyway."

She looked shocked by that disclosure. "That's not possible."

"Oh yes it is. He can go up to a full week without really sleeping."

"And not have a psychotic episode?"

Syn shrugged. "With him? Who could tell?"

Her expression less than amused, she turned back toward her bed.

Syn cursed under his breath as he felt his stomach twist. He really couldn't stand to see a woman suffer. It ate at him like acid. "Don't look at me with those doleful eyes. Geez, you remind me of a condemned man headed for execution. I can't stand that look."

A single tear fled down her cheek which shredded the last of his resistance. He groaned and dropped the blankets. "C'mon." He led her to her bed. "Tell me what happened before I got here."

She gave him a startled, hurt look.

Syn felt like a louse as he sat down on the mattress. Hell, he hadn't done anything wrong, why should he feel awful? "Nykyrian wanted me to tell you he was sorry for whatever he said. Knowing him, it was probably brutal, but don't take it to your soul. When he's wounded, he blurts out all sorts of stupidity. He really doesn't mean it. It's just his way of communicating. Sucks to be on the receiving end of it when it happens, but, really, pay no attention to it."

She wiped away her tear. "I hate to cry." Her voice

was laced with venom, but he could tell it was directed at herself and not him. She looked up and met his gaze. "What happened tonight? How did he get hurt?"

His anger built as he remembered their mission. "We went to meet with an informant. Unfortunately, some of Bredeh's dogs beat us to him. By the time we got there, the informant was dead and the bastards had taken the guy's kid as a hostage. Since I was with Nykyrian, one of us had to get wounded before we could legally take the buggers out."

She gaped. "He let them shoot him?"

"Yeah, so that I could get the kid to safety while he took care of the others. I shouldn't have gone with him—it's not like we don't know the risks when I'm around, but I thought we were just going to talk to the informant and come back. And when it comes to questioning people, I have a lot more finesse than High King Let's Beat The Shit Out Of Them Until They Answer Us. The nonviolent art of interrogating someone is totally lost on Kip."

Her expression lightened only a tad. "Will he be all right?"

"Definitely. I've seen him through a lot worse than this."

She tilted her head to look at him with a probing stare. "You two been friends that long?"

"A few decades."

This time, he saw her brain working on that. "How did you meet?"

His anger returned. He wasn't about to give her anything she could use against Nykyrian. How they met was none of her damned business. "I'm not that drunk, woman. I don't answer personal questions about my friends." He got up and moved to the door. "I'll see you in the morning."

Kiara sat on the bed, stunned by Syn's quick departure. She had no idea why her question had upset him. All she'd wanted was to understand the two of them.

But obviously they liked hiding in the shadows and tonight she was too tired to pursue them.

Nykyrian woke first to find Syn asleep on the floor, right next to the couch where he'd slept. On his side, facing the door, Syn had one hand resting on his unholstered blaster and the other on his flask, which he cuddled like a baby under his chin. It saddened him what had become of the man who'd once been so full of life and hope.

In one heartbeat and because of one asshole, Syn's entire life had been stripped from him. For that alone, Nykyrian gave him latitudes he would never allow someone else.

Tempted to snatch the flask, he knew Syn would most likely shoot him if he tried.

Next time, buddy, that shit gets tossed.

Silently so that he wouldn't wake him, Nykyrian stepped over Syn's sleeping body. The pain in his side had ebbed to a dull ache.

Damn, next time he'd let them shoot Syn.

But he knew better. He'd never let one of his men get hurt in his stead.

As he reached the bathroom door, Kiara's bedroom door opened. Before he could think to avert his eyes, she saw them.

Shit . . .

Kiara's mouth dropped as she finally saw what Nykyrian really looked like.

Holy crippin' flips.

With his white hair down and flowing around his broad shoulders, he was gorgeous. The eyes staring at her were nothing like she'd imagined. They were clear and the lightest, prettiest shade of green she'd ever seen, with just a hint of a brown band around the outer edge of the iris.

His eyes were human and they were beautiful.

Her throat tightened in happiness. Those eyes gave her the first true glimpse of his soul. In them, she saw all the mistrust, anger, and bitterness.

It was like seeing him naked.

Biting her lip, she shifted her gaze to take in his entire face. There, she had no surprise. He was every bit as handsome as she'd suspected.

He blinked and looked away, seemingly embarrassed. "I'm sorry about what I said last night," he whispered, meeting her gaze for a moment to show her his sincerity before he looked away again.

She bit her lip at the sudden thrill that skittered up her spine. This was the one person she was sure didn't utter an apology often. "Syn told me last night. I'm sorry, too for what I said. I didn't mean to be so harsh."

"Don't worry about it. It didn't even register on my pain scale." He entered the bathroom and shut the door.

Kiara stood there, staring at the closed door as she trembled in her newfound knowledge. Without his shades, he wasn't a fearsome, half-known phantom who haunted her dreams.

He was a man.

Gorgeous and real, with eyes unlike any she'd ever seen before. What a tragedy to keep them hidden from the world. Eyes like his needed to be savored.

But he would never allow anyone to behold him like that. And that was the greatest tragedy of all.

Nykyrian's hands shook as he dragged them over his face. He cursed himself for having allowed her to see his eyes.

I'm such a fucking idiot.

Now it would begin. The initial pity would be first—poor, deformed halfling—then the worst part, the eventual hatred of his mixed blood, of the fact that he bore too many characteristics of both races.

People had never seen anything more in him than the manifestation of their own fears, not realizing or caring that he could be hurt by their scorn. The humans saw him as a predatorial animal with no soul. Brutal and lacking all feelings. The Andarions saw him as a weak, pathetic insect who wasn't fit to breathe their air.

Over and over, images of the past tore through him. The mockery and insults.

Even though he was now the fiercest assassin ever trained, there was still that part of him he couldn't destroy that was the same small, frightened child who'd been brutalized by others. The child who'd wanted only to be held and told that he wasn't so bad. That he didn't deserve what life had handed him.

Freak. Animal. Despicable. Worm. Deformed.

Why couldn't he silence those voices?

But it was useless. Even after all this time, the scars were still there, biting and tearing, and they refused to heal.

Clenching his teeth, he ripped the bandage from his side, taking a small amount of satisfaction from the throbbing protest of his now raw skin. Physical pain was easy to deal with and it took his mind off other things such as his brothers, both genetic and adoptive, and their "kindness" toward him.

Disrobing, he stepped into the shower.

The water burned as it slid against his wound. Despite the pain, an image of Kiara's welcoming smile the night before tormented him. No one had ever given him so great a present.

She'd actually been glad to see him.

For the first time, he understood what had possessed Syn when he'd asked Mara to marry him. And he wanted Kiara to look at him like that forever.

But it was a stupid dream.

He was garbage and she deserved a man to love her, not some half-formed animal wanted by every known government.

She was only a client. That was all she'd ever be.

He would make sure of it.

Kiara smiled at Nykyrian as he joined her in the kitchen, but to her chagrin, his dark shades were back in place. His long white hair was still wet and brushed back from his handsome face. She handed him a plate. "I've seen your eyes, you know. You can dispense with the shades now."

He didn't comment.

She filled a plate for herself and sat across from him. "How do you feel?"

"Like I've been shot," he replied drily.

"Gee, I wonder why?"

He glanced up at her, then quickly looked back at his food. "I'm surprised you're speaking to me after what I said to you last night. I really am sorry for insulting you. You didn't deserve it."

Kiara was still stung by the words, but she wasn't willing to hold them against him when he'd been hurt. "My father tutored me well on amnesia. He always said it was a necessary ingredient for any friendship."

Nykyrian sipped his juice. "Your father's very wise."

"Good day," Syn yawned, stretching as he entered the kitchen. "What smells so good?"

"Frisanian tarts." Kiara returned his smile.

Syn walked over to the warmer and pulled a couple

off. After tasting one, he turned around and winked wickedly. "If you want a man in your life, love, call me anytime. Ah, man, these are *good*."

Kiara laughed, amazed at how handsome he was without the eyeliner ringing his eyes, or hoops in his ears or nose. He really could stop traffic, but even so, he paled in comparison to Nykyrian's angelic features.

"Don't you have a hangover?" Nykyrian asked.

Syn licked his fingers. "Like a motherfucker. But I'm used to the brain damage. I'll eventually drink enough to make it go away."

Nykyrian shook his head.

Kiara decided to change the subject. "Will I be blessed with both of you today?"

Syn sat next to her. "Cursed would be more apropos. In which case, I reply affirmatively." He pulled his flask out and poured a large amount of alcohol into his juice. "Kip will no doubt, and you can see proof by the look on his face, object to my hanging around."

"I don't need a nursemaid."

"Well, in my case it's a nurseman. So don't bother with your usual bluster, I'm committed."

"You should be."

Kiara burst into laughter at Nykyrian's dry, even-toned response.

Syn sputtered. "Kiara, please. Don't encourage him to abuse me, he does enough damage on his own."

Nykyrian set his fork down and eyed Syn with a dark frown. "You know, I always wondered what it would feel like to strangle a Ritadarion."

Kiara glanced to Syn, not sure if Nykyrian was joking.

Syn continued to smile. "You missed your chance three years ago on Tondara."

"And never got over it."

Kiara continued to listen to their bantering. She was amazed at how well they got along and was certain Nykyrian wouldn't allow anyone else to treat him so lightly.

After a few minutes, Nykyrian excused himself and went to the main room.

"Is he really all right?" Kiara whispered to Syn.

Syn leaned over toward her. "Whispering does absolutely no good around him, he can hear from miles away. It's one of those damnable Andarion traits." He straightened up and continued talking in a normal tone. "He's just sullen as a swollen gimfry. Ignore him." He popped his knuckles. "So what trouble shall we get into?"

"I thought you had too much to do to be hanging out in this place." Nykyrian's voice traveled into the kitchen without his shouting.

Kiara raised her eyebrows, surprised he really could hear them.

Syn winked at her. "I do, but you're completely bended if you think I'm leaving this sweet thing in your surly presence."

Nykyrian said something else in that strange language he used with Syn.

Syn's eyes widened before he shot from the kitchen.

CHAPTER 14

"Bredeh's coming for her," Nykyrian said in Ritadarion to Syn so that Kiara couldn't understand what was going on . . . yet.

He glanced up as she joined them from the kitchen.

"Do you think he'll bomb the building?"

Nykyrian shrugged. "I don't know. He's completely psycho and too hot after both of us. Either way, we've got to move her. Call her father on a secured line, tell him he has less than a half hour to get here and see her before we leave."

Syn nodded and moved to comply.

Nykyrian beckoned Kiara to come to him.

She hesitated for a moment before walking forward.

Taking a stylus on his computer ledger, Nykyrian wrote his commands for her: *We have reason to believe we're being monitored. I need you to pack enough clothes for several days. We have to move quickly.*

Her eyes widened as she read the note. "Oh God," she whispered and ran from the room.

Kiara trembled in fear. Who was monitoring them? Was it this mysterious Aksel?

Or was it someone worse?

She opened her bedroom door and heard Syn arguing with her father over the telelink next to her bed.

Through the view screen, she could see the worry on her father's face as he glared at Syn. Cold, clammy sweat chilled her hands.

She stepped into range for the camera and interrupted his long list of what he intended to do to Syn. "Papa. Everything is fine. I trust them completely."

"I don't," he snarled, eyeing Syn with a murderous glare. "And I don't see why you have to take her someplace I don't know about."

"Then trust my instincts, please." She placed a hand on Syn's shoulder to prove her words.

Instead of calming her father, the gesture seemed to push his anger to full boil. "Don't you *dare* move her until I get there, or you'll wish to God you had stayed in whatever hole you crawled out from!" He cut the transmission.

"Geez," Syn snorted. "What a grouch."

"He's just worried about me."

Syn scratched the stubble on his cheek. "Yeah, well, the man needs a couple of drinks."

Before Kiara could reply, Nykyrian leaned through the door and tossed Syn his blaster. "The attack's already started."

Kiara went cold.

Nykyrian stepped back as Syn ran to the front.

"I'm scared," she whispered, half expecting to drop into a faint at any moment.

Nykyrian touched her arm reassuringly. "Don't be. They've got to come through me and I'm no easy obstacle."

"Yeah, but you're wounded."

"Won't matter." He held his blaster in his left hand and stretched his right hand out to her.

The fact that he would let her touch him surprised her and told her exactly how deadly a situation this was. Not that she'd doubted the severity of it in the least.

Without hesitation, she placed her icy hand into his large, gloved one.

He pulled her with him out into the hallway. They crouched together beside the bar. Nykyrian draped a poncho over her and placed the hood of it over her head. "It'll protect you." He surrounded her with warmth, her back against his chest. She could smell the clean scent of soap from his skin.

Syn hid behind the chair closest to the door while Nykyrian braided his hair to keep it out of his way. Kiara stared at the laser cutting through the door, remembering her brief time on board her kidnapper's shuttle.

She swallowed her panic, telling herself Nykyrian was here this time and he would see her to safety. She believed in him.

As if he knew her thoughts, he rubbed a comforting hand down her arm. She stared at his left hand held out near her face and watched him click back the release of his blaster.

Waiting.

The hissing of the torch grew louder.

"When they come through, be prepared to run," Nykyrian whispered to her, his warm breath stirring her hair and raising a chill on her cheek.

She nodded.

"Meet me at the rendezvous," he shouted to Syn over the sound of her door splintering.

Kiara's heart pounded in her ears, deafening her to all other sounds. The charred stench stuck in her throat and choked her. Fear restricted her vision and all she could focus on was the weakening door that separated them from the men who wanted to kill her.

Where was the building's security? Her father's? Had the men outside killed them already?

She prayed.

With a cloud of smoke and a loud triumphant shout, a group of men came through the door. Syn fired, killing the first two. He made a holy gesture to his lips and ran into the chaos of the hallway.

She couldn't believe her eyes.

Was he insane?

The sound of insults, curses, laser fire, and blaster shots echoed.

Nykyrian wrapped his right arm around her waist like a safety belt, then pulled her to her feet. "Stay under the cloak."

She trembled in fear, praying she wouldn't trip and cost them their lives. Nykyrian held her against him, his body shielding her from the blasters' fire. She stumbled against him as he led her into the smoke-infested hallway.

He fired his blaster. His arm tightened around her. In spite of her fear, she wanted to see what was happening.

"Don't look," Nykyrian said calmly before pulling her behind him. He spun around and fired at something behind them.

He led her down the corridor, away from the lift. Kicking open the stairwell, he scanned the stairs, then pushed her through the door. He pulled a device from his pocket and used it to seal the door closed behind them.

"Wait here, I need—"

"Don't leave me!" Kiara locked her hands on his forearm as the horror of her mother's death poured through her. "Please!"

Nykyrian's throat tightened at the sound of fear in her trembling voice. Taking a deep breath, he took her hand and led her down the stairs and into the landing bay in the basement of the building.

Kiara's entire body was shaking so badly that she was terrified of falling on her face. Nykyrian on the other hand looked as if he were just out for a stroll. "How can you be so calm?"

He shrugged and continued leading her behind the docked shuttles and parked transports. "Either we'll make it, or they'll kill us. If they kill us, they can't torture us. It's a win-win situation."

She didn't find that funny at all.

Then, she heard them. They were calling to each other as they swept the area, looking for her and Nykyrian.

Nykyrian covered her lips with his finger and motioned her into the shadows of the landing bay.

As the assassin several yards away moved on, out of range, Nykyrian removed his finger from her lips. "Listen," he whispered in her ear, pulling her close enough so that the sound amps the assassins would be using wouldn't pick up his voice. "I have to leave you alone. Just for a few minutes, I promise. I have to clear the sentries from my ship or we'll never make it out of here, okay?"

She rubbed the chills on her arms. "I'm scared."

"Don't be." He handed her a small blaster. "If I go down, Syn will be here in a matter of seconds. You won't get hurt. I swear it." He touched the comlink in his ear. "Syn? Location."

Nykryian nodded in response to whatever answer Syn gave him. "Stay there. I'm about to do something you can't be a part of." Clicking it off, he reached his gloved hand out to cup her cheek with a tenderness he'd never shown her before. "Courage, *mu Tara*. They won't take you today."

Then he was gone.

Kiara crouched down behind the fighter, straining her ears to hear what was going on. Footsteps returned and she pressed herself deeper into the shadows. After a second, she found a hidden spot that allowed her to watch as Nykyrian flipped himself onto a transport.

Nykyrian took a second to tuck his coat into the clips that would keep it out of the way of his reaching for his weapons. He removed his earpiece and slid it into his front pocket. He couldn't afford to have his hearing impaired in any way. With everything in place, he moved atop the ships as silent as the specter for which he'd been named.

From his hearing, he deduced there were roughly fifteen assassins in the bay. The most concerning for him were the two together by his ship and one roaming about to his left.

He ID'd the targets and his ship, then glanced back to where Kiara was hiding as he made the necessary mental calculations on time, distance, and how many he'd have to kill to get out of this alive.

Time to do business.

He rolled off the ship and came to a standing position between the two assassins.

One spun to face him, the man's mouth falling open and moving spastically like a fish. The man gasped before bringing his weapon up. Nykyrian let fly the knife in his left hand, then spun about to catch the second assassin before the soldier could shoot him in the back. The throwing knives caught them both in the throat, piercing their necks completely and cutting off their windpipes which ensured they wouldn't be able to call for help.

Nykyrian took a second to make sure they were both dead and then drained their blasters. He retrieved his knives, wiping them clean on the bodies before he swept forward with them in hand.

A chill raised the hair on the back of his neck.

"I've got your bitch, freak!"

Nykyrian clenched his teeth in frustration at a voice that had haunted him in his youth. It wasn't Aksel.

It was worse.

His much more demented younger brother.

"Turn yourself over to Aksel, and I might let her go."

"Yeah, right," Nykyrian muttered, resetting his blaster for a stronger and smaller shot. "And I'm a one-legged dung dealer."

Damn. How had Arast found her?

His hearing was not what it used to be.

Nykyrian skirted around the ships until he was where the idiot stood, his blaster aimed at Kiara's head. Her face was a mask of complete terror, but her eyes were dry. That look tore through him and he hated the little son of a bitch for making her feel like that.

Arast jerked in a nervous circle as he looked around for Nykyrian. "Hybrid! You have one minute before I spray her brains all over the pavement."

"Nykyrian, run!" Kiara shouted bravely.

That was almost enough to make him laugh.

He'd never run a day in his life and he damn sure wasn't going to run from the maggot holding her.

Arast tightened his grip around her throat. "Another word, *harita,* and I'll snap your neck."

Kiara let loose a dry sob before she regained control of herself.

Nykyrian knew he had one chance and one chance only. "You want a piece of me, Ari?"

Arast spun around, looking for the direction it came from. "Where are you, hybrid?"

He moved before he answered that to keep Arast from pinpointing his location. "It's not where I am that should concern you, brother. It's where my knife is going to land if you don't let her go and put your weapon down."

"And let you shoot me?" Arast laughed sadistically. "I'm not stupid."

"About as smart as my boots," Nykyrian muttered, doubting his own intelligence for letting the imbecile get the drop on him.

"Send me your blaster or I'll kill her right now!"

Arast really was an idiot. Did he think a blaster was needed? Or that he only had one?

Damn, the money spent on Academy training had been seriously wasted on that piece of shit. No wonder The League had tossed his ass out.

Might as well humor the punk. Nykyrian slid his blaster across the floor. The hollow, piercing sound of metal against pavement grated against his sensitive ears.

Arast laughed in triumph.

Laugh it up, lardass. It's one of the last sounds you're going to make.

A wave of inevitability settled over him. Nykyrian had always known it would come to this one day. In all honesty, he was surprised it'd taken so long to get here.

Now it wasn't his life they threatened, it was Kiara's. For that alone, they would die. He'd done his best to avoid killing them out of respect for . . . hell if he really knew.

But today Arast and Aksel had crossed the line for the last time.

So be it.

Nykyrian started forward.

An assassin came at him. "Arast, I got—"

His words died as Nykyrian swung around and killed him before he could even finish the next syllable. Death spasms made the assassin's hands tighten and his blaster fired. It arced a stream over the bay, searing the ceiling and several nearby transports. Nykyrian pulled it from the man's hand and drained the charge before leaving it behind just in case the identifier in the grip had been programmed to work with someone else's handprint.

Arast started sweating. "Kero? You there, man?"

"Dead," Nykyrian said. "Let her go, Ari, and you'll get the chance you've been waiting for."

"Come on, you worthless bastard. I'm ready." Arast slung Kiara away from him.

Nykyrian walked calmly out of the shadows with his hands held out to his sides, away from his body. "You have one shot before I kill you, Ari. You better make it count."

Kiara bit back a scream as the next few seconds happened so fast she could barely follow their sequence. But the one thing that stood out vividly was the cold-blooded grace of Nykyrian's movements.

Assassins came out of nowhere to attack him. He spun, his coat flaring out with an eerie beauty, and shot two with a blaster strike before he holstered it and caught the ones nearest him with his hands. In a terrifying death ballet, he used his knives to cut their throats and bring them down one by one until the only ones standing were him and the man he obviously knew.

Arast.

Her abductor aimed for his head and shot. Nykyrian dodged the blast and rolled on the ground before he came to rest in a graceful crouch. He launched two knives that spun toward Arast and landed in his shoulders.

Arast screamed out. He tried to lift his blaster toward Nykyrian and couldn't. He grabbed a knife and went for Nykyrian, who caught his hand as soon as he reached him, and head-butted him back.

Arast shrieked in frustration. "You're a freak. I should have killed you while you slept."

Nykyrian's tone was even and flat. "Yes, you should have." He snapped Arast's arm with a sickening sound.

With his good arm, Arast brought his blaster up to aim for Nykyrian's heart, but before he could pull the trigger, Nykyrian caught him about the head and twisted. Kiara cringed at the sound of grinding bone a split second before blood gushed out of the assassin's mouth and he crumpled slowly to the ground to rest at Nykyrian's feet.

Nykyrian knelt down and felt for a pulse. Satisfied Arast was dead, he pulled his knives out of the man's body, wiped the blood off on the sleeve of his coat and sheathed them without so much as hesitating.

Kiara's heart pounded in fear. For the first time, she fully realized what Nykyrian really was and what he could do. She'd known what the term "assassin" meant, but his kindness toward her these past few days had dulled the brutality of that word.

He'd let Pitala and his partner go.

Twice.

But this . . .

She looked at the bodies he'd left in his wake. At least a dozen men were now soaking in pools of blood. The last minute of horror and pain was permanently etched into their features.

The stench of blood clung to Nykyrian, choking her.

This was cold and it was brutal. Most of all, it brought home exactly what sort of creature he really was. One who brutally killed without hesitation or remorse.

"We have to go." Nykyrian held his hand out to her. "The others are coming."

She couldn't move as she stared at him with new sight. He was ruthless. It was one thing to know he could kill. Another to see him do it.

He'd snapped a human being's neck with his bare hands and it hadn't affected him at all.

How could he have wiped their blood off on his own sleeve without even cringing?

He'd killed them with the same knives he'd used to prepare her meal . . .

For a minute, she thought she'd be sick.

"Kiara. We have to leave. There are others here and it won't take them long to find us." He hauled her by her arm to his ship.

Somehow, she managed to climb up the ladder and seat herself in the cockpit. Her heart hammered in her chest as he joined her while she continued to stare at the bodies on the ground.

Nykyrian wasn't even breathing hard . . .

He'd just strapped them in when his body went rigid.

She looked up to see more soldiers entering the bay. Nykyrian flipped switches in front of her with that same calmness that was now disturbing to her. The engines fired with a deafening roar as lights danced across his control panel.

In true battle formation, the assassins took up positions to fire at them. One man stood out at the head of the group, glaring at her and Nykyrian with a handsome, cold face that mirrored cruelty and hatred.

He made a military gesture at Nykyrian that was unmistakable. *You and me to the death.*

Nykyrian made an obscene gesture back at him before he launched the ship.

Aksel growled in frustration as his men fired uselessly on the *Arcana,* knowing Nykyrian had once more slipped from his grasp. The bastard and his slut flew right over their heads.

In that moment, he wanted to rip apart every soldier with him. He slammed his fist into the face of the assassin who was dumb enough to be closest to his arm's reach. "You fucking women. Worthless! All of you!"

It was then he noticed the body of his baby brother lying dead on the ground a few feet away. Raw, unmitigated fury tore through him.

"Find them!" he snarled at his men. "I will have that hybrid's life, or your own!"

Shoving them from his path, Aksel made his way back to his own ship.

This was far from over. He would claim Nykyrian's life no matter what. And when he did, that freak of nature would beg like a sniveling child wanting a toy.

The princess was just bonus pay.

CHAPTER 15

Kiara trembled in shock and fear. Over and over, she saw Nykyrian breaking the assassin's neck, heard the snapping of bones, saw the look of horror on the man's face as he realized Nykyrian had killed him . . .

It'd been grisly and cold.

The blood on Nykyrian's clothes . . . Dear God, he'd callously wiped their blood on his own sleeve. A sleeve she stared at as he flew them to wherever they were headed.

He was absolutely stoic over the horror of it all. What kind of monster could do such a thing and not feel even a twinge of *something?* He'd treated it with no more emotion than someone putting on their shoes.

Those memories merged with the ones of her mother's death—the way the assassins had mocked them both and ruthlessly beat her mother while terrifying her. It made her sick and confused and terrified.

She just wanted to run away. To find a place where things like this didn't happen.

Where people like Nykyrian didn't exist.

There's no place safe. Not for you.

The truth scalded her.

Not since that beautiful spring morning when she'd

been eight years old, eating in the garden with her mother before they'd been kidnapped, had she felt safe.

She struggled for her sanity and a way to grasp what had just happened.

Nykyrian felt her pain as he flew them to the neighboring planet where Syn lived. He knew he should say something to her, but he didn't know what. He remembered the first time he'd killed someone. The horror of it still haunted him. That moment when his vic had realized the blow was fatal.

Over time, he'd become so acquainted with the blood and gore that it no longer fazed him at all. It was a tragic waste, but everyone died.

Better them than him.

Kiara clutched her mouth to keep from being sick as he banked and her stomach lurched. He finally docked his fighter in the attached bay of a high-rise building.

The scent of warm, sticky blood, of death, clung to him.

When he moved his hand away from the controls, his gloved handprint, in blood, was right there in front of her.

He was completely oblivious to it.

Bile choked her.

"We need to go."

She tried to rise from the seat, but her limbs wouldn't cooperate.

Gently, Nykyrian wrapped his arms around her and carried her through the bay, up the lift, and into an immaculate apartment on the top floor that had a breathtaking view of the bustling city below. There was something hauntingly familiar about Nykyrian's actions, something her subconscious told her to pay attention to, but she was too upset to catch it.

Inside the apartment, everything was perfectly clean.

Sterile. Most of all, it was *huge*. The main room alone was bigger than her entire flat. But even so, the furnishings were sparse.

"Where are we?"

His answer was dispassionate. "Syn's."

She shook her head. No one would ever dream this elegant place belonged to another killer—like them, on the surface, it appeared so . . .

Normal.

There was a black desk, with nothing on top of it, set against the wall, turned toward the floor-to-ceiling windows. A highly polished white piano faced out toward the balcony. In the middle of the room, perfectly positioned, were two black leather sofas and a small black table that contrasted sharply with the white walls and carpeting.

And as she hurriedly skimmed the room, she realized why the walls and carpet were white. It was so that no color would compete with the expensive art pieces he'd collected . . . or maybe stolen.

Truly it was a master's collection. From the paintings on the walls to the statues and other objets d'art scattered about. A museum would kill to have a collection this extensive.

Along the far wall was a fully stocked bar with bottles of whisky and wine she knew went for over a thousand credits each.

The only personal photo in the room was set on the corner of the bar's black countertop. Nestled in the arms of a well-loved stuffed lorina was a frame that showed a slideshow of a small boy.

The incongruity of that sight actually stunned her. Syn had a son? Surely he didn't live here with him.

Did he?

More to the point, did he know what his father was?

How could these people have families?

Without faltering, Nykyrian reset the security system. The latest and most expensive system made. A DNA skimmer that wouldn't allow anyone inside unless the scanner recognized them. Proof that the man who lived here was as fierce and dangerous as the one holding her.

Kiara wanted the strength to push Nykyrian away, to bathe the smell of blood from her body. She wasn't sure if she'd ever feel clean again.

He took her straight to the bathroom and set her down on the floor before the toilet. Raising the lid for her convenience, he stood back as she unloaded all the contents of her stomach.

Kiara wasn't sure how he knew what she'd been holding back, but she was grateful for his quick actions. She felt so ill, physically and mentally. Her entire body quaked as she tried to regain control of herself.

As unaffected by her sickness as he'd been by killing those men, Nykyrian wet a cold washcloth and held it against the back of her neck until she was finished.

He handed the cloth to her and flushed the toilet. "Feeling better?"

She couldn't meet his gaze. Instead, she stared at the dark stains on his coat and shirt. "You have blood all over you."

He looked down at it. "It happens."

That made her sick again.

His elbows on his knees, Nykyrian crouched beside her in silence as he listened to her regurgitating. Her cheeks were flushed and the horror in her eyes kicked him straight in the gut. He knew what a monster he was.

But seeing that monster through her amber eyes was the most painful thing he'd ever endured.

You're nothing but an animal, unfit to be around decent people. No wonder your parents threw you away.

Trying to push the hurt away, he got up and found one of Syn's unopened toothbrushes. The little paranoid OCD bastard always kept extras so that he could change them out every few weeks. Nykyrian handed one to Kiara and stayed with her while she straightened herself up.

He would clean the blood off his own clothes, but the sight of it smeared over Syn's white linens would only make it worse for her. There was nothing more nauseating than blood on white—which was why he wore black and all of his linens were black.

When she was finished, he reached across her to get a towel.

She flinched and stepped back.

His heart twisted at her involuntary reaction. Did she really think after all they'd been through and shared that he could hurt *her*?

You wanted her to hate you. Congratulations. She does.

But he'd never wanted *her* to look at him that way— like he was unfeeling garbage. Just because he didn't show his feelings, it didn't mean he didn't have them.

You should be used to it by now. Everyone had looked at him like that at some point. Even Syn.

I am what I am.

What they'd made him. Nothing was ever going to change that.

He moved away and watched as she pulled the towel he'd been reaching for to her. When she was finished brushing her teeth and washing her face, she walked into the main room and refused to look at him as she sat down on the couch.

God, how he wanted to comfort her, but she'd never allow that now. She'd looked straight into the beast inside him and, like everyone else who'd seen it, she'd never be the same with him again.

The door opened.

Nykyrian spun about at the sound, his blaster leveling at the body in the doorway.

Syn held up his hands as the red dot lay steady on his forehead. "Whoa. Friend!" He tapped his chest twice. "Really good guy. 'Member me?"

Nykyrian holstered his blaster. "You should have used the link, asshole."

"Didn't think about that since I was entering, you know, *my house*. Thank the gods you're not like Darling. Shoot first and then sort it out after we're all bloody." Syn dumped his pack by the bar. "Whatever you did to Aksel, you got him screaming mad. He's sent his men all over looking for you. I heard he already beat two informants to death trying to find out where you live."

Syn paused as he noticed Kiara sitting on the sofa as if she were in shock while she stared silently into space. "Is she all right?"

Nykyrian shook his head, his guilt mounting. He moved to stand beside Syn so that Kiara couldn't hear him and spoke in Ritadarion to make sure that even if she heard, she wouldn't understand. "I killed Arast in the bay before we left . . . right in front of her. She's coping with it about as well as you could hope for with a civilian . . ." He paused before he spoke again. "Don't let me forget I owe you a toothbrush."

Syn paled. "You okay?"

He gave his friend a dry stare. "When has death ever bothered me? Besides, it was a payday long overdue." He looked at Kiara over his shoulder. "I have some things to do. Get her to the safe zone."

Syn inclined his head.

Kiara heard Nykyrian leave, but she didn't bother looking up. Right now, she was trying not to be sick again.

"Here."

She jumped as Syn handed her a glass of brika—a very potent alcohol. "I don't drink that stuff."

"Today you do. The sugar in it will help with the shock and the minerals will help with the nausea." He pressed it into her hand.

Without further argument, she tossed the scorching liquid down her throat where it burned a path to her stomach. She gasped, her eyes watering.

"Good girl."

She handed the glass back to Syn as new fears washed through her. "How many people have you killed?"

He shrugged before he took the glass over to the bar and set it down. "I don't think about it."

"How can you not?"

He avoided looking at the picture of his son as he reached for a bottle of whisky and poured it into another glass. "Because if I hadn't killed them, they would have killed me. No offense . . . my life, suckass though it is, means more to me than theirs." He took a deep swig. "I leave the world alone and I figure if someone is dumb enough to put me in their targeting sights, then they deserve what they get."

She shook her head. "On one hand I agree with that, but to take a life . . . I just don't understand how someone can do it without feeling *anything*. Nykyrian took them down so fast they had no chance whatsoever."

Syn sputtered as anger tore through him. How dare she judge them so. She, who'd lived her precious life full of love and doting while people like them risked their lives to keep her safe.

What's more, she'd lied to him when she told him that they weren't trash. That she wasn't like others—that she saw the good within them no matter what.

And now . . .

She wasn't a bit better than the rest of the maggots in the universe.

Just like his ex-wife and son. Didn't matter how much love you gave them. How good you treated them. How you gave them everything you wish to the gods you'd had, including respect. It didn't matter how much you hated the life you'd been forced against your will to live or how hard you'd try to put the past behind you.

They cursed you for surviving and judged you on a past you despised even more than they did.

He and Nykyrian were the ones who'd lived in hell, and these assholes who had no understanding of the world dared to look down on them for it.

He wanted to hit the bitch for her smug, sanctimonious condemnation.

Thanks for proving me right, princess . . .

Most of all he was angry at himself for believing her when she'd lied to him.

When was he ever going to learn?

He wanted her blood, especially since Nykyrian had almost died while protecting her crybaby ass. "Tell me exactly how many assassins were there today?"

"I don't know. Fifteen. Twenty maybe."

He gave her a snide glare. "Twenty trained assassins against one guy who had his guts lasered last night . . . Lady, I think they had more than a fair shot at surviving and we're damn lucky you and Kip are alive right now. Instead of being upset with him, you should be grateful."

Kiara hadn't thought of it that way. He was right and yet . . . she couldn't get over the cold ruthlessness of what Nykyrian had done. "But I don't understand it. I just don't. Both of you let Pitala go. Twice. Twice!" She reemphasized the word. "Nykyrian mowed them down without even trying to talk them out of it. He just started killing like it was nothing."

Syn set his glass down on the low table in front of her. There was a raw anger to him that she didn't understand. It was like he wanted to lash out and hurt her. "That's because with Pitala, it wasn't personal. You're a paycheck to him and not worth his life. He's a bully and if you let him know you're a bigger asshole willing to cut off his body parts, he will back off and find his credits somewhere else. But with Bredeh, it's not the money he's after. It's the prestige. Once he takes a target, he will kill it and nothing is going to stop him. Ever."

She shook her head in denial. "But Nykyrian didn't kill Bredeh. He killed other people. And he didn't try to reason with them first."

"No shit, he didn't try to reason with them. They may not have been Bredeh, but they were his men and he would have killed them had they allowed you two to escape. I assure you, there's no reasoning to be had with men who know it's kill or be killed. And lady, you better get your head out of your spoiled little ass and wake up. Kip didn't kill Bredeh, he killed his brother, who followed the same code of misconduct. Believe me, Kip has spent his entire life trying to avoid doing what he did today."

"What do you mean?"

He gave her a bitter stare that sent a chill down her spine. One that only increased with his next words. "Aksel Bredeh's birth name and Arast's last name are the same." He gave a long pause before he spoke again. "Quiakides."

Her mouth fell open. *No, surely not . . .*

"What?"

"Nykyrian is their adopted brother. He was raised with them."

She stifled another round of nausea. "Oh my God . . . How could he do such a thing? What kind of monster is he?"

Syn leaned over the arm of the couch, forcing her to lean back. He braced his arms on each side of her, penning her in. She didn't like being cornered.

His eyes blazed and, for a moment, she thought he might actually strike her.

"You think you're so unsullied. How dare *you* sit there like some high queen dispensing her judgment on us." His alcohol-laced breath fell against her cheek in angry pulses that punctuated each biting word. "Don't waste pity on Arast. If he'd been given the chance, he'd have raped you slowly and in ways you can't even conceive of, then cut you into little pieces and fed you to his dogs. All except your head with your contorted fear permanently twisted on your pretty little face—that he would have sent home to your father as a present, but only after he'd been paid. And that's nice compared to what he'd have done to Nykyrian. To what he's done to Nykyrian in the past."

Kiara stared at him, wondering if he were telling her the truth. She tried to remember the verbal exchanges between Nykyrian and Arast, but all she could see was their brief fight.

"I just don't see how anyone can be so cold."

Syn shoved himself away from her. "And you should be grateful, little girl, to whatever god you worship, that you can say that. In the world we come from, I don't understand how anyone can be anything *but* cold."

"I'm not a child. Don't talk to me like I am."

He scoffed at her. "No, you're worse. You're an adult who still thinks the world is a beautiful place, filled with people who will help you just for the sake of being nice. Wake up and smell the bloodbath and humility the rest of us have to cope with."

"Don't you dare mock me. I've seen more pain than you can even imagine."

He snorted cruelly. "Yeah, your mother was shot dead in front of you. Boo-hoo. So what? You think you're the only one who ever lived through that? My father was publicly executed for the entire Ichidian Universe to watch. The saddest part of that is I just wish I'd been the one who'd gassed the bastard."

Kiara drew a sharp breath in at what he described. Only the most brutal criminals were publicly executed. "Who was your father?"

His breathing ragged, he gave her a cold, harsh stare. "Idirian Wade."

Kiara shot off the couch as terror filled her. Oh dear God . . . Idirian Wade had been the most feared criminal to ever live. He'd gleefully mutilated and killed hundreds of people. Men, women, children. It didn't matter. He'd cared for nothing and no one. Mothers still used his name to terrify their misbehaving children.

What horrific atrocities would the son of such a man be capable of doing?

Syn curled his lip. "Don't look at me that way, *harita*. I'm not my father. That look on your face right now takes me to places you don't want me to go, especially while I'm drunk."

Kiara looked away as indignation filled her. How dare he compare her mother's execution with that of an animal like his father. "My mother wasn't a psychotic criminal."

"No. I'm sure she was a wonderful lady who loved

you dearly. That she held you when you cried, probably even baked you cookies and gave you hugs and kisses before she sent you off to bed at night," he spat those words mockingly, "and it's a damn shame a decent woman like her died so tragically.

"My mother, whore that she was, abandoned me and my sister to our father so that she could return to her cushy life and pretend we didn't exist while she left us in that house with a man whose name, even though he's been dead for decades, can still make an assassin wet his pants. And if you think his cruelty was reserved for strangers, think again. My sister and I were target practice for him. So don't you dare talk to me about pain. My father wrote the book on it and he rammed it down my throat every day of my childhood until they killed him. And the real kicker is, my life under his demented fist was a lot better than Nykyrian's. At least I was able to hide sometimes from the ones trying to kill me."

His tirade stunned her.

Syn pulled his link out of his pocket. "You want me to call your daddy, baby? Go right ahead. I'll be more than happy to take you to him. But know that Aksel will have his hands on you in a matter of hours. *Then* you'll be able to talk to me about pain and you'll finally have an idea of what we've endured. You won't live long enough to apologize, but true clarity will be yours before you die."

A loud knock pounded on the door.

Kiara jumped and bit back a scream as Syn leveled his blaster at the door faster than she could blink.

"You wonder why I drink," Syn muttered. "Stay down." He moved to the bar and flicked on the video console that showed Darling on the other side of the door, looking bored.

Syn holstered his blaster.

Crossing the room, he opened the door and hauled Darling into the apartment by the front of his shirt.

"Hey!" Darling snapped, shoving him back. "What the hell are you doing?"

Syn locked the door. "Aksel's after us. You're lucky he didn't shoot you while you were jacking off in the hallway."

"Nice language in front of the lady, bud. Thanks for the image. But at least it explains why Nykyrian was edgier than normal." He looked at her and nodded a greeting.

Kiara had to force herself not to react to the black eye marring the exposed side of Darling's face. His eye was red and the whole cheek swollen. There was blood crusted around his nose, and the center of his upper lip was also scabbed over.

Syn grimaced as he took Darling's chin in his hand to study the bruises. "What the hell happened to you?"

Darling gave him a droll stare. "What do you think?"

Syn cursed. "I swear I'm going to kill that bastard someday."

"Get in line."

Syn sighed as he released him. "What was it over this time?"

"Dumbass thinks I'm dating the manwhore of all time."

Syn scowled in incredulous disbelief. "Dagan?"

"Yeah," Darling said with a sarcastic laugh. "You know anyone else who can compete with his record?"

Syn shook his head. "I'd pay good money to see you hook up with him."

"I would too, but then Caillen would have my ass in a sling and I'd be dead so it wouldn't do me any good."

Syn returned for his whisky. "Why would he think that anyway?"

"Private fu—" he broke his word off as he looked at Kiara, "investigator. Caught me at a bar with Caillen while he was trolling for his nightly concubine and I was trying to relax. The photo he took was of Caillen leaning over to whisper something to me and I have to admit, it's pretty damning to anyone unaware of the fact that I don't have the proper anatomy to entice him. Of course, Arturo wouldn't believe it was innocent so here you go." He gestured at his face.

Syn lifted his hair to look at the other side of his face. "Did you see a doctor?"

"Yeah. It'll heal."

"Did your mom say anything?"

"Clean the blood out of the carpet before it sets." Darling cleared his throat. "What could she say? Better me than her."

Kiara was horrified by what he described and, by his face, she could tell he wasn't exaggerating.

"Anyway, Nyk sent me here to get those files you've been working on for him."

Syn's scowl deepened. "Why?"

"As if he'd tell me? I don't even know what I'm getting. All he said was to grab and upload the data since you weren't supposed to be here."

"Then why did you knock?"

"Just in case you *were* home. I don't want to get hit again and my peripheral vision is seriously compromised right now. So if you copped one of your notorious right hooks at me, I wouldn't see it coming in time to duck."

Syn let out a tired breath. "I'd never hit you, Cruel. I only fantasize about strangling you."

"You're a sick bastard to waste a perfectly good fantasy on *that*."

Syn laughed. "It's in the safe in my room. The red

drive." He met Kiara's eyes. "And on that note, I hate to be rude, but I've got to get her *highness*"—he sneered the word—"to safety before you know who figures out where I live. Unlike Kip, my address isn't that hard to find. Lock the door and don't forget to reactivate the scanner."

"Done."

Syn held his hand out to her. "Are you staying with us, your queenship?"

Kiara hesitated. She was terrified of them, but they had saved her three times now when her father's people hadn't. No matter what her personal opinions about them, this did seem the safest course of action.

At least as long as she wanted to stay alive.

Please don't let me regret this . . .

Swallowing the lump of fear in her throat, she took his hand, not really sure if what she did was for the best. "For now."

Syn pulled her to her feet and they headed toward the door. He led the way through the building and to his ship. His hand stayed on the grip of his weapon, ready to pull it out in a heartbeat. He kept his head low as if listening and watching.

Something that made her more aware herself and drove home to her exactly how tenuous her safety was. She'd never seen Syn this nervous—not even when they were about to be blown to pieces.

Unwilling to distract him, Kiara didn't speak again until they were safely tucked inside Syn's two-seated fighter and out of the planet's orbit.

"What happened to Darling's face?"

His voice dripped sarcasm as it echoed from the speakers in her helmet. "It got hit. Repeatedly."

She rolled her eyes. "By whom? His boyfriend?"

He scoffed. "Cruel isn't stupid enough to hook up

with someone who'd beat him and if anyone ever made that mistake, he'd hand their heart to them. You know . . . Nykyrian style."

She cringed at his cruelty in reminding her of what Nykyrian had done. "Then what happened to him?"

He flipped a switch, then banked. "You know anything about the Caronese?"

"Not much."

"Yeah, well, they're a strange race. Their male children aren't considered adults until they're thirty. Four more years for Darling. In the meantime, he falls under the guardianship of his uncle, who can't stand the fact that Darling isn't interested in women. Anytime he catches Darling associating with men, Darling gets a visit from his fists."

She winced at that. "Why does he tolerate it?"

"His uncle happens to be their Grand Counsel. Darling causes any trouble or pisses him off and he can have him put in jail or a mental facility, which he's done in the past, or have him executed. If he tries to leave, Arturo has him dragged back in chains. Believe me, we've tried to extract him from there many times. It always backfires on Darling."

Kiara sighed. Syn had been right. She couldn't fathom their backgrounds. The brutality and horror.

Her mother had died trying to keep her safe and her father wouldn't hesitate to do the same. The worst thing her parents had ever done was yell at her. "What about his mother? Can't she do something?"

"On Caron, women have no authority and are considered perpetual children. While she loves Darling, there's nothing she can do, and so long as she stays out of it, Darling's younger sister and brother are left alone. If she interferes, it goes worse on Darling. Not to mention, she then becomes the one abused. So Darling has told her to do nothing and let the beatings fall as they may. As he said, better him than his frail mother."

She ground her teeth at the injustice of that. "So he pays the price for all of them?"

"Yep. The world sucks, doesn't it?"

But that knowledge made her even more curious about Darling's friendship with them. "If his uncle is so controlling, how is it he works for The Sentella?"

"His uncle doesn't know that. The man's a bit thick. He thinks he's hired Kip to guard Darling and that we're keeping him out of trouble."

"But if he's hired private investigators—"

"They report what they find, and if there's one thing we're all good at, it's manipulating things. No one knows what goes on inside The Sentella."

"You mean falsifying documents?"

"You say to-may-to, I say to-mah-to."

"Aren't you afraid I'll report this?"

"You have to live first, and even if you do, you have to find the real files to prove the existing ones are false. Trust me, you won't."

She stared at the back of his head. "What about Nemesis?"

"What about him?"

"How does he figure into all of this?"

"Do you really think I'm going to answer that?"

No, she didn't. So she switched to something she might have more luck with. "Where are you taking me?"

"Kip's house."

Kiara couldn't have been more shocked had Syn turned around and shot her. "I'm surprised he'd allow me near it."

"Me, too." Syn shifted in the seat.

She frowned in confusion. "Then why are you taking me there?"

"Because he told me to."

"You always do what he tells you to?"

"Absolutely."

With that simple statement of loyalty, she remained quiet and watched the stars zoom past outside as she thought about everything she'd seen and learned today.

It wasn't even noon yet and she felt battered and weary. How could so much happen in such a short period of time?

And how much worse would it get? She was almost afraid to ask that question even in her head for fear of the powers that be dumping more down on her.

But in spite of it all, she found herself relaxing a bit as she tried to come to terms with the two polar extremes of the men around her.

Fierce protectors and vicious killers.

How could they be both?

It didn't take long to reach Nykyrian's planet. Kiara stared at the swirling orange and yellow mists. It seemed so peaceful and isolated. An untouched piece of heaven.

Syn landed outside a floating house that was almost as large as her entire housing building. He docked in the bay and pressed a button.

"We have to wait for the bay to pressurize and a breathable atmosphere to mix."

She didn't say anything as she glanced about the bay where another fighter was parked. The engine to it was in pieces around it. From the condition of the fighter and the way everything was laid out, she figured it must be a long-term project of Nykyrian's and it made her wonder if he'd restored the fighter he flew, too.

The bay itself was large enough to accommodate six ships and, aside from that organized mess where he was working on the other ship, everything was sparkling clean and unbelievably orderly.

After a couple of minutes, Syn lifted the hatch and helped her down.

As soon as he reached the door and gave a palm scan, he held her back. "Careful." He opened the door.

Expecting a booby trap or alarm, she was stunned as they were bombarded by a huge lorina. The animal jumped up on her, licking her cheek with its large, rough tongue. Three more danced around them.

"I hate these things." Syn pushed them away from him. "They think they're lap pets. Down, Ilyse." He extricated himself from the smallest one. "Down!"

Kiara smiled, petting the one licking her arm. "Are there just the four?"

"Yeah. Believe me, four's plenty. Come on in and make yourself at home. There's no telling when Kip'll return."

Syn walked through the house, switching on lights with a hand control. "This is the kitchen," he said, showing her the huge, gleaming white area to the right of the door. It was a chef's dream, with an industrial steel stove, huge cooling unit, and a full array of gourmet pots and pans hanging from hooks in the ceiling. His knives were lined in perfect symmetry along the wall on a magnetic strip.

Syn moved toward the shining black staircase. "Kip's room is up those stairs." He held up his remote to show the controls to her. "Everything in the house is wired to this. You can lighten the ceiling to see the sky, and the same for the upstairs wall where Nykyrian sleeps." He held down a button and, sure enough, the ceiling became transparent to let her see the bright stars twinkling in the heavens.

How absolutely beautiful.

Syn led her through the main room that was flanked by a media room on one side and an exercise room on the other. A study and computer rooms were in the back, along with two bathrooms, two more bedrooms, a massive library, a weapons room, and a tribal court. Everything was pristine and top of the line. No expense had been spared in building or maintaining the house.

"This is an impressive place," she breathed, awed by the heated marble floors and gold-leaf trim. "I didn't realize he had so much money."

Syn shrugged. "Murder's a profitable business."

Kiara stiffened at his obvious dig at her. "Why are you being so cruel?"

"Honestly? Because I believed your bullshit lies when you spewed them and I don't often make that mistake. I should have listened to myself and known that in the end, you're just like every other sanctimonious ass out there who dares to call *us* callous and unfeeling."

She felt struck by his unwarranted condemnation. "I *never* lied to you."

"Of course you did—you said you could see the real us—that we weren't as bad as we claimed. But you didn't and, just like everyone else, so long as we risk our lives to protect and save you, we're okay. But the moment we have to make a choice not ours, the moment you see what our pasts have made us, you're horrified by the truth and hate us for it like we had some kind of choice in what we are."

"Everyone has a choice."

He scoffed coldly. "No, princess, they don't. Choices aren't always up to us. Life and circumstances can shred even the stoutest soul. No matter how pure and untainted you think you are, I promise you that you, too, can be shoved into the darkness just like we were."

She didn't buy his excuses. Everyone had control of what they did. It was the one principal her father had raised her on. All choices were those of the people who made them and the least they could do was be men enough to accept responsibility for the monsters they'd become. "Nykyrian left The League. He could stop killing any time he wanted to."

"And had he done that, princess, you'd be dead right now and so would I." His eyes blazed with indignant fury as he took a step toward her. "Believe me, baby, no one ran harder or faster from their past than I did. And in one moment, one fucking whore brought it all home and laid it back at my feet. Even though I'd clawed my way out of the gutter, turned my back on everyone and everything I'd ever known and become respectable. Even though I'd buried my past so deep that I thought I was untouchable. It didn't matter. I was still shit to the world and the moment the woman I'd sold my soul to saw me for what I was, she ruined me and left me with nothing except the drunken bitterness you see now. You want to know why I drink? It's because I can't escape my past and I hate what I am. What I was forced to endure just to survive."

He raked a scathing glare over her body. "I hate this fucking life and, most of all, I hate people like you who can't see past the surface. You judge us on one deed alone without seeing all the other things we are. Damn you for that, Kiara Zamir. Had I known you were just like everyone else, I would have left you chained in Chenz's ship." Curling his lip in repugnance, he turned and headed back down the hallway. "Do whatever you want. But stay away from me."

Those words struck her like blows. Kiara wanted to chase him down and apologize, but he was too angry at her for that. Besides, she'd done nothing wrong. Anyone would have been horrified at the way Nykyrian mowed down those men.

And since she didn't know what Syn was capable of—if he was worse than Nykyrian—she decided it would be best to give him room.

So, instead, she went into the library to see if Nykyrian had something she could read. Turning the light up, she was stunned by the number of languages represented on the black shelves that lined all four walls from floor to ceiling. She dragged her finger down the leather spines until she reached the trophy cabinet.

Her jaw went slack. There were trophies for sharpshooting, flying, and archery, knife throwing, language translations, and commendations for his service to The League. But the one most stunning was his commission certificate.

To the youngest being to ever reach the rank of Command Assassin.

The words leapt out at her. But more than the words was the fact that it, along with all the other awards, had no name listed on the certificate. They were all given to Hybrid Andarion.

Hybrid Andarion . . .

Not even that cold piece of paper recognized the fact that Nykyrian was human . . .

Hybrid Andarion was also listed on his certificate of completion for The League's prestigious Pontari Academy. A sad smile curved her lips as she saw a notation that he'd graduated with honors and at the top of his class.

But it made her heart ache to know that no one had thought enough of Nykyrian to give him a name.

Wincing at that harsh reality, she turned and left the library. In the hallway, she paused outside the clear door that showed his weapons room. She'd never seen a more comprehensive collection. A testament to his brutal trade.

She clenched her teeth and moved up the hallway toward the media room.

Syn was in the office on the computer.

Deciding to avoid him, she ducked into the media room and closed the door. Maybe she'd be able to find something to occupy her mind and allow her to forget the nightmare of this day.

Completely windowless, the room was painted dark brown, trimmed in black. Black speakers lined the walls, but there were no pictures anywhere—in fact Nykyrian had nothing on any of his walls. What a strange thing, given how much art Syn collected.

A long, dark brown couch was set before the huge screen. The media case and player were to the right.

With a heavy sigh, she walked to the cabinet, opened the glass door, and flipped through Nykyrian's vid collection.

A half smile curved her lips as she realized several discs were of her past performances. He hadn't been lying when he said he was a fan. For some reason that made no sense, a small thrill went through her.

And since she couldn't stand to see herself perform, because all she could do was find fault with everything she did, she pushed them aside to see what else he had.

Most were action or horror movies and true crime programs she couldn't stand to watch.

But under those . . .

It was a box labeled private. Opening it up, her heart stopped. The overhead light made the discs sparkle in a bright rainbow of colors. Her conscience told her to put them back, that she had no right to pry into his past, but she was too compelled to see what they contained. Her private discs were recitals and birthday parties. What were his?

Tucking her conscience away, Kiara inserted her handful into the machine. She picked up the control and switched on the viewer. She plopped down on the sofa to see just what his horrible secrets were.

The first vid was in a sterile hospital room. She wasn't sure who or what was lying on the bed with padded restraints around wrists and ankles. She couldn't even tell the gender or age of the patient. The patient had a leather mask fastened around the face, obscuring everything except the eyes. The patient's head was bald and a doctor was making notes on a ledger while the tense patient watched her with wary eyes.

The doctor went to touch the patient's leg. A shriek of rage was followed by the patient trying to move the leg away from her grasp.

"It's all right, boy. I'm not going to hurt you."

He screamed and fought like a wild animal, regardless of her assurances.

"Why don't you sedate him?"

The doctor turned as Huwin Quiakides entered the room. Tall and slender, he was younger than Kiara had remembered him. His handsome face was marked with a cold, calculating look.

"I tried earlier and he had some . . . interesting side effects."

Horror filled her as she realized this was Nykyrian as a child.

The commander moved forward to look down at the leather mask. "I thought you were going to remove that."

"We tried."

"But?"

"He's worn it for so long that parts of it have fused

with his skin. It's literally grown into his face." She moved closer to show the commander. "As you can see, part of his skin around it is also infected. Removing it will require minor surgery and right now, we can't figure out a way to put him under with normal anesthesia."

Kiara felt sick as she realized now what the scars on Nykyrian's face had come from.

"Then cut it off while he's conscious."

Kiara's stomach jerked in response to the heartless order.

"Yes, sir." The doctor made a note.

Huwin moved to touch Nykyrian's face.

Nykyrian thrashed about, trying to get away or to attack. It was hard to tell. But there was no denying his ferocious anger.

Huwin smiled. "Look at him. Like some wild animal trying to tear me apart. I couldn't ask for a better specimen."

Kiara gasped at the sick pride in the commander's voice. It was a child he spoke about, not some specimen.

The doctor swallowed. "Commander, I'm not sure about your plans where he's concerned."

He turned on her with a scowl so severe, she took a step back. "What do you mean?"

"He's really . . ." The doctor paused as if trying to find the correct word. "Damaged."

"And you will repair him."

The doctor looked skeptical. "Sir, I don't think you realize the extent of what's been done to him. He's had multiple compound fractures over a period of years and none of them were ever set. His right arm alone will have to be rebroken in eight places and reset. It might never work right again."

The doctor lifted Nykyrian's fingers even while he

struggled against her. "They've crudely torn his nails out. I assume the nails must have been Andarion hence the removal, but for an Andarion taking the nails is like amputating a limb. His fingers are completely deformed now. And I can't even begin to count how many times his hands have been broken. It looks like someone stomped on them repeatedly. As you can see from his movements, he can't even make a fist."

While Kiara was ill from the disclosure, the commander appeared completely unaffected. "All of that can be fixed. Is there anything else?"

"Just the severe malnutrition, dehydration, and starvation."

Just? Kiara shook her head at the woman's blase tone.

Huwin handed the doctor a small collar. "Make sure you put this on him as soon as you can."

"What is this?"

"It's a training collar we use on League soldiers. It'll make it so that we won't have to restrain him." He handed over a small silver box. "And I want him tagged as soon as possible, too—just in case he tries to run."

The doctor bowed. "Yes, sir." Then she left him alone with Nykyrian.

Huwin picked up the ledger from the bedside table. He smirked at the notes. "Parents unknown. Age unknown. Name unknown. Hmmm . . . I wonder if you know any of that?"

Nykyrian didn't answer. He merely stared at him with raw hatred.

The commander smiled cruelly. "You, hybrid, are going to be the greatest legacy I can give to The League. When I finish with you, you will be unrivaled in skill and savagery." He reached for Nykyrian's mask.

Nykyrian bucked and fought.

The commander laughed. "Just look at you. You're already halfway there."

Cringing and unable to take it, Kiara clicked to the next disc.

It showed Nykyrian in his mid-teens, at school. He sat alone outside under a tree, reading from an electronic reader. There were other kids all around him, socializing and laughing. Dressed in plain black clothes and with this white hair cropped short, Nykyrian looked beautiful except for the left side of his face, which was discolored from healing bruises. The scars on his face from the leather mask were a bit more prominent then than they were now.

A boy was shoved down not far from him.

"C'mon you little nadico, give us your credits."

Kiara flinched at the harsh condemnation of the boy's manhood.

The boy cringed, trying to escape. "Leave me alone, Aksel. I gave you everything this morning."

"Bullshit!" Aksel kicked him hard in the groin.

The boy started crying as he tried to crawl away.

"Let me!" Another boy came forward to kick him in the same place. This boy was Arast.

When Arast moved to kick again, Nykyrian launched himself at him and sent him flying.

Aksel turned on Nykyrian with a laugh. "The freak wants some more. What's the matter, we didn't beat you bad enough last night?"

Nykyrian started forward, but Aksel held his arm up to show him a control bracelet. "You know you can't hit me, asshole. Not as long as you're collared like a dog." He looked at the boy Nykyrian had shoved. "Get him, Ari."

Arast launched himself at Nykyrian, who was now powerless to fight back.

Kiara couldn't breathe as she watched the virulent hatred of the two of them stomping and beating Nykyrian.

It seemed like forever before a male teacher came forward to stop them.

"What's going on here?"

Aksel gestured to the boy he'd attacked initially. "The hybrid was bullying Terrence. Arast and I stopped it."

Nykyrian pushed himself up into a sitting position. His nose and mouth were bleeding profusely. But his eyes were completely dry. He wiped a trembling hand over his nose, smearing the blood across his cheek.

The teacher snatched Nykyrian up by his arm. "What have we told you about fighting?"

Nykyrian glared at Aksel and Arast, but said nothing in defense of himself.

"You should call our father and let him know. He said he wanted to be notified if the hybrid got into trouble again."

Nykyrian's face paled three shades.

"Don't worry, we will."

Kiara was baffled by Nykyrian's actions. Why wouldn't he tell them the truth? Why didn't Terrence tell them what had happened? Couldn't they have simply watched the video?

Instead Nykyrian was taken to the administrator's office where he was spanked with a metal paddle.

And when the commander arrived, Nykyrian, still bleeding, was hauled to his feet by his hair. He didn't even grimace. The commander thanked the staff for letting him know what had happened.

"Wait until I get you home," he promised Nykyrian in a tone so threatening it raised chills on her arms.

But it was the empty resignation on Nykyrian's young face that brought tears to her eyes.

God, what more had he suffered?

She clicked to another file.

This one was also of Nykyrian in school. It was a camera shot of the academy's cafeteria. Even though it was packed with students, Nykyrian sat alone in the corner with no one around him, eating a sandwich while he read from the same electronic reader set on the table in front of him.

One side of his head had been shaved and a row of stitches marked the skin from the top of his ear to his eyebrow. His right arm bore a cast and was held to his side in a dark blue sling. He looked terrible and it was obvious from his slow movements and grimaces as he ate and read that he was in a lot of pain.

As soon as he was finished eating, he rose and picked up his tray to walk it to the cleaning window. He'd only taken a few steps when Arast slid up behind him and hit him hard on his injured arm.

Nykyrian gasped before the tray and its contents went flying.

"Watch where you're going, freak." Arast shoved at him, then laughed before he rejoined Aksel at a nearby table.

The pain on Nykyrian's face was searing as he knelt down to clean up the mess.

A tall, slender Andarion boy came up to help him. It took her a second to realize that it was Hauk as a young teenager.

Nykyrian shoved his hands away.

"Let me help," Hauk said, his tone sincere.

Nykyrian raked him with a sneer. "I'm not dumb enough to fall for that trick again. Get away from me." He finished picking up the garbage and his reader, then rose to his feet. He gave a long, hard glare of hatred to Hauk before he headed to the window.

Hauk watched him leave, his face a mask of sadness.

"What the hell are you doing, Dancer?"

Kiara grimaced at the sight of the crowned Andarion prince and heir. She'd always hated that smug prick.
There was something about him that made her flesh
crawl.

Hauk bowed low to him. "He saved my life, Highness. I was only trying to pay him back."

Jullien arched one regal, scathing brow. "You'd better
remember where your loyalties lie, pleb. Or else you'll
find yourself sharing his misery."

Kiara winced as she looked down at the remote in
her hand. "Come on. There has to be a good moment in
here somewhere." She skipped ahead to another random file.

This time Nykyrian was older. Maybe fifteen or sixteen. He was entering into an elaborate home with a
beautiful older woman by his side. She looked vaguely
familiar, but Kiara couldn't place her.

Again his face was battered and he held his one arm
as if it was injured again. There were more bruises on
his neck and he looked as if he hadn't slept for days. As
before, his movements were slow and methodical as
they'd been last night in her flat. She now realized it was
the way he moved whenever he was seriously hurt.

The woman shut the door behind them. "Go upstairs
and get showered. I'll call the doctor for you."

He gave her a slight, awkward bow. "Thank you,
Lady Quiakides."

Kiara smiled as she realized the woman was his
adoptive mother. Kindness marked the woman's face as
she watched him head for the stairs.

Well, at least someone appeared kind to him.

But Nykyrian didn't make it to the staircase before

Aksel and Arast joined him. Aksel from the stairs and Arast from a neighboring room to pin Nykyrian between them.

The look on his face was one of restrained fury.

Aksel popped Nykyrian on the side of the face so hard, Nykyrian's head snapped back. The bloodlust in Nykyrian's eyes should have frightened him. But obviously he'd been getting away with years of torturing him so Aksel had learned not to fear his glares. "Well, look what Mom dragged home. What was it like in jail? Huh, freak?"

Nykyrian tried to push past him, but Aksel wouldn't let him.

He shoved Nykyrian back toward Arast. "C'mon. Tell us. I have to know how many prisoners went deep drilling on you."

Rage darkened Nykyrian's eyes at the crude expression. He lunged for Aksel, but only managed two steps before he screamed out.

Arast held a control in his hands and laughed. "I love your shock collar, dog. Bark for me." He twisted the dial.

Nykyrian fell to his knees, panting and trying to claw the collar from his throat.

"Ari, stop!" his mother shouted, trying to get it out of his hands.

"Lock his limbs!" Aksel shouted with a cruel laugh as he kicked Nykyrian in his injured arm.

Fighting her, Arast did and he turned the shock dial up all the way.

For the first time, Kiara saw tears in Nykyrian's eyes as he lay on the ground, unable to move. The collar hummed evilly, leaving her to speculate on how much agony it was delivering to a boy who could do nothing more than take it.

Finally, their mother wrenched it out of Arast's hands and turned it off. The moment she did, the commander came slamming through the front door.

He glared at his wife as if he'd like to beat her. "I told you to leave him in jail. How dare you go behind my back like this!"

"He's just a boy, Huwin. He doesn't belong in a holding cell with hardened criminals. My God, you should have seen where they kept him, and naked no less. That was completely unnecessary for a child his age."

"He's not a child. He's an animal." The commander grabbed Nykyrian by his hair and hauled him to his feet as he started searching his clothes. "Where is it?"

"I didn't take it, sir."

The commander backhanded him so hard, it split his lip and caused his nose to bleed. "Don't lie to me." He seized Nykyrian by the neck and drove his head back against the wall. Four times.

Kiara covered her mouth as a wave of nausea swelled at the horror.

What had he done to cause so much anger?

Nykyrian didn't respond at all as the commander slung him across the room. The force of it was so great that he tripped and fell through a glass door on the opposite side of the foyer. The glass shattered instantly, spraying fragments over Nykyrian. Blood covered him as he tried to stand.

"Stop it, Huwin!" Lady Quiakides put herself between the commander and Nykyrian, who slowly pulled himself up. Panting, he leaned against the door frame with one bloodied hand.

The commander raked her with a furious glower. "Don't get in the way, Terraga. I won't suffer a thief in my home. Ever!"

His wife refused to budge. "Why in the name of the

gods would the hybrid steal the ring of a prince? What would he do with it?"

The hybrid. Not even she had a name for him.

Kiara winced.

"I don't care why he did it. I will not be embarrassed like this. Not after I took his mongrel ass in and fed and clothed it."

Nykyrian stared at the commander without a single tear even though he was bleeding profusely. "I didn't take it, sir. I swear."

The commander grabbed him, shoved him against the wall and started searching through his clothes again.

Terraga pulled her husband back. "He's already been given two full body-cavity searches and everything he had was taken and searched. They found nothing."

"Why would the prince lie?" The commander turned to glare at Nykyrian. "Have you an answer?"

"No, sir."

Aksel snorted. "The animal probably gave it to that girl he has a crush on."

The commander turned to look at Aksel. "What did you say?"

"Ambassador Brill's daughter. I saw them dancing together when the hybrid was supposed to be on watch duty with her."

There was no mistaking the terrified panic on Nykyrian's face.

Or the fury on the commander's. "Leave us!"

Terraga cast a sympathetic glance at Nykyrian before she made her way to the back of the house. Arast and Aksel looked smug and ecstatic as they made their way up the stairs.

Nykyrian stood there with his gaze on the floor while he cradled his left arm against his side, his face impassive. It was as if he knew better than to beg for mercy since there was no way he'd receive any.

"Is that the truth?"

Nykyrian swallowed. "She only wanted someone to dance with her for one song when she had to have an escort. She knew I wouldn't touch her inappropriately. It's the only time I was near her. I swear it." His voice quivered in panic. "I did my job, sir. I protected her and kept my hands to myself."

His face contorted by rage, the commander went to the stand just inside the door where umbrellas and three canes were kept. He picked up the thickest cane and turned back toward Nykyrian, who stiffened in response. He beat the large silver ball against the palm of his hand. "What have I told you?"

"I'm an animal unfit to be in human company."

Those words tore through Kiara as she heard the emptiness in his tone.

"And why do you have no name?"

"I'm not worthy of one."

The commander nodded approvingly. "Get on your knees."

Nykyrian hesitated before he complied. He leaned forward so that he was on all fours while trying to keep his weight off the one injured arm.

The commander brutally let fly the cane across Nykyrian's back. "What else have I told you?"

Nykyrian's voice was taut with pain. "I'm here only by your good grace and I should be grateful for everything you've given a freakish monster like me."

He lashed him again. "And?"

"I will do as I'm told. I will not bring disgrace to you."

"Now repeat it all."

Nykyrian did, but it wasn't enough to save him from

being beaten again and again until he was no longer able to hold himself up.

The commander kicked him over and put his foot on Nykyrian's throat. "I ever find you with a woman again and so help me, I will finish what they started with you in your orphanage. I am not going to suffer another hybrid dog like you to live. If you ever show such a weakness again, I will geld you myself. Do you understand?"

"Yes, sir."

"Now get up and clean this mess. You have twenty minutes." He delivered one last kick before he left him there.

Nykyrian was shaking as he pushed himself up. The commander's wife came in, but said nothing as she watched him clean the mess.

"I can't call a doctor for you. He won't allow it."

Nykyrian inclined his head respectfully. "Thank you, ma'am."

Her eyes were filled with misery as she brushed past him to head upstairs.

Kiara wanted to cry for the sheer agony of his existence. Afraid of the next clip, she pushed the button and held her breath.

This one stunned her so badly she dropped the remote. It was Nykyrian in his mid-twenties. Stark naked. He was in bed with a gorgeous woman. By their flushed skin and ragged breathing, Kiara could tell they'd just had sex.

Lying next to the woman's side, Nykyrian rolled over to touch her arm. She shoved him away. "You can go now."

He frowned. "But I thought—"

"What? That we were going to have a relationship?" She laughed. "I was morbidly curious what it'd be like to sleep with a hybrid. Now I know. You're more human than Andarion—and that's not a compliment. Now get out and if you tell anyone about this, Commander, I'll ruin you. Remember who outranks who."

There was no emotion on his face at all as he left the bed to dress. But his eyes . . .

The hurt there made her want to cry for him.

Kiara bent down to pick up the remote and flip again. This one appeared to go back in time. Nykyrian looked a few years younger than the last one, but it was hard to tell exactly how old. Maybe his late teens. His long hair was braided and he was in full League uniform.

He had that slow methodical walk as he moved in the shadows of a dark alley. It wasn't until he walked under a lamp that she saw why.

He was bleeding profusely. His face and body looked like he'd been on the bad end of a machete.

Pausing, he leaned against the wall. Another shadow moved. Nykyrian spun on it so fast that Kiara couldn't even tell what was happening until he had a smaller teenager on the ground pinned under one knee while he held a knife to the kid's throat.

The boy didn't even flinch as he stared up at him. "Do it," he growled.

Dear God, it was Syn . . .

Nykyrian sat back, releasing him. He pulled his wallet out and threw it at Syn. "Take it. You look like you could use it more than me anyway."

Syn scowled as he held the wallet to his chest and watched him in fear—as if he expected it to be a trick.

Nykyrian moved away and sat down in the shadows.

Syn rolled over, pushed himself to his feet, then started to run away with the wallet in his tight fist. He'd only gone three steps before he stopped to look back at Nykyrian, who now had his eyes closed as blood pooled around him.

The debate in those dark eyes was searing. Finally, Syn slid the wallet into his pocket and went back to Nykyrian. When he reached for Nykyrian, Nykyrian pulled his blaster out and aimed it at his head.

"Get out, rat."

Syn knocked the blaster aside. "You're going to die if you don't get help."

Nykyrian holstered his weapon. "I don't care."

"Normally I wouldn't either, but you bastard, you did me a favor and I don't let those go unanswered. You could have killed me and you didn't. Now get up. I know someone who can help."

Nykyrian, his head tilted back against the wall, just looked at him with a blank expression. "Just take the money and go."

But he didn't.

Instead, Syn helped him to his feet. "C'mon."

Nykyrian hesitated. "Wait . . . My tracer. It fell out of my wrist. I have to have it."

Syn let go of him to pick it up from the ground where it lay covered in blood.

"What are you doing?"

Kiara jumped at Nykyrian's furious snarl, which came from behind her. She'd never heard such a sound from him before. He'd always been so calm, but now . . .

She saw the blood in his eyes as she turned to face him. Heat stung her cheeks at being caught in her snooping.

Rushing forward, Nykyrian cut the power to the viewer. "How dare you!"

She averted her eyes in guilt. "I just wanted to see what you were like as a child. I had no idea . . . I am so sorry."

He ran his hand over his bicep as he continued to glare at her. Kiara could swear his hand trembled.

"Don't you *ever* watch one of my personal files again. I swear to the gods, I'll kill you if you do." He stormed from the room.

Despondency, guilt, and pain for him consumed her as she sat there holding the remote in her hand.

Now she understood only too well why they kept their pasts hidden. She'd only glimpsed a few scenes from his life.

Nykyrian had lived and suffered through those and who knew how many more. Not as a horrified observer, but as the recipient of the pain and hatred of the world. How much more was there and how much worse did it get?

No wonder he'd made the comment about his lover not liking him . . .

Syn had been right. Her pain, severe though it was, didn't compare at all. She'd been sheltered by her parents. Loved. Cherished.

Nykyrian had had no one.

Not even a name.

I condemned him for killing someone who'd tortured him while he'd been powerless to fight back . . .

Someone he'd never hurt even though he should have beat Arast long before today. And the only reason he'd done what he had was to keep her safe.

Having seen what he could really do today, she realized something. The fact that he hadn't tracked Aksel and Arast down and killed them long before now for what they'd done to him . . . that was much more a testament of his character than what he'd done in the hangar bay.

Regret tore through her. *I'm so stupid.* She'd seen his kindness. The way he'd held her when she cried. The way he'd tended her in Syn's apartment.

He wasn't a monster. He was a man who'd been battered by everyone in his life.

I won't be another one.

Drawing a ragged sigh, she went to find him and apologize for everything.

Kiara hesitated in the hallway just before entering the main room.

Nykyrian sat at the desk, holding his head in his hands, looking more miserable than anything she'd ever seen. She glanced around for Syn, but he must have left.

Hesitant over her reception, she moved forward and knelt beside his chair. "I'm so sorry, Nykyrian. I didn't mean to pry."

Nykyrian stared down at her apologetic face and wanted to curse. He couldn't believe she'd found his files. Bitter, agonizing memories tore through him. All the times in his life he'd needed someone to talk to, to hold him, flashed before his mind and he felt like crying.

What was the use?

He was nothing but a piece of shit.

But as he stared at the pain on Kiara's face as she watched him, he didn't see her scorn or condemnation. In her beautiful eyes, he saw the sincere caring he'd always craved.

She looked at him like he was human.

Something inside him shattered under the weight of her expression. How easy it would be to trust just this one person. He wanted to be able to trust someone.

Just once.

But he knew better. Look at what Mara had done to Syn. People weren't trustworthy. They'd kill for a single credit. Would mutilate another person's entire life over something as petty as hurt feelings.

People were vicious and they were cold.

He knew that firsthand and yet he didn't listen to the voice inside him and all the warnings it shouted.

For the first time in his life, he listened to his heart.

And he reached out to touch her.

CHAPTER 16

Nykyrian's hand stopped millimeters from her face.

Kiara knew that he couldn't bring himself to go any further and, having seen the horrors of his past, she finally understood why. Smiling at the gesture, she clasped his gloved hand in both of hers and kissed his fingertips. His hand, which was always so steady, trembled as she held onto it.

A hand that had been damaged so badly by other people's brutality that Nykyrian hadn't even been able to make a fist as a child.

The same hand that had soothed and protected her. That had killed others . . .

A hand he always kept covered . . .

His features unreadable, he laid that hand against her cheek while his thumb stroked her chin. He buried his other hand under her hair, his fingers lightly stroking her scalp, causing chills to form all the way down her body. Desire erupted inside her, and she knew tonight she wouldn't, couldn't, let him go. Not after what she'd seen of his past.

He'd spent his whole life in solitude and for reasons she couldn't even begin to fathom, she cared about him. She wanted to give him what no one had ever given him before. Things that she'd taken for granted her entire life. Things that every being deserved to have.

Someone to hold him when he needed it. Someone who wouldn't judge, betray, or hurt him.

His arms tightened and he pulled her up to his mouth. His lips claimed hers with a passion born of desperate need. Kiara moaned with the pleasure of it as she cupped his face in her hands. She heard his ragged breathing as he gently nipped her lips with his fangs. Opening her mouth, she welcomed him.

He slid from his chair, his hands working magic on her body. Everywhere he touched, she burned, aching for more. Her heart thundered as she ran her hands down the soft silk of his shirt, delighting in the way his hard muscles flexed beneath her fingertips.

She wanted him more than she had ever wanted anything.

Nykyrian buried his lips against Kiara's neck, finally inhaling the sweet fragrance of her exotic perfume. She was so soft and warm. So very beautiful. And the way she held him . . .

Like he mattered.

In this one moment, he didn't feel like a freak. Surely she wouldn't touch someone who was. He laid his cheek against her so that he could feel the warmth of her as her breath tingled his skin. He shook with the force of his need and lost himself in the first true bliss he could recall ever feeling.

Her precious arms held him to her in a tender embrace. Desire surged through his veins like liquid fire. He clung to her, needing her, wanting her.

Chills formed under the heat of her hands across his back. He gasped as her tongue played along the tendons of his neck, her teeth gently nipping. He closed his eyes to the sensation.

Reclaiming her lips, he kissed her deeply.

Kiara's body throbbed in an aching need that demanded the feel of his naked body against hers. She ran her fingers under the collar of his shirt, but that didn't appease her, it only whet her appetite more.

She moaned as he moved his hand over her breast, down her stomach, and underneath the hem of her dress. Chills formed beneath his gloved hand as he stroked the skin of her stomach. Kiara kissed him fiercely, wanting to keep him with her.

Nykyrian growled at how good she tasted. For the first time in his life, he felt desired.

Wanted.

It's a lie . . .

Don't you dare buy it.

I was morbidly curious what it'd be like to sleep with a hybrid. Tasha's cold words tore through him.

You're a freak. I wish I'd never touched you. You ever tell anyone what happened and I'll have you killed! He winced at the memory of Driana's last words to him.

Pulling away, he looked down at Kiara and saw the same desire they'd held . . .

But it wasn't real. He was well aquainted with this game. He'd played it enough and lost to know better than to even try his hand. She was no different than they were. Today had proven that.

You're shit and shit is all you'll ever be. Not even your own mother could bear to look at you.

Leave her now before she turns you into the same drunken waste Syn has become.

Unable to bear anymore, he rose and moved away from her. His breath came in labored gasps. He stared at Kiara's confused expression, his cock aching in painful arousal. All he wanted was to feel her body against his, but it wasn't worth the pain that would come later when she kicked him out of her bed and told him she didn't want anyone to know what they'd done.

He would *never* do that to himself again. Better to jack off than be hurt.

"I'm sorry."

Kiara blinked, his apology confusing her more than his sudden retreat. "For what?"

He turned away and brushed his hand through his hair. "I had no right to touch you. Forgive me, princess."

Kiara's heart lurched at his pain-filled words.

Walking to him, she ran her hand over his back. "You have more right than anyone else." She gripped his upper arm and turned him around to face her. When she reached up to remove his shades, he dodged her hand.

Disheartened, but determined, she ran her hand down his cheek, her palm scraped by his whiskers. "I want you, Nykyrian."

He tore away from her as if her touch burned him. "You pity me. I don't need it, or want it."

The anger in his tone set fire to her own. "Don't tell me what I feel." She crossed the floor to stand in front of him again.

Once more he tried to move away, but she grabbed his arm and kept him by her side. "You can't walk away from me, I won't let you."

His jaw tensed. "Maybe I don't want you."

One corner of her mouth lifted. She remembered the number of discs in his cabinet of her performances, the look on his face as he reached out to her just moments ago. "If that were true, you would stay still and not keep moving away from me. Face it, soldier, you want me more than anything." She looked down and gave a pointed stare at the part of his body that showed her exactly how interested he was. "Your lips can deny it all they want, but *that* says it all."

He shrugged her touch away. "You don't want me. Not really. I'm just a morbid curiosity to you and nothing more." He grabbed his long, black coat from the couch where he'd draped it. "You're safe here. I'll be back in a little while."

Desperation filled her. If he left without this settled, she knew he would be gone from her forever. "By God, hybrid," she shouted. "Don't you dare walk away from me!"

The murderous look he gave her when he turned around caused her to take a step back. He clenched his hand at his side and she had the distinct feeling he wanted to kill her. "Don't you *ever* call me that again."

Kiara gave him no quarter as she closed the distance between them. "I thought soldiers were trained to meet conflict, not run from it. What is it about me that frightens you so?"

He didn't answer.

Kiara wanted to scream in frustration.

"I'll be back later." In a single graceful move, he flared his coat out and put it on before he headed for the door.

In that moment, she had total clarity as she realized he'd quoted the bitch in the video to her. *I'm just a morbid curiosity to you.*

That was it . . . That was why he was running from her. He thought she'd do him the same way his commanding officer had done. That she'd kick him out of bed the moment they were through and tell him to keep his mouth shut.

Her heart splintered with the thought of all the needless and cruel pain and rejection he'd carried throughout his life. Pain she wanted to soothe and banish. "Why do you think you can't be loved?"

He froze with his back to her.

"That's it, isn't it? That's why you live here, light-years away from everyone. Why you don't even trust your best friend. You've closed yourself off from everyone and everything to the point you can't even touch me." She closed the distance between them and put her hand on his shoulder. "I won't hurt you, Nykyrian. I'm not like those others."

He looked at her over his shoulder. "I'm not blind, princess. I saw the look on your face today when I reached for a towel to help you. I disgust you. You can't deny it. You *are* just like everyone else who's ever looked at me."

She shook her head. "You don't disgust me, Nykyrian, and that's the truth. You learned to forgive Hauk for hurting you. Can you not forgive me, too?"

She ran her hand down his arm, to his wrist where his League tattoo began. "What you did today hurt *me*. It made me remember things from my past that I didn't want to—it shoved them straight into my face and it took me time to separate those monsters who killed my mother and shot me from the man you are." Wrapping her arms around his lean waist, she pressed her front against his back and laid her head against his spine. "Let me love you tonight, Nykyrian. Just once."

Nykyrian couldn't breathe as he heard words he'd never thought to hear. And when combined with her embrace . . .

It shattered his defenses.

Leave. Now. Before it's too late.

But he didn't want to. He wanted to be held. Just once. To make love to a woman who didn't stare at him like he was a foreign species. To have a woman see him as he was.

Acceptance.

Was that too much to ask?

Nykyrian turned around slowly as he ignored every single piece of common sense he had. He cupped her face in his hand as he tried to discern the truth in her eyes.

Will you betray me, too?

How could she not?

He was so battered from his life. He didn't know if he was strong enough to take another blow.

Dare he take the chance?

Kiara struggled to breathe as she realized her words had somehow made it through his defensive core. He was standing his ground.

Reaching up, she touched his shades.

He didn't move away.

Her hand trembling, she pulled them off so that she could stare into those beautiful, green, human eyes that laid bare his own fears and uncertainties. The soul she saw there wasn't frightening or cruel. It was the soul of a man who'd been thrown away one time too many.

She cupped his face in her hand and offered him the smile he deserved.

Nykyrian drew her into his arms, crushing her against him as he kissed her breathless. She could feel the pounding beat of his heart against her chest while his warmth surrounded her. And she never wanted to leave this spot of paradise. Here, in the arms of the most dangerous being in the universe, she was safe.

She nipped at his lips and smiled up at him. "Let me love you, Nykyrian. Let me prove to you that I'm not one of the monsters in this world."

Nykyrian couldn't breathe as she whispered those

precious words to him. No one had ever offered him such kindness before. Scared and unsure, he saw the sincerity in her amber eyes.

Please don't be lying to me . . .

Before he could stop himself, he tightened his arms around her, picked her up from the floor, and headed for the stairs.

Kiara gasped in terror at what he was doing. "Your wound. You're going to hurt yourself."

"Believe me, princess, right now the only pain I feel is the one in my groin."

As soon as they were in his room, he tossed her on the huge black bed. Kiara barely had time to blink before he stretched out on top of her, pinning her to the mattress. As he stared into her eyes, she realized just how heavy he was.

She wrinkled her nose as she struggled to breathe. "No offense, sweetie, but you weigh a ton . . . And you're crushing me."

He hissed as he pulled away from her. "It's the coat. Sorry. I forget how heavy it is." He shrugged it off and it landed on the floor with a most disconcerting thud.

Her eyes widened at the sound. How did he wear that thing without being hunchback from the weight? "Should I even ask?"

He stepped back, his face instantly apprehensive as if she'd struck a sour chord.

Kiara tsked at him as she rose up on her knees and reached for his belt. Pulling him closer to her, she removed it and tried not to think about the weapons fastened to it. "I know what you do, Nykyrian. I saw it today and I'm not afraid now." She let the belt and holsters fall to the floor.

That made him step back. "I don't like being unarmed."

She scoffed at him. "You think I can hurt you?"

He swallowed as he placed one hand on her shoulder so that he could play with her earlobe. He stared at her as if he were searching her soul to find the truth of her character. "If we go through with this, Kiara, you will live in a place inside me where only you *can* do me harm. And if you plan to savage me the same way Mara did Syn, then I hope you're woman enough to kill me instead of leaving me like him."

She took his hand into hers and placed a kiss on his gloved knuckles. "I won't do that to you. I swear."

Nykyrian flinched as she started tugging at his glove. He balled his hand into a fist. "Don't. I'll take them off later."

But she didn't listen. Instead, she uncurled his fingers one by one. "I want to see."

He ground his teeth as he forced himself to endure this. It'd been almost twenty years since he last touched a woman. Twenty long, *hard* years.

Please don't reject me.

He held his breath, waiting for her to cringe as she uncovered his scarred hands and laid them bare. His hands were hideous and no woman wanted him to touch her once she saw them. Not that he blamed them for that. He couldn't stand to look at his hands either. It was why he always wore gloves.

But for her curiosity, he endured this humiliation.

Kiara forced herself not to react as she saw what had been done to him. Each fingernail had been torn out, leaving behind a twisted nail bed that looked as if someone had fused or cauterized it to keep the nail from growing back. The two middle fingers were twisted from all the injuries that had been done to them and his entire hand was scarred from wounds she could only guess at.

Meeting his gaze, she brought his hand to her lips and kissed each scar.

Nykyrian shook as she did what no one ever had. And when she kissed his palm . . . He was lost to her now. He would never again have any power over her.

She owned a part of him that he hadn't even known he possessed any longer.

His bloody heart.

She reached for his other hand and repeated the same slow, methodical torture. How was she able to do it? To touch and kiss something so sickening?

Hands that had taken so many lives . . .

Surely if she could ignore that, there was hope that she could . . .

Don't even go there.

But he couldn't help himself. She awakened things within him that he'd buried so long ago he'd forgotten about them. Needs that he wanted to deny.

She was beauty personified and he was all that was ugly in the universe.

When she got to the sheaths on his arms, she hesitated. "Are these spring-loaded?"

Nodding, he pulled them off so that they wouldn't accidentally hurt her. Next he removed the ones on his biceps.

She laughed. "It's like disarming the entire League West Fleet."

One corner of his mouth twitched. Until she started unbuttoning his shirt.

Kiara licked her lips as she uncovered more and more of his deep, tawny flesh. Scars sliced through every part of him.

How had he withstood it all? His strength amazed her, especially when she pulled the shirt off and saw the whole of his League tattoo. Bright ink covered his arm from wrist to shoulder. Black, burgundy, dark green, white, and yellow. The colors of the skull, daggers, and bone blended together in a work of art. Grisly and harsh, it was designed to inspire fear.

And that it did to anyone who saw it. The mark of a Command Assassin of the First Order.

The deadliest of them all.

Her heart breaking, she leaned forward to kiss the dagger's hilt.

Nykyrian sucked his breath in sharply at the tenderness of her touch. Wanting to please her, he reached for her dress.

Her cheeks turned bright pink as if she were suddenly embarrassed and shy.

"Do you want me to darken the room?" he asked.

"Please."

He reached for the control on the table next to his bed.

Kiara bit her lip as the lights went low and the ceiling above her head faded to transparency. A thousand stars twinkled brightly, their light bathing the room in a soft, white glow. "It looks like a dream," she whispered, awed by the beauty. "No wonder you like it here."

He sat down on the side of the bed and pulled his boots off. "They're not half as beautiful as you are."

His voice was so low, Kiara wondered if he'd said it, or if she'd imagined it. She leaned against his bare back. His sharp intake of breath brought a smile to her face. She ran her hands down his arms, delighting in the sensation of his muscles bunching and relaxing under her hands as she laid her cheek against the bones of his spine.

He smelled of leather and man. A heady concoction that made her want to breathe him in forever.

Suddenly, all four lorinas hit the bed at once. The biggest one butted at Kiara, trying to separate her from Nykyrian.

Nykyrian mumbled a curse. "Pixley, down!"

Kiara stroked the smallest one behind the ears as it nuzzled her. "What are their names?"

Nykyrian was trying to regain control of them. "The one you're petting is Ilyse, Pixley is the biggest, Ulf is the one with the white patch and the other is Centara." He wrestled them out of the room, then locked the door. "And stay out, you little beasts."

Kiara laughed. "How long have you had them?"

"Eight years." He started undoing his pants.

Shyness overcame her—she'd never seen a naked man in the flesh before. Her mouth dried at the expanse of tanned skin she wanted to run her hands and tongue across. He left his pants on and undone as he loosened his hair and shook it free to fall around his wide shoulders.

The bed dipped under his weight again as he returned to her side. He stretched out beside her, his head propped on his hand as he studied her with an intensity she found unsettling.

Kiara mimicked the gesture.

After several seconds, he reached his hand out and touched her hair, spreading it out along the black fur covers.

She reached out to finger the harsh scars on his face where the mask had been. She desperately wanted to ask him why they'd done that to him as a child, but didn't want to bring up a topic she knew would only hurt him.

In spite of all the scars crossing his flesh, she thought Nykyrian had the best body she'd ever seen. She touched the deepest scar that ran along his collarbone, just above the tattoo. It looked as if something had dug a huge claw into his neck. Sadness welled up in her throat, choking her as she thought of all the pain he'd suffered in his life.

Nykyrian pulled his hand away from her hair. "You've changed your mind."

The despondency in his voice wrenched her stomach. "No," she whispered.

He frowned, smoothing a curl from her cheek, stroking her cheekbone with his thumb. "You look so sad."

She held his hand to her cheek, reveling in the feel of his calloused palm against her skin. She moved his hand to her lips and kissed his scarred knuckles. "I wish I could take away your pain. I wish I could go back to when you were born and take you somewhere safe. Far away from all the people who've hurt you."

His eyes were liquid emeralds. "You're doing that now." He leaned forward and kissed her lips.

Kiara welcomed the feel of him pressing her down on the mattress. He was still heavy, but this time the weight was not only tolerable, it was wonderful.

His lips traveled over her body, blazing a trail of fire everywhere they touched.

He lifted the hem of her dress and placed a kiss on her bared stomach. Kiara clutched his head to her in dizzy ecstasy that overrode her shyness as he scraped her skin with his fangs and whiskers. He removed her dress and let it fall to the floor. She watched him explore her body, each nerve alive and attuned to him. She laughed and jerked as his lips and whiskers tickled her flesh.

He locked gazes with her before leaving her and removing his pants.

She trailed her gaze down his magnificent body, warmth singing her cheeks. He was extremely large and frightening. Yet she knew he would never hurt her.

Not intentionally.

Curious about his body which was so different from her own, Kiara leaned over him and ran her hand down the scars of his chest to the small trail of hair below his navel. Smiling, she nipped at the skin of his hard stomach, taking care not to hurt the injury that was still heartbreakingly obvious.

She was the cause of that. For her, he'd been wounded . . .

He closed his eyes and drew a ragged breath. When her hand moved lower to touch his swollen shaft, he gasped.

"You're mine now," she said devilishly, nibbling his hipbone. "I'll never let go of you."

Nykyrian couldn't think rationally as she hesitantly stroked and tongued him. It'd been so long since anyone other than him had touched his cock. He'd forgotten how good it felt. In The League, they were forbidden to take lovers—not that they always listened. But to be caught was to be punished severely.

He'd only been with two women before her and only one time each. Neither experience had gone well for him.

But they had never made him feel like Kiara did. Nor had they explored him so fully. A quick groping and a bungled coupling, then it was over and he was humiliated.

He'd been nothing to them except a passing curiosity. To Kiara, he was a man, and the care in her touch branded him. The difference was astounding.

Most of all, it was incredible.

Needing more of her, he reached around to open her bra.

Kiara's breath caught as he moved his hands over her exposed breasts. Sharp heat pulsed in her veins until she wanted to shout with the bittersweet ache.

His mouth replaced his hands on her breasts and his

warm breath drove her to an even dizzier height. She leaned her head back, surrendering herself to him completely. His strong, warm hands circled her waist and roamed up her spine.

Gently, he leaned her back against the mattress, his kiss deepening. Kiara twined her fingers in the soft strands of white hair, holding him to her.

His eyes blazing, Nykyrian pulled away and removed her panties, exposing her completely. A shiver went over her as she fought an urge to cover herself. No doubt he'd take that the wrong way and she wanted nothing as trivial as modesty to destroy what they were sharing.

"What are you thinking?" She smoothed the frown on his face.

"How frail you are. I don't want to hurt you by accident."

She smiled at him. "I'm not as frail as I appear. I know from lots of experience that I bounce really well."

He laid his fingers against her cheekbone before he placed a tender kiss there. "I would kill anyone who hurt you."

"I know." He already had, and instead of scaring or repulsing her, she took comfort in that fact.

For the first time in her entire life, she felt safe. This was the one person no one could get through to reach her. Nykyrian would always keep her safe.

Kiara kissed him with all her passion and spread her legs as his hand skimmed along the inside of her thigh. When he touched the part of her that craved him, she groaned in pleasure.

Nykyrian buried his lips in the crook of her neck as he felt how wet she was for him. The heat of her skin scorched him. Nervous and unsure, he moved to cover her with his body.

Had he waited long enough? Had he pleased her

enough? He had so little experience with women that he wasn't sure. He would ask her, but he didn't want her to mock him for his ineptitude.

I forgot how bad assassins suck in bed. Nice to know you're no exception.

He flinched at words that still haunted him. Would Kiara mock him, too?

But as he looked into her eyes, he saw her tenderness. No one had ever looked at him like that before.

Like she cared.

She nipped at his chin as her arms held him close. There was a connection in this moment that he'd never known. He took her hand in his and laced their fingers together.

Kissing her lips, he drove himself home and hissed at how good she felt.

Kiara gasped at the sudden pain that ripped through her pleasure as he entered her. It was raw and biting, and it was all she could do not to cry out loud.

Nykyrian went rigidly still. Releasing her hand, he leaned back on one arm to stare down at her. "You're a virgin?"

"Not anymore."

He started to move away, but she wrapped her body around his and kept him in place.

"Stay with me, Nykyrian. Let me love you tonight."

A tic started in his jaw and, for a moment, she feared he would leave her, as he avoided meeting her gaze.

"I want you." She cupped his face in her hands and forced him to look at her. "I see you, Nykyrian, and I want to be with you. In all the universe, you are the only one who makes me feel like this. Don't walk away. Please."

Nykyrian was terrified by those words. How could

she say that to him? Now he totally understood Syn's stupidity.

Even when it was bad, it was good.

He had no right to be with her. No right to touch her. Except for the fact that she wanted him . . .

She kissed his lips and shattered the last shred of his resistance. Slowly, he began to rock his hips against hers. "Tell me if it hurts."

Kiara reveled in the feeling of his cheek against hers as he made love to her as if she were the most precious thing he'd ever touched. In all her dreams and fantasies, she'd never imagined anything more wonderful than the way he felt inside her.

After a time, the pain ebbed and was replaced by a new pleasure. She breathed heavily as he moved even faster and she met his strokes, driving him even deeper into her body. She ran her hands over his shoulders, feeling the strength of him as he pleased her.

He was hers and she intended to keep him with her no matter what.

A new demand built inside her. Kiara rocked her hips against his. She matched his rhythm, amazed at the sharp, intensifying pleasure. Just when she thought she couldn't stand anymore, her world exploded into a titillation she'd never dreamed of.

Nykyrian buried his face in her hair and joined her release. He breathed in the sweet fragrance of the silken strands. Her soft arms and legs wrapped tightly around him, obliterating all the pain in his soul. Her hand played in his hair, holding him against her.

He lay there unable to believe it was real. That someone could hold him like this . . .

The fact that it was a woman he'd been longing for all these years . . .

He expected to wake at any moment and find himself alone and that the entire night had been nothing more than a cruel dream. But then he wondered if the reality of this night would be even more cruel than the dream itself.

Because in the end, he knew this couldn't last. Any minute she'd curse him for this.

"Why?" he breathed against her cheek.

"Why what?"

"Why did you sleep with me?"

Kiara heard the pain in that simple question. "I care about you."

He withdrew from her and left her feeling suddenly cold as he rolled to his back. "You don't even know me."

She rose up to look down at him. "That's not true. I've seen the beauty inside you. The part of you that protects your friends even while you expect treachery from them. The part of you that hides from the world."

Kiara ran her hand through his soft hair . . . It and his lips were the only parts of him that weren't as hard as steel. "It's weird. I went through a period in finishing school where I wanted to lose my virginity at any cost, but every time I started to go through with it, I couldn't bring myself to squander it on boys who didn't really care about me." But she knew Nykyrian wouldn't take it for granted or brag about this.

She meant something to him. She knew it.

"So you squandered it on me?"

She screwed her face up in anger over his even thinking that for a second. "Of course not. I gave you what I've never given to anyone because you deserve to have something uniquely yours. I wanted you to know how much I care about you and I couldn't think of a better way."

He scoffed at her. "A thank you card would have sufficed."

She gaped at his random oddity. "A thank you card?"

He shrugged. "No one's ever given me one of those either and it would have been less painful for you."

She punched playfully at his stomach for that. "You're awful."

He pulled her into his arms and held her close. Kiara listened to his heartbeat as she lay her head on his chest, wishing she knew a way to really reach him.

For now, she would give him what she could and hope that one day soon he would realize she could be trusted inside his comfortable world of solitude.

CHAPTER 17

Nykyrian watched the sky lighten. Kiara, still asleep, snored softly beside him as she lay tucked in his arms. He'd been here for hours, watching her sleep, feeling the warmth of her body tucked into his.

The scent of her skin hung heavy in his nostrils while he ran his hand down her silken arm in a tender caress. Her rear pressed against his cock which was already swollen again.

But he'd hurt her enough. He wouldn't press her for anymore.

He took her hand into his and studied the perfection of her fingers compared to the ugliness of his own. Her nails were polished and dainty. Beautiful.

His stomach lurched as he remembered them tearing his nails out when his mother's men had dumped him in the human orphanage. After that, they'd dipped his fingers in acid to keep his Andarion claws from growing back.

You won't be hurting any of our children, you fucking animal!

He'd fought as hard as he could, but it hadn't been enough. They'd held him down and put that damned mask over his face to keep him from being able to bite. Then he'd been chained down in the bathroom, naked, and kept there for years, until the commander's wife had seen him.

He could still see her looking at him as he cowered in the corner, ready to strike out at her if she attacked him like the others had done repeatedly over the years. Even on that day, he'd had one broken arm from an attack the night before—one of the guards had a sister who'd been killed by an Andarion. So the guard had used Nykyrian as the scapegoat for the Andarion's action and the guard's fury. The guard had beaten him so badly that his face was still burning. His back and arms . . . and other things he didn't want to think about.

All he'd wanted was to be left alone in his pain to heal. It was why he'd been laying on his stomach on the floor when she'd entered the facilities as part of a charity tour.

The moment they'd come in, he'd forced himself to sit up in spite of the pain and hide as best he could in the far corner of the last stall. He'd stared out from under his matted hair and held the chains around his wrists to try and keep them from making a noise that would betray him. If he was as still as possible, hopefully they'd ignore him and go away.

But the commander's wife had drawn closer to him.

"Don't get too close, mistress. He's an Andarion and prone to attack."

She'd frowned at the shackles on his ankles and wrists. "Why is he chained so?"

"To protect the children. We don't know what he's capable of, so we make sure there's no way for him to harm them."

Terraga had tilted her head to watch him. "He doesn't look dangerous."

"Trust me, he is. Vicious. We even use a pole to push his food near him when he's fed at night."

Nykyrian had scoffed at the caretaker's words. Fed? The leftover, half-eaten scraps were bad enough, the fact that they usually spat in them before they handed them over was worse.

As for water . . .

He looked at the toilets where he was forced to find drink. Like an animal.

No, even animals were treated better than he was.

The commander's wife had pulled back in horror. "You feed him here in the bathroom?"

"Of course. He's not allowed to leave."

Nykyrian had glanced up at the window not far from him. When no one was in here, he'd crawl over to it and lay his head on the sill so that he could look outside and pretend he wasn't locked away in here. That was his only contact with the outside world and he was grateful his chains were long enough to allow him that one small freedom.

Terraga turned back toward him with sadness in her eyes as the commander joined her in the doorway.

He'd taken one look at Nykyrian and curled his lip in disgust. "What are you doing?"

She pointed at Nykyrian. "I want to adopt him."

Huwin's snarl had only grown more severe. "It's pathetic and weak. Look at it." The commander had moved forward to kick him.

Unwilling to be hit without returning the blow, Nykyrian had lunged at the commander with everything he had.

Huwin had laughed as he brought him down hard on the tiled floor. Nykyrian had screamed out in rage as he did his best to break free. But it was no use. He was too weak and injured.

The commander picked him up again and slammed him so hard against the floor that it'd dazed him. "You do have spirit, don't you?" He grabbed Nykyrian's face to examine it. "Not a single tear." A cruel smile had twisted his lips. "We'll take him. Have him cleaned and brought to my ship."

Nykyrian winced as more memories surged. He hated to think of the past. To remember. There was nothing there even remotely pleasurable.

He leaned his head against Kiara's hair and inhaled her scent that drove away those horrors. She was the beauty that had been missing for so long from his world.

And he never wanted to let her go.

Unfortunately, he couldn't stay here in bed with her much longer. He didn't want to move, but he had too many things to do to lie in bed while she kept sleeping. As gently as he could, he pulled her arms away from him and slid out of bed.

He watched Kiara situate herself on the mattress, her hips wiggling provocatively. A smile played at the edges of his mouth. He covered her with a sheet, then darkened the ceiling against the dawning sun.

Kiara was beautiful in his bed. And the memory of her touch was branded into his soul.

Reluctantly, he moved to the bathroom to shower. Over and over, he castigated himself for what he'd done last night. It was so wrong to touch her. She belonged to the day, to warmth and sunshine. Her world was light and wonderful, filled with love and laughter.

And he was born of night. His mother was the darkness, her cold embrace was all he had a right to crave. Just as the sun destroyed the night, he was sure she would destroy him, provided their enemies didn't kill her first.

He refused to watch her die.

A lump burned raw in his throat. He would treasure

the memory of last night forever, but that would be all.

She would have to be returned to her father before she did any more damage to him. Holding that close, he quickly bathed, dressed, and headed downstairs without looking at her tempting form.

The lorinas assailed him downstairs, unhappy about being banned from his room. Nykyrian grabbed a glass of juice and headed to his work. Switching on the monitor, he ran his hand through his wet hair. Without paying much attention, he scanned the new contracts.

He drank his juice and switched the screen to the most recent contracts.

He choked.

No fucking way . . .

He reached for his link.

It took several nerve-wrenching minutes before Syn answered with a menacing curse. "I told you Hauk, I'm not going. You can roast your overgrown—"

"Syn, it's me."

Nykyrian heard a yawn over the link. "Damn it, Kip. Have you any idea what time it is here? Unlike you, I do need to sleep, and damn it, my head hurts. Tell me again how being sober is good for me?"

Nykyrian didn't bother answering his question. "Zamir has issued a death contract on both of us. Clear your flat and get here immediately."

"Bullshit. I clear my space for nothing. Be damned if some half-wit politician is going to drive me into hiding."

"What about Aksel or Shahara? They're the names signed on your contract."

He heard Syn knock something off his bedside table, no doubt bolting upright in shock. "Shahara Dagan?"

"Yeah."

Syn cursed again. "Does Caillen know his sister's coming after us?"

"I doubt it. But it doesn't matter. I need you to get information about the two of them and where they're living. ASAP. As much money as Zamir's offered, and after I terminated Arast, Aksel's not going to stop until my brains are in his trophy jar."

"Yeah, no kidding. I'll be there shortly."

Nykyrian tossed the link away and reread the contract. It made all the other offers on his life look like jokes. Zamir had given his enemies full immunity from any prosecution, which meant they could forget League rules and come after him unbarred.

That was all Aksel needed. Now Kiara was in more danger than ever before. Her father had to have the IQ of a half-formed zygote to do something this stupid.

How the hell did someone so fucking dumb run a government?

What was he supposed to do now?

"With a frown like that, you could frighten small children and elders," Kiara said, startling him.

He flipped the screen off before she could see it, then turned in his chair to see her approach. The sight of her in his black shirt with her shapely legs bared made him instantly hard. God, she looked good in his clothes. "I didn't know you were awake."

Kiara was puzzled by his distant mood. Worse, his shades and gloves were back in place. What would it take to make him set them aside even in his own home?

Feeling sexier than she ever had before, she slid into his lap, half expecting him to stop her. He didn't. With his usual stoicism, he watched her every move.

She straddled his hips and pulled the shades off before placing them on his desk.

For once he didn't protest.

She ran one hand over his jaw and smiled at him. "Is something wrong?"

His eyes dark, he traced the dip in her shirt to touch the small valley between her breasts. "Your father wants me dead."

Her mouth dropped in shock. He had to be kidding. But with his deadpan tone it was hard to tell. "What?"

Nykyrian turned his monitor on and pointed to it. "For that amount of money, I'm tempted to turn myself in and collect it."

Kiara tensed. "You're not funny," she snapped, unable to believe her father would be so ruthless. The contract detailed how her father wanted Nykyrian executed in minute description. "How could he do such a thing?"

Nykyrian looked at her, his eyes blank as he skimmed his hands up her thighs. "He's worried about you. Given the condition we left your flat in yesterday, who knows what he thinks has happened to you? I'd want the balls of the man who took my daughter, too."

She narrowed her eyes at him as she reached for his link. Frowning, she tried to dial her father, but Nykyrian's set was unlike anything she'd ever seen before. She handed it to him. "How do you use this?"

"He's not going to listen."

"I have to try."

The look on his face was one of priceless disbelief as he tuned the link in. "Nykyrian Quiakides to speak to his excellency."

Kiara knew the moment her father took the line.

Nykyrian snatched the piece away from his ear.

"You fucking whoreson! I want my daughter back right now! Do you hear me, you freak?"

Her heart wrenched at the insults and threats that

Nykyrian didn't even react to. Taking the link from his gloved hand, she held it close enough to her ear to hear words she'd never heard her father use before, but far enough away that he didn't damage her hearing with his shouts.

"Papa?"

He stopped midstream. "Angel?"

She put the piece in her ear. "Hey, Daddy, it's me."

"Are you all right?"

"I'm fine, but I don't understand what's going on. Nykyrian—"

"Nemesis signed the contract for your life yesterday. The Sentella is against you."

Kiara's throat closed in shock. "What?"

"They've turned and I have to get you away from them before they hurt you."

She scowled at his words as she looked at Nykyrian. "No, I don't believe it."

A tic worked in Nykyrian's jaw. "Because it's not true. Nemesis didn't sign shit yesterday—he wasn't even near a computer."

She'd forgotten about his sharp hearing as her father warned her about their ferocity.

Her father didn't take his words well. "Let me speak to that freak. Now."

"He's not a freak, Papa."

"You don't know his kind the way I do. Now put him on."

Kiara held the link toward him.

Nykyrian took it. "Is this going to be productive, or are you just going to insult me some more?"

"Listen to me, you little prick. I don't know what game you're playing, but if you harm so much as one hair on her head, I will torture you in ways you can't imagine."

He had to bite his tongue to keep from scoffing at that ludicrous threat.

"If you return her in the next two hours, I'll rescind the contracts."

"If I return her in the next two hours, she'll be dead before the third one. I don't think you understand what—"

"You're the one who doesn't understand, hybrid freak. I will spare no resources bringing you in."

Nykyrian rolled his eyes. "And I will not see your daughter dead because her father's a first-rank moron."

"Bring her back! Now!"

"Fuck you, asshole." He hung up the link.

Kiara gave him an irritated glare.

"What?" he asked innocently.

"That wasn't helpful. Why did you say that to him?"

Nykyrian sputtered in indignation. "He's the one wanting my balls cut off."

"Nykyrian! You didn't help me calm him down."

"He's not going to calm down until you're back with him, and you know what I do . . . Aksel won't stop just because he rescinds the contract on me. His brother died because of you. Believe me, I know how he thinks and I know how he acts. The only hope you have is to stay with me."

"And if I stay with you, my father will kill you. I don't want you hurt because of me."

"He's not going to kill me, Kiara. Better men than him have tried and I'm still here."

She cupped his face in her hands and leaned her forehead against his. "You are the most stubborn man I've ever met."

"I pale in comparison to you." He ran his hands up under her shirt to cup her bottom and scoot her closer.

His lips claimed hers with a heat so hot, she melted.

The sound of an engine outside in the bay broke them apart.

"Syn," Nykyrian sighed as he pulled away. "I told him to stay here until we sort this out." His gaze went over her, making her hot. "You'd better get dressed."

She nodded before she scooted off his lap. He reached for his shades and replaced them.

"Nykyrian?" She waited until he looked at her. "I don't want anything to happen to you."

"Feeling's mutual."

She heard Syn cursing outside. With one last glance his way, she rushed up the stairs to get dressed before Syn saw her near-naked state.

Syn came through the door with enough anger to fuel the energy source of a small planet. "I want blood!" He stalked over to where Nykyrian sat at his desk. "Two of Aksel's dogs cornered me near Tondara. They shot me," he growled incredulously. "Those bastards actually shot a hole in my stabilizer the size of Mirala."

Nykyrian just stared at him.

"Aren't you going to say something?"

"Were you hurt?"

Syn shifted, some of his anger diminishing. "No."

"Then why are you having a fit?"

Syn laughed. "I don't know, it just felt right. You see why I don't like being sober? I overreact like an old woman." He opened his flask, then slammed it down on Nykyrian's desk. "Figures the damned thing would be empty."

Nykyrian shook his head at him. "Was there much damage done to your ship?"

Syn moved to stand behind Nykyrian so that he could read over his shoulder. "No, not really. Just enough to seriously piss me off and ruin my suckass day." He let out a low whistle as he scanned the contract for them. "Geez," he breathed. "He's not playing around with that, is he?"

"No, he's not."

Crossing his arms over his chest, Syn moved away. "So what are we going to do about it? My vote is we terminate the *gratter*."

Nykyrian gave him a menacing glare.

"What the hell is that look for? You finally grow a conscience?"

"No, but we can't go around assassinating respected officials."

Syn snorted as his anger snapped even more. He was tired of being hunted and playing these stupid political games. "I think we should forget this protection crap and jettison her royal pain in the ass back on a remote shuttle." He moved to lay down on one of the sofas.

The door upstairs opened. The softened look on Nykyrian's face as he stared up at the dancer made Syn grind his teeth. He glanced up from the couch and caught Kiara's blush, and in that moment, he knew what the two of them had been up to. "Please, by all the blessed saints and their bladders, tell me you two didn't . . ."

Nykyrian shot him a lethal glare.

Kiara's blush deepened.

His stomach churned to the point he thought he'd vomit. Syn slung his legs over the couch and moved back to where Nykyrian sat. "Have you lost all semblance of intelligence?"

Nykyrian came to his feet and Syn recognized the angry twitch in his jaw. "It's none of your concern."

Clenching his teeth, Syn backed down even though he wanted to beat his friend until he saw reason. "Fine. Whatever."

Nykyrian pulled his coat off the couch and shrugged it on. "Kiara and I have a few things to do this morning. I need you to stay here and work on locating Aksel and Shahara. When I get back, we'll repair your ship."

Syn ground his teeth even harder, wanting to say a million things that would only cause Nykyrian to shoot him. He'd been in those shoes, and he knew exactly how stupid Kip was being, and he knew his friend would never listen to reason.

No more than he had.

Damn it to hell.

"Fine. I need a new plate for my rear thruster."

"No problem." Nykyrian headed up the stairs. "I need to change, then we'll leave."

Syn turned his glare to Kiara. *Yeah, you better put on something armored, you stupid son of a bitch.*

Too bad he hadn't kept it around his heart.

I expected better from you. Having seen the hell Mara had put him through, he couldn't believe Kip didn't have better sense. Why? Why? Why?

After a few seconds, Nykyrian called down to him. "I need you to find an address for Aksel's wife. Her name is Driana Bredeh. She should be in the Solaras System."

Syn frowned. "When did he get married?"

Nykyrian didn't answer.

Kiara walked around the couch, a strange look on her face as she neared him. "Why does Aksel hate Nykyrian so?"

Syn shrugged. "Hell if I know." He glanced upstairs, wondering if Nykyrian could hear him. Maliciously, he decided he didn't care and continued, "Huwin found Nykyrian in an orphanage. From the moment they met, Aksel hated him. Then when Nykyrian graduated top of his class and went into The League as the youngest commissioned officer in history, Aksel couldn't take it. He's been mental toward him ever since."

Kiara opened her mouth to ask him another question, but Nykyrian returned.

Syn recognized the warning glower on Kip's face that he should keep his mouth shut around Kiara. Yeah, and someone should keep his dick in his pants. A vengeful smile curved his lips as he silently dared him to say anything.

At least Nykyrian wore his usual street clothes. The long black coat that concealed his weapons, his shades, and the silver-inlaid boots with retractable blades.

In those clothes, his friend was a virtual tank.

He knew Nykyrian could take care of himself, but he still wished Kip would see reason and stop this crap with Kiara before it was too late for all of them.

Nykyrian held his hand out to Kiara and Syn cursed under his breath as she took it.

With his temper barely restrained, he watched the two of them leave. Stroking Ilyse's head, he listened to the engines fire outside.

"I hope you know what you're doing. Most of all, I hope she's worth it."

But even as he said the words, he had a strange premonition Nykyrian was headed straight into death.

CHAPTER 18

Kiara stared out at the brightly lit landing bay on a planet she'd never been to before. But as she saw the subversive people who used this place, she realized why it was so bright . . . so the workers could keep an eye on the people who all appeared to be looking for victims.

"Where are we?"

Nykyrian locked down the engines. "Verta."

A thrill rushed through her. She'd always wanted to visit the infamous shops lining Paraf Run, but common sense had kept her from it. Every manner of questionable merchandise—including slaves—was bought and sold here by some of the universe's most dangerous beings.

"Are you sure this is a good idea?"

Nykyrian released the hatch. "Don't worry. I'm well known here and no one's stupid enough to cross me. The last person who tried . . . let's just say it didn't go well for him. Unlike other places, the Vertan enforcers ensure that high-profile people like me can come and go without complications."

Because they had the serious money the stores here catered to, and if the outlaws couldn't shop . . .

Yeah, it was a strange universe they lived in where

the criminals were usually better protected than the law-abiding citizens. But that was the way of things.

An impish thought occurred to her as she removed her helmet. "What if some high-ranking aristocrat sees me and demands my *private* services?"

His hands tensed around her safety strap. "I'd rip his heart out and feed it to him." There was no missing the deadly undertone of those words.

Kiara wasn't sure if she liked his answer. Nykyrian was one of the few people she knew who could make good that threat. "Why are we here, anyway?"

He cradled her against him as he said in a low tone in her ear, "As much as I like the sight of you in my shirts or better yet, completely naked, I thought you might want to have something else to wear. I'm sure your one dress and underwear will only last so long."

She frowned at his words. "We're shopping?"

"Just a quick trip to get the necessities you need."

His thoughtfulness amazed her. "After what happened last time, I'm surprised you'd go near another store."

"As I said, they know me here." Once he'd freed her of the safety straps, Nykyrian helped her down and led the way out of the bay, into a crowded street. "Stay with me and don't wander off." He wrapped an arm possessively around her shoulders.

That move would have thrilled her had she not realized that he wasn't doing it to be sweet—he was doing it because this place was just that dangerous and he wanted to publicly claim her so the rest of the people around them would leave her alone.

Swallowing her fear, Kiara scanned the street, astonished at the variety of beings and cultures represented. She saw everything from wealthy princes and princesses arrayed in the finest materials available, to

filthy street urchins who barely wore enough to cover
their nudity. But it was the thugs who scanned the
crowd looking for marks that stood out the most.

What a strange mixture . . .

As they passed an alley, she heard a boy cry out.
"Get off me!"

Nykyrian pulled her to a stop.

"Shut up, you little bastard."

He dropped his arm from her shoulders and took her
hand, making sure to keep himself between her and
whoever was in the alley as he went to investigate the
loud voices.

She was horrified as she saw the man mauling a boy
who appeared to be around the age of twelve. Three
other men were with him, laughing at the struggling
child.

Anger, fear and horror went through her as she remembered the men who'd once done her the same way.

*That's it, bitch, keep crying. Mommy can't help
you.*

Why did people have to be so cruel? She'd never
understand it.

Releasing her hand, Nykyrian shot across the alley.
He kicked the man tormenting the boy into one of his
cronies so hard that the two of them hit the ground. In
one fluid move, he picked the boy up and put him down
out of the crossfire, then spun around and caught a
third man in his jaw, knocking him away.

He flipped the fourth one over his back to the ground.
He delivered three punches to his head that were so
fierce, she could almost feel them.

The boy started back into the fray.

"Jana, stay with the lady," Nykyrian growled before
he spun to catch the man who'd picked up a board and
was about to hit him with it.

Nykyrian raised his forearm to deflect the board before he kicked the man into a Dumpster.

The boy shot toward her. Kiara wrapped her arms around him to keep him safe while Nykyrian dealt with his attackers. A few inches taller than her, the boy was so emaciated she could feel his bones, but even so, he had a handsome face that told her he'd be stunning once he grew into his own.

"Who the fuck are you?" the first man asked, pushing himself up.

Nykyrian lowered his head threateningly. "I'm the last thing you're going to see if you *ever* touch a kid again."

Kiara saw the desire in the men's eyes to keep fighting, but their common sense prevailed. Extremely bloodied and bruised now, they pushed themselves to their feet.

Nykyrian turned toward her and Jana.

The moment he did, the first man attacked again. Before she could make a single sound of warning, Nykyrian spun about and caught him with a hard punch to his jaw that lifted him up from his feet and sent him straight to the ground, flat on his back. A second man went to return the hit. Nykyrian caught his arm and twisted it.

She cringed at the sound of breaking bone.

Nykyrian delivered another hit to the man's midsection hard enough to drive him to his knees. "Had enough? Or do I have to kill all of you?"

"Enough." The man panted.

Nykyrian wrenched the man's arm, causing him to scream out before he released him. "Next time, pick on someone a little closer to your size." Leaving the men to whimper on the ground, Nykyrian took her and Jana out of the alley.

He let out a tired sigh as he looked at her. "I know. I'm an animal."

Kiara shook her head. "No, you're not. You were too merciful."

He frowned at her.

She offered him a smile and patted Jana's shoulder. "I'm beginning to understand your world, Nykyrian. I'm not going to judge you for it."

As soon as they were on the street and had put enough distance between them and the alley, he pulled Jana to a stop. "What were you doing there?" he demanded of the boy in a firm, yet gentle voice. "You should know better."

The boy swallowed. "I didn't do nothing, Nykyrian, I swear it on my life. I was minding my own business when they jumped me and dragged me into the alley. I tried to fight them off, but they were too big."

Nykyrian's stern face softened. "How many times have I told you to be careful? You have to stay away from Paraf Run. Have you any idea what could have happened to you had I been five minutes later?"

"I know and I listened. It's just . . ." His blue eyes misted. "Me mum died two days ago, and they threw me out of her brothel. The authorities want to take me to an orphanage or to a League academy. And I ain't doing that shit. Paraf Run is the only place where the enforcers don't patrol for bastards to arrest. Have you any idea what they do to boys in those places? I promised me mum when she died that I wouldn't let them take me."

There was a subtle tightening to Nykyrian's features that made her wonder what ghosts tormented him. "It's all right, Jana. I won't let them do that to you."

A lump choked Kiara's throat as she watched the tender way he directed the boy down the street in front of them.

Jana hesitated. "Where are you taking me?"

"To a friend's place where you'll be safe."

Jana gave him a suspicious glare. "How do I know that?"

"You have my word."

Jana nodded as if that was all he needed.

Kiara watched the two of them. While it was obvious they knew each other, she wanted to know how. Had Nykyrian been a client of Jana's mother? While the thought didn't thrill her, it wasn't really any of her business.

"So how did you two meet?"

Jana flashed a sheepish grin at her. "I tried to pick Nykyrian's pocket last year."

She gaped at Nykyrian. "And you let him live?"

There was a subtle lifting at the corners of his mouth. "I have an age requirement before I kill someone."

Jana slowed down so that he could walk beside her. "He actually bought me dinner, then took me to me mum and told her to keep me off the streets. Not that she listened. She was a whore."

Nykyrian's features tightened, and when he spoke, his tone was sharp. "Your mother loved you, Jana. One day you'll understand how rare a thing that is. Don't disparage her memory by reducing her down to the occupation she had that kept you fed and clothed. She deserves better than that."

Jana's anger deflated as he lowered his head. "Sorry."

Kiara studied Nykyrian as they walked. His ability to assess people still amazed her. And even though he was an assassin, he had an astonishing amount of compassion.

They walked in silence as he led them through a small alley to the back of an office. He removed his shades and knocked on the rear door where they waited until an elderwoman appeared. With dark brown eyes and black hair laced with gray, she was heavyset and beautiful.

"Nykyrian," she breathed happily, pushing open the screen door to look him up and down like a mother seeing her son after a long absence. Yet she made no move whatsoever to touch him.

That alone told Kiara exactly how familiar she was with Nykyrian and his habits.

He stood back to indicate her and Jana. "Hi, Orinthe. May we come in?"

"You know you're welcome here any time." She opened the door wider.

Nykyrian stood back and allowed Kiara to enter first. The elderwoman led her through an immaculate storeroom of foodstuffs and into a small lounge to the right. Jana looked at the food with such longing, it made Kiara want to cry for him.

Nykyrian directed Jana to one of four brown leather chairs that encircled a small, round table. Orinthe reached up on a shelf and brought out a bowl of fruit and a covered plate of pastries.

With a tender smile, she set it before Jana, who eagerly tore into it. A strange look crossed Orinthe's face as she watched Jana shove an entire pastry into his mouth. "He reminds me of another boy I knew a long time ago." She glanced over to Nykyrian. He didn't respond at all.

Orinthe went to get a glass of milk for the boy, who was doing his best to inhale the food. Kiara's heart wrenched as she thought of how many times in her life she'd joked she was starving when she really had no concept of the hunger Jana knew.

The hunger Nykyrian had endured . . .

When Orinthe sat down, Nykyrian met her gaze. "His mother died and he has no place to live. I was wondering—"

"I could use help here in the office. My regular errand boy quit three days ago to go off and run with one of the local gangs, and I haven't had the time to look for another. There's a room for him upstairs."

Jana looked up from his food, his eyes wide. "Stay here?" he asked in awe. "With all this food?"

Orinthe's bright smile warmed Kiara's heart. "Are you willing to work for it?"

He narrowed his eyes suspiciously. "Are you going to cheat me?"

Orinthe glanced at Nykyrian. "He's *just* like someone else I know." She smiled kindly at Jana. "No, child. I've never cheated anyone in my life. As long as you do a little work and don't steal, you're welcome here and I'll make sure you have as much food as you can hold."

Jana beamed.

Orinthe cleaned up the remains of the food. "Nykyrian, would you mind showing him upstairs to the guest room and get him cleaned up a bit?"

"Sure." He helped Jana carry the rest of his fruit out of the room.

Once they were gone, Orinthe turned her attention to Kiara with a probing stare that told her she wouldn't be able to hide anything from the elderwoman. "Are you Nykyrian's woman?"

Kiara shook her head. "No. We're just friends."

Orinthe narrowed her gaze. "I've never seen him so relaxed with anyone else—he actually allowed you to stand at his back, and he seldom considers anyone his friend. It's a term he's never taken for granted and it's something he doesn't offer lightly." She wiped a damp cloth over the surface of the table, removing the crumbs

Jana had left behind in his eagerness to eat his fill. "What's your name, child?"

"Kiara."

Her smile widened. "A name as beautiful as the one who bears it."

"Thank you."

Orinthe folded the cloth and set it on the table before them.

Kiara watched the kind elderwoman, a thousand questions swirling in her mind about Nykyrian. "How do you know Nykyrian?"

Orinthe bit her bottom lip, then stood and closed the door to the stairs where Nykyrian had taken Jana. She returned to her chair, motioning for Kiara to lean closer to her. "He can hear from long distances, you know?"

"Yes, I do."

Orinthe leaned in so that she could speak in the lowest possible whisper. "I was the psychologist Commander Quiakides hired after Nykyrian's adoption to . . ." She paused as if seeking the right words. "Nykyrian had a lot of trouble adjusting."

"How do you mean?"

Tears misted in her eyes as she swallowed audibly. "I've been a child therapist and psychologist for almost sixty years, and I've seen some of the worst cases you can imagine. Things that would make you ill to even hear about. Yet none of them haunt me the way his case does. The things that were done to him . . ." She blinked back tears. "He's a *good* man. I don't know how someone like him emerged out of the horrors of his past, but he did."

She glanced at the stairway. "If you are his friend, you have no idea how lucky that makes you. Nykyrian has trouble bonding to people."

"I don't understand."

"Because of the way he was abandoned and treated, he doesn't trust people at all. He doesn't even open up much to me. He's afraid to let anyone know him for fear of their rejecting him as his parents did. Because of that inner fear, he rejects others before they have a chance to hurt him."

Kiara scooted closer. "I've noticed that he never talks about his childhood."

"I don't blame him." Orinthe toyed with the cloth on the table as if she needed the distraction to speak. "He was thrown into a human orphanage where he was only allowed garbage for nourishment. The workers there feared giving him meat. They thought the taste of it might drive his Andarion blood into a feeding frenzy and so they . . ."

Orinthe winced as if the horror of it was too much to bear even now. "He drank out of toilets. And then when he was taken into the commander's home . . . they weren't any better to him. Sometimes I think it was even worse because the commander and his children were trying to kill the last human part of him." She sighed heavily. "The commander even put a training collar on him. Do you know what those are?"

"I've seen them, but I don't really know how they work."

"They can lock down the entire nervous system so that a person can't move—or more to the point, defend themselves. You can feel, but you can't move. They also have a shocking device. They're the worst kind of torture. But the commander demanded it, and so . . ."

Orinthe wiped a trembling hand over her face. "The commander never listened. I can still remember arguing with him when he sent Nykyrian to school. I knew it was too soon and . . ." She shook her head. "That poor boy used to sleep on the floor, underneath his own bed in their home."

"Why?"

"For protection. The commander's sons used to sneak up on him in the middle of the night to beat him. So he learned to stay up for days and still does. He only sleeps when he absolutely cannot go another moment without it."

Kiara finally understood. She remembered what he'd said to her when they met. "Because when he sleeps, he's vulnerable."

Orinthe nodded. "I'll be honest, I told the commander to put him down for his own good. Given the horror of his childhood, I didn't think there was any hope for him at all. But that was what the commander wanted. A killing machine incapable of human feelings."

Kiara was horrified that the woman before her had actually called for Nykyrian to be killed. "Why would you want him put down?"

"You have no idea what he was like back then. He was so fierce as a child. He would attack without stopping until someone overpowered him. And then one day as I was observing him in a park while he did his homework, a small child came up and hit him for no reason. I was terrified and tried to get to them. I was sure he'd kill the child before I could reach them. But instead, Nykyrian looked up and stared at the child, and did nothing. As soon as I reached him, the child ran off and when I asked Nykyrian why he didn't attack, he looked at me blankly and said the child wasn't old enough to know better. Then he went back to his reading as if nothing had happened. It was then I knew that somehow, against all odds and against everything my books had told me about psychology, he understood right and wrong. I realized then that when he attacked it was to protect himself. He doesn't attack out of anger or maliciousness."

"He attacks out of necessity."

"Exactly."

And he understood who would be a threat later and who wouldn't. Like Syn had said. It was why Pitala and the bullies in the alley had been spared.

But Kiara was still trying to reconcile what she'd seen in the video with the man she knew. "What about the commander's wife? Did she—"

"I always felt sorry for her. I could tell she wanted to help where Nykyrian was concerned, but every time she tried, her sons and husband would mock her for it. In the end, she wasn't much better off than Nykyrian was, and so she tried to stay out of things as much as she could. But she wasn't the worst to hurt him . . ."

CHAPTER 19

Kiara opened her mouth to ask Orinthe more, but Nykyrian returned.

He stood beside Orinthe's chair. "Jana's taking a nap."

"Good," she said with a tender smile. "I'll let him sleep until dinner."

Nykyrian inclined his head to her. "I'll transfer funds to your account for him."

Orinthe sputtered at his words. "You'll do no such thing. Heaven knows you already give me more than enough as it is. Even if it is for the children, you're too generous."

For a moment, Kiara thought he actually blushed. "Thank you for taking Jana in. If he gives you any trouble, call me and I'll talk to him."

"I have a feeling he won't be a problem."

Nykyrian held his hand out to Kiara. She didn't hesitate to take it.

A frown covered Orinthe's face. "You're not leaving now?"

He nodded before replacing his shades. "If you need anything, call me or Syn and we'll take care of it."

Orinthe sighed in a way that made Kiara think Nykyrian's words embarrassed her. She looked up at

Nykyrian and her friendly, warm smile returned.
"You take care of yourself and this pretty lady. The
two of you make a handsome couple."

Kiara smiled at the gentle woman. "Thank you."

By Nykyrian's face, Kiara could tell the compliment
made him uncomfortable. "I'll check on the two of you
in a couple of weeks."

Orinthe nodded and showed them to the door.

Nykyrian led the way back down the street. Kiara
knew by his rigid spine that something was bother-
ing him.

"What's wrong?"

A tic worked in his jaw. "I wish Orinthe hadn't told
you what she did about me."

Was there anything that ever got past this man's
hearing? "I wish you'd told me yourself."

Nykyrian hesitated and looked down at her. Kiara
wished he didn't have his shades on so she could read
his emotions.

After a moment, he shifted. "Why do you want to
know about my childhood? I prefer not to think about
those days. They're gone and forgotten."

Kiara shook her head in denial. "It's not forgotten,
Nykyrian. Horrors like that don't just fade. Take it from
someone who knows. No matter how hard we fight, no
matter how hard we try, they sneak up on us and drag
us back with a clarity that is as vibrant as it was when
they first happened. I like to pretend my past isn't there,
too, but it doesn't change the fact that I still can't stand
to be alone in the dark."

Nykyrian paused as her words touched him. The
fact that she understood . . . It made him feel close to
her. But it didn't change the pain he carried with him.
"I would never leave you in the dark."

"And I feel the same toward you."

The smile she gave him weakened his knees and made him feel the stirring of something he didn't even want to contemplate. Unwilling to think about that, he took her to the large shopping complex at the end of the street.

Kiara gaped at the dizzying variety of colors and merchandise that blended with shoppers from all cultures. The store they entered had huge glass counters filled with accessories and trims—any and everything a person could possibly want. Clothing styles were hung over abstract mannequins, showing how they might look on various life-forms.

As she browsed, she realized the clothes here were obscenely priced. Even her extravagant father would faint over these. She stepped back from the rack. "Is there another place to buy clothes?"

"Don't you like them?"

She widened her eyes as she leaned into him to whisper. "Did you see the price?"

Nykyrian snorted. "I'm more than capable of supplying you with several wardrobes from here."

"But—"

"But nothing, *mu Tara*. Start shopping."

Kiara bit her lip in agitation, unwilling to give in so easily. No one needed clothing that cost this much. "This really isn't—"

"Kiara," he growled low in his throat. "Buy clothes or go naked. Personally, naked works for me."

How could she be both annoyed and amused by him? "Fine. When you're homeless and bankrupt, remember I tried to stop you."

A smile curved his lips.

Stunned, she stood there unable to move as she saw the one thing she'd never thought to see from him. A real, full-blown smile. The man was absolutely gorgeous.

"My God, you have dimples."

His smile vanished instantly. "I know."

"No, no, no, no, no!" she said, reaching up to touch his cheek. "Don't you dare hide those. They're beautiful."

He dodged her touch. "They look stupid."

She let out an aggravated breath. "They are sexy as all get-out. Trust me. Dimples like those will definitely get you laid."

That almost succeeded in making him smile again . . . At least until they were interrupted.

"Kiara Zamir!"

Kiara turned around to face an excited salesclerk. The young woman stared at her with huge, animated brown eyes.

"Oh my God, I love you!" she gushed. "I saw *Silent Prayer* last year and thought it was the best thing ever produced. You are the best."

Kiara grinned, warmed by the compliment. "Thank you."

"My name's Terra and whatever you need, just let me know. Oh my God. I can't wait to tell my mother, she'll never believe this!" And Nykyrian had been right. Unlike on Gouran, Terra didn't judge or react to him. No wonder he was willing to pay so much. Here he was normal.

Kiara glanced at Nykyrian to see how he was taking the clerk's continuing adoration. He watched them quietly, his features patient and his stance unobtrusive. Oh, thank goodness he wasn't chafing like other people, including her father, did. He seemed completely content to stand in the background and let her have time with her fan.

That meant a lot to her.

She allowed the clerk to take her by the arm and

show her a variety of pieces. For all the generosity of her father, Kiara realized she'd never seen such extravagant materials. Each piece was light and airy with the most delicate, silky texture.

Terra explained many of the fabrics were from non-human worlds, brought to the store only by an exorbitant price. She glanced over her shoulder, unsure how much Nykyrian was willing to spend on her clothes.

"I like that one," he said, indicating the dress Terra held.

Kiara cringed. It was absolutely stunning, but . . . "I don't know . . . it's the GNP of a small planet."

He let out a slow, aggravated breath. "Don't worry about the price, princess, just buy whatever you need."

Terra smiled at him. "Ooo, I like you. If you're not counting coins, I have an even better line in back."

At his nod, Terra moved them to the exclusive section.

In spite of her reluctance, Nykyrian and Terra fitted her with enough clothes to last for a solid month. As Terra left to place the order, Kiara faced him with one arched brow. "How long are you planning to keep me?"

Again there was no emotion whatsoever from him. "Until you're safe."

She looked at the pile of samples they'd gone through and the bigger pile of ones he'd approved to purchase. "That's a lot of clothes . . . I can't believe you spent so much on me."

He shrugged.

"You're terrible, Nykyrian." She wished she could see his eyes. Instead, her irritated reflection glared back at her from the dark lenses.

"I want you to have it. You deserve beautiful things and I took you from your own clothes."

"No, Aksel did that." She trailed her gaze over his

tall, sexy body. He leaned back against the mirrored column with his boots crossed at the ankles and his arms folded over his chest. Deceptively relaxed, he was alert to everything around them.

And she was highly attuned to him. She walked herself into his arms, forcing him to straighten up.

He stiffened until she wrapped her arms around his waist and kissed him lightly on the cheek.

"Thank you, Nykyrian."

Nykyrian was at a complete loss of words as his hormones fired. He really didn't know how to deal with her kindness.

Terra returned with her computer ledger and Nykyrian quickly signed his name and indicated where the packages were to be delivered to his ship.

"Do you need anything else?" he asked Kiara, handing the ledger back to Terra.

"Not hardly."

With a nod to Terra, he took Kiara's hand and led her from the store. "We need to get Syn's part next."

"Can you buy him a new attitude while we're at it?"

Nykyrian frowned. "Why?"

"He's been just a little cranky lately. Haven't you noticed?"

"Not really. He's usually acerbic when he drinks."

Kiara was puzzled by his answer since she had yet to see a time when Syn wasn't guzzling alcohol. "Then why are you friends?"

He paused to look down at her. "He saved my life."

Kiara was stunned that he'd admit that. Had he suffered a head injury in the earlier fight? "Really?"

He moved away and started walking again. "Yeah. I was on an assignment . . . one of my first, and it didn't go quite as I'd planned."

"You were hurt?"

"Bleeding like a mother. I knew I didn't have long before I bled out. I was in so much pain, I don't remember much really. Somehow I ended up sitting in an alley, waiting to die."

"And Syn helped you."

He rubbed his hand over his jaw. "Actually, he tried to mug me. I started to kill him until I realized he was just a hungry kid. So I gave him my wallet. I figured since I was dying, I didn't need it, anyway."

She didn't dare tell him she'd seen that history on his files, and that his charity still astonished her. But that was the part of him that touched her most.

"He didn't leave?"

"No. He took me back to his . . . I would call it a place, but it was disgusting. He'd rigged a home in an abandoned factory that was barely fit for rodent habitation. But it was his and it was safe. It took a couple of days for me to recover enough to go back to The League, and he split what little food he had with me while I healed."

"They didn't come looking for you?"

"No. It doesn't work that way. Since executing a target takes time, you're given a time frame to carry out the mission. So unless you miss the check-ins or go AWOL, they keep their distance."

She'd always wondered how they did that. "I still don't understand how you became friends with him."

"He saved my life. I paid him back by giving him one, too."

"How so?"

This time she sensed the pain he kept cloaked inside him. "I gave him what he wanted. Paid for him to go to school. Set him up in an apartment and . . . fucked him over royally in the end. Sometimes I think he'd have been better off had I left him in the gutter. He'd have earned enough money eventually to get out on his own. All I did was show him a life he could never have."

"What do you mean?"

She saw the torment on his face and it made her ache for him. "With my help, he crawled out of the gutter. Got a great career he adored, a wife he loved, and a kid he worshiped. Everything was perfect. Then this damned reporter came in and started asking questions about his past and his father. His wife found out who his father was and that Syn had also been in prison. Without a second thought and forgetting everything he'd done for her and given her, she threw him out and ruined him. In less than twenty-four hours, he lost everything."

Kiara's throat tightened at the horror of what he described. No wonder Syn was so bitter. "He could have fought harder to keep it."

Nykyrian shook his head. "Believe me, no one could have fought harder for his life than Syn did. In the end, it wasn't enough. By trying to save him, I shattered him even more."

She reached out to touch his arm and for once he let her. "It wasn't your fault."

"I tell myself that. But I was the one who sold him on a dream. I told him I could bury his past and no one would ever find it. Gah, if I could just go back."

"And do what?"

"Stop him from making the worst mistake of his life."

Kiara thought about that for a minute, but knowing Syn, she doubted if there had been anything Nykyrian could have done to change things. As her father so often said, there were some lessons only personal experience could teach. "I don't think he would have listened."

Nykyrian paused and looked at her. For the first time, he realized how right she was. Syn wouldn't have listened to reason no matter how hard he would or could have tried.

Just like he wouldn't listen to Syn where she was concerned. He finally understood why Syn had been so willing to risk everything.

Including his life.

Sometimes those chances were worth taking. But would Kiara be like Syn's wife and throw him to the dogs one day?

"You know I've never told anyone any of that."

She smiled. "I won't breathe a word of it. Ever."

He didn't know why, but he believed that.

Then she reached out and took his hand in hers. His automatic response was to let go and snap at her. But he forced himself not to. Honestly, he liked the way she claimed him in public—like she wasn't embarrassed to be seen with him.

No one had ever treated him like that before.

Suddenly she stopped in the middle of the sidewalk and tugged him back in the opposite direction. Laughing, she pulled him into a small store. "Have you ever had Sprinkles?"

He was completely baffled. The store was some kind of eatery that sold treats. "No."

"Oh, you have to try these," she said with a breathless excitement that made her amber eyes glow. "When I was a little girl, my mother used to take me for them every Saturday after dance practice." She closed her eyes as if savoring the memory. "They're like biting into heaven."

He wanted to smile at the way she danced to the counter with childlike enthusiasm and ordered two flavors of something that didn't look particularly edible. He wrinkled his nose at the "food" that looked more like unappetizing balls of excrement. "What is it?"

"Freeze-dried cream." She reached up and popped him playfully on his nose. "Stop making faces, you'll love it."

Nykyrian couldn't have been more stunned had she slapped him. Indeed, *that* he would have expected. This playful side of her that dismissed the fact he could snap her in two with his bare hands was unexpected and . . .

Fun.

The clerk handed her the containers while he paid for it.

She bit her lip before she dipped her spoon in and took a bite. The look of ecstasy on her face made him instantly hard as she savored the food.

"Oh, this is the best." Her eyes bright, she dipped her spoon in and then offered him a bite.

Before he could stop himself, he opened his lips and let her feed him. Syn would shit sideways if he ever saw this. For that matter, the rest of his crew would fall over dead.

But as the flavor hit his tastebuds, he choked on it. Cringing, he had to swallow fast to try and kill the taste. "What is *that*?"

"It's supposed to be good."

Nykyrian shook his head, trying to dispel it from his mouth. "I'm not used to things that are that sweet."

Her face fell. "I'm sorry. I thought you'd like it."

He wiped a small trace of melted cream from her chin. "I like that you like it. But it's definitely not for me."

Kiara had never been more touched by anything in her life. It wasn't just what he said, it was the look on his face. The gentleness of his caress. Before she could think better of it, she rose up on her tiptoes and kissed him.

Nykyrian froze as her tongue swept against his . . . in public. That quick, simple kiss scorched every part of his body. She treated him like he was normal and they were . . .

Lovers.

Taking his hand, she led him back to the street.

"Do you want this?" he asked, holding his container out to her.

She pouted teasingly as she licked the back of her spoon in a way that made his cock twitch. "Are you sure you don't?"

"Yes."

She tsked before she added his to hers and then tossed away his container. "You have no idea what you're missing."

Right now what he was missing was being in bed with her. Most of all, he was dying to be the spoon she kept sucking on.

Trying to get that thought out of his head, he led her to the part store to get Syn's repairs.

But all he could think about was how beautiful she was licking that spoon.

I wish she were licking my *spoon . . .*

Stop it!

No wonder The League banned them from relationships. There was nothing more distracting.

As soon as he had the part, he tucked it under his arm and realized how late it was. He could go all day without eating, but now that he thought about it, Kiara had been a little too eager to eat her treat. "Are you hungry?"

"Famished."

"Well, there's some of everything nearby. What are you in the mood for?"

Kiara smiled. Licking her lips, she raked a wistful look over his tall, gorgeous body. "Andarion."

"Really? Most humans find it too spicy."

She started to correct him, but ended up biting back

a laugh as she realized he wasn't used to women flirt-
ing with him. Not that she minded. She was actually
glad he wasn't like the playboys she was used to. She
found it charming and sweet.

Yeah, right. Two words that definitely flew in the
face of his lethal facade.

She shook her head as he opened the door to an Andarion restaurant and allowed her to enter first. She
frowned as they waited to be seated and she noticed
something about him. "It's very strange that here, in
one of the most dangerous, most crime-ridden places
we could possibly be, you're more relaxed than I think
I've ever seen you. How is that?"

He leaned over to whisper. "Not true. The most relaxed I've ever been was last night after I made love
to you."

She blushed profusely. "Out of the bedroom . . ."

He shrugged. "The people here are more honest.
You know they're looking for a shot at your back and
they know you know, so they tend to live and let live.
So long as you're not a snap, you're safe."

"Snap . . . Syn used that term."

"Single. Naive. Amateur. Person. A walking vic."

A shiver went down her spine. "And you guys would
be. . . . ?"

"In a word . . . predators."

That definitely suited him.

He didn't speak to the Andarion waitress who raked
a speculative glare over them. He merely held up his
hand to indicate two of them.

The waitress led them to a table in the back. Kiara
sat down first and noted that Nykyrian took a seat with
his back to the wall so that he could watch everyone in
the café.

Some habits died hard.

She frowned at the menu that was written in an alphabet she'd never seen before. She wasn't even sure if she was holding it right-side up. "Don't they have menus in Universal?"

"No. Andarions are assholes. If you can't read it, they don't want you to eat it." He leaned over to explain the menu choices to her.

Kiara was hesitant. "There's no human meat on here, is there?"

He shook his head. "While there are still those who partake of human flesh, they confine that delicacy to Andaria. The rest of the universe tends to consider it murder. It's all beef or vegetable on your menu."

She let out a relieved breath. "So what do you recommend?"

"You would probably like the *Fitau Cour Bariyone*."

A chill went down her spine at the way those words rolled off his tongue. He had an incredibly sexy voice, especially when he spoke in his native tongue. "And that would be?"

"Lightly seasoned beef with a yellow herb cream sauce and stewed vegetables. It's not as spicy as the other items."

She'd forgotten what a gourmet he was. "That does sound good. I'll try it."

As soon as the waitress returned, Nykyrian ordered.

The moment the waitress saw his long canine teeth, she spoke in Andarion to him. Nykyrian's response was tinged with condescension—something Kiara had never heard from him before, and it made her wonder what the waitress had said to cause it.

When they were alone again, she sat forward. "What was all that about?"

"She wanted to know why I bleached my hair and was with a human."

"And you said?"

"That a servant shouldn't question me."

"That was harsh," she chided.

He didn't react at all. "I'm a trained warrior, Kiara. On Andaria, the only thing that outranks me is the aristocracy. Had I answered her questions, I would have ceded my status and become inferior to her. She would have attacked us both. The caste order is sacred in their world. If I considered myself a true Andarion, she'd have been beaten for even questioning me. As bad as you think Hauk is off-world, you should be around him when he's with his people. He's really a nasty bastard then."

She'd forgotten just how warring and brutal the Andarions were. "I'll bet you're glad you weren't raised there, huh?"

As soon as the question was out of her mouth, she realized how stupid and thoughtless it was. "I'm so sorry, Nykyrian. I wasn't thinking."

"It's all right. It didn't go any better for me on Andaria than it did in the orphanage. I see no real difference between humanity and them. Both races prey on the weak and defenseless."

Kiara hated the fact that he was right. In the end, it was only a dental anomaly that really differentiated them from each other.

"Do you remember your mother at all?"

He gave the subtlest of nods.

She opened her mouth to ask more, but a chill went down her spine.

"Kiara Zamir . . . you're the last person I expected to see here."

Nykyrian went completely still as he heard the one voice that spun him into a level of pissed-off that not even Syn's drinking could match.

Jullien eton Anatole. The crowned Andarion prince.

Nykyrian steeled himself to keep from leaping at him and killing him where he stood. Jullien had been bad enough to stomach before he'd been sent off to the orphanage.

But it was the cruelty of the bastard in school that still haunted him. A bully and a ringleader, the prince hadn't been content to pick on him, knowing he couldn't fight back so long as he wore a training collar. The little bastard had accused him of stealing his sacred signet ring.

He ground his teeth at the memory. He'd been put through three weeks of hell—the highlights of which had been two brutal body-cavity searches and then spending two days in jail while having his arm broken in the process.

Meanwhile, the prince had hidden the ring in his own gym bag and conspired with his asshole crew to frame Nykyrian for no other reason than he didn't like him. If not for Hauk coming forward to say he'd found the missing ring, Nykyrian would probably still be in jail for a theft he hadn't committed.

And now, having almost ruined his entire life, the bastard didn't even recognize him . . .

This was priceless.

Kiara turned around in her chair to see Prince Jullien behind her. She smiled even though she wanted to curse. Jullien had a bad habit of turning up in places she'd rather he not. She didn't know why, but she'd never liked him. He just put off a nasty aura that made her want to cringe anytime he drew near.

Corpulent and slimy, he wore an expensive dark pewter suit that dripped gaudy jewels. His long black hair always looked greasy—today was no exception. He carried a silver-tipped black cane that was more for fashion than necessity. The cane also allowed him to flash his prince's signet ring for the world to see when he posed with it.

As he joined her, she noticed his guards withdrew to a discreet distance in the café to give them space.

Yippee that.

Without a word of courtesy, Jullien took a seat beside Kiara and lifted her hand in his soft, fat palm. She stifled her cringe at the uncharacteristicly swollen white flesh—most Andarions had dark tawny skin. What made the prince think she had any desire to be touched by him?

But he was nothing if not haughty, and in his world, all females, regardless of species, craved his corpulent form.

It was all she could do not to be sick.

"It's a such pleasure to see you again." Jullien smiled a confident smile that told her how much arrogance the ugly thing possessed.

She smiled stiffly. "It's a pleasure to see you again, Your Highness." *Now go away and get out of my face.* She pried his hand away from hers.

Flipping a lock of coal-black hair from his shoulder, he took her dismissal in stride.

Kiara glanced at Nykyrian. He appeared calm, and yet she had the distinct feeling it was taking all of his self-control not to leap at Jullien and strangle the prince.

Why?

Facing Jullien, she met his gaze and had to stifle a shudder at his mutated greenish-brown eyes ringed in blood red.

His smile widened. "I've spoken with my father about bringing you back to Triosa to perform. He's as enthralled with your beauty and talent almost as much as I. But my people have had trouble getting yours to commit. I'm sure it's just an oversight. After all, think of how good it would be for your career to be seen on our stage."

What did he think? She was some ingenue begging for a job? His offer was as insulting as the way he drooled over her.

Nykyrian cleared his throat. "Emperor Aros is exceedingly generous to say such things."

Jullien raised a disbelieving eyebrow and turned around in his chair to face Nykyrian.

Kiara held her breath, unsure of what would follow. No one spoke to a prince unless acknowledged beforehand. As Nykyrian had pointed out, their caste system was set in stone.

"Did I speak to you?"

Nykryian responded to him in Andarion.

Jullien's eyes narrowed and for a moment, Kiara thought he might call his guards to arrest Nykyrian. "You are one of my subjects. I demand proper respect!"

"*Titana tu.*"

Kiara didn't know what Nykyrian's deadpan response was, but by the amount of color suffusing the prince's cheeks, she knew it wasn't polite. She prayed Nykyrian calmed down before Jullien's guards attacked him.

"*Giakon,*" Jullien sneered.

Nykyrian rose to his feet, his entire being coiled to strike.

"Your Highness," Kiara interrupted before the tensing guards launched themselves at Nykyrian. "I would be honored to perform on Triosa. If you could contact my manager, I'm sure something can be arranged." She offered Jullien a false smile.

Jullien glared intensely at Nykyrian. "Very well, *mu*

Tara. Unlike your *fritalla*, I have no desire to further embarrass you." Jullien stood, his eyes locked on Nykyrian's face.

Nykyrian didn't move until Jullien and his guards had been seated far away from them.

"What was all of that?" she asked him.

"Nothing."

She was aghast at his answer. "Nothing? You lecture me on the higher order of Andarion etiquette and then you insult their crown prince? We're both lucky they didn't arrest you."

"They wouldn't have lived long enough to regret that mistake."

Kiara paused as she noted the bitter undercurrent in his voice. There was history there. Then she remembered the bit in his files . . .

"You went to school with him?"

Nykyrian didn't answer as the waitress brought out their food.

Kiara wasn't willing to let this go. "Nykyrian? Why did you attack him that way? What did he do to offend you?"

"He was born, and I don't want to discuss it." He indicated her plate. "We should eat and get back."

"You're locking me out again, aren't you?"

His grip tightened on his silverware. "In spite of Jullien calling me your girlfriend, I'm not a woman, Kiara. I'm a mercenary assassin and I really don't want to talk about my feelings."

The wall around him was back in place. She could almost weep in frustration. They'd had such a pleasant day.

Now it was ruined.

Sighing, she ate in silence while she pondered everything she'd learned today.

But what disturbed her most was how easily Nykyrian could shut her out and retreat back into himself. As if she wasn't even here.

How she envied him that ability, because all she could feel was him, and it hurt to know she could be so easily dismissed.

Nykyrian searched his mind for some way to ease the awkward tension between them. He wanted to go back to the playful Kiara who'd fed him her disgusting treat.

But he didn't know how. *I suck at human relations.* He always had. Jayne and Darling said he was too brutally honest. Syn called him socially awkward.

It was easier to stay silent and just observe others.

And yet, he wanted to know how to make her happy again.

Why bother? She's just a client.

No, she was much more than that.

She'd made love to him. Most of all, she'd touched him in a way no one ever had before and she made him feel things he'd never even dreamed possible.

Damn you, Jullien, for ruining this.

One day he was going to kill that bastard . . .

After they finished eating, they picked up her clothing packages in the hangar, and made their way back to Nykyrian's fighter and then his house.

Kiara remained silent as she entered the house first and patted the lorinas on their furry heads.

Syn appeared relieved by their taut silence as he helped unload the fighter. The only words Nykyrian spoke to her were to tell her where to store her purchases. Other than that, he quickly changed and made his way out to the bay to work on Syn's ship.

In angry, irate jerks, Kiara pulled her clothes out of the bags and boxes, and set about putting them away. As each second passed, she became angrier and angrier at

herself for caring what Nykyrian thought anyway. She
was acting like some lovesick teenager. If he didn't
want to talk to her, fine.

So what if he kept her at a distance? It was his pre-
rogative.

And yet it wasn't that easy. She wanted him to let
her in. She wanted . . .

Kiara wasn't even sure. She just knew that he'd
somehow changed her, and it wasn't fair that after all
they'd shared, he would cut her out so easily.

I'm nothing to him.

And that was what stung most of all.

"So what did you two do today?" Syn helped Nykyrian
jerk open the panel on his stabilizer.

Nykyrian picked up a socket wrench. "Grabbed some
clothes for her and your part." Unwilling to elaborate
beyond that, he changed the subject. "Did you find Driana's address?"

Syn nodded, his stare probing Nykyrian in a way
that always made him want to throw something at the
man. "I also found out some interesting tidbits about
you and Driana."

Nykyrian narrowed his gaze. He definitely wanted to
throw something at Syn. "You weren't supposed to go
into her personal file, or mine for that matter."

Syn shrugged and unwrapped the new part. "You
know me. Couldn't resist."

Nykyrian held his breath, waiting for Syn to build
up enough courage to ask him the next question.

Sure enough, he found his courage. "So how did she
end up married to Aksel and not you?"

"You know the answer. I was already engaged to The
League." Nykyrian loosened the plate's bolt, his mind
whirling with memories he didn't like to think about.

"Yeah, but from what I read—"

"Enough!" Nykyrian roared. "I don't want to think about this anymore. It was a long time ago." And what had happened between them still tore through him with serrated talons. The parting words Driana had sneered at him were forever carved into his heart. "Leave it alone."

Kiara stroked Ilyse's ears as she drew a ragged sigh. A few weeks ago, she'd known exactly who she was and what she wanted out of her life—to retire after a brilliant career and marry a nice, loving aristocrat her Father approved of and start a family.

Now, she wasn't sure of anything. Instead of dreaming of her polite, sweet man, she was haunted by the presence of someone who lived his life on the edge. A man more lethal than anyone she'd ever met.

One who saved people even when it flew in the face of his ruthlessness.

Why was she so attracted to someone who didn't seem to care about her at all? Yes, he'd slept with her, but that wasn't love. Men wanted sex, and she'd made a mistake by sleeping with him.

Why am I so stupid?

With a trembling sigh, she pushed herself off the bed and continued folding her clothes. She didn't understand why Nykyrian did anything.

Why did he buy her so much, then push her away?

He'd been so tender last night that she'd convinced herself he cared for her . . . that he needed her. Then the morning had dawned, and again he was distant.

Clenching her teeth against the miserable pain in her heart, she pushed the button to open the closet door.

A flash of light from the windows caught her attention and she looked out of the clear wall next to the closed-off bathroom to see Nykyrian and Syn working on Syn's ship.

From inside the closet, Syn's voice was muffled, but clearly audible as they talked, and for once, they spoke in a language she could understand.

"You are out of your fucking mind," Syn snarled, tossing a tool up to Nykyrian.

Nykyrian caught it with one hand and leaned back into the engine well. "Stay out of it, Syn. Kiara's my concern."

"No, she's all of ours. My God, with one word, she could destroy you. Hell, *all* of us, for that matter."

Nykyrian grimaced as he tugged on a part. "So could you."

Syn made a sound of disgust. "You know better than that. Be reasonable. We've worked too hard for what we have for you to just toss it away because of some *harita*. If all you want is a piece of—"

Syn barely had time to dodge the tool that flew past his head.

Nykyrian jumped off the ship and grabbed Syn by the collar of his shirt.

Kiara held her breath, afraid of what he might do.

"Don't ever insult her again." he snarled, his hands tightening around Syn's shirt. "It's my life I risk, not yours."

Anger clouded Syn's face and for a moment, Kiara feared they might begin fighting. "Goddammit, don't do this. You're all I've got. She's not worth your life, don't you understand? You saw what Mara did to me. How quickly she turned. Do you really think for one minute that the princess"—he sneered the word— "would be a bit better in the end? She'll betray you before the end of it. Mark my words. Dump her now before it's too late."

Nykyrian shoved him back. "I've had so many people dictate my life for me. I'm tired of doing what I'm told. I thought you of all people would understand what it's like to want something and then once you get it, not let go."

Syn shook his head, his lips in a tight line. "C'mon, you know better than this. Since when are women reliable? They leave the first time anything gets difficult."

Nykyrian snorted. "That's not true."

"Isn't it? She'll never leave her career to be with you and you know it. And you can't live out in the open. If you try, you know how long it'll take before a League assassin cuts your throat and hers just for good measure."

Nykyrian slammed his hand into the side of the ship. The hollow sound echoed in the bay. "I've spent my entire life listening to people tell me why I can't be loved and how I'm nothing but a worthless piece of shit." The bitterness in his voice tore through Kiara. "I always told myself that I didn't care, that I didn't need anyone else."

He raked his hand through his hair and leveled his gaze on Syn. "It was a lie, you know. I do care and I want Kiara. If it costs me my life to be with her, it doesn't matter. I've already lived past my prime, anyway. I get up every morning with more pain in my joints than the day before. If I have to die, I'd rather die knowing someone cared about me, just once. Is that really too much to ask?"

"For us? Yes. It is. We are the gutter and the gutter is all we'll ever be. Don't reach out for the stars. They'll burn you until there's nothing left."

"Then let me burn."

Kiara slid down the wall in the closet as a thousand thoughts went through her.

But above it all was the one that mattered most.

Nykyrian cared for her.

Even though their relationship made no sense. Even though it was ludicrous and unorthodox . . .

And in that moment, she realized her own truth. She loved him. That was why she'd slept with him. That was why his moodiness hurt her.

She cared. Every part of her wanted what only he could give her. No other man had ever made her feel so safe. So desired.

And somehow she was going to breach his defenses and show him that she wasn't like Syn's wife. She would never betray him.

Your father will never allow you to be with someone like Nykyrian.

Neither would her dance company.

Reality crushed her. And yet she didn't want to listen to any of it. There had to be some way to work this out. And by all that was holy, she was going to find it even if it killed her.

And it bloody well might.

CHAPTER 20

Nykyrian stepped out of the shower and dried himself off. Maybe Syn was right—maybe Kiara would be his death. But then, death had been something he'd craved most of his life, anyway.

Orinthe had asked him once why he didn't kill himself. He'd never had a real answer to that question. Maybe it was sheer stubbornness or just blind stupidity.

He didn't fear death, but neither did he welcome it. So here he was, waiting ambivalently until it came for him.

With a tired sigh, he wrapped the towel around his hips and opened the door.

He froze.

Kiara lay on his bed in a filmy black negligee, her hair combed out around her. His blood raced at the sight as he went instantly hard. He steeled himself, trying to remain distant while knowing it was absolutely futile. "I thought you were downstairs."

She smiled warmly. "Obviously not."

He reached to retrieve his clothes from under her. Her silken hand covered his. Nykyrian's flesh burned at the gentle touch. He wanted her body wrapped around his more than he'd ever wanted anything. His gaze traveled from her hand, up her supple arm, to the beauty of her face. Her soft, amber eyes sparkled in the dim light of the room in an open invitation for him to kiss her.

"I'm sorry for what happened earlier today," she whispered. "I think we both need to work on our communications skills."

"I tried that once."

"And?"

"Darling told me that I could never hold a job as a suicide counselor or hostage negotiator. He said my failure rate would become the stuff of legends."

She laughed.

Nykyrian pulled his clothes out from under her. She lifted her hips in a way that made him ache. Trying not to think about that, he dropped his towel.

Kiara's face turned bright red before she averted her eyes from his body.

Pulling on his clothes, he studied her profile. What was it about her that made him feel so much at ease? That soothed the ache inside him? All he wanted was to crawl into her arms and stay there for eternity.

There was so much he wanted to tell her and so much he feared telling her. He took a deep breath. Either way, there were things she had to know. He owed her that much.

Kiara looked back at Nykyrian when the bed dipped under his weight. He was fully dressed, right down to his gloves, and staring at her with a strange look she couldn't fathom. She sat up, wondering if he'd tell her what was on his mind.

He reached his hand out and toyed with several of the curls laying on her shoulder. "You have the most beautiful hair."

"You know you can take your gloves off to touch me. I won't protest."

To her amazement, he did.

She smiled again, taking his hand in hers. When she opened her mouth to speak, he placed a finger on her lips to silence her.

"I have some things to tell you and I need you to listen."

She swallowed, curious about his grave tone.

He stared at her for the longest time as if he wanted to memorize her face. "I'm not what you think. No," he said, cupping her cheek as she started to protest. "Listen. I've done a lot of things in my life that I regret. But I've never raped a woman or hurt a child." He looked away from her and his hand fell away. "I'm hollow inside, Kiara, and I've always been that way."

Kiara wanted desperately to bring his warm touch back to her skin. To tell him she didn't care about his past, that he could never do anything to drive her away.

Not after what she'd heard earlier. She understood him now and she wasn't afraid.

Nykyrian sighed, his gaze still focused on the wall. "I used to tell myself what I did was right, that the killings I performed protected governments and innocent lives. That I was on the right side, only taking the lives of people who'd earned their death sentences." An angry tic beat a determined rhythm in his cheek. "Then I learned the bitter truth."

When he didn't elaborate, she ran her hand down his back and prompted him. "What happened?"

"It was a mission like hundreds of others I'd done. Only this time it was a family they wanted swabbed. Father, mother . . . child."

Horror filled her. "Why?"

"To save the order of Tondara. The family had been exiled after Prater took office. Since they had blood ties to the former leadership, The League was afraid that insurgents would rally to them and overthrow Prater's authority."

"You killed them?"

He met her gaze and she saw the truth there. "I thought I could. I killed the father and then went after the mother and child. I didn't realize how small the child would be. How innocent. She looked up at me like I was the monster everyone had called me and for the first time, I saw myself in her eyes for what I really was and I hated it. And her mother . . ."

Kiara brushed his loose hair back from his face. "What about her?"

"She didn't ask me to spare her life. Only her daughter's. In that moment, I knew my life was over. I couldn't kill them. Even though I knew what The League would do to me if they caught me, I couldn't kill a woman who was so loving."

"And that's a good thing, Nykyrian."

He shook his head as if he disagreed. "That night, I decided that my days of being a mindless pawn were over. No more would I be a tool for The League . . ." His green-eyed gaze locked with hers. The heat of that look scorched her. "That's when I became Nemesis."

Her smile faded as his unexpected words hit her like a blow. "What?"

"I'm Nemesis."

Kiara's mind went numb. Over and over, she had heard newscasts informing the public of the grisly killings performed by Nemesis. This was a creature who took pride in inflicting pain on others.

For a moment, she thought she'd be sick. "You rip people into pieces. You . . . you eat pieces of them before you dump their bodies. How could you?"

Nykyrian looked away. Without another word, he left her alone in the room.

Kiara sat on the bed, trying to make sense of all this. She just couldn't accept what he'd told her.

He was Nemesis.

And yet some part of her had known that. It was what her mind had tried to tell her when he'd carried her into Syn's flat. The familiarity of that action had tugged at her mind. She knew he was being honest with her and it horrified her.

Dear God, what had she involved herself in? No wonder Syn was so afraid of her. With this knowledge, she could hand Nykyrian over to the authorities and end the entire Sentella.

All of their lives were now in her hands.

Nemesis. The most feared creature in the entire Ichidian Universe, and she'd slept with him . . .

An image of Jana flashed through her mind. The way Nykyrian had protected, then soothed the boy before taking him to safety. Images of his past replayed through her mind. The cruelty and abuse . . .

Was it any wonder he'd grown into a mercenary assassin?

But Nemesis. Of all the things to be . . .

Nemesis.

Kiara took a deep breath to slow the frantic beating of her heart as she focused on the most important fact.

Nykyrian had trusted her. He'd given her the most sought-after secret in the universe, and he'd laid his life at her feet. He could have kept his secret.

But he'd trusted her. A man who expected betrayal from everyone. A man who didn't like to feel vulnerable. One who'd withdrawn so far from others that he lived on a remote planet alone . . .

He'd trusted her.

She sat there for close to an hour as she sifted through her warring emotions. The fear and uncertainty. Part of her wanted to do the right thing and turn him in—it was what her father had raised her to do. Abide by their laws always. But her heart and soul wouldn't let her.

Nykyrian wasn't a brutal killer—well . . . that wasn't entirely true. He *could* kill brutally. But there was a lot more to him than that. He had a heart.

A true, kind heart, and even though she should be terrified of him, she wasn't. He'd protected her. Cared for her. Most of all, he touched a part of her that no one ever had before.

And that was the part of her that loved him.

Wanting to put his mind at ease, she left the bedroom and went to find him in his monstrously large house. It took her a few minutes to wade through the lorinas, who were begging for attention. Pushing them aside, she searched the media room, his office.

She finally found him in the exercise room, stripped to the waist, pounding a weight bag. His hair was pulled back into a ponytail as sweat glistened over the muscles that were taut and honed. Each blow he delivered to the bag was one in studied fury, and they caused stats written in what appeared to be Andarion to flash on a monitor across from her. She could feel his anger and pain as if it were her own. And every strike emphasized not only his power, but his lethal beauty.

"Nykyrian," she said softly.

He hesitated, looking over at her. The bag swung back, knocking him sideways.

Grunting, he pushed the bag away and cursed.

Kiara stifled her laughter over the shocked look on his face.

He curled his lip at her. "What are you doing here?" He struck the bag again with his fist. "I might get blood on you."

She swallowed the lump in her throat as he turned to deliver a succession of fast, angry blows to the bag.

Kiara watched his hands pound into the rough canvas and was distracted by the sound and lights on the monitor. "What are those colors that keep flashing?"

He delivered a staggering blow. "When it turns red, it lets me know that I hit hard enough to shatter human bones." He slammed a fist into the top part of it. The monitor turned black. "That tells me that if the bag were human, I'd have snapped the neck and splintered the skull." Again, he struck a series of blows and the monitor flashed several colors that he named off. "Black, orange, red, and purple are death blows. The colors just let me know how much pain they'll feel before they die."

She glared at him as a much too graphic image went through her head. "You say crap like that intentionally to horrify me, don't you?"

He spun about and kicked the bag with his foot. Again it flashed red—another death blow. "I am what I am. Nothing will ever change that." His hand flew into the bag with a heavy thud that caused the chains suspending it from the ceiling to rattle—black flashed. "And I don't expect a damned thing from you. Just take your prissy"—orange—"spoiled"—purple—"ass out of my sight before I show you just what Nemesis *is* capable of." The monitor flashed red, black, and purple simultaneously.

Kiara's common sense told her to leave, that he was too angry to talk to, but she couldn't.

Before she could rethink her actions, she crossed the room and shoved him away from the bag.

Stumbling two steps before he caught himself, he gave her an astonished look. The bag swung in an arc between them. "Are you out of your fucking mind?"

"Apparently. 'Cause I'd have to be to shove at you after what I just saw, but it got your attention, didn't it? And now you're going to talk to me."

Nykyrian raked her with a sneer. "Or what? Don't think for one minute you can do anything to me someone else hasn't done already."

And that was what cut her deepest as she looked at the scars marring his flesh. The horrors of his past would always be there so close to the surface that all it would take was one thoughtless word to remind him of the degradation.

Just like her . . .

Kiara lowered her gaze from his face as pain consumed her, wanting some way to break through his overdeveloped defenses. Then she saw his knuckles. They were dripping blood.

"What did you do?" she snarled, crossing the distance between them to take his bleeding, swollen knuckles into her own hands.

He tried to pull them away, but she held fast. "It doesn't hurt. I'm used to it."

She let out a sound of utter disgust. "Why aren't you wearing your gloves? Of all the times to be without them! What were you thinking?" Then it dawned on her. He'd done it intentionally.

The physical pain numbed the inner one.

He closed his eyes and pulled away.

"Nykyrian, talk to me, please. I swear I'll listen. I know you aren't capable of tearing someone apart."

Instead of soothing him as she'd intended, her words angered him more. He spun on her with a snarl, pushing her back against the wall. His light green eyes raged with emotions she couldn't even begin to name.

"Do you really think I couldn't tear someone into pieces?" he ground out in rage. "I was trained to tear men apart so fast that they had the opportunity to see whatever organ I ripped out of them before they hit the floor dead." His arms, braced on either side of her, tensed. "Have you ever held a beating heart in your hand? Felt the warm, sticky blood slide between your fingers while it pulsed?"

"No, I haven't," she breathed, trying to stay calm. He had a soul, she knew it. She'd seen him do too many things that contradicted such brutality. "I asked you once before if you enjoyed killing. Do you?"

He looked away from her.

For a moment, she didn't think he'd answer, then he shook his head. "I hated it," he whispered, pushing himself away from her. "Every damned minute of it. But it wasn't ever that hard to do. All I had to do was reach just below the surface where all my rage dwells . . . all the times when I was wronged and abused. And I pretended they were the ones who'd hurt me. That was all it took to mutilate them."

He turned around and stared at her with all the horrors of his life burning in his eyes. "You have no idea what lives inside me, Kiara. The absolute need to crush people who are around me. There are times when it's so commanding that I don't even know how I pull it back."

"And yet you do."

"No. Sometimes it escapes in spite of my best efforts."

Kiara pulled him into her arms. "I would never hurt you, Nykyrian. But you have to give me time to adjust to the things you tell me." She cupped his face. "I know you, but I have to reconcile what I've heard of you and what I've seen with my own eyes. You are a scary person. You know that. But it doesn't mean I don't love you."

Nykyrian froze at what she'd said to him. Disbelief floored him. "What?"

"I love you."

He jerked back from her, unable to accept that. It wasn't possible. "No, you don't."

"Don't tell me what I feel. I know exactly what's inside my heart."

Still, he refused to believe her. He had to make her understand what she was dealing with. While he might have been worth something as a child, he'd long since damned himself by his own actions. "I'm a killer, princess. Plain and simple. It's all I'll ever be."

"You can be, but you're also the man who holds me while I sleep. The one who tenderly cared for me when I was sick even while I cursed you. You're not just one thing, Nykyrian. Like you told Jana, no one should judge you for what you've done to feed and clothe yourself. Look me in the eyes and tell me the truth. Have you ever once killed purely for profit?"

"No."

"Would you ever kill for the money?"

He shook his head.

"Have you ever killed a child?"

"God, no."

"Then you're not an animal."

He stared at her in awe. How did she do it? How was she able to see him—to look at his bare face and eyes—and not sneer or curl her lip when everyone else had?

She brushed a stray piece of hair back from his face and cupped his cheek. "While your past may shock me at times, I promise that it won't change how I feel about you. Unless you've been slaughtering baby bunnies on the side . . ."

He wasn't amused. "I've butchered people."

"And I've seen you do it. But I wouldn't consider

them people. People don't take pleasure in hurting others. Even when you killed Arast, did it give you pleasure?"

"No."

"Then you're a better person than most, and that is why I love you."

Stepping away from her, he leaned against the wall, watching her with hooded eyes. "I don't care if you turn me in, but I want you to swear to me you'll never betray Hauk, Syn, Darling, or Jayne."

"I would never betray *any* of you."

Nykyrian nodded as she closed the distance between them. He took her hands and turned them upwards. "In your palms, I've placed my life, my secrets," he whispered, his breath falling against her cheek, making her skin tingle. "I give you freedom to leave me at any time. I'm not easy to love. No one ever has. All I ask is that you always keep your silence, if not for me, then for the families of the others you'd destroy."

Kiara blinked back tears at the sound of resignation in his voice. He expected her to turn on him just like Syn's wife. But she would never do that.

"I could never hurt you, Nykyrian. You can trust me. I swear it."

His lips covered hers, burning her as he kissed her passionately. Kiara welcomed the feel of his warm mouth, the hunger of his need. She clutched him to her, needing the feel of his body against her.

She ran her hands over the hard, muscled flesh of his ribs. To her shock, Nykyrian jerked and laughed.

She stilled her hands and looked up at his face. "Was that a laugh?"

He looked as baffled as she did. "I think I'm ticklish."

Devilishly, Kiara ran her hands back over his ribs.

True enough, he was ticklish. His rich, throaty laughter filled her ears and her heart with happiness. She kept tickling him, delighting in the way he squirmed.

"Mercy," he cried at last, his eyes bright.

She gave one last rub before she pulled her hands back. "Okay." She kissed his cheek.

He pulled her to him, his eyes serious, and wrapped his arms around her shoulders. "Don't ever leave me," he said in a ragged voice that tore through her.

"I won't leave you."

In one deft movement, he pulled her nightgown from her body and lowered her to the floor. Kiara welcomed the feel of his skin against hers even though he was sweaty. Strangely enough, he didn't stink. It was a warm musky scent that made her instantly wet.

She caressed the hard tendons of his back that were covered with deep scars, wanting to keep him with her forever. "You lied to me, you know."

He scowled at her. "How?"

"You told me you slept with Nemesis every night."

His gorgeous dimpled smile teased her. "No, I said I fucked him, which I do. I screw myself over pretty much every day, or at least on a regular basis."

She rubbed her nose against his. "You're terrible."

Not around you, I'm not. Nykyrian stared at her in amazement. What was it about her that tamed the anger inside him . . . well, not when she pissed him off. But right now, her touch quieted all the fury that lived inside him. His soul was at peace.

How did she do that?

Lowering his head, he took possession of her mouth and tasted her. Her scent and soft skin succored him like nothing ever had.

For this he would be willing to die.

She wrapped her legs around his waist. He pressed his cheek to hers as he savored the sensation of being held. Her breasts pressed against his chest as he breathed her in. He pulled back to stare down into those eyes that reflected his face back at him. It was the first time he could look at his reflection and not a sneer.

The child's eyes had shown him a monster.

Kiara's showed him the man.

And he wanted to be that person she stared at so adoringly. Rolling over, he set her on top of his bare stomach. The hairs at the juncture of her thighs teased his skin and made him even harder.

Kiara took Nykyrian's hand and grimaced at the blood still on his knuckles. "We should take care of this."

He pulled a towel to him that was on the floor a small distance away and wiped at the blood. "Trust me, I don't feel it."

She took his thumb in her hand and nibbled the pad, tasting the salt of his skin. "You are a masochist, aren't you?"

"Most assassins are." He traced his free hand over her breast, toying with her nipple. "You know, I've never had sex with the same woman twice."

Dropping his hand, she arched a brow at that. "You really do stink at social skills, don't you? Telling me you've been with a bunch of different women isn't exactly the thing to do . . . especially right now. Just so you know, it's really a buzz kill."

He took her hand back into his. "That's not what I meant. I've only been with two women. Neither of them would have me again."

"Why not?"

He didn't answer, but she saw the pain in his eyes.

"They were fools, Nykyrian." She ran her tongue up his neck until she reached his lips. "There's no one else I'd ever want to be with."

Nykyrian closed his eyes as those words tugged at his heart. Reaching behind her, he opened his pants and slid them off.

Kiara was impressed by his ability to do that while she still sat on his stomach. "You are a strong, flexible little booger, aren't you?"

"I have my moments." He sat up under her so that he could taste her breasts.

Leaning back, she gave him full access as she cradled his head to her chest. His tongue stroked her nipple, making her stomach contract while pleasure spiked through her. She felt his cock pressing against her stomach as he took his time tasting her.

Unable to stand it, she lifted herself up and set herself down on him. They groaned in unison.

Nykyrian ground his teeth as he pulled back to watch her ride him. She lifted her hips up and sank down, taking him in all the way to the hilt. Her warm skin slid against his in a velvet caress. Biting his lip, he raised his hips, driving himself even deeper inside her. He took her hands into his and kissed her delicate fingers.

She was so frail, and yet one unkind word from her lips could shatter him. How could she have so much power over him? He wanted to hate her for that.

If only he could.

Kiara leaned forward as she quickened her strokes. She wanted to please him so much . . .

His gaze locked on hers, he reached down between their bodies to stroke her. She let out a gasp as he increased her pleasure.

A slow smile spread across his face. "You like that."

She wrinkled her nose at him as his fingers stroked her in time to her thrusts.

Nykyrian held his breath until he saw and felt her come. She almost fell off him. Catching her, he rolled over and quickened his thrusts, intensifying her orgasm. She clung to him.

He buried his face against her neck and let her scent send him over the edge so that he could join her. Growling, he kept himself deep inside her until he was completely spent.

He laid himself down on top of her, careful not to put too much weight on her. Her hands played in his hair. "I'm yours completely."

She laughed. "I somehow doubt that."

And she would be wrong. Right now there was nothing he would deny her.

Suddenly, a loud whistle rent the air. Nykyrian looked up with a jerk.

"What is it?" she asked breathlessly.

He let out an irritated growl. "My link. Ten to one it's Syn's stupid ass needing something stupid."

"You're hung up on that word, aren't you?"

He grunted as he reluctantly withdrew. This had damn well better be important. Otherwise Syn was going to be wedged somewhere very uncomfortable.

Kiara pulled her gown to her while he picked up his pants and left the room. As soon as she was dressed, she went to see what was going on.

Nykyrian, now wearing just his pants, switched the link off and tossed it back on the low table. He rubbed his hands over his face, a deep grimace lining his features.

"Is something wrong?"

"Yeah. We're about to have company."

CHAPTER 21

Kiara's heart clenched at his dire tone. "What do you mean?"

"Arturo beat Darling up again. Since Syn's place isn't secure, there's no other safe place to take him to keep him out of Arturo's reach." He cursed foully. "I knew I should have killed that bastard."

She moved to stand behind him so that she could rub his back and offer whatever comfort she could. "Honestly, I'm surprised you haven't."

"Yeah. But Darling doesn't want that. End of the day, it's his uncle and he says he loves him. God, he's an idiot. How can he love someone who beats the shit out of him?"

"People are complicated. Didn't a part of you love Commander Quiakides?"

He gave her a droll stare over his shoulder. "Kiara, I'm the one who killed him."

She stepped back, stunned by the disclosure. "What?"

"I killed him. He crossed the wrong person at the wrong time and The League justices called for his death. It was one of the few missions I volunteered for—it's also the one that got me my commission so early. My CO said my ability to carry out their orders so swiftly and coldly against my own father showed ideal discipline. Ironic, really, when you think about the fact that it was all the commander wanted me for and his death is what actualized his dream." He shook his head. "You should have seen the look on his face when I cut his throat."

She struggled to breathe at what he was telling her. "You killed the man who adopted you?"

He ground his teeth. "And now I've horrified you again. See why I'm better off not telling you anything?"

She held her hand up and tilted her head as she tried to quell her emotions. "I told you when you drop these little bombs on me that you have to give me a chance to cope. Some of these are harder to take in than others. I know from what little I saw of your past that the commander was a complete bastard. I get it. But even you have to admit that was harsh."

"No." His gaze blazed with fury. "Harsh was leaving me in jail for two days because he was embarrassed by something I didn't do and insisting that I be put in with the class-three felons."

"Class-three felons?"

"Rapists and pedophiles."

Kiara felt ill as she remembered what Aksel had said to him when the commander's wife had brought him home. He must have known what his father had done and the fact that he would rub Nykyrian's nose in it . . .

They were sick.

She looked up at Nykyrian. "Are you saying . . . did they . . ." She couldn't even bring herself to use the word. It was too nightmarish to even contemplate.

His expression was completely dead. "Yes, they did. As bad as everything else was, nothing compares to those forty-six hours of being degraded while I wore a collar that kept me from being able to fight back as I was attacked . . . repeatedly and without mercy. You want to know why I hate Jullien? He was the one who accused me of theft when he had the ring the whole time. Because he was a prince and I was the bastard the commander wouldn't even give his name to who outscored him on a test, he wanted me hurt and it was the best revenge on me he could think of. The school officials seized me and searched me, then handed me over to Jullien's guards, who beat and interrogated me for hours before they called the commander to tell him what'd happened. He told them to do what Jullien's father had called for—send me to jail, and they did." The furious pain in his eyes scorched her. "I was barely fourteen, Kiara."

She hugged him close. "I'm so sorry, Nykyrian. Why would he do that?"

He wrapped his arms around her and rested his chin on her head. "For the same reason Aksel and Arast hated me. I was beneath them and yet I outscored them. How dare *I*, a mongrel life form that should never have been born, outperform them in any way. I told you that I live with a rage so fierce it's consuming, and on that night, I unleashed it all against Commander Quia-kides."

And now she understood why. She couldn't blame him for what he'd done, not after everything they'd put him through.

"I can't believe Jullien didn't recognize you today."

"That's how little I mattered to him. I wasn't even worth remembering."

Yet he was worth ruining for no other reason than Jullien was a jealous snipe. He'd scarred Nykyrian in a way no one should ever be scarred. And it made her wish she had Nykyrian's skills. "I vote we go out and beat the little snot until his head explodes. That would serve him."

Nykyrian scowled at her even though he tightened his arms. He loved whenever she defended him. With a quick kiss to her cheek, he pulled away. "C'mon, we need to get dressed before Syn and Darling arrive." He led her upstairs. "Luckily my bedroom walls are soundproof." His devilish smile brought heat to her cheeks.

After they cleaned up and dressed, they ended up in the media room. Kiara wrinkled her nose at everything he pulled out for them to watch. "Don't you have anything that isn't gory?"

"Not really."

"You don't have a single comedy?"

He shook his head. "I have you performing."

She rolled her eyes and laughed. "I think I'm offended that I said comedy and *that* was your suggestion."

He laughed.

"Do you get any broadcasts out here?"

"Yeah." He handed her the controls. "Download whatever makes you happy."

"Even if it makes you miserable?"

"I've suffered through worse, I'm sure." He went to lie down on the couch while she scrolled through the downloadable movies.

Ooooh, there was a romantic comedy she'd been dying to see . . . She looked over her shoulder and sighed. She wouldn't torture him.

"You can watch it if you want."

"Watch what?"

"That sappy crap you paused on."

She hesitated. "You sure?"

"Yeah."

Smiling at him, she pressed the order button and went to join him on the couch. He got up and let her sit, then he did the most amazing thing of all.

He actually laid his head in her lap.

Stunned, she stared down at him.

He caught her look and tensed. "You don't mind, do you? I had a bad eye injury a few years back and tend to get vicious headaches if I watch sitting up."

"Baby, I don't mind at all. I was just shocked that you'd do that after the way you cringe every time I touch you."

"I don't cringe *every* time you touch me."

She smiled down at him. No, he was getting better about being touched. Completely content, she brushed her hand through his soft hair as the movie started playing.

Kiara couldn't believe she had what she'd wanted.

He trusted her.

A lump constricted her throat as she looked down at him. His long eyelashes fluttered while he watched the movie. She pulled his hair away from his neck to see the short, baby hairs curling around his nape. Using her fingernails, she gently brushed them. Chills formed on his neck and he closed his eyes with a sigh.

With her fingertip, she traced the line of his cheek and lips while her heart lurched at the sight of the faint scars left behind by his mask and other injuries. How she wished he'd had the childhood he deserved.

Turning his head, he opened his eyes to meet hers. The tenderness inside the light green eyes scorched her.

He reached his hand up and brought her head down to his so that he could kiss her. Kiara moaned, her body igniting at his touch. His arms tensed.

Syn's engines thundered in the bay.

Nykyrian let out an irritated sigh. "Remember this position for future reference."

He stood up and she wanted to curse in frustration. Pausing the movie, she followed him to the main room to wait for Darling and Syn. It took several minutes before the door finally opened.

Kiara gasped.

Syn supported Darling with his shoulder. Darling was slumped heavily against Syn's side, unable to walk without assistance. Darling's face, bloodied and bruised, could barely be recognized. His left arm dangled in an awkward position and Kiara realized it was broken.

Nykyrian cursed, then swung Darling up in his arms. Syn ran ahead to the back bedrooms. Kiara followed behind them, her heart twisting at the sight of Darling's beaten condition.

The cruelty of it made her want to hurt whoever had done that to him, and it brought home exactly how awful Nykyrian's past really was. It was one thing to be told about it, to even see it through the sterility of a vid, but to see it face to face . . .

This was raw and real.

Syn pulled the covers back. "Let me pull up the sheet."

"To hell with the sheet," Nykyrian snarled.

Syn nodded, then met Kiara's eyes. The hostility in his gaze made her take a step back.

Oblivious to the hate-filled look, Nykyrian laid Darling down on the bed. Syn broke eye contact with her to tend Darling. Kiara stood in the doorway, the lorinas curling around her legs as they rubbed against her.

She frowned as she saw for the first time why Darling kept his hair over the left side of his face. A deep, white scar traveled down his face from hairline to chin. What in the world would leave a scar like that?

Her throat tightened at the amount of blood covering him. Never in her life had she seen anyone so abused. She glanced at Nykyrian, his jaw tight, and wondered how many times he'd been beaten into a similar condition.

"I'm going to kill Arturo," Nykyrian ground out between clenched teeth.

Darling reached out and touched Nykyrian's arm. "Leave him alone."

Nykyrian let fly a vicious curse.

Kiara couldn't believe he was still conscious given the severity of his injuries.

Syn injected a painkiller into Darling's arm, then moved to set the break. How did Darling stand it without crying out or at least cursing? He just lay there so quiet and still he didn't look real. The only reason she knew he was still conscious was his open eyes that stared up at the ceiling.

Nykyrian looked at her. He crossed the floor, took her by the elbow and led her outside. "I think it best if you went upstairs and waited for me."

Kiara nodded. "Is he going to be all right?"

Nykyrian brushed a strand of hair from her cheek. "He'll be fine," he said before giving her a quick kiss on the lips.

Kiara started to leave, then paused. "Nykyrian?" She waited until he turned around to look at her. "I hope you do beat Arturo." And with that, she headed to their bedroom to wait for him.

It was an hour later when Nykyrian joined her in the bed. Without a word, he pulled her into his arms and held her close, his face buried in her neck. His warm breath caressed her nape through her hair.

Kiara wished for the words to make him feel better, to ease some of the tenseness in his muscles that surrounded her.

"How's he doing?"

Nykyrian sighed and pulled back from her neck. He stroked her bare arm with his hand. "He's asleep. He'll be fine, all things considered."

She bit her lip, her throat tight. "Do you know what I've been thinking about while I laid here?"

A short laugh rumbled behind her, bringing a tiny thrill to her body despite the seriousness of her mood. "I hope you were thinking about me and not another man." He kissed the lobe of her ear.

She caught his hand in hers and brought it to her cheek. "The irony of life."

She felt him stiffen around her.

Kiara closed her eyes and held his warm hand closer to her. "I've been thinking about how much I wanted to leave my father's house growing up because he never respected me or my privacy." She sighed, her thoughts tripping over each other. "I always thought he was so cruel to check up on me and intimidate and interrogate my friends like they were criminals. He'd never let me out of his sight without siccing one of his soldiers on me." She winced as she remembered all the arguments they'd had about his restrictions for her. "I was so stupid. My mother used to tell me my life wasn't so horrible. Now I fully understand what she meant. God, I've been so blind."

His hand tightened around hers and he raised it to his lips where he placed a gentle kiss on her fingers. "I'm glad your father protected you. I wouldn't want to have to kill him, too."

Kiara gave a bittersweet laugh. "All I wanted growing up was to be free." She rolled over onto her back and faced him. "Is that what you wanted, to be free of your father?"

His eyes darkened. "Truthfully?"

She nodded.

"All I wanted was to die like a man, without tears or pleading."

That made her want to weep for him. "And now?" she whispered, afraid that he still wanted to die.

He kissed her heatedly. His lips trailed over her body with an insistence she couldn't deny. Kiara welcomed him to her as he pulled her gown from her body and kissed his way from her lips, to her breasts, then lower over her stomach until his lips were buried where she craved him most.

She cried out in pleasure as his tongue teased and tormented her until her body exploded. Still he licked and played until she'd had three more orgasms.

Only then did he take his own pleasure. He made love to her slowly, with the stars twinkling all around them.

When he was finally sated, he held her tightly in his arms, as if he were afraid to let her go.

It wasn't until later when she was drifting off to sleep that she realized he'd never answered her question.

To Kiara's amazement, Darling left his bed the next morning. His movements were slow and studied, but he was able to get about by himself. After seeing him the night before, she'd been certain Darling would be bedridden for days.

Darling sat at the kitchen table eating muffins with Kiara as Nykyrian joined them and made a cup of tea. "I always wondered where you lived. Now that I know how nice it is, I'll be sure to pass the info on to the rest of the group. This'll make a nice crash pad for us."

Nykyrian looked up from his cup, a smile twitching the edges of his lips. "Finish your food before I finish what Arturo started."

Syn checked the lorinas' feeder in the kitchen. "Where are the mongrels?"

Nykyrian took a sip of tea before he answered. "They were confused by all the people. Last I saw of them, they were hiding out in my bed."

Darling frowned. "They don't bite, do they?"

Nykyrian scoffed. "I'm the only thing that bites in this house."

Kiara had to stifle a laugh at his dry response. Her neck still tingled from the bite he'd given her last night after he'd joined her in bed. Though he tried to be careful with his fangs, every now and again he did catch a bit of her skin.

Darling scratched at his plaster cast. "What are we doing today?"

Syn crossed the room to join Nykyrian. "You're going to rest."

Nykyrian downed the last of his tea, put the cup in the sink, then donned his long black coat. "And since you're here, you can keep Kiara company while we go after a couple of Aksel's men."

Kiara's heart stopped beating as fear for him consumed her. "I wish you wouldn't."

"We have to."

Gah, how she hated his stubbornness. She could argue, but in the end, she knew it wouldn't do her a bit of good.

Syn grabbed his bag off the floor and gave Kiara a nasty glare. His glare intensified as Nykyrian pulled her into his arms to kiss her good-bye.

With a heated curse, Syn entered the bay.

"We'll be back around dark," Nykyrian said, squeezing her arm reassuringly.

Kiara watched him leave, her heart heavy with fear and worry. *Be careful, baby.*

"Should I ask about what I just saw?"

Darling's voice distracted her from her thoughts. Kiara shrugged.

A tiny smile curved one corner of his mouth. "Now that I think about it, I slept in the room with Syn. Where did you sleep?" Darling stared at her with an intensity she found a bit disturbing. Then it faded to a teasing look as he wagged his brows at her.

Laughing at his expression, she took a seat across from him. "Why are you so interested?"

"I've had a severe crush on Nykyrian for years. If not for fear of my life, I would have made a pass at him long ago. But I know I'm too hairy for his tastes."

She watched the way Darling cut up his food with one hand. "May I ask a personal question?"

He looked up at her. "Depends on the question."

"How did you get the scar on your face?"

He went so still, Kiara wished she could take the question back. Self-consciously, Darling put his fork down and rubbed the cheek covered by his hair. "It's disgusting, isn't it?"

"No," she answered honestly. "But it is deep."

He sighed. "Yeah, you should have seen it sixteen operations ago."

Her eyes widened in shock. "What happened?"

He shrugged as if the matter didn't really bother him, but she knew better. "My eldest brother, Ryn. We got into a fight a few years ago and this," he tucked his hair behind his ear to display the scar, "is what happened."

"Your brother did that?" Kiara was aghast. Didn't any of them have a happy childhood?

Darling nodded. "It was an accident. At least I think it was."

Compassion welled up inside her as she surveyed the scar. While it was far more noticeable than Nykyrian's, it really didn't detract from his handsomeness. "You know, you're still extremely good-looking."

He gave her a look that told her he thought she'd lost her mind. "If only you were a man, love. Unfortunately, most people curl their lips and run."

"Most people are idiots."

He laughed. "No argument on that." Then he turned serious. Draping his uninjured arm over the back of his chair, he studied her face for several minutes. "I want you to promise me something."

Kiara glanced sideways, her mind thinking of several things he might want from her. "What?"

"I want you to take care of Nykyrian. I can't explain it, but he's different now that you're here. Happier, I guess. He doesn't seem so serious and emotionless anymore." His eyes narrowed into an intense stare that probed her soul. "I want you to promise me you won't hurt him."

"I would never hurt him."

Darling nodded. "Good, now let's go digging around and see what kind of trouble we can find."

She laughed, happy to find Darling such an easy person to befriend. Leading him to the library, she tried to keep her mind from worrying over Nykyrian and the trouble *he* might find. The last time he went out, he'd been shot on her behalf, and that was the last thing she wanted.

Hours later, Nykyrian and Syn sat in the backroom of the Bended Maiden sipping drinks. Nykyrian juice and

Syn . . . he might as well be injecting alcohol straight into his bloodstream.

Nykyrian's head pounded from a vicious headache. He hated when his vision screwed up like this. Damn his injuries. But there was nothing he could do except suffer with it.

They continued to review their findings for the afternoon, to little avail.

He growled at the time they'd wasted. Aksel beat his dogs well. They were all so afraid of him, none of them would betray him for fear of his retaliation.

Bloody bastards.

All he wanted was an end to this contract. So long as Aksel was on the hunt, Kiara wasn't safe. And God help her if Aksel got his hands on her.

Agitated at the apparent futility of his day, he sifted through the sheets of printouts that lined the tabletop.

The bare, tan walls kept out the noise of the clientele in the bar area fairly well, but every now and again a loud laugh or shout would interrupt their quiet.

Antilles brought them another round of drinks. Nykyrian watched the elderman fight his way around all the boxes and barrels that stored his supplies.

The old man smiled at them, setting their drinks on the table. "It's good to have the two of you back. It's been too long."

Nykyrian inclined his head in appreciation and handed him payment.

Syn sat back and cupped his hands around his head. "Has Ambassador Cruel arrived yet?" His tone was irritated. Like him, Syn had grown bored with the wait long ago.

Antilles offered Syn a look of apology. "He hasn't yet, but I promise to send him back here as soon as he does."

When they were alone again, Syn let out an aggravated growl. "Shahara is my main worry. Aksel comes in full force, blasters blazing. You can't miss him. She slips up from behind and drives a blade into your lung. Lethal *harita.*"

Nykyrian agreed. Shahara was one of the best bounty hunters ever born. A fully trained Seax, she was to tracing what he was to the assassin's guild. No one ever escaped her.

And Syn was right. She never acted out in the open. Had she been an assassin, she would have given even him a run for his money.

Nykyrian moved his drink out of the way. "I'll go to Tondara tonight and try to find Driana at the club they told us about." Aksel kept his address as guarded as they did—they couldn't even pinpoint which planet the scab lived on. The only lead they had was that Driana went to the same Tondarian dive every weekend, which ironically was an old haunt of theirs. "If we can find her she'll gladly give me Aksel's plans, and knowing him, he's run his mouth in front of her, thinking she'd never betray him."

Syn swilled his drink. "From my reports, I'm surprised Aksel hasn't killed her. Everything I have says they hate each other."

"Aksel won't kill her because of her trust fund. If they divorce or she dies under mysterious circumstances, all her money reverts to her family. Aksel's too greedy to let something like hatred interfere with his wealth."

"Why doesn't she divorce him?"

"He'd kill her and her family. You have to remember, Aksel's one psycho bastard."

"Why are you talking about that scum?"

Nykyrian turned to see Ryn approaching them. Ryn's red hair was a shade darker than his brother Darling's, but his eyes were an identical shade of blue.

Even though Ryn had a jaded past, he, like Darling, showed no traces of being anything other than a high-ranking aristocrat. Their past was completely shielded behind a mask of arrogant disdain.

Dressed in bright imperial robes, Ryn looked like he'd just left a council meeting.

"We were discussing ways to kill him. Want to join the fun?"

Ryn ignored Syn's sarcastic question as he took a seat in front of Nykryian. "So how's my renegade little brother? He still running with you guys?"

Knowing Darling wouldn't want his brother, who couldn't help him, anyway, informed about his condition, Nykyrian shrugged the question off. Besides, it wasn't like Ryn didn't know what Arturo did behind closed doors—he'd fallen under the man's fists too many years to not be well acquainted with his brutality. But unlike Darling, he'd at least had their father to run interference. "He's fine."

"Good." Ryn took a seat and handed Nykyrian a copy of the Probekeins' latest contract on Kiara's life. "That hasn't been posted yet," he said, adjusting the voluminous yards of his robe—the only sign he gave of not being completely at ease with his duties. "But it goes up first thing in the morning. They've quadrupled the bounty and upgraded from bill-kill to spill-kill. They're getting antsy that she has yet to die."

Nykyrian ground his teeth at the news. Spill-kill meant anyone around her was considered fair game. The messier, the better, and each vic would have a lesser fee paid for their assassination, too.

Zamir had screwed up royally where she was concerned.

Syn scowled. "Why are they so hot to kill her, anyway? I would think by now they'd let it go and move on."

Ryn sighed. "All I could find out about what set them off was that Zamir told Emperor Abenbi to burn in a very uncomfortable position for a long time. At this point, Abenbi refuses to call the contract off even if Zamir gives him the surata. His honor has been too abused by President Zamir, so Kiara must die."

Syn smirked. "I could've learned that online."

Ryn frowned at Nykyrian. "What did you do to put him in such a foul mood?"

Syn flipped him off.

Ignoring him, Ryn continued talking to Nykyrian. "Abenbi also wants the weapon to go after the Fremick territory. He feels since they're his neighbors, they should be part of his territories. I really wish you guys would put a stop to him."

Syn crossed his arms over his chest. "Pay our fee."

Ryn glared, but again wisely chose to ignore him. "That's all I know. I hope it helped."

At Syn's scoff, Ryn faced Nykyrian. "You should keep him on a leash."

Nykyrian barely had time to grab Syn's arm before his fist made contact with the ambassador's chin. "Calm your ass down."

Grudgingly, Syn retook his seat.

Nykyrian shook Ryn's hand. "Your information helped a lot. Thanks."

Syn rolled his eyes as Ryn took his leave. "We waited all this time for *that*?"

Nykyrian jerked the papers off the table. "What the hell is wrong with you?"

Syn slammed his hand down on the table so hard it almost upended his drink. "You slept with her last night. I waited up half the night hoping you'd come back downstairs. But you didn't. You stayed with her."

"I know where I spent the night."

Syn's gaze narrowed dangerously. "When she betrays us, just remember *I* warned you."

Nykyrian clenched his fist, tempted to send Syn flying. Their friendship was the only thing that saved Syn's jaw from being shattered. He tried to remind himself that Syn's anger was only because his friend was watching out for him, but right now, he was sick of hearing Syn's shit. "How could I forget, since you'll no doubt remind me every day of my life?"

From the clenched fists Syn kept at his own side, Nykyrian knew he wanted to knock his head from his shoulders.

After a few tense minutes, Syn snatched his papers up. "It's your funeral." He stormed out of the room.

With Syn's dire warning echoing in his head, Nykyrian made his way slowly to his ship. Maybe Syn was right. Things had been going too good. His life never went smoothly. Just when things seemed to improve, something always happened to screw it up.

Nykyrian climbed aboard his ship. He sat in the leather seat, thinking. His thumb played across the trigger for his lasers. A bad feeling crept along his spine.

Checking his power grid and fuel levels, he didn't see anything out of the ordinary.

Still the dread feeling persisted—he could literally see himself in a massive dogfight with his ship damaged—it was as clear as day.

And if he'd learned anything in his life, it was to always trust his instincts, and now those instincts were buzzing loudly in alarm.

Something awful was definitely going to happen and he was going to be in the middle of it.

CHAPTER 22

Nykyrian froze as he found Kiara dancing in his training room. The embodiment of grace and gentle beauty, she twirled around his instruments of death. The dichotomy of that wasn't lost on him.

And as he watched her, he remembered the sensation of her making love to him last night. The way her lips had felt as she tongued his nipples—who knew how much pleasure *that* could hold? It'd startled him at first, but once the initial shock had faded, he'd willingly submitted to her painstaking exploration. He was still getting used to allowing another person complete access to his body. It was so odd to lie there and not have to protect himself from her.

The fact that she didn't hurt him never ceased to amaze him.

Kiara twirled and caught sight of him watching her. The smile that spread over her face made his gut wrench.

Would he ever get used to her being happy to see him? The way her eyes lit up and her cheeks rushed with color . . .

It made him feel so welcomed and wanted, and to his complete horror, it made him return her smile.

She walked into his arms and planted a sweet kiss on his cheek. "How'd it go?"

"Not as good as it could have, but it was basically uneventful."

"Meaning?"

"I didn't kill anyone."

She rolled her eyes at him, then stepped back and tugged at his arm. "Come dance with me."

"I really don't dance."

Kiara tightened her grip on his hand. Having seen the vid of his past, she understood why—the only time he'd danced, he'd been beaten ferociously over it, but she wanted to replace his bad memories with good ones. She wanted him to trust her.

Most of all, she wanted him to love her as much as she loved him.

"Dance with me, Nykyrian," she insisted.

Nykyrian wanted to decline, but the look on her face . . .

He hated disappointing her. Growling at her playfully, he allowed her to pull him deeper into the room. The music started in a slow ballad.

She wrapped her arms around his neck, swaying gently to the music. "See, it doesn't hurt."

Not entirely true. It raised a lump in his throat that burned as he ached to stay like this forever. Closing his eyes, he savored the sensation of her arms wrapped around him, her breasts pressing against his chest as the music teleported him to a realm of heaven he'd never imagined.

Kiara buried her face against the opening of his shirt and inhaled the warm scent of his skin. She loved the feeling of his arms wrapped around her. He always held her as if she were unspeakably precious. As if he were afraid of hurting her. The strength of him never ceased to amaze her. His body was so hard and yet his touch gentle.

Adoring him, she tilted her head up to kiss him as they danced. His fangs scraped against her tongue, sending a chill down her spine.

She felt him tense before he pulled back. "Let's not start this fire while Darling's here. Otherwise, I'm going to toss you over my shoulder, take you upstairs and make love to you until we're both limping."

Smiling at his threat, she twisted her hand playfully in the small hairs at the nape of his neck. "You said the room was soundproof."

He smiled at that. "You are an evil temptress."

She kissed his cheek. "Only for you, baby. Only for you." Reluctantly, she stepped back and released him. But not before she nipped at his chin. "Go on with your bad self. I need to finish working out."

Nykyrian had to force himself to let go of her. With one last smile at him, she headed back to her dancing. Her touch and scent lingered on his skin as he realized why he couldn't listen to Syn.

Kiara healed him.

Somehow she took all the ugliness of his past and made it not matter to him anymore. Yes, it still stung when he thought about it, but with her here, it wasn't as severe.

I'm a fucking idiot.

No, he was a man in love with a woman who meant the entire universe to him.

Like I said, you're a fucking idiot.

And for the first time in his life, he was happy being stupid because the only alternative would be existing without her, and now that he'd tasted the sunlight she brought into his world, he never wanted to live in darkness again.

Please don't send me back to the night.

Hours later, Nykyrian, Darling and Hauk stood in the main room of Nykyrian's house waiting for Kiara to join them.

I can't believe I'm doing this. What kind of moron would even contemplate taking her to Club Blood?

He didn't like the answer to that question since it was *him*.

If only she hadn't pleaded with those big amber eyes, he might have been able to stand fast and make her stay behind. But he was entirely too weak-willed where she was concerned, and her disappointed pout completely overrode his common sense.

"Your advice didn't help," Hauk said darkly, eyeing the stairs.

Nykyrian turned around to see Kiara descending. As he'd requested, she'd pulled her hair back from her face into a severe bun. The old, ragged battlesuit that added inches to her waist didn't deter from her beauty in the least.

Damn.

And even worse was the major hard-on he had just looking at her.

Just what I need—more blood drained from my already impaired brain.

Darling let out a loud sigh. "What else can we do?"

"Put something over her head." Hauk's tone was completely dry.

Kiara's face flushed bright pink. "Why don't you wear something over your head, you big, hairy—"

"That's it," Nykyrian said, interrupting her before she said something that might piss the Andarion off.

"Keep her mad. She looks like she could kick ass now."

Hauk didn't comment as he came forward to strap a blaster and a belt of knives around her waist.   .

Kiara frowned. She hadn't realized before how much things like this weighed. It was a wonder Nykyrian and the others could move, never mind fight when armed. "What are you doing with those? I've never been able to shoot straight."

Hauk snorted. "No one else has to know that. Just consider them for show and make sure that if you do pull out the blaster, warn me so I can duck before you pull the trigger."

Kiara scoffed at him as Nykyrian went to the closet and pulled out a thick, padded leather jacket that was four times her size. He brought it over to her. "What are you doing? I already look like a shuttlecraft."

Nykyrian winked. "That's the idea."

Kiara pursed her lips, no longer sure if she should go with them, given their behavior. When Darling had told her what type of club it was, her curiosity had gotten the best of her.

But now . . .

Maybe she should stay here.

While Nykyrian helped her into the jacket, her gaze drifted over his hot, taut body. He wore a pair of tight leather pants and an oversized leather jacket without a shirt on beneath it as a show of strength and power—*I'm such a badass that I don't need protection from your unworthy attempts to hurt me.* An act of silent defiance that was helped by the presence of scars that advertised exactly how many battles and fights he'd been in.

And obviously survived.

But it was the sight of his well-defined eight-pack that left her all but drooling.

His tanned, muscled flesh begged her hand to touch him. If not for Hauk and Darling, she'd pull him back upstairs and make him beg her for mercy. She licked her dry lips as she met Nykyrian's eyes.

Color stained Nykyrian's cheeks at her hungry look.

Hauk's laugh rang out. "That may actually be the first time in my life I've seen that boy blush. Damn, someone grab a pic quick. We might be able to use it for blackmail later."

Nykyrian cast him a dark scowl.

Hauk took a step back, still laughing.

Muttering a curse about the Andarion, Nykyrian undid Kiara's hair and gently plaited it into three braids, then the three into one. He stood up the collar of her jacket and turned her to face Darling and Hauk.

"Now what do you think?"

Hauk grimaced. "I still think she's too damned attractive. She's going to get us killed."

Darling shoved playfully at him. "Relax. Shahara goes there all the time and no one ever bothers her."

Hauk gave him a droll stare. "That's because she'd kill you for nothing more than asking her the time of day."

Kiara hesitated as she looked up at Nykyrian. "I would love to go with you, but . . ."

"We'll keep our eyes on you. Don't worry. If anything happens to you, I'll kill Hauk for it." Nykyrian took her hand in his gloved one.

Hauk arched a brow, but wisely said nothing as he followed them out to the landing bay and they boarded their ships.

Time passed quickly for Kiara as they made their way to the large planet of Tondara and the thriving port city called Touras.

They landed and docked outside the grimiest bay

Kiara had ever seen. When they'd told her the club was filled with riff-raff, she'd assumed they would at least attend to basic hygiene, but apparently she was wrong.

As the hatch raised, she choked on the pungent odor of rotting garbage and body odor—now she understood where Chenz had learned his cleanliness from. Maybe she should have listened to Hauk and stayed home after all. This place was disgusting.

She pressed her hand to her nose to help block the odors.

Nykyrian unstrapped her. "You'll have to jump down unassisted. Act like you know what you're doing and if anyone looks at you, snarl at them like you're going to kill them where they stand."

"Are you serious?"

"Very."

She definitely wanted to go home. But it was too late. She'd argued with all of them to come, so the least she could do was be a woman about. Trying to look tough, she got out and did just as he told her. When her feet hit the pavement, pain jarred through her knees.

"Ow," she breathed. But at least the fierce grimace on her face was real.

And she did great maintaining her kick-ass facade until several unidentifiable vermin squeaked past her feet, rushing under a nearby garbage heap. Unable to stand it, she made a most undignified shriek and ran to Hauk for protection.

Several beings turned to stare at her with interest.

Hauk let out a disgusted sigh as he pried her hands loose from his arm and scowled at the people who were now eyeing them.

Nykyrian jumped down beside her.

Like Hauk, he gave the onlookers a fierce scowl that

threatened total dismemberment. This time, they paid attention and quickly averted their gazes.

Nykyrian placed his arm around her shoulders in an act of overt possession.

Darling joined them. He glared at Nykyrian. "My knees hate the shit out of you, boss."

Nykyrian shrugged. "Mine don't think much of me, either."

Hauk narrowed his eyes as he glanced around the area. "Looks crowded tonight. I think we should turn back before we get pulverized."

Nykyrian pushed Hauk toward the entrance.

Kiara tilted her head down and used her peripheral vision to pinpoint the lethal predators around them who watched them intently. It was obvious their group was being sized up and judged by them.

Luckily, she was with the deadliest of the bunch.

Nykyrian leaned down to whisper in her ear. "Don't meet anyone's gaze."

Kiara nodded even though a lump of dread settled in her stomach. When the doors to the club opened, she flinched. Loud music blared at a level that pulsed in her body like a second heartbeat.

Her curiosity faded in the wake of true panic. *This is a major mistake . . .* After being with Nykyrian and his group, she'd mistakenly thought most outlaws were similar to them, but she was wrong. The men, women and aliens moving inside the dark club were the roughest, most intimidating individuals she'd ever seen and she had no doubt any of them would kill someone for nothing more than looking at them askance.

Dim lights blinked wildly overhead and flashed off elaborate outfits and weaponry. The stench of cheap alcohol and expensive perfume and aftershave lodged in her throat. Creatures tumbled over one another, shoving, snarling, picking fights.

Or, more to the point, picking pockets.

Nykyrian paid their fee before he led her in. "You won't be hurt so long as you stay with us." He pulled a pair of filters from his pocket and held them out to her.

Grateful for them, she put them in her ears so they would muffle the throbbing sound. No wonder Nykyrian wasn't flinching from his sensitive hearing.

She let out a relieved breath as the music and voices dropped to a tolerable level. *Thank you!* she mouthed at him.

He inclined his head to her.

Hauk put his hand on her shoulder, letting her know he was behind her. Literally.

Darling indicated a table with a jerk of his chin. "There's an open table." He cut through the crowd ahead of them to get to it before someone else claimed it.

Once she was seated between Darling and Nykyrian, Kiara breathed a sigh of relief that no one had bothered them.

Yet.

Hopefully it would stay that way. And at least the table section didn't appear nearly as crowded. She cringed as she realized why.

There were illegal transactions taking place all around her. Drugs, prostitution and weapons.

What have I gotten myself into?

But more than that was how at ease Nykyrian, Darling and Hauk were here. This was the world they lived in. No wonder they were so jaded. She'd known these kinds of places existed, but it was entirely different to experience it. It opened her eyes up to them and it made her appreciate why Nykyrian was so withdrawn. Why he had a hard time opening himself up to her.

And why Syn was so angry with her now. This was the world he'd grown up in. On the streets. Completely alone.

She watched as a young man around the age of twenty sold an illegally marked blaster in the corner. Gah, her father would have a stroke if he knew she was here.

Suddenly, a shadow fell over her. Kiara looked up, slightly startled to find a waiter from an unknown species who'd brought the men drinks.

"She's new," the waiter lisped between bubbled lips. "What does she favor?"

Nykyrian indicated Kiara with a tilt of his head. "Grenna."

The server appeared to smile, but Kiara couldn't quite tell with the strangely shaped lips. "It's good to see you again. I'd begun to worry that someone had gotten in a lucky shot with you boys."

Nykyrian smirked. "You know better than that, Vrasna. I go down for no one." He glanced over at Kiara and amended his comment. "At least not when I'm fighting."

Her face flushed at his words, but she knew he wouldn't embarrass her without reason.

Vrasna gave Kiara a once-over that made her want to sink under the table. "Is she yours?"

Nykyrian nodded.

Vrasna adjusted the tray. "I'll make sure to pass that around. No need for unnecessary bloodshed. We just got the window fixed from the last bloody brawl."

Kiara watched the creature leave on four tentacled legs. "What species is our waiter?"

One corner of Nykyrian's mouth lifted. "You can't pronounce it because of the way our palates are formed, but she's female and very nice unless you step on her limbs or call her a male. That'll get you choked out." Nykyrian handed her his drink.

Kiara took a small sip, then gasped as the tart, thick liquid almost burned a hole in her tongue and through her lips. Tears stung her eyes.

"Damn, Nykyrian, you should have warned her." Darling switched his drink with hers.

"What is that?" she gasped when her voice was finally able to work again.

Nykyrian answered. "Tondarian Fire."

She sucked air in to cool her mouth while it continued to burn. "How does Syn drink that crap?"

Darling shrugged. "Hell if I know. I'm told you can use it to strip rust from lead, though. Personally, I believe it."

So did she.

Darling urged her to take his drink.

Skeptical this time, she eyed it warily.

"Relax. It's colored juice so that no one knows I can't stand the shit they serve here."

"Thank you." She took a deep drink to put out the fire on her tastebuds.

Nykyrian ran a gentle hand through her hair. "I'm sorry. I should have warned you."

"It's all right. Just remember in the future that I have the tastebuds of a girl."

Instead of being amused as she'd intended, he tensed before moving away from her and made a hand gesture at Hauk that said to guard her closely.

Hauk nodded, then Nykyrian took off through the crowd.

Worried and upset about his quick departure, Kiara watched as the crowd shrank from his path as if they knew just by looking at him what he was capable of. She didn't know who he was after or why, but she prayed he wasn't running into danger.

Of course that thought ended a few moments later when he cut across the room and met up with an extremely attractive blonde woman. Kiara's gaze narrowed as an unfamiliar wave of jealousy tore through her so fiercely, she was tempted to push her way through the crowd and snatch the woman's hair out by the roots. Then, when Nykyrian led the cheap-looking ho off to the back, she burned even more.

Hauk's rumbling laugh filled her ears as he caught the expression on her face. "Relax. Nykyrian needs information, nothing more."

That'd better be all he's after or he's going to be hurting later tonight. Unlike the people in this club, she didn't live in fear of his moods.

But if he had any sense at all, he'd better live in fear of hers . . .

After a few minutes, Hauk excused himself to chase after an old friend as Vrasna brought them more drinks.

"So what do you think?" Darling asked.

"I think all of you live in a very dangerous place. And now I understand why my father has always been so overprotective of me."

A strange look darkened his features. "I hear you."

She studied the refinement that bled from his pores the same way savagery bled from Nykyrian and tried to understand how it was he'd come to be friends with The Sentella members. "Hauk told me you do explosives."

He nodded. "I live to blow shit up."

"It seems like a strange occupation for an aristocrat."

He took a drink before he answered. "Not really. I

loved chemistry in school and got into demolition as a hobby. The skill it takes . . . I don't know, there's nothing like it . . . but my father wanted me to be a politician."

"Would that be so bad?"

He smirked. "I don't like people well enough to play nice with them. It's why I treasure Nyk, Hauk, Syn and Jayne so much. With them you always know exactly where you stand. If you're getting on their nerves, they tell you—granted, sometimes gruffly, but they do tell you. There's no backstabbing bullshit or manipulation. They don't play head games or lie. There's no deception. Believe me, it's a rare thing and I don't want to be nice to someone I can't stand because I have to be politically correct. If I hate you, I want to be able to tell you to get out of my face and go die."

She could more than understand that and she admired him for being able to stand up for himself even when others were trying to knock him down. The bruises still marring his face were a testament to his strength and convictions. "Yeah, I don't like playing those games, either."

He held his drink up to her. "Here's to life without drama."

She smiled and clinked her glass to his. "Amen, my brother. Amen."

She set her drink down and scanned the crowd, noting the members who were still watching them. "Do you think any of the people here know about the bounty on my life?"

"Probably. But the good news is virtually everyone here has a price tag on them. Those who don't are wishing they did."

"And this is a good thing, how?"

He laughed. "They know better than to try and build their reputation with the clientele here. And those like

Aksel who are hunting you would *never* think to look in Club Blood for you. You're hiding in plain sight. No place safer."

She hoped he was right. "And what about the woman Nykyrian's with? Who is she?"

"Aksel's wife."

Kiara's eyes widened. "What?"

He patted her hand. "Relax. She hates him and it's how we know none of his people are here. If they were, she wouldn't have come."

Kiara wasn't so sure about that, but she trusted them. Most of all, she trusted Nykyrian.

"Cruel, you slimy little bastard."

Kiara jumped at the shout in her ear.

A tall, handsome man sat down in the chair on the other side of Darling. He winced as he saw Darling's injuries. "No offense, but you look like hell, buddy. You want me to kill someone?"

"Thanks, Cai, but I got it."

Kiara studied the newcomer's gorgeous face. Ebony eyebrows slashed above hazel eyes that glowed with intelligence and mischievousness. His dark hair was shoulder-length and worn in a short ponytail. There was an air of playful exuberance that was tempered by an equal aura of "You mess with me and I'll feed you your own liver."

Leaning forward, he whispered something in Darling's ear that made Darling laugh, then he looked over at her. A slow, seductive smile curved his lips. "Greetings, beautiful." He extended his hand to her.

Kiara could just imagine how many females had fallen to that debonaire smile.

Darling tsked at his friend's actions. "Kiara, this is my best friend, Caillen Dagan, smuggler extraordinaire and lady-killer extreme."

"Nice to meet you." She shook Caillen's hand.

He raised her hand to his lips and placed a warm kiss across her knuckles as he wickedly caressed her fingers. One corner of his mouth lifted in a way Kiara was sure would have set most women off into giggles.

"As in the most talented Kiara Zamir?"

At her nod, his smile widened. "It's an even greater privilege to swap drinks with you, princess. I've always been enamored of your beauty and work that no other dancer can touch."

Darling shoved playfully at Caillen's shoulder. "Don't start on her." He faced Kiara. "Caillen's harmless enough, he just thinks every woman breathing is dying to crawl into his bed and stay there."

Caillen finally released her hand to reach for Darling's drink. "In case it's missed your attention, Darling, most are." He took a sip and grinned. "You're moving up in the world. When did you start drinking the hard shit?"

"Hi, Caillen." An attractive redhead leaned over Caillen's shoulder to kiss his cheek.

Caillen wrinkled his nose and sent the woman away.

Kiara looked at Darling, who was giving Caillen an incredulous stare.

He shook his head in disbelief. "I think that may be the fist time since you hit puberty you've let a beautiful woman get away unmolested."

Caillen shrugged as he downed his whisky in one gulp. "Yeah, well, Lila's a ubiquitous slut. Someone should paint an *X* on her back and mark it 'This side down.' "

Kiara's eyes widened at his crude response.

Caillen returned his attention to her, his irresistible smile back in place. "I'm sorry if I shocked you, princess, but I tend to let my manners slip at the damnedest times."

He swapped his empty glass for Darling's other drink, then leaned across the table and gave her a seductive grin. "I hope you're not here on Darling's arm."

"She's Nykyrian's," Darling answered for her.

Caillen's face blanched as he withdrew so fast, he left a vapor trail. "I'm out of here." He bolted to his feet, then turned around and glared at Darling. "Why didn't you tell me he was here? That I was making passes at his female? Geez, Darling, what're you trying to do, get me disemboweled?"

Darling shrugged innocently. "Actually, I enjoyed watching you embarrass yourself. It was kind of fun."

"Hah, hah." Caillen gave Kiara a sheepish look. His face turned serious. "By the way, some of Arturo's men came by Kasen's place a little while ago asking about you. I told them you were visiting Ryn last I heard. I don't think they believed me, so watch your back."

"I will."

With a nod to them, Caillen drifted off into the crowd.

Kiara watched him go and pick up a woman off the dance floor and carry her through the crowd. "That was an interesting human."

"You've no idea. But he's worth his weight in comic relief and he's a hell of a man to have at your back in a fight."

Kiara twisted the straw in Nykyrian's glass with her fingers. "I thought Nykyrian was your best friend?"

He leaned back in his chair and studied her face. "Nykyrian protects me and I love him for it, but he's too serious. Caillen, on the other hand, takes life in stride, always with a joke about it." He reached for his juice that Caillen had been drinking. "I don't know, he just makes me laugh when no one else can."

She nodded, understanding all too well the importance of laughter. "Are you and Caillen lovers?"

Darling laughed. "No, Caillen is strictly heterosexual." He glanced around the crowd. "You still nervous?"

She took a deep breath. "A little."

He picked her hand up off the table and traced the line of her fingers. "Don't worry. Nothing's going to happen to you."

"Touching," a malevolent voice snarled between them.

Darling went rigid as he turned to face three men dressed in Caronese uniforms. "What are you doing here?"

The man who'd spoken was glaring in rage. A handsome, older man, he had a few faint lines flanking his cruel mouth. His graying, sandy-brown hair was cropped short and steely blue eyes raked her with a cold stare.

"We were told to fetch you home . . . highness." Could there have been any more loathing in that one word?

Panicking for Darling, Kiara scanned the crowd, trying to find Nykyrian, Hauk, or Caillen, but she didn't see anyone who looked familiar.

Darling lobbed several coins at him. "Pretend you didn't see me."

The guard looked at his companions and smirked. "Well, we know what our orders were should you resist us." His next response was a vicious backhand.

Darling fell against the table, upturning it. Without thinking, Kiara ran forward and shoved the guard away from Darling.

She barely budged him.

With a ringing curse, he slapped her hard, knocking

her backward into a group of men. Ignoring her stinging cheek, Kiara pushed herself off them, intending to
return to the fight, but found herself surrounded by the
ones she'd bumped into.

"Excuse me." She tried to break through them.

They refused to part or move in any way.

"Just where do you think you're going, lovely?"

"I don't think she's going anywhere," another answered before grabbing her by the waist and pulling
her back into the center of the group.

Terror engulfed her. She had to do something.

Kiara fought against the man's hold, clawing at his
hands. With a heated curse, he slung her over his shoulder and headed for the door. She shrieked and screamed
as she fought as hard as she could against his hold.

He didn't relent at all.

Infuriated and frustrated, she watched as the guards
dragged Darling through a rear door. She renewed her
struggle with vigor. She had to get free to help him.

The man holding her laughed at her attempts and
bounced her hard against his shoulder. Her breath left
her with a loud, painful *woof.* Pulling at his hair, she
clawed at his exposed neck.

He took her outside to the landing bay and threw her
onto the filthy ground where she landed with a solid
thud. She moaned at the pain pounding through her
body. Her ribs and back ached to the point where she
feared they were broken.

"You'll pay for that, *harita.*" He drew a huge dagger
out of his boot.

She shook all over, her mind seeing Chenz coming
after her again with his cruel blade.

The others in his group surrounded her so that she
had no way to freedom.

What was it Nykyrian had taught her?

Eyes, head . . .

No . . . throat.

Nose.

Go for his nose . . .

No, the groin.

Clenching her teeth, she did exactly what Nykyrian had taught her. She landed a hard kick straight in his groin.

He cursed as he doubled over. "Get that little bitch!"

The others moved in on her. Kiara spun around, trying to catch them like Nykyrian had said, but he hadn't told her what to do when she was so outnumbered.

They were going to kill her.

Suddenly, they started hitting the ground around her feet. One by one, they dropped until she saw Nykyrian standing there, his face a mask of fury.

The one she'd kicked made the mistake of running at him.

Nykyrian caught him and spun him about. Out of nowhere he manifested a knife and held it tight to the man's jaw. "What do you think you're doing?"

A bead of sweat ran down the man's temple. "This is human business, Andarion."

The cold look on Nykyrian's face sent a shiver down Kiara's throbbing spine. "She's my mate, asshole. What you do with her *is* my business."

The man started shaking uncontrollably. He looked to her, to Nykyrian, then back at her. "You're his mate?" he squeaked.

"Yes," Kiara answered with conviction.

Nykyrian dragged the knife under the man's chin, leaving a small trail of blood before shoving him away. He extended his hand to Kiara. Grabbing it like a lifeline, she allowed him to pull her to her feet.

The man gulped as he wiped the blood from his face

with the back of his hand. "I'm really sorry. She crashed into us. I had no idea. I mean . . . we—"

"I suggest you leave. Now." Nykyrian bared his fangs threateningly.

The group ran faster than Kiara would have given them credit for being able to. Shaking with her relief, she buried her head in Nykyrian's shoulder. "Had you said 'boo,' I think they would have wet themselves."

He held her against him, his arms soothing her completely. "What happened?"

"Arturo's guards grabbed Darling and I tried to stop them."

His body went rigid. "Where'd they go?"

"Out the back door."

Nykyrian led her back into the club and through the crowd. As they passed Hauk, Nykyrian grabbed him by his shirt and, with a furious curse, hauled him behind them. They burst through the back door into an empty street. There were a few people hanging out, two who looked like they were doing something illegal. But no sign of Darling or the guards.

Nykyrian paced around, scanning the area. He paused to glare at Hauk. "Remind me later to kill you."

Hauk frowned in confusion. "What's happened?"

Nykyrian curled his lip. "Nothing of any great importance. Kiara was grabbed by a rape gang and Arturo's men have Darling."

"Shit!" Hauk raked his hands through his braids. "Where do you think they went?"

"Most likely back to Caron." Nykyrian pulled his link out and tried to call Darling. When that failed, he snatched it out of his ear, then punched coordinates into his wrist computer. After a few seconds, he cursed again. "They must have removed his tracer and link. Damn it to hell."

Caillen came running through the back door. He pulled to a stop as he caught sight of them. "Where's Darling?"

Nykyrian cast a look of disgust at Hauk. "Arturo's men have him."

Caillen let out a curse so foul it brought heat to Kiara's cheeks. "Kasen just told me she saw him being taken out of here a few minutes ago. So help me, I'm going to kill my sister for waiting to speak up. Idiot!"

"Do you have any idea what holding facility Arturo's men would take him to?" Nykyrian asked Caillen.

"Maybe."

Nykyrian replaced his link and called Syn and Jayne to start a search. He tossed his link to Caillen. "Keep in touch with them and tell them where to start looking. I'll take Kiara home, then join you."

Caillen put the link in his ear. "How will we keep up with you?"

"I have another link at home."

Caillen nodded. "All right, then. Let's burn out." He struck his fist against Nykyrian's as a mark of solidarity before he and Hauk took off.

Guilt gnawed at Kiara while Nykyrian led her to his ship. If not for her getting into trouble again, Nykyrian might have been able to get to Darling in time.

"I'm so sorry," she whispered as they reached his ship and he helped her up the ladder.

His grip tightened on her waist. "You didn't do anything wrong. I should have known better than to leave Hauk with the two of you. Sometimes he just doesn't think."

Kiara nodded as she got in and waited for him to join her.

Before long, they were launched and headed back to his house.

She remained quiet the rest of the trip, her thoughts whirling over what had happened. She prayed for Darling's safety, unsure if she'd be able to forgive herself if something happened to him.

Nykyrian rushed her inside his house, grabbed his link and was gone before she could even wish him luck. Her heart heavy, she made her way up to bed with the lorinas following after her.

Stroking their soft fur, she lay for hours watching the stars twinkling above her head. Her thoughts drifted between all of the men she'd befriended. Hauk and his surly personality. Syn, who was basically bipolar, and Darling's sweet disposition.

Most of all, she thought of Nykyrian and his pain. Who would have ever believed that four people could come to mean so much to her in such a short amount of time?

Yet they did. And she prayed for all of them.

When she finally saw Nykyrian's fighter fly over, her heart pounded in relief.

Please let it be good news.

Grabbing her robe, she dashed downstairs to wait for him to enter. The lorinas curled about her legs, mewing softly.

Exhausted, Nykyrian came through the door. He dropped his helmet to the floor and opened his arms to receive her tight squeeze. "We found him," he said in a tired voice.

"I hope you beat them into pieces."

Nykyrian held out one of his hands. The knuckles were swollen and bloody. "Just don't hate me for it."

Kiara kissed his hand, then reached up to pull the shades from his eyes. "Where's Darling?"

Nykyrian moved away from her toward the stairs

and shrugged his jacket off, baring his ripped back. Goodness, she could see every single muscle ripple as he moved. And the colors of his tattoos were always striking . . .

"He's staying with Jayne and her husband."

He paused on the second step and turned to face her. "I'd give anything if you'd carry me upstairs."

Kiara laughed at his almost juvenile pout. "Come on, soldier. Up you go." She pushed at him playfully.

A groan escaped him as her hand accidentally slid between his thighs. "If you keep doing that, I might revive myself after all."

She tsked at him as they entered the bedroom. "Listen to you . . . and after the way you ran after that blonde tonight, too."

Nykyrian threw himself across the bed. "I needed information." He yawned into the pillow before he reached into his nightstand and pulled out a small container.

"What's that?"

He let out another yawn. "My mouthpiece. I can't sleep without it."

"Why?"

"An old injury. My fangs will shred the soft tissue of my month if I don't have it." He slid the piece in and dropped the container on the floor.

Kiara shook her head at the slow way he moved. "If The League could see Nemesis right now, I doubt they'd find you such a terrible threat."

She waited for him to respond.

"Nykyrian?" Kiara leaned over him and realized he was sound asleep.

With her standing at his unarmed back . . .

A smile curved her lips. Orinthe had told her he

would get tired like this. Nykyrian hated sleeping and would run himself solid until he hit a wall and his body forced him to sleep.

Grateful he was finally resting, she turned down the lights to only the softest glow and darkened the ceiling. She had to tug him over onto his back so that she could pull off his boots and pants. She paused at the weight of his boots and belt.

Her poor Nemesis. Always ready for battle.

She ran her gaze over his naked body, amazed at the beauty that had been marred by a brutal world. There was barely any part of him that hadn't been scarred. She pulled his gloves off and placed them on the nightstand, knowing he'd want them as soon as he got up. The only time he didn't wear them was when he made love to her or showered.

A warm tingle pulsed in her breasts as she watched him in the dull glow of the room. He looked so peaceful. She prayed he would sleep soundly tonight, and with that thought foremost in her mind, she closed the door to keep the lorinas out and then darkened the walls more.

He needed his rest.

Pulling his hair away from his cheek, she kissed the stubbly area right in front of his ear. "I love you, Nykyrian," she breathed.

She spread a blanket over him, then crawled into bed by his side and wrapped her arms around him. With a contented sigh, she drifted off to sleep.

Nykyrian slowly came awake to a strange sensation.

Something was pressing on him . . .

At first he thought it was one the lorinas, until he realized it was Kiara's silken body entwined with his. Her thigh rested high between his, pressing nicely against his balls while her right hand was tangled in his hair. Her gown had ridden up, exposing her entire bottom as she slept like an angel beside him.

For a full minute he couldn't breathe as it dawned on him what he'd done.

He'd spent the night asleep with someone touching him. Never had he done that before. In the past, he'd always known if anyone came near him and jolted awake.

But not with her. Even his subconscious welcomed her.

Astonished by that, he cupped her head in his hands and kissed her brow.

She blinked her eyes open to stare up at him. As soon as her gaze focused on his face, she smiled. "Good morning, baby."

He cherished every syllable. "Good morning."

She started to move her leg, but he caught it. "Easy . . . you're dangerously close to hurting me."

Her face blushed bright red as she realized how hard he was and where her thigh rested.

"Sorry." She withdrew more carefully. Yawning, she stretched, arching her back until her breasts were clearly outlined by her nightgown.

His cock jerked as he reached out to cup her right breast in his hand. She didn't complain in the least. Smiling, he brushed his fingers over the hard nipple hidden by the light pink silk. "Do you realize you married me last night?"

She froze in the middle of her stretch to gape at him. "I did what?"

He slid her gown aside so that he could touch her without the silk barrier. "Andarion law states that any two people who profess, uncoerced, to be mates before another individual are married."

She arched one brow. "Are you serious?"

He pulled his hand away from her. He didn't know why, but her unenthusiastic reaction cut him. "I take it you want a divorce."

Kiara bit her bottom lip as the full implication of it hit her. She was "married" to Nykyrian? She should be completely horrified and yet . . .

There was a part of her actually thrilled with the prospect.

"Is that really all it takes?"

His features blank, he touched her cheek, his hand burning a trail along her chin. "It is. Andarions aren't big on illustrious ceremonies. But don't worry, a divorce is just as easy to get. All we have to do is tell someone else we're divorced and it's done."

That time she heard the underlying note of hurt in his voice.

We're married . . . Those words echoed in her head as reality sifted through what it would mean to her. *If you're married to him, you can hang up your career forever.* No one would ever hire her to perform again. She couldn't be a public figure while married to Nykyrian.

He's an outlaw. And not just any outlaw. *He was Nemesis.*

Your father will have a stroke . . .

It was all true. Nothing in her life would ever be the same again.

And with that thought came the realization that everything had already changed. She wasn't the same person who'd been kidnapped by Chenz. She no longer wanted the same things that she'd wanted a few weeks ago.

While she still loved to dance, she hated the politics

and people. The best dance of her life had been the one with Nykyrian downstairs in his training room. The one with no audience except for him. He didn't care if she slipped or if her costume was a little tight. In his eyes, she was beautiful, and for the first time in her life, she really felt beautiful. When he was with her, she was calm. Most of all, she felt safe—even in a club filled with the scum of the universe, she'd felt safe.

He'd changed her forever.

Her life was no longer her own.

It belonged to him and she didn't want to live if that meant existing without him.

She cupped his jaw in her hand and narrowed her gaze teasingly on his face. "Oh, no, you don't, boy. You're stuck with me now. I'm not about to divorce you."

Nykyrian couldn't breathe as he heard the last thing he'd expected. "Don't tease me, Kiara."

She brushed the backs of her fingers down his face while her amber eyes stared at him with total sincerity. "I'm not teasing you, Nykyrian. I willingly give to you my heart, my life, and my devotion. I will put no one before you, not even myself, and I will gladly be here when you need me, to support you forever."

Those were the Gourish marriage vows she spoke. "There's no priest here to sanctify that oath."

She smiled. "I don't need one. God hears me and you hear me. That's good enough for me."

And in that moment, he could almost believe in a higher deity.

Hell, in this moment, he felt like he could fly. If someone as innocent and pure as her could love something as repulsive and corrupt as him, anything was possible.

"I will make myself worthy of you. I promise."

She scowled at him. "You're more than worthy of me."

No, he wasn't. He knew the truth. But the fact that she believed it touched him deep inside his heart.

Kiara watched as his expression darkened. What was tainting this for him? "What's wrong?"

He kissed the top of her head. "I thought I'd take you to your father today."

That was the last thing she'd expected him to say.

She studied his lovely green eyes, not entirely sure she wanted to go home. But it was wrong to leave her father worried about her. There was no telling how insane her absence had made him.

And while her current arrangement might not fly too well with her father, she was sure she could win him over. Like Nykyrian, he only had so much willpower where she was concerned.

"You know, my father might shoot you if he finds out we're married," she said with a smile, running her hand under their blanket.

"I definitely would if I were him." He jerked as she touched the tip of his cock.

She bit her lip, giving him her most seductive smile. "Is the marriage legal without consummation?"

Before Kiara could blink, he had her pinned on her back, to the mattress. He pulled out his mouthpiece and set it on his nightstand.

She welcomed his kiss, the strength of his hands on her body. He trailed kisses to her ear, gently nibbling the lobe. Chills shot white-hot through her body.

Everywhere he touched, she ached in pleasure. She dug her heels into the mattress and arched her back to meet him. Never had she felt so desired, so alive.

He was so hungry with her. She'd never seen him like this, like he had to be touching her body.

She ran her hands over the planes of his back, feeling the scars. He belonged to her and no one would ever take him away, she would make sure of it.

His kiss was frenzied and possessive as he parted her legs with his knees and filled her. She reveled in the feel of him deep inside her as he thrust against her hips. The power of him, the strength . . . she loved being joined to him like this.

His features intense, he stared down at her as he held her close. "You are mine, Kiara."

"I know."

He quickened his strokes, shooting ecstasy through her until she couldn't stand it anymore. When she came, it was explosive and more intense than anything she'd ever felt before. Throwing her head back, she cried out his name.

Nykyrian stared down at her in awe as she clutched him to her and wrapped her legs around his hips. It still amazed him that she could accept him so completely. That she could look at him like she was doing right now and see him as a man.

He was lost to those amber depths. Staring into her eyes, he felt himself slipping as his orgasm claimed him. He buried himself deep inside her and held her close as he breathed in her precious scent.

If he died right now, he'd be grateful. Because the last thing he wanted was for her to learn to hate him.

Stop it! Don't ruin this.

But it was so hard not to. Nothing good ever happened to him. Nothing.

And he knew this would be fleeting.

Don't take her to her father. Keep her here forever. Just the two of you.

But that would be selfish and it'd be wrong. Her father loved her as much as he did. And she loved her father. Sooner or later, she'd demand to see him.

Better to get it over with. Like ripping off a bandage. Get the hurt out of the way so the healing could begin.

Because in his heart, he knew this would be the end of them. There was no way Zamir would let her return with him.

Their time was over.

It's best this way. Let her go now before she learned to hate him. Before the new and shiny wore off their relationship and she saw the flaws in him.

Before she became like Mara and turned him in to the authorities out of spite. Syn had barely survived.

You're going to die without her.

No, he would live. Just as he always had. Alone and in solitude.

Pain is your friend.

His heart screamed, but he ignored it. This was the best for both of them. He knew where Aksel was and he could drop her off with her father, then kill the bastard and keep her safe.

No one would ever hunt her again. He'd make sure of it.

Kiara brushed her hand through his soft hair as he lay on top of her, his strong body melding to hers. She forgot about her career, her life. All she wanted was Nykyrian.

Kissing his lips, she hoped her father wouldn't stay angry at them for too long. She wanted the two men she loved most to be friends and to respect each other as much as she respected them.

As they lay silently, Kiara felt his heartbeat slow down to a normal rhythm. She kissed the salty flesh of his neck, reveling in the deep masculine scent of his skin. She could breathe him in all day long.

"Care to join me for a bath?"

Kiara smiled. "I'd love to."

It didn't take long for them to bathe and dress. Almost too soon, they were in his fighter and headed to Gouran. How different it was this time from the last time they'd done this.

Then she'd all but hated Nykyrian. She'd feared him and been looking forward to going home.

Now . . .

She dreaded meeting her father. She didn't know how he'd react to their news, but she was sure it wouldn't be gracious. *Please don't be completely unreasonable.* There were times when she was sure her father would overreact to something and he didn't.

Let this be one of them.

When Gouran came into sight, a really bad feeling went through her. She wanted to urge Nykyrian to turn around and take them back. But she knew she couldn't. Her father was worried about her. She owed him this meeting and telling him she'd married someone wasn't something to be done over a link.

She just prayed he would listen to reason and not jail Nykyrian immediately upon their arrival.

As soon as they entered Gourish airspace, a hundred fighters surrounded them.

Nykyrian let out a low whistle. "Baby, I think your father's just a tad upset at me."

She could have done without his sarcasm. "You're not funny." She stared aghast at the number of ships. Her father definitely wasn't playing around and if they ran at this point, she was sure they'd open fire on them.

We have to see this through.

"Drop your shield and disengage your main thruster," the controller ordered.

Nykyrian tensed as a warning light went off notifying

them they were targeted by another ship's weapons system. "Drop target. There's no need for this kind of hostility," he said in that calm, dispassionate voice he always reverted to when threatened.

"You'll know hostility after you land, you sonovabitch!" Her father's loud shout echoed in her ears.

Kiara swallowed her fear. *Maybe he'll be better once we land.* Yeah, and the world was filled with happy puppies and rainbows, too.

"Papa, everything's fine. I'm in the ship. Please don't open fire."

"Angel?" His voice quivered. "Thank God you're alive." Then his tone turned lethal again. "You have the coordinates to land. You make one tiny variable and so help me, I'll have you slaughtered where you sit."

"He's just such a nice man."

She rolled her eyes at Nykyrian's mocking tone. "He's worried."

Nykyrian snorted. "Honestly, I'm not exactly jumping for joy over here, either. I don't like having this many targets on my forehead."

"I know, sweetie." The knot in her stomach coiled tighter. "We'll be fine. You'll see."

Nykyrian bit back another sarcastic quip. He wished he was as naive as she was, but he knew better

Her father was out for blood.

His blood.

Pushing his emotions aside so that he could think clearly, he followed the route in. *You've had worse odds.*

Yeah, he bore the scars from those, too. But there was nothing to be done about it.

He landed inside the main landing bay for the palace. The moment the ship stopped, at least six battalions came out with weapons trained on his ship. There were so many targeting lasers dancing over them, it looked like a light show.

Kiara trembled in apprehension. When her father was this angry, he was completely unreasonable. Never had she seen so many soldiers.

Her father strode out in the middle of them to glare up at their hatch. "Send Kiara down first!" he shouted.

Nykyrian's strong hands unstrapped her helmet and her safety harness. "It's all right," he whispered. "Do what he says. Just move slowly and keep your hands away from your body so that none of the others get nervous or mistake your intent."

Kiara nodded. Her head light with panic, fear, and anger, she stepped out and descended the ladder. Like Nykyrian had instructed, she moved slowly toward her father, with her hands held out at her sides.

She glared at her father as she reached him. "What is the meaning of this, Father?"

Keifer placed two icy hands on her cheeks, then drew her into his arms in a crushing embrace. She hugged him back, thinking he must be calmer now that he was sure she was fine.

Letting out a relieved breath, she stepped back and smiled up at him. "As I told you, I'm all right." She turned back to see the guards hauling Nykyrian out of his ship at gunpoint.

They snatched his helmet off and held a blaster to his temple while he kept his hands behind his head and his fingers laced.

Anger tore through her at his treatment.

He could fight them and get away, but because of her, he was submitting. His humiliation on her behalf made her want to claw their eyes out.

Glaring at her father, she snarled, "It's time you stopped this madness."

"You're right, angel." He smiled at her. "It is time to put a stop to this. Someone has to." His arms tightened around her as he looked up at his men. "Shoot him!"

Her father's order tore through her.

"No!" she screamed, trying to pull free.

Her father's grip tightened as she fought against him. He held her by her arms, preventing her from running to Nykyrian.

Light erupted inside the bay as the soldiers opened fire on him. Terror and disbelief tore through her as everything seemed to slow down.

Nykyrian recoiled from the shots and fell to the ground where he lay unmoving. Blood ran out from under his body, staining the light gray pavement.

Kiara went cold. No sound would leave her lips as she crumpled to the floor, unable to cope with what had happened. A denial screamed inside her soul. Nykyrian was dead.

Dead.

Because of her.

No, because of her father.

Her father's hands were still locked on her, preventing her from running to her husband.

She couldn't breathe. All she could do was stare at Nykyrian as a soldier moved forward to feel for a pulse.

"He's dead, sir."

Tears flowed down her cheeks as sobs racked her body. It couldn't be. It was a nightmare. It had to be. *Wake up!*

But she didn't. She wanted to die as excruciating agony tore through her soul.

The look of prideful satisfaction on her father's face nauseated her. "Dispose of the body. Troops dismissed."

When he moved to help her to her feet, she slapped

and shoved at him. "I hate you, you bastard!" she screamed. "I hate you! I hate you!"

But those words were weak in comparison to what she really felt. She wanted to kill her father.

Wailing, she lay on the ground, too weak to move or to really fight.

All she wanted was to have this go away.

But it was too late. Her father scooped her up in his arms and carried her away from the one man she'd promised never to leave.

Nykyrian did his best not to breathe deeply as he watched his own blood pooling around his hand. He ached more now than he ever had in his entire life. At least four shots had hit him at point-blank range. And there was no telling how many more had torn through him.

Gah, it hurt . . .

Why couldn't some of those bastards have missed?

"We're so dead," Tameron whispered as he draped a sheet over Nykyrian's head to help shield him from the others. "If Zamir finds out about this, he'll have my balls."

"He won't know unless you tell him," Nykyrian whispered, thankful for the loyalty of his Sentella members. There were times when spies were extremely valuable.

This was definitely one of them.

Tameron cursed as he scanned the bay and the handful of soldiers who were still milling about. "Just how the hell are we supposed to get you and your fighter out?"

Nykyrian closed his eyes against a wave of pain. "Tell control you're driving my fighter out on remote to get rid of it and me."

Tameron smiled. "Brilliant."

That's why they pay me the big credits.

Nykyrian forced himself to remain limp as Tameron and Jayde picked him up and dumped him into the seat of his fighter. He had to bite back a curse at their roughness. But they all had to make it look real or die.

Kiara's screams echoed in his ears and he wished for a way to let her know he was still alive.

Unfortunately, if he tried, he really would be dead.

Tameron threw his helmet against his stomach. Pain erupted through his body and for a moment, he feared he might pass out.

One, two, three . . . breathe.

He focused on the rhythm to distract himself from the physical misery. From the emotional damage of hearing Kiara's sobs.

And yet a part of him treasured the sound. She wouldn't have cried like that had she not cared about him. Those sounds couldn't be faked.

She did love him.

The thought warmed him as they jettisoned his fighter out by remote.

Still, he wasn't out of danger. Blood covered him to the point that he couldn't figure out where he was wounded. If he didn't get help soon, he'd bleed out.

He waited until he'd cleared orbit before he sat up and took control of his craft. Pain clouded his mind, dulling his thoughts. Every second seemed to bring more throbbing agony than the one before it.

By the time he reached home, it was all he could do to move at all.

Get out and get in. C'mon, boy, you can do it. He had to stop the bleeding.

Nykyrian staggered out of his ship, his eyesight

dimming. He had to call Syn and get help with his wounds. He didn't have much time left . . .

In spite of the sweat covering his body, he was freezing. He opened the door to his house, blood smearing over the white controls.

He let his helmet fall from his numbed hands. The lorinas ran forward, confused by the smell of blood. *Think of Kiara. You can't die. Not right now.*

She's still not safe.

You have to live to stop Aksel.

Nykyrian took a step forward and fell to his knees. *Get up, asshole.*

He tried to rise, but the pain was too much. He had to move, he had to.

Instead, he collapsed against the floor. His last conscious thought was of a tiny dancer who had promised never to leave him.

CHAPTER 23

"The Probekeins repealed their contract on your life! You're safe!"

Kiara barely heard Tiyana's jubilant shout. Honestly, she didn't care. Her life had ended eight weeks ago when her father had killed Nykyrian right in front of her eyes.

Nothing else had mattered since.

Nothing.

Tiyana squatted down beside the chair where Kiara sat in the palace's garden, wrapped in her mother's old woolen shawl—something she always wore whenever she was upset. It made her feel like her mother was still with her.

Every day, her father had her marched out here to the garden by his soldiers, thinking the beauty would soothe her and create some freakish miracle that could drive Nykyrian's memory from her.

But all it did was sicken her, body and soul. How could she see any form of beauty when her heart had been shattered?

"Kiara, didn't you hear me? You can return to the theater and dance again."

Like she cared. How could Tiyana think that

something so trivial would make her happy? In truth, she hadn't danced since she'd held Nykyrian in her arms.

And she had no desire to ever dance again without him. The memory was more than she could bear.

"I heard you."

Sighing, Tiyana took a seat in the identical white, wrought-iron chair across from her.

Kiara used to love sitting in the well-manicured garden behind the palace, breathing in the scent of all the flowers blooming around her, sunlight warming her skin, not doing anything except enjoying the sweet air, gossiping with Tiyana.

But those days were gone.

I don't think I'll ever smile again.

Tiyana looked past Kiara's shoulder and shook her head. By that action she knew her father must be standing behind her. She didn't bother to look. She really couldn't care less where her father was.

"Tiyana," he said roughly. "Could you excuse us for a moment?"

"Sure, Your Excellency." She stood and touched Kiara's hand. "I'll be back in a minute. Do you want anything?"

Kiara shook her head, stifling a sob. The only thing she wanted was her husband and nothing could bring Nykyrian back from what they'd done to him.

With a trembling breath, Kiara looked away from her father as he took Tiyana's chair.

"Angel?"

"Don't call me that anymore." Every time she heard it now, it made her think of her father calling out for Nykyrian's death, and of the countless other horrible things he'd put her through since then—in the name of "protecting" her. He'd made her take a rape test and marched her through countless psychologists who came up with all kinds of names for her "condition."

"It makes my skin crawl," she snapped.

He took a deep breath and extended a long, manila folder toward her. "Your medical report came back. I wish to God I could kill all those bastards for what they did to you."

Kiara ground her teeth, wanting to claw his eyes out for that statement—she was so sick of him calling down the wrath of all incarnations to destroy The Sentella when all they'd done was protect her. Of course, it would help if the psychologists would stop calling it Captive Syndrome—the victim learns to identify with her captor and in time will even begin to think that she cares for him.

How stupid could they be? But they were experts and so her father listened to them and their psychobabble instead of hearing her when she spoke.

She refused to take the folder from his hand. She didn't want anything from him. Ever.

Her father believed that she'd been raped by all of The Sentella men, and no matter how much she tried to explain what had happened between her and Nykyrian, her father kept saying she'd been brainwashed.

Why wouldn't he listen to her? How many times had she tried to tell him no one did anything to her she didn't want done?

When he spoke, his voice was full of bitterness. "You're pregnant."

Those words hit her like a sledgehammer.

"What?"

"You're pregnant," he sneered as he repeated the word.

Kiara gasped as reality hit her. For the first time in weeks, she felt like laughing.

She carried Nykyrian's baby . . . The miracle of that floored her. Placing her hand over her flat stomach, she tried to imagine the child forming there.

And in her mind, she imagined telling Nykyrian . . . imagined him wrapping his arms around her as he gave her that dimpled smile and shared her happiness over what they'd created together.

She grabbed the folder, opened it and searched the documents until she found the sonogram of her infant. The baby looked like a tiny bean of a creature, but there was no mistaking it. And to think she'd assumed her illness and lethargy were from her grief.

How could she not have known?

"The doctor said he can terminate the pregnancy without any problems."

She glared at her father. "Absolutely not. No one touches my baby."

Keifer stood, his face dark and foreboding. "Be reasonable. A child will end your career. Is that really what you want after you've worked so hard and for so long? To lose your career over *this*? Why would you want to give up your life because of some bastard seed?"

Kiara trembled in rage. Never in her life had she wanted to strike her father, but at the moment she doubted anything else would give her more satisfaction. She rose to her feet to confront him. "It was my husband you killed. My baby is not a bastard! It's all I have left of Nykyrian. How dare you insult either of them. I . . ." Her words broke off into a sob. Why should she even bother?

He never heard her.

And she wasn't about to let him ruin this moment for her. Tightening her mother's shawl around her shoulders and wishing she were here to comfort her, she left him to his brooding and returned to her room.

All she wanted was to go back to their last day together. To touch Nykyrian one more time and to see the look on his face when she told him he was going to be a father.

Instead, she touched her stomach where the last piece of him flourished. She would give their baby all the love she'd wanted to give Nykyrian—all the love Nykyrian had been denied his entire life.

Her baby would never doubt the love of its mother. She would make sure of it.

"You have to return to the theater, Kiara. It's miserable there without you."

Kiara sighed heavily as Tiyana continued to beg her while they walked down a busy street. It was the first outing she'd been on and she wanted to look for baby items. She'd already found a beautiful layette and placed an order for the baby's crib.

Honestly, she couldn't remember the last time anything had excited her more.

And Tiyana seemed as eager to ruin her joy, and she was determined not to let her. She suspected her father was putting Tiyana up to the incessant begging. "I've told you a thousand times I'm through dancing. I don't want that life anymore. I have a baby to think about now."

"How can you walk away from your fame at the height of your career? Do you know how many people, myself included, would kill to have what you're throwing away?"

And therein was most of the problem. She knew and she was sick of dodging those digs and smiling while they clawed pettily at her for no other reason than they were jealous.

Nykyrian had shown her a world where she was free

of that misery. And now she had a much better reason to live.

Kiara placed her hand over her belly, which was just barely starting to round, longing for the day when she would see real proof of her baby. "There are other things more important to me now."

"Such as?"

She stiffened. "My baby, for one."

"You can dance for a few more months, you know? Return to the show and finish out the run."

"I am not going to put my body through those rigors and risk hurting the baby. I'm retired, Tiyana. Accept it. And for the love of heaven, stop with the nagging before you suck the rest of the joy out of my day."

Her friend growled at her. "It just kills me, Kiara. I would sell my soul for your fame."

She opened her mouth to reply that she would sell her soul to have Nykyrian back, but as she looked up, she saw Darling eating lunch inside the café they were passing.

Shock riveted her to the sidewalk as she stopped midstride.

He looked so good there . . .

A happy thrill rushed through her. Without another word to Tiyana, she doubled back and entered the café. But as she drew near him, she hesitated in uncertainty. Surely he grieved as much for Nykyrian's loss as she did. She didn't want to hurt him, and yet, she wanted to touch that part of her brief past.

Darling looked up and caught sight of her standing in the doorway. A smile spread across his face as he rose slowly to his feet. "Kiara?"

She closed the distance between them. Darling grabbed her into a fierce hug.

He placed a kiss on her cheek as he tightened his

embrace, then released her. "It's so good to see you. I've been wondering how you were doing."

She returned his smile. "You look great. I've been wanting to talk to you guys, but I didn't know how to get in touch with any of you." Apparently The Sentella didn't believe in passing messages to them from women. "What are you doing here?"

"Waiting on Caillen, as usual. I swear that man's going to be late to his own funeral."

She laughed at his dire tone.

"Kiara?" Tiyana was hesitant as she joined them.

"Tiyana, this is my friend, Darling."

They shook hands and Darling pulled a chair out for Kiara to join him. "It's really good to see you. After the way Nykyrian's been acting lately, I'd started to think—"

"What?" Kiara gasped, interrupting him as her stomach hit the floor.

It couldn't be possible. Surely she'd misheard that.

Darling looked at her and his face turned the shade of his hair. "I probably shouldn't have said that."

Her mind spun with the knowledge as her emotions spiraled out of control—something not helped by her pregnant hormones. "Nykyrian's alive?"

Darling nodded.

She shook her head in disbelief. No, it wasn't true. If Nykyrian lived, he would have come for her. He wouldn't be so callous or cruel as to leave her in so much pain for no reason.

"I saw him killed right in front of me." The soldiers had been adamant.

Darling glanced at Tiyana. "He was severely wounded, but a couple of Sentella members shielded him from your father's soldiers and helped him get home."

Kiara struggled to breathe as that reality slammed into her.

Nykyrian was alive and he didn't want her.

All this time, she'd told herself he loved her, yet he hadn't even bothered to tell her he was alive. Oh, how she wished she were a man. She'd hunt him down and beat him within an inch of his worthless, cold life.

The bastard!

Darling swallowed. "Are you all right?"

She lifted her chin, unwilling to let him know how much pain she was in. Be damned if he'd report *that* back to his boss. "I'm fine," she said, her voice as icy as the bitter feeling consuming her. "It was nice seeing you today." She extended her hand to Darling. "I wish I could spend more time with you, but I'm afraid I have to call my manager and accept a job. Give my best to the others."

Kiara sensed Tiyana's confusion as she turned and made her way back to the street with a calmness she definitely didn't feel. Right now, she wanted to pummel someone.

A tall, blond asshole!

"What gives?" Tiyana glanced back in the direction of the café. "Who was that guy?"

Kiara seethed in humiliation and hurt. "He's no one." How could Nykyrian do this to her? How could he put her through this? He was inhuman, and she was through wasting her life, pining for him.

"Where are you going now?"

Kiara gave her an arch stare. "You heard what I said. I'm calling Mortie and coming out of retirement."

CHAPTER 24

Nykyrian stroked Ulf's soft belly while he watched a taped performance of one of Kiara's ballets. His heart heavy, he knew he should go after her. No, *needed* to go after her, he corrected himself. But he couldn't.

She was better off thinking him dead. Let her go on with her life without any reminders of him to hold her back. It was better this way.

And if being without Kiara wasn't hell enough, Syn was missing, too. His flat had been torn apart and no one had any clue who'd done it. They'd been searching for weeks, but no one could find a trace to Syn's whereabouts.

He was most likely dead, otherwise he'd have contacted them.

Pain gripped him and Nykyrian tossed back another shot of whisky. He was alone like he'd always wanted to be. But he'd never guessed just how painful true solitude was.

Or maybe it was because Kiara had shown him heaven and now he was relegated to hell.

He sighed in weary frustration as he watched her. But he wasn't satisfied with this anymore. He knew what her touch felt like. The sound of her laughter and her tears.

I can't stand this . . .

At least she was performing tonight on Gouran. She had her old life back.

A sliver of satisfaction crept over him. His threats had worked. Nemesis had been able to intimidate the Probekeins enough that they revoked their contract. She was safe and no longer hunted.

There was so much he wished he could tell her. If he could just touch her one last time . . .

Aw, hell, what did it matter? He'd spent his whole life wishing for what could've been. As Syn would say if he were here, he had two choices. He could either continue to wallow in his useless self-pity or he could try to see Kiara.

Neither option seemed promising at the moment.

Lights flashed in Kiara's face, blinding her. She turned her head away and made a few quotable responses to the reporters as she pried her way between them with the help of her security detail and headed for her dressing room.

After her brief, mysterious disappearance, she seemed to be the hottest topic in the media. Well, let them gossip. What did she care, anyway?

Just wait until they learned about her baby, then they really would swarm her for juicy tidbits.

With a weary sigh, she fell into her room and closed the door against the overzealous reporters as her detail held them back.

Leaning against the closed door, she took several calming breaths, grateful to have a few seconds of silence without a light in her face or someone shouting a question at her.

How had she ever thought this was enjoyable?

Tonight had been particularly grueling, and she was sick of all the backbiting politics and eager young dancers out to bring a performer down, all the two-faced promoters who wanted to make a *sola* with one hand and shove the other down her dress.

This is what you wanted.

She had no right to complain and yet . . .

She wouldn't think about Nykyrian. Not now when her fury and hurt were so raw.

Pushing herself away from the door, she grabbed a towel from her dressing table and wiped the perspiration from her brow.

"Kiara?"

She froze, knowing that deep, accented voice that continued to haunt her dreams.

Nykyrian stepped out of the shadows to her left. Dressed all in black with his shades in place, he was the embodiment of fierce, lethal grace. She stared at him, noting the tenseness around his lips. Stubble lined his handsome face as if he hadn't shaved in several days.

Despite her anger and pain, her body throbbed with desire. How could she still want to make love to him after what he'd put her through?

He'd abandoned her and their baby without so much as a goodbye.

But in spite of it all, she wanted to run to him and hold him close. To beg him to take her away from this and keep her safe.

He doesn't want you. If he had, he would never have been able to put her through the hell of thinking him dead.

With that thought, she steeled herself. She wasn't about to let him know how hurt she was. "What do you want?"

He reached his hand out to touch her, then drew it back. "I wanted to explain."

She turned away and jerked the zipper down the back of her costume, cursing as it caught in her hair and ripped out several strands. "I don't want to hear your excuses. What you did was wrong. You let me think you were dead."

As expected, his face was impassive.

Unshed tears blurred her vision as she remembered seeing him shot. The agony of that moment and the hatred she'd borne for her father over it . . . All the while Nykyrian could have called her and let her know he was fine. Her anger over that burned. "I thought you were dead because of *me*. You selfish bastard. How could you do such a thing?"

He looked away and brushed his hand through his unbound hair. "Don't you think I've suffered, too?" His voice was a faint, unemotional whisper that barely reached her. "I almost did die."

"I wish to God you had."

His jaw ticced, but he showed no other reaction. Without a word, he disappeared through the open doors of the balcony.

Kiara told herself she was glad he was gone. She didn't want to see him after what he'd done.

He had left *her*.

Her heart didn't listen.

She ran to the balcony to call him back. "Nykyrian!"

But it was too late. He was already gone.

The street below was as empty as her soul, her life. There was no sign of him anywhere. He'd vanished into the night like he was part of it.

A light breeze rippled through her hair while she

stood there trying to find him, reminding her of gentle fingers that used to play there instead.

"What have I done?"

But she already knew the answer. She'd ruined her life and there was no way to repair it.

CHAPTER 25

Kiara took a deep breath, relieved to finally be finished with the talkshow interview that promoted the last week of her show's run. Weak and nauseated, she just wanted to go home and rest. While she loved being pregnant, there were times when it was hard and debilitating.

Her father and Tiyana walked down the station's glaring white hallway by her side, chatting away about the interview while three guards trailed them. Their feet tapped a solemn rhythm on the gray porcelain floor.

"I think you did great." Tiyana smiled. "One of the best interviews ever."

Her father nodded. "I'm just glad to have you back in the game. You look so happy."

Funny, she didn't feel that way. She couldn't remember a time in her life when she was less so.

Kiara rubbed the chills from her arms. She hated being here. And at this point the only thing she was looking forward to was having her baby—something her father refused to even talk about.

"Are you all right?" her father asked, his voice warm with concern.

Her father had become much more understanding and loving since she'd returned to dancing, but he still refused to call the baby anything more personal than "it."

She'd ceased to be angry with her father anymore—it was pointless, since he hadn't killed Nykyrian. Now her impotent rage stayed focused on another source, one who had gorgeous blond hair and deep dimples.

One she would really like to kill.

"Just tired." Kiara tightened her cloak around her shoulders.

As they rounded a corner, she caught a movement out of the corner of her eye. She turned just in time to see a blaster level at her chest.

A scream rippled up through her lungs as her father pushed her out of the way. Pain, intense and throbbing, burst across her arm as she fell on the floor.

More shots were fired, but she couldn't tell what was going on from her position under her father. Shouts filled the hallway and someone ran past her.

"Kiara? Are you all right?"

She blinked at Nykyrian's deep, worried voice, the pain of her arm forgotten.

Her father rolled off of her and attacked.

Nykyrian sent him headfirst into a wall before he seized her in an iron hold and pulled her to her feet.

"Release her!" her father roared, starting for them.

Nykyrian leveled his blaster at her father's head. "Don't."

Her father froze. His gaze darted over them as he mentally calculated his options.

She struggled fiercely against Nykyrian's hold until she saw the blood covering her upper body. Cold dread and fear consumed her.

Her baby!

"I've been shot?" she gasped, unable to comprehend why she didn't feel more pain.

Nykyrian scooped her up in his arms and sprinted down the hallway.

More shots were fired at them. In stunned disbelief at what was happening, she remained silent, praying her wound wouldn't endanger her baby.

What was going on here?

Out of nowhere, Hauk appeared, firing his blaster at attackers she couldn't see. "I've got you covered," he shouted to Nykyrian. "Get her out of here."

Nykyrian hesitated for only a second before he opened the stairwell and ran down it as fast as he could with her cradled in his arms.

She wanted to fight, but until she knew what was going on, or more to the point, who was threatening her, she remained as still as possible.

The most important thing was to get to safety and get help for her wound.

Nykyrian finally put her down next to his ship, but his right hand stayed firmly on her arm while he holstered his blaster with his left.

Fury descended over her as she realized he intended to take her with him.

Oh, hell no!

She wasn't about to go anywhere with him ever again. She fought against him, striking out at his tight grip with all of her might. "Let go of me!"

He pulled her up against him so she couldn't hit his hand anymore. "Aksel's men have this place surrounded. Their mission is to capture *you*."

She shook her head in denial. "You're lying. There's no contract on me. I'm safe."

The venomous look in his eyes chilled her. "It's me he's after and you're the bait he's going to use to lure me with."

Her blood left her cheeks. For a moment she thought he might be lying, but the cold seriousness of his face warned her of the truth.

She was bait . . .

Numbed, she allowed him to push her up into his fighter and speed them away from Gouran.

Her head spun and for a moment, she thought she might pass out. A wave of nausea consumed her, but she managed to fight it down. "Where are you taking me?" She tried to staunch the blood coursing down her arm. "I need a doctor."

His rough hands ripped her dress away from the wound on her shoulder. "It's a flesh wound," he said, pulling a piece of cloth out from under their seat. "Hold this on it. It'll stop bleeding before we get home."

Kiara's lips trembled. He was furious at her, proof of it was in his hardened voice as he spoke.

What had she done to *him*?

"How dare you be mad at me. This isn't my fault."

He didn't answer her.

Her vision dimming, she wiped at the blood. "I want to go home to Gouran."

His hand tightened around the throttle. "You can't. You won't be safe there."

Kiara didn't bother arguing with him. She knew she'd get back home no matter what. She wasn't about to stay with him, not after he'd abandoned her.

He was being an insensitive pig and . . .

She gagged.

"Don't you dare get sick in my ship."

"I don't really have a choice."

Nykyrian barely pulled out a bag for her before she unloaded the contents of her stomach.

Inwardly, he cursed. Not because she was sick, but because he'd upset her so much and he hated himself for that weakness. Why should he care after what she'd said to him?

For her, he'd almost died. More than that, he'd risked his life with the Probekiens and put his ass on the line with The League—just to keep her safe.

Meanwhile, she cursed him for it.

You should have told her you weren't dead.

To what point? To have her cry for him?

It doesn't matter.

He was used to people hating him. What difference did it really make if she was one more of them?

Pushing the thought aside, he focused on the trip back to his house.

Kiara wanted to lean back and rest. She felt so sick still. The stress of it all was more than she could bear right now. Leaning her head back, she felt Nykyrian jerk at the contact.

Serves you right for not having a bigger ship.

The hostile silence wore on her nerves, but she knew breaking it would be even worse than bearing it.

Not soon enough, they were finally in his bay. He released the hatch and let her climb down unassisted while he cleaned up her mess.

When he was done, he led the way into the house. He didn't bother looking at her or helping her inside.

Kiara clenched her teeth in aggravation. She stood in the doorway between the bay and his house, her legs caressed by the lorinas.

Still not looking at her, Nykyrian opened a closet in the kitchen and retrieved a medical bag. He pulled out antiseptic and a white cloth. Completely silent, he cleaned and dressed her wound, then went upstairs.

He paused in the doorway of his bedroom and turned to face her. Not a single emotion was evident. "You're to sleep in the back guest room. The bed's already made up for you, and your clothes and personal items are there." Then he went into his room and closed the door.

Kiara gripped the bottle of antiseptic, wanting to throw it at his head. How dare he treat her this way. Fuming, she went to her room to change her clothes and brush her teeth, all the while cursing him.

She paused in the doorway. One of her gowns was laying neatly on the turned-down bed. Even in anger, he watched out for her. Her throat tightened. It would be so easy to rush upstairs and pound on the door until he opened it, but she couldn't.

Not after what he'd done.

Still she wanted him, burned for him. But he didn't care for her at all. If he did, he'd have never allowed her to go through all those weeks of misery thinking he was dead.

Tears coursed down her cheeks as she sat on the edge of the bed. She wiped at them, despising the fact that her baby made her so weepy.

She looked down at her stomach. "If you ever act like your father, I swear I'll beat you until you bleed."

Nykyrian watched the stars above him. He tipped the almost empty bottle of alcohol back against his lips, letting the liquid burn down his throat.

Syn had been right, the stars were a hell of a lot more interesting when you were flagged than sober.

He sighed, aching for a friend he knew was dead, aching for a woman he knew he couldn't have. If Driana hadn't contacted Hauk this afternoon, Kiara would now be dead and it would have been all his fault.

God, if he'd been two seconds later this afternoon, she'd be captured or dead. His gut twisted. He took another swig of whisky.

What a life.

Before he could stop himself, he left the room and headed downstairs to Kiara's room. He could tell by her breathing pattern through the door that she was asleep—a trick he'd learned courtesy of The League.

He pushed open the door, careful not to make a sound.

His heart rate intensified as desire pounded in his veins, demanding he do something more than just stand here like a gaping, lovesick fool. But he knew to-night he wouldn't listen to the part of him that loved Kiara, that part of him that would die for her.

Keep your distance.

Bitter longing welled up inside him as he watched her chest rise and fall in peaceful slumber. She lay on her side, her curly hair fanning out behind her while one hand was tucked beneath her chin.

His hand tingled with the memory of what those strands felt like in his palm and he wanted to bury his face in the curve of her neck and just breathe her in un-til he was drunk from it. He clenched his teeth. His body throbbed and for a moment, he feared he might yield to the fire in his blood after all.

"Nykyrian?" Kiara whispered, opening her eyes to look up at him with a pitiful, sad face.

He gripped the doorframe in indecision. He had to let her go. Aksel was just one of a hundred assassins who would do anything to bring him down.

Anything.

She was the one weakness he couldn't afford to have.

Ever.

"Go back to sleep," he snarled and slammed the door.

Kiara stared at where he'd stood watching her, her heart breaking. Why had he come to her?

Why did she care?

She placed her hand over her stomach, tempted to

tell him about the baby, but she couldn't. With his present temperament, who knew how he would react. The last thing she needed was an even more irate assassin roaming around the house while she slept.

Besides, it was her child she nurtured. A remembrance of a happy time she doubted would ever return.

"Aren't you ready yet?" Nykyrian snarled as Kiara plaited the last piece of her hair while she stood in his main room.

"Stop snapping at me."

So he glared at her instead.

Wishing he'd put his shades on, Kiara ground her teeth in aggravation. All he'd done since he growled at her to get up this morning was snap and hiss. "Where are you taking me, anyway?"

"Out."

Disgusted, Kiara sighed. "You're such a font of information. Maybe you should consider a job in the media?"

By his face, she could tell her sarcasm struck home. "If you're through making asinine comments, I'm supposed to be meeting someone."

Kiara froze. "Why are you taking me along?"

Anger and hatred blazed at her from his light green eyes. She took a step back, afraid of him.

"Syn's gone. And I have no idea who knows about my house now. If I leave you here, with my luck and yours, someone will find you."

She frowned at him. "Syn's gone?" she repeated, her body going numb. "What do you mean?"

Nykyrian pulled his coat on with irate jerks instead of his usual grace. "I mean he's vanished. No one has seen him in weeks and his flat was torn to pieces. We're assuming someone acted on your father's contract and killed him. I suppose I should go to your father's office and see if Syn's severed head has been delivered to him as he requested."

"No," she whispered, unable to believe what he was telling her. In spite of Syn's later hostility, she'd liked him a great deal. "I'm so sorry."

He curled his lip at her. "I should have killed your father when I saved you."

Kiara lifted her chin, refusing to show him how much that comment hurt. "Then why didn't you?"

"I don't know," he mumbled. "I don't know why I do anything anymore."

Kiara reached out to touch him, but he turned away. "Just get into the fighter and leave me alone."

"You really do suck when it comes to social skills." She knew she should be mad at him, curse him, something. But at the moment all she could do was see images of Syn teasing him. Syn had been the one person he was closest to.

Now . . .

He was in pain, and for that she'd give him some latitude. But the man had to start giving her some consideration, too.

Kiara climbed into the ship and remained silent as he joined her and then launched.

She watched the stars zoom past as they flew to a destination she didn't even bother to ask about again. She was tired of being snapped at. All she wanted was a day of peace. To return to those gentle days of when the two of them had actually gotten along.

It didn't take too long to reach a small outpost planet. Nykyrian landed them with a severe jolt.

Kiara gasped, her body aching. She frowned at him, wondering about the rough landing, but held her tongue.

Without a word, he led her out of the craft and from

the small, sterile bay toward a row of average-sized houses. She looked around, trying to get her bearings, but nothing seemed familiar.

She followed him down several back streets before he finally came to a large, white house. He glanced up and down the street in a manner that reminded her of the night he'd first started protecting her—like he was looking for someone to attack them—then he knocked sharply on the door.

He pushed her to the side of the door and unholstered his blaster.

She swallowed in fear. What was waiting for them inside?

The door opened to display the attractive blonde from the club they'd gone to all those weeks ago. "If you like, you may search the entire place, but I assure you he's not here." The woman smirked, opening the door wide enough for them to enter. "I'm sick of the way you guys go around expecting an ambush. For the sake of the gods, put your weapon away."

Kiara didn't miss the underlying hatred in the woman's voice.

Nykyrian pushed Kiara into the house. But even so, she sensed his unease, as if he still expected them to be attacked.

Worried and unsure, she glanced about the main room. A teenage girl sat on the floor, looking up at them with large, luminous green eyes. Her eyes widened even more as she studied Nykyrian's size and fierce demeanor.

His features softened immediately. "I'm not dangerous," he said in a gentle voice.

The girl looked to her mother for confirmation.

"He's all right, Thia. Now run along to your room."

The girl shot from the floor like a doom squad was

hot on her heels. Kiara frowned, wondering why a girl her age would be *that* afraid of strangers.

Driana held her hand out to the couch. "You two have a seat, and I'll get the discs."

Kiara didn't move. Instead, she watched the odd way Nykyrian stared after the girl.

"How old is she, Driana?" He faced the woman with a stern frown. There was a strange emotion darkening his features.

Driana shifted uncomfortably under his stare.

"Is she mine?" he asked and Kiara felt her world tilt.

Her breathing ragged, she looked back at Driana and the beautiful, cold grace ingrained in the woman's face and mannerisms.

"No, she's not."

Nykyrian cursed. "You never could lie worth a damn. Your nose always crinkles."

Self-consciously, Driana rubbed her fingers across the bridge of her nose. Tears gathered in Driana's eyes as she looked back at Nykyrian. "Thia knows Aksel isn't her father. I couldn't bear the thought of her calling *him* Papa."

Nykyrian met Kiara's gaze. What she wouldn't give to know what thoughts were playing through his mind, but he kept every hint of his mood concealed.

For that matter, she wished she could sort through her own feelings about this discovery. The worst was a sense of betrayal, though to be honest she didn't understand the source of that one, since it was obvious he'd slept with Driana long before they'd ever met.

"Why didn't you tell me?"

Anger clouded Driana's eyes. "To what purpose? After what the commander did to you when he found out we'd only danced together, I didn't dare tell anyone

I'd slept with you. I still have nightmares over the beating you received." She rubbed her arms and looked at the floor. "Aksel isn't sure you're the father. He suspects. But I have no idea what he'd do to her if he ever learned the truth."

"Is she why you asked me here?"

Driana glanced at Kiara. "Who is she?"

"My wife."

Kiara was stunned he'd bother claiming her after the way he'd treated her since he'd saved her at the station.

Driana drew a ragged breath. "No wonder Aksel's been trying to get to her. He raved all last night because he didn't capture her yesterday."

"He touches her, I will kill him in ways not even he can imagine."

"I know."

Nykyrian picked up a picture of his daughter from the low table. "Can I spend time with her?"

Driana bit her lip. "I would like that, but I don't know. Aksel has her afraid of everything. He reminds me so much of your father it's not even funny." She broke off as intense fear and sadness darkened her eyes. "I might be able to arrange something in a week or so when Aksel goes off on one of his self-indulgent binges." She gave Kiara a hard look. "That is, if you don't mind?"

Kiara glanced at Nykyrian, who was studying her intently. "I don't mind at all," she said, amazed by the honesty of her response. Thia was as much a part of him as her own child was, and she'd been every bit as innocent in her own conception.

How could she ever hold something like that against a child?

Driana nodded. "If you want, you can see her now while I get the discs."

Kiara followed Nykyrian as Driana led them down the hallway to a back bedroom. As they entered, Thia jumped up from her desk with a startled gasp.

"Mama, don't burst in here like that. You know it makes me crazy."

Nykyrian tensed at the gesture.

"Thia, these are some friends of mine. Will you keep them company while I do something?"

"Sure." She righted her upturned chair.

Driana inclined her head at them, then made her way out of the room.

Kiara stayed in the doorway, not wanting to impose on Nykyrian's precious time with his daughter. She glanced around at all the pink and lace. The room was beautiful and sweet, much like the girl who lived here.

It made her wonder if her baby would be another daughter or a son.

Nykyrian approached the girl slowly. Kiara watched his reaction carefully, knowing this would enable her to tell how receptive he'd be to her own surprise for him.

Reflexively, she rubbed her hand across her stomach.

Thia scratched her head, studying Nykyrian's tall stature. "Are you a friend of Aksel's?"

"No." He took a seat in the chair beside her. "Truthfully, I can't stand him."

"Good. Me, either. He's a total . . . dirtbag." She studied his shades. "What about you?"

"Not a *total* dirtbag."

That made her smile. She looked down at the picture she'd been drawing, then glanced back up at him. "Are you my real father?"

"Why would you ask that?"

"Mom doesn't let strangers in here, especially men. Aksel gets too bent over it." She tilted her head. "What color are your eyes?"

Nykyrian reached up and removed his shades.

Thia's lips parted as she saw eyes that were identical to hers.

Nykryian didn't say anything while he stared at his daughter in awe and fear. She was an exact copy of her mother, except for the eyes that betrayed his DNA. Did she have any of the abnormalities he had?

Her teeth appeared human, as did the rest of her. But was she harmed in other ways by his screwed-up genes?

He wanted to hold her, and yet he was afraid to even reach out toward her. Who would have thought that one clumsy, embarrassing fifteen minutes with Driana could have produced such a beautiful child?

Flinching, he still remembered the way Driana had shoved him away after he'd failed to please her. *"That's* it? *You're worthless."*

He brushed his hand over a stack of books piled next to her desk, trying to distract himself from the bitter memory of Thia's conception. Picking one up, he thumbed through it. "Do you read these?"

"I do. I study languages in school, but no one other than my instructors can talk to me in them."

Kiara leaned against the doorframe as she watched them. Nykyrian said something to Thia that Kiara couldn't understand.

Thia's eyes widened as she responded in the same language. Warmth rushed through her when Thia smiled and displayed a set of dimples identical to Nykyrian's.

They were beautiful together, and it gave her hope for their future.

"How many languages do you know?" Thia asked excitedly.

"I've never really counted. But if you wish, I could

help you with them. I've lived on a lot of the planets where these languages are spoken."

"Were they beautiful?" Thia's eyes were dreamy. "Aksel won't let me leave here. He says that I'm not worth enough to pay for the fuel to visit them." A frown flitted across her face, then disappeared behind another smile. "I've only visited them online. At night, I like to dream about going off and exploring each one."

"If your mother okays it, I'd love to take you to some of them."

Kiara thought she might burst into tears. This was the Nykyrian she'd fallen in love with. The gentle, kind man who would do anything for the ones he cared about.

"Aksel's coming!" Driana's shout broke through their conversation.

Kiara met Nykyrian's gaze, her heart pounding in fear. By his expression, she could tell he was torn between leaving and staying.

Replacing his shades, he stood. "Is she safe here?"

Driana curled her lip. "She is unless Aksel catches you here. Do you really think I'd take a chance with my daughter's life?"

He ignored that last barb. "Is there a back way out?"

Driana inclined her head. "The balcony behind you."

He opened the door and helped Kiara through. Driana handed him the discs.

He paused for a moment, staring at Thia. "I'll be back for her."

"I'm counting on it."

With one last look at his daughter, who'd come to her feet to watch them leave, he ducked out the window.

They made it safely down the trellis and to the street below without running into any of Aksel's people.

Kiara breathed a sigh of relief, grateful for once that they didn't have to fight their way out. She looked at Nykyrian, but as usual, he gave her no clue about how he was feeling.

He took her arm and led her back toward their ship. At least this time, his grip was gentler than before.

She touched his hand and gave it a light squeeze. "So you're a father. How does that make you feel?"

After the tender way he'd spoken with Thia and the promise he'd made to Driana, Kiara expected him to beam with satisfaction, to smile and be happy, but what she got was a deep growl.

His hand tightened on her arm. "I feel like total shit."

A chill went down Kiara's spine. She rubbed her hand across her stomach. "Why would you say that?"

He stopped in the alley and glared at her. "First, she's more than half grown—I've missed most of her life already. Second, a child is the last thing I need in my life. One more helpless person depending on me to protect them. I can't even protect myself, Syn . . ." His voice trailed off as that familiar muscle worked in his jaw, letting her know he was furious.

She shifted nervously, wishing for something she could say to soothe the pain that bled from every part of him.

He shook his head. "I'm not fit to be a parent. What's she supposed to do, introduce me to her friends, 'Hi, this is my Dad. He's wanted dead by more governments than I can count'?"

Kiara stiffened. "You don't have to be so sarcastic."

He gave her an expression filled with loathing, but until he spoke she couldn't tell if it was directed at her or himself. "Come on, Kiara. Even you aren't that naive. Aksel's after you to get to me. What do you think my enemies will do if they ever learn I have a daughter? Her life won't be worth a lead *sola*."

Kiara let his words fall over her, and with each one she cringed a little more. She knew exactly what he was saying. At eight, she'd been just such a target.

She was a target even now because of her father and husband. Bile rose in her throat as she finally understood the horror her mother must have faced that day they'd been taken. Her mother hadn't feared for her own life.

Her mother had feared most for hers. Just as she feared for the life of her baby . . . She would rather they tear out her heart than touch her child.

Her heart pounding in agonized beats, she realized she had to make a decision.

Her husband or her baby.

There was no way she could have both. Nykyrian's world was too harsh for that. Swallowing the lump of remorse that burned in her throat, she knew what her answer must be. She'd have to shelter her child from the truth just as Driana had done with Thia.

Nykyrian could never know about their baby, and she could never live with him as his wife.

CHAPTER 26

Nykyrian stood in the shambles of what had been Syn's flat. Everything had been destroyed. Everything. Even the paintings had been torn from the walls and slashed. The statuary busted. The bottles of alcohol shattered.

This was how he knew Syn was dead. Because Syn had been raised on the streets with absolutely nothing but filth to call his own for the first part of his life, he was a packrat who fiercely protected his den.

For someone to come in and do this . . .

Syn would have called down the wrath of Nemesis to track the bastards and kill them.

Had he been alive.

I shouldn't have come. This was the first time he'd seen it for himself. But he wanted Kiara to understand, and *he* needed this cold reminder as to why he couldn't stay with her.

Now that she was back, he was weakening every second he was around her. He kept making excuses and telling himself that he could protect her and keep her safe.

The wreck of this apartment shouted loud and clear that none of them, no matter how fierce or well trained, was above the noose that hung perpetually over their heads. Her father had an army and couldn't keep her safe. How could he?

From the corner of his eye, he looked at her and ached to hold her close.

I won't be your death.

But that was exactly what he'd be if he didn't let her go. And for that reason, he would never touch her again. He couldn't take the chance of his love weakening him to the point of stupidity.

Kiara blinked away her tears as she took in the horror of what had been done to Syn's home. His scanner was torn out of the wall. His furniture upturned. Even his mattress had been violently slashed and everything maliciously stomped or broken. This wasn't a burglary or something random. Whoever had done this had been angry and had wanted to hurt Syn in the worst possible way.

What had they done to him?

Terror consumed her as she glanced at Nykyrian. He stood rigidly still with no emotion whatsoever. But she knew better. This was his best friend, and he had to be taking all of this hard.

She closed the distance between them, intending to touch him, but he stepped away. "Do you know who did this?"

He shook his head. "We haven't a clue. There are so many contracts out for us, so many who want us dead . . . you can pretty much take your pick."

As she searched the room, coldness consumed her. "Do you really think my father is responsible for this?"

"I have no idea."

She raked a trembling hand through her hair as that reality tore through her. Until Nykyrian, she'd never seen her father's ruthless side. Yes, she'd heard him threaten people in anger. She'd known he was a feared military commander, but the man who'd raised her had been kind and loving. Doting and sweet.

The same two opposing sides Nykyrian showed.

Nykyrian headed for the door. "We need to go. Whoever did this could come back or be observing us."

She followed him to the lifts. "Do you want to talk about this?"

Even though she couldn't see his eyes, she had the distinct impression he was giving her a droll stare. "I'm not a woman, Kiara. I don't want to talk about my feelings." His tone was rife with sarcasm.

"Sorry." She entered the lift and glanced back to where Syn's flat was. On the outside, there was no hint of the violence within.

Like Nykyrian. It all looked so calm and normal. It wasn't until you entered that the truth slammed into you.

And the brutal reality of his world settled over her like a pall, reminding her just why she would have to give up her husband.

As they left the building, he walked slightly ahead of her. She searched for words to make him feel better, knowing none existed. His best friend was most likely dead. No, not just dead, he'd most likely been tortured and mutilated.

Now Nykyrian was distant—as if he resented being around her. As if he wanted to forget she existed.

Yet . . .

She caught up to him and pulled him to a stop. "Why did you tell Driana we were married?"

That weighed on her. If he wanted no part of her, why would he keep claiming her as his wife?

Nykyrian faced her with his usual stoicism. He wore his shades again, making it impossible for her to have any trace whatsoever of his mood.

"Whoever got to Syn is most likely headed for me

next. If they took down that paranoid SOB so fast he couldn't even make a call to me, I doubt I have the skills to escape them. I told Driana about us so that you're now entitled to my estate once they kill me."

Kiara's stomach twisted at the blasé way he spoke about his death and the cold rationale behind his actions. It wasn't that he wanted the world to know about them or that he loved her. It was all business, and that hurt her on a level she hadn't even known she could be hurt on. "Why not tell Darling, Jayne, or Hauk?"

"One's legally a minor and the other two are outlaws, *mu Tara*. Driana is the daughter of a well-connected ambassador. All you have to do is contact her after my death and everything I own is yours."

How could he be so callous . . . ?

But then she knew. It was all he'd ever known. "I don't want your money, Nykyrian."

He didn't move. "Fine. Let the banks have it, then. I really couldn't care less."

Turning around, he continued down the street. Kiara flicked her hands at him in anger, wanting to pummel him until he saw reason. How could a man so astute with everything else be so blind when it came to her and her feelings?

When had he lost his ability to see her as clearly as he saw the rest of the world?

"Kyrian?"

Kiara almost walked into Nykyrian, he stopped so suddenly and without warning.

Frowning, she glanced about the street to see what had made him lock up like that.

A beautiful Andarion woman let go of the shop door she was holding to come rushing toward them. The woman paused a few feet away, her face a cross between disbelief, agony and joy as she covered her mouth with a trembling hand. She was almost as tall as Nykyrian.

Her red and white eyes scanned his body in a possessive manner Kiara didn't like at all. The woman's long, black hair was partially concealed by a golden diadem that framed the fragile, pale features of her face.

"Kyrian?" she asked again, her voice filled with wonder and fear as she reached a graceful hand out to him. Just as she would have touched him, she jerked it back.

He stood ramrod stiff, not acknowledging the woman in the least.

Another Andarion lady came running up to them, followed by their guards. She gave the woman talking to them a stern frown. "Cairistiona. Don't ever leave us like that again! You know it's not safe." She placed her arms around the woman's shoulders and tried to walk her away from them.

But Cairistiona refused to leave. She wrenched herself away from the other woman and stared up at Nykyrian as if he were a ghost. "It's my Kyrian, can't you see? He's finally come back to me."

The woman shook her head at Kiara and Nykyrian. "I'm so sorry. She's not been right since her son died as a child." She put her arms back on Cairistiona and patted her gently. "Come along, Carie, he's not your Nykyrian, you know that. Nykyrian's long dead."

"No . . . I know my son. It's him." The agony of Cairistiona's voice was heart-wrenching.

Kiara's blood left her cheeks. She placed her hand on Nykyrian's arm and felt the degree of tenseness in his body. That alone told her the truth.

This was his mother . . .

Cairistiona's eerie eyes pleaded with him. "Tell her who you are, baby." She gestured to the woman beside her. "Please."

Nykyrian started to move away, but Kiara grabbed him and kept him there.

"You know her, don't you?" she asked, wishing she could see his eyes.

He gently removed her hand from his arm. "Let go of me."

Kiara glanced at Cairistiona, then back at him. "Is she your mother?"

The woman holding Cairistiona gasped.

He tensed even more, but Kiara wasn't about to let this go until she knew the truth. "Nykyrian, answer me. Is she your mother?"

Nykyrian stared at Kiara, his stomach knotted. This couldn't be happening. Why today of all days did he have to bump into his bitch of a mother?

Wasn't his life in turmoil enough? The last thing he wanted was to come face to face with the one person he hated most.

"Kyrian?"

He cringed at his mother's voice, the same voice that had haunted him for years. As a child, he'd prayed to hear the sound of her voice again. To have her come get him and apologize for what she'd done to him.

But she never came, and his nightmares had only worsened until the only part of her he craved was her death.

Memories tore through him.

I don't belong here! It's a mistake. My mother will kill you for this. Let me go!

His mother's guards had told the humans not to believe any claim he made about his identity.

He could still see the cold administrator's face as she registered him. *What's his name?*

The guards had sneered at him. *He's a filthy lying mongrel and has no name. He makes them up.*

Nykyrian had fought and tried to tell them who he was—to call for his mother to come get him, but once the administrator had muzzled him, he'd been unable to claim anything.

Still, he'd known the truth, and it'd carved so much hatred inside him that nothing could erase it.

His mother sobbed. She was so much frailer than she'd been when she sent him away. Older and obviously heavily sedated. "You have to tell them who you are."

Why? So they could mock him again? Why should he care about her tears when she hadn't cared about his?

Let go of me, you filth. The disdain on her face as she'd pried his small hand from her arm had haunted him for years.

What did she want from him now? Absolution?

Forget it, he wasn't in a forgiving mood.

"I don't have a mother," he sneered at her. "I never had one."

Oblivious to the staring passers-by, Cairistiona burst into tears and wailed as if she'd been slapped.

Nykyrian tried to move past Kiara, but she held fast and refused to let him leave. At the moment, he wanted to kill her, too.

"Get out of my way," he said in a low tone that never failed to intimidate people. For once, it didn't work. She just stared at him with those damned amber eyes, demanding with them that he do something he knew would only hurt him more.

Kiara wasn't about to let him escape. Not if what she suspected was true. Holding him firm, she glanced to his mother. "Your Nykyrian . . . did he have green human eyes?"

Nykyrian's arms flexed threateningly underneath her hands.

The woman holding Cairistiona paled.

"Yes, yes, he did—just like his father." Cairistiona breathed excitedly, her eyes never wavering from Nykyrian's rigid back.

"Kiara," Nykyrian growled angrily.

She ignored him.

Nykyrian pulled away from her.

In one last move to defy him for his own good, Kiara stood on her tiptoes and swiped the shades off his face.

The look he gave her made her take a step back.

"Oh, God," the other woman gasped as she saw his bare face. Her hands fell away from Cairistiona.

Cairistiona let out a happy laugh as she ran for him. "I knew you were alive."

"Don't you dare touch me," Nykyrian snapped with enough venom to drain all the joy out of his mother's face.

The other woman moved forward, shaking her head. "This can't be. You're supposed to be dead." She looked at Kiara with her red and white eyes, like Cairistiona's. "I saw the charred remains myself and the tests." Her gaze shifted back to Nykyrian. "I was there when they buried you."

"I told you then that boy wasn't my son. But you wouldn't listen. All of you thought I was crazy." She bit her quivering lip. "They wouldn't even allow me to search for you."

Nykyrian bared his fangs, anger darkening his eyes. "Don't you fucking lie to me. You knew exactly where I was . . . where *you* had sent me to die. You didn't want a human in line for inheritance. I was an embarrassment to all of you, so you threw me to the dogs hoping I'd die before I could return and make a claim to your beloved throne."

Kiara staggered back at those words as realization struck her so hard, it stole her breath. No. It couldn't be.

Her gaze drifted over the women's expensive, imperial robes, the imperial guards. Her throat dried. The woman before her was Princess Cairistiona, the lady holding her was Princess Tylie, which made Nykyrian . . .

Nykyrian barely caught Kiara against him as she fainted.

Tylie frowned at them. "Is she all right?"

Nykyrian clenched his teeth, fear pouring over him. This wasn't like her . . . and for the first time in his adult life, he tasted true panic as he swung her limp body up into his arms. "I don't know."

"Our shuttle's docked behind this building. Carie's personal physician is on board. Even though she's human, that would probably be the closest place to take her for care."

Nykyrian glared at his aunt, wanting to get as far away from them as he could. But Kiara came first. He nodded and followed them to their craft.

His mother kept looking back at him, her smile wide. Every time he saw her, he was torn between welcoming it and wanting to drive one of his knives straight through her unfeeling heart.

It seemed an eternity before they were on board the shuttle and the Andarion doctor came out of the back, bitching about having to treat a human patient. The prejudice ate at Nykyrian's control.

Gently, he laid Kiara in a soft, cushioned seat. His

heart thudded in his chest as he watched her pale beauty, aching for her to wake up so they could leave these people.

Then he spun on the doctor and grabbed his shirt in his fist. "You will treat her. You will respect her. Or by the gods, I will rip out your heart and shove it down your throat."

The doctor's face turned three shades paler. "Don't worry. Their anatomy isn't that different from ours. I'll take good care of her. Now if you'll excuse us, I need a little privacy."

"Just remember her life is tied to yours."

He nodded.

Reluctantly, Nykyrian allowed his mother to pull him to the back of the shuttle where she and Tylie could talk to him.

Tylie sat down first. "Who is the woman?"

"My wife," he said coldly.

His mother appeared elated by the news. "You're married? How wonderful."

He just glared at her. Was she completely stupid? She seemed to function on the level of a child.

Or was it the drugs? By the dull tone of her skin and the dilation of her eyes, he could tell she was seriously sedated.

Tylie frowned at him. "What happened to you? After we sent you off to school, we were told you died in a fire."

Nykyrian snorted at her bullshit. "You never sent me to school, so don't bother lying."

His mother and aunt exchanged puzzled scowls.

Cairistiona cocked her head as if she couldn't understand what he was talking about. "You were sent to Pontari Academy after you placed so high on the entry test. They sent an escort for you and everything."

His temper boiled. Why were they playing this game with him? "*You* sent me to a human orphanage and your guards instructed them to never believe my claims of being a prince. They told them I was the mentally defective bastard son of a dead whore. Don't think for one minute that those words aren't carved into my memory."

Both of their faces lost color.

"Mother," Tylie breathed as she took her sister's hand. "Dear God, I never thought she'd do something so horrible."

Nykyrian's frown deepened. "What are you talking about?"

Cairistiona swallowed as she clutched at her necklace. "She always hated you. She said Jullien could pass for an Andarion, but that you would always look too human."

Tylie nodded. "It was her idea for you to go to Pontari early. She thought you would be better off there." The bitter anger in his aunt's voice surprised him.

Cairistiona shook her head. "We should have known better than to trust her."

Tylie's eyes teared up. "Everything was a lie. And all this time, we kept you," Tylie turned to face his mother, "drugged so you wouldn't search for him. How did you know he was alive?"

"I just did."

Nykyrian refused to believe them. "Why are you lying to me? You were the one who put me on the shuttle yourself. You pried my hands off your arm and told me that I sickened you. That you—"

"I never said that!" his mother shouted, her tone indignant.

"Fuck, yeah, you did. I don't know what the drugs have done to your mind, but nothing has ever dulled the cold look on your face or those harsh words from my memory."

Tylie raked her hand over her face. "Parisa. It had to be."

His mother pulled a small photo chip from her bag. She turned it on and handed it to him. "Is this the woman you saw?"

Nykyrian started to tell her to shove it, but for some reason he took it from her and looked.

His stomach hit the floor. There in the picture was his mother, standing beside another woman who looked so much like her, they appeared to be twins. Nothing differentiated them. Not their hair color, or height.

"What the . . ."

"She's our cousin." Tylie cursed. "As kids she and Carie used to pretend to be each other to fool the adults."

"We thought it was funny. How could she do this to me?"

"Mother bribed her, I'm sure. Parisa's father was a ne'er-do-well who squandered all their money and she's always been jealous of us." Tylie let out a disgusted sigh. "She may have even done it just to get back at you for being an heiress."

"I swear I'll kill her."

Nykryian sat in shock, not knowing what to believe anymore. He stared at the photo, trying to sort through all the emotions tumbling through him: rage, pain, grief, loss.

Were they telling him the truth?

Did it even matter if they were? Nothing changed his past. It was still horrific and cold.

But if his mother had wanted him . . .

You're not a child anymore. Who cares?

And yet deep inside, he did care and there was no denying it.

Tylie drew a ragged breath. "Mother's committed a terrible crime. What are we going to do?"

Cairistiona looked at Nykyrian with a love in her eyes that tore through all the defenses he kept around his heart. It was the look he'd always wanted to see on his mother's face. "Were they kind to you in the orphanage?"

Nykyrian shrugged, not wanting to remember. There was nothing she could do to ease the ache in his soul or correct the wrongs that had been done to him. Only Kiara seemed able to do that. "I was adopted," he said at last, deciding that would be the easiest thing to disclose.

Her expression turned hopeful. "By good people?"

Yeah. The best quality imaginable.

A lump closed his throat and he stifled the urge to curl his lip. "Commander Huwin Quiakides."

His mother's smile widened. "My father knew him well. They went through League training together. He always said that for a human, Huwin was almost Andarion in his beliefs." She said that like it was a good thing. "Are you a soldier, too?"

Nykyrian looked at her, his soul screaming out for vengeance, and he wanted to hurt her because of it. "I was a League assassin."

The look of shock on her face didn't give him the satisfaction he'd thought it would.

"But you have a wife . . ."

"As I said, I *was* an assassin. I left The League."

Before she could respond, the doctor cleared his throat. Nykyrian came to his feet immediately to face him. "Is she all right?"

The doctor nodded. "She must have had a shock or something. Not unusual for a woman in her condition. I've heard many human women faint when expecting."

"When expecting what?" Nykyrian asked with a scowl.

A second later total understanding dawned on him, and he felt completely stupid for having asked the question.

Suddenly, he couldn't breathe. The walls seemed to close in on him.

What had he done?

The doctor raked him with a cold look. "Didn't you know she was pregnant?"

Unable to respond, Nykyrian stared at his mother's face, wishing he could feel the same happiness she beamed. Instead, all he could think of was how many people were out to kill him. No, not just kill him—to tear apart anyone they could to get to him.

For lack of simple birth control, he'd signed Kiara's death contract more effectively than if he'd hired the assassins himself.

His mother stepped forward, her forehead wrinkled with worry. "Are you all right?"

Nykyrian didn't know how to answer.

No, he wasn't all right. He'd killed the only person he'd ever loved . . .

What was he going to do?

"Is she awake?" he asked the doctor.

"Not yet, but I could revive her if you like."

"Please."

His mother's cold hand touched his cheek. "Are you leaving us?" Her voice trembled.

"I have to."

Large tears rolled down her cheeks and he finally understood how Syn felt when he saw a woman cry. It was debilitating.

"You don't plan on coming back to me, do you?"

He clenched his teeth in anger and pain. "What do you want from me? From where I stand, you're the one who threw me away years ago."

"Please, don't do this. You have no idea what I've been through over your loss. I love you. I've always loved you, more so than even Jullien because you reminded me so much of your father . . . I wasn't a whore, Nykyrian. Ever. I fell in love with a beautiful man I couldn't have because of my political station and his, and I gave him two sons who have always meant the world to me." She opened the necklace she wore and there, inside, was a picture of him as a small child. "You've never been far from my heart."

And in that moment, he remembered things he'd purposefully buried because they were too painful to face. Images of his mother singing to him and holding him . . .

He knew she wasn't lying. She meant every word.

She had loved him once . . .

"Would you at least meet us for dinner?" Tylie asked. "One meal, and then you never have to see us again if you don't want to."

"Please," his mother begged.

Nykyrian looked away, unable to bear the agony in their eyes. Before his common sense could intervene, he nodded. "Where do you want me to meet you?"

His mother smiled. "Here at Camry's. Do you know the place?"

"I do."

Tylie's smile matched his mother's. "Six-thirty?"

"I'll be there." Nykyrian stepped back as Kiara joined them. Her pale features worried him. "How are you feeling?"

She rubbed her arms. "A little shaky, but I'll be fine. What happened?"

"You fainted."

"I don't faint."

He brushed back a strand of her hair before he could stop himself. "Yes, you do." With a goodbye to his mother and aunt, Nykyrian wrapped his arm around Kiara's shoulders and helped her from the shuttle.

He remained silent until they were inside his fighter and headed back to his house. Only then did he bring up what was foremost on his mind. "Why didn't you tell me you were pregnant?"

Kiara went cold at his question. Why did he have to ask her that when she was strapped in and unable to look at him? "How did you find out?"

His hand jerked on the throttle and Kiara wondered what his first reaction to the news had been. Had he felt any joy whatsoever?

Or was he only angry at her?

"The doctor told me."

She hated the lack of emotion in his voice. "Oh . . . Are you happy?"

"What do you think?"

Her heart sank. She remembered his rage at finding Thia and knew this didn't thrill him half as much as that. "So what does this mean to us?" She was terrified of the answer, but needed to know his take on the situation.

His body tensed around her. She felt his heart pounding under her shoulder blade and wanted so much to comfort him, but knew she couldn't.

"What do you want to do about it?"

Tears gathered in her eyes. "He's not an it, Nykyrian. The baby is our child." And what she *wanted* was to live with her baby's father and raise her family like her parents had done. To watch Nykyrian play with their child, teach the baby all the languages he knew, hold him or her when he or she cried and needed soothing.

But all of that was a futile dream.

Nykyrian would never stay with her.

"I was planning to raise the baby on Gouran."

"Probably for the best. Once I finish with Aksel, no one else should ever bother you again. I know Driana won't tell anyone about you and I'm sure my mother won't, either."

Kiara's stomach churned with dread of the next question she had to ask. "Will I ever see you?"

Nykyrian tensed as pain tore through him. He couldn't stand the thought of living without her, of returning to his solitude, especially now that she carried a part of him with her.

The fact that she would keep their baby . . .

How he wanted to pull her into his arms and kiss her. To keep her with him forever. But he couldn't be that selfish.

And if he were to ever see her with his child, he knew he would forget his common sense, his survival skills, and stay with them.

But he couldn't. He refused to risk their lives for his own selfish desires. "No."

Kiara winced. She'd known his answer before she asked the question. Once he killed Aksel, she would lose him forever.

Her soul screamed out in pain. She didn't want to live without him, she wasn't even sure if she could.

You're going to have to. Because she had a baby who needed her now.

She stared down at Nykyrian's gloved hands, re-membering how good they'd felt on her body as they created the new being inside of her.

And she refused to let him go. *I will find some way to keep you, Nykyrian. The rest of the world may have thrown you away, but I won't.* Somehow, she was going to make her dreams come true, no matter what it took.

Even if it was dangerous. She didn't care anymore. Life wasn't for the timid. It was harsh and it was biting.

But the one thing that made it bearable was the people you cared for. It was finding that light in the darkness. That peace in hell.

It was being with the man she loved . . . the father of her baby, even when the rest of the world plotted against them, and she wasn't going to let her fears tear that away.

Yes, he had enemies. She had them, too.

But the best revenge was to live their lives while thumbing their noses at them. To love each other even while those people tried to rip them apart.

That was what she was going to give to her child and, most of all, to Nykyrian.

Even if she had to beat him to do it.

CHAPTER 27

Jullien sat in the security room of the embassy, his temper boiling. The moment his mother and aunt had returned from their shopping trip, he'd known the bitches were up to something by the furtive glances they'd cast about the hallway before they secreted themselves in the study.

He'd learned a long time ago to beware his Aunt Tylie's treachery. That bitch hated him, and she seemed to delight in getting him into trouble.

Now, as he listened to them talking about his missing twin brother through the hidden mic, he realized just how dangerous a position he was in.

While everyone had been told of Nykyrian's supposed death as a child, his grandmother had confided the whole sordid story to him several years ago of how she'd bribed his cousin to pretend to be their mother—a final act of cruelty for which his grandmother was famous. Parisa had put Nykyrian on a shuttle and the bastard was supposed to be dead. God knows, his grandmother had paid enough money to the orphanage to see his brother starved and abused.

No one should have survived his treatment.

Unlike his grandmother, he knew better than to trust a hireling. If you wanted something done right, you had to do it yourself, especially when it involved murder.

He clenched his fists in anger. If his mother and aunt had their way, they would reinstate Nykyrian back into the empire. He would have to split all his inheritance.

And there was just no way he'd do that. Ever.

Jullien tapped his fingers against the wooden desk, his mind whirling with various plots. His mother had to be stopped. He would be the sole heir to the Trioson and Andarion empires.

By God, he would tolerate no encroacher!

But what could he do?

His knees shook with nervous energy as he planned action against Nykyrian. He would secure his position as sole heir no matter the cost.

Kiara adjusted the black lace of her robe, then fluffed a few wisps of her hair around her face.

Nykyrian was in his office, working at his computer. They still had four hours before they were to meet his mother for dinner, and she'd decided she wasn't going to give him a reprieve.

Any day, Nykyrian might have Aksel, and send her away. But she wasn't going to be expelled without a fight.

An image of Syn's flat went through her mind, followed by the afternoon she and her mother had been kidnaped.

I will not be intimidated.

She replaced those images with the ones she wanted to have as memories. Nykyrian holding their baby.

That was what she was fighting for. Since he knew about the child, she was going to make him part of their lives.

With her resolve set, she opened the door and headed for him.

Nykyrian's neck tingled like someone was watching him. He looked up from his screen to see Kiara standing in the doorway, her long hair swirling about her lithe body that was covered by a robe so thin he could see her nipples standing firm underneath the silk.

His breath caught in his throat.

No! I won't touch her. I know better.

She stared at him with those amber eyes as she closed the distance between them. As soon as she reached his side, she slowly undid her belt and shrugged the robe from her body. It pooled at her feet, leaving her completely naked before him.

Oh, she was fighting dirty.

Before he could move, she took his hand and led it to her stomach, which was just starting to show her pregnancy. He stared at his gloved hand, aching with the memory of how soft her skin was.

He knew what he did was wrong, but he couldn't stop himself. He was drawn to her against all his reasons that told him this was suicide.

Kiara sensed his defenses, but she'd breached them enough times to know what she had to do to keep him from pulling away. She ran one hand over the stubble of his cheek and buried it in the silken, white hair while she removed his shades with the other and placed them on his desk.

He closed his eyes and kissed the inside of her elbow. Giddiness welled up inside her. With him here with her now, his leaving her alone these past weeks didn't seem to matter. Even the pain over him not coming for her was gone.

She doubted if he could ever do anything she

wouldn't forgive. She loved him too much to hold a grudge.

At least for too long.

Nykyrian watched her in awe as she sank to the ground in front of his chair. He didn't know what she intended until she moved her hands to his fly. His breath catching, he watched as she undid his pants and freed his erection. She ran her fingers down the underside of his cock, making his body jerk in response.

Locking gazes with him, she slowly lowered her mouth to take him in.

Holy saints . . .

His eyes rolled back in his head as her lips and tongue caressed him. Never had anything felt more incredible. Snatching his gloves off, he buried his hand in her hair as he spread her hair out over his lap.

The sight of her on him . . .

His resistence to her shattered. How could he have ever thought to live without her?

"Kiara, please . . ."

She gave one luscious lick to him before she pulled back. "Please what?"

Don't leave me. But he couldn't say those words. They hung heavy in his throat and heart.

Unable to stand the pain of the reality that couldn't allow him to keep her and the need to hold on to her forever, he pulled her to his lips so that he could kiss her. His head swam as he lifted her up and set her down in his lap.

Kiara gasped as he filled her completely. She opened his shirt as she rode him slowly and ran her hands over his flesh.

Nykyrian allowed her to pull his shirt off and drop it to the floor.

"I love you, Nykyrian," she whispered before she brushed her tongue over his fangs.

How could she do this? How could she love him after he'd abandoned her?

"I love you, too, Kiara."

Kiara froze at the words she'd never expected him to say. "What?"

Instead of answering her, he kissed her deeply, with more passion than she'd ever experienced.

He slung his hand out over his desk, sending everything on it straight to the floor—including his computer. Without leaving her body, he stood up and laid her back against it.

His thrusts were furious now, pounding through her as he braced one hand on the desk and cupped her breast with the other. Arching her back, she tightened her legs around him, drawing him in ever deeper.

Nykyrian stared down at her, savoring the feel of her body. He pulled back enough so that he could see where they were joined and watched as he slammed into her.

Kiara didn't know why, but she felt so exposed to him like this. As if he were seeing her completely naked— something that made no sense since he'd seen her naked many times before.

And yet . . .

She ran her thumb over his lips, letting his fangs graze her knuckle before she trailed her hand down his chest over his stomach and then lower until she could feel him sliding between her fingers, into her body.

Her covered her hand with his and the look of complete pleasure and possession on his face sent her over the edge. Crying out, she came with the fiercest orgasm she'd ever had.

Nykyrian let go of her hand to cup her head in his

hands as he quickened his thrusts, intensifying her pleasure. Her warm body enveloped his, sending him over
the edge until he joined her release.

Entwined, they stayed there while he felt her heartbeat thumping furiously against his chest.

She touched his face. "Are you still wearing your
pants?"

He laughed as he realized that he was also wearing
his boots. "Yeah."

She tsked at him. "I think I should be insulted by
that."

"Trust me, baby, it's not an insult. It's a tribute to
how bad I wanted you." He started to pull away, but she
tightened her legs around him.

He stared down at her naked body as he ran his hand
over her breast.

"I love the way you feel inside me."

"Kiara—"

She put her fingers over his lips, silencing him. "I
will always be yours, Nykyrian. Always."

His link's whistle rent the air. "Nykyrian!"

He cursed as she opened her legs and released him.
Kneeling down, he scooped up his link from the floor
where it'd landed. Then he made the mistake of looking up for the best view of his life.

"Nykyrian? Are you there?"

Kiara . . . emergency . . . Kiara . . . emergency . . .

The emergency won out, but only barely and only
because he was afraid it might impact her safety.

"What the hell do you want, Caillen? And this better
be worth your life."

"Fuck you. We have a major problem here. I'm pretty
sure this is Syn's link that I found at my sister's place,
along with a contract signed by her for his life . . . and
yours. I haven't seen her, Syn, Tessa, or Kasen for weeks.

I came over here to find Shahara, and instead I find what looks like a war zone . . . Just what the hell's going on?"

Nykyrian went numb as Kiara sat up to stare at him with wide, concerned eyes. "Where are you now?"

"Shahara's condo."

"Is there anything else of Syn's there?"

The pause stretched out. Nykyrian's fear increased every second that went by without a response. What the hell had happened?

Where was Syn?

"Yeah. I've got his flight jacket—you know, the one he loves to wear."

Nykyrian bit back a curse. Syn wouldn't have left that behind if he'd had a choice.

When Caillen spoke, there was a hesitancy to his voice. "You don't think Shahara's hurt him, do you?"

Nykyrian clenched his teeth and looked at Kiara. "How should I know? She's your sister."

"If she'd killed him, she wouldn't have taken trophies. That's not her way. They have to be together somewhere."

Yeah, but the question was where, and more importantly, why?

Nykyrian ground his teeth as he tried to sort this out. "Can you tell when they were last there?"

"Judging by the condition of the milk left out, I'd say a few days at least."

He looked at Kiara and debated what to do. He wanted to take off right now to find Syn, but he didn't dare leave her here alone, unprotected.

The safest place would be to take her to his mother. Aksel would *never* look for her there. No one knew anything about his mother, and as a royal heiress, she had the best guards in the business. Surely his mother would do this one favor for him . . .

"Look, I have something I have to take care of first. Why don't you meet me at Jayne's around ten and we can try to figure out this mess?"

"All right. I'll keep trying to contact my sisters until then."

Nykyrian tossed the link aside and rubbed his hands across his face. "And the hits just keep on coming . . ."

Kiara brushed her hand through his hair, trying to soothe the pain she saw in his eyes. "Isn't this good news? Doesn't it mean Syn's alive?"

He kissed the palm of her hand. "I don't know what it means."

She reached down and tickled him until he laughed. "Stop being so dour. Lighten up a bit. Syn didn't die in his flat. He might be all right."

"How can you believe that?"

"I have faith that things will work out."

He shook his head, amazed by her optimism. "I don't know how I'm going to let you go," he whispered in a ragged voice.

"Then don't."

His eyes went dead. "We both know that's impossible."

Kiara traced the line of his lips. "I bet if someone had told you six months ago that you would smile for me, you'd have said the same thing."

Nykyrian moved to pull away, but Kiara wrapped her arms and legs around him, holding him close to her. "I'm not giving up on you, Nykyrian. People have done that to you your entire life. And I intend to fight for you—no matter what. I'll die for you if I have to."

"And that's exactly what I'm afraid of, Kiara." He slipped out of her hold.

Kiara laid there as the significance of those words

hit her. The man who feared nothing, not even death, had finally admitted to fearing something.

Losing her.

She listened to him entering the bathroom across the hall. Her heart beat a painful rhythm in her breast as she pulled her robe up from the floor and put it on.

She'd always thought love was supposed to be easy. When you found that special someone, the two of you lived out your lives together, forever happy . . .

Why hadn't someone warned her that love didn't answer all of life's problems, it just created more?

Stop it! She wouldn't let her doubts and fears ruin this. So long as they were alive, there was hope, and so long as she had hope, she wasn't going to give up on this.

She would *not* give up on Nykryian.

CHAPTER 28

The crowd at Camry's was huge. Kiara's stomach rumbled in protest as she dreaded the long wait ahead of them. She paused at the end of the line, surprised when Nykyrian tugged at her elbow to keep her moving.

"What are you doing?" she whispered, trying to ignore the angry glares from the other people who'd been waiting ahead of them.

People who weren't polite enough to use low tones as they criticized their actions. "Who do they think they are?"

"The nerve of them!"

Nykyrian didn't bother to whisper in return. "I can't stand out here on the street. Too many people would like to shoot me." He cast an amused expression at the ones closest to him who'd been the rudest. "As well as any asshole unlucky enough to be near me when they open fire."

Several of the more disgruntled people actually took a step back to give them a clear path to the door.

Kiara shook her head. "You're incorrigible."

Nykyrian shrugged nonchalantly. "I'm just saying . . ."

The maitre d' looked up from his podium, his smile bright when he saw Nykyrian. "How nice to see you again, Commander, your party is already seated and waiting."

Kiara paused in confusion. "How did he know you were a commander?"

The maitre d' grinned at her. "He saved my son's life."

Nykyrian shifted in discomfort as if the gratitude embarrassed him.

Kiara was impressed. "Aren't you full of unexpected surprises. What did you do?"

The maitre d' was the one who answered. "Assassins were after a target who took my boy hostage. The commander got him out of there without even a scratch."

"Really? How?"

Nykyrian cleared his throat. "I have good aim."

"And impeccable speed and timing." The maitre d' inclined his head to lead them to the right. "I took the liberty of having your favorite dish prepared for you, Commander. The others have already placed their orders."

Kiara followed him past the intricate rows of crowded tables with Nykyrian just a few steps behind her. Even though Nykyrian walked fluidly, she could tell he was more than aware of everything around them.

The maitre d' took them to the back of the restaurant where the private dining rooms were reserved for prominent guests.

A wave of surrealism hit her as she remembered that Nykyrian was a prince . . .

The tragic reality of that only worsened the horror of his past. How awful it had to have been for him to know the truth, to know that he should have been sheltered and loved, and then to be subjected to the nightmare of his life.

And it made her wonder if Jullien had known who he was when he'd picked on him in school.

Or was Jullien just that stupid?

The maitre d' opened a door and ushered them in. Kiara hesitated as she recognized Emperor Aros seated at the table with Nykyrian's mother and aunt. Now that she saw Nykyrian and his father together, she didn't know how she'd missed it before . . . They looked so much alike that only a fool would mistake them for anything other than father and son. They even shared the same height.

While the emperor's white hair was cut short and his unscarred face was older than Nykyrian's, he still held the same sharp features and green eyes.

Of course, the similarity in their faces wasn't quite as obvious since Nykyrian wore his shades.

But without them . . .

There was no doubt who his father was.

Nykyrian bit back a curse as he saw his father waiting on them. It was bad enough to be here with his mother and aunt—he still hadn't reconciled his past where they were concerned or come to terms with their parts in it.

But to have his father here, too . . .

He felt awkward and out of place with these people. Any time he'd ever been near the aristocracy it hadn't gone well for him.

A part of him kept waiting for this to be a trick and for them to have him shot or arrested. He had no trust whatsoever where they were concerned.

Especially not his father . . .

His mother came to her feet. "There you are," she breathed happily. "We'd begun to worry that you had changed your mind."

He should have, but unlike them, when he gave his word about something, he abided by it.

The maitre d' excused himself and left them to a modicum of privacy.

His father rose more slowly, and by that, Nykyrian knew he was nervous. He could also tell his father wasn't used to being uncertain about himself. "I hope you don't mind my presence. When Carie told me she'd found you, I insisted that I attend as well."

Kiara took his hand and gave an encouraging squeeze. He returned the gesture even though he still wanted to bolt for the door.

For several awkward seconds, no one spoke.

Nykyrian finally broke the tense silence. "This is my wife, Kiara."

Aros inclined his head respectfully to her. "We've already met, but it is a pleasure to see you again."

Kiara returned his smile as she curtseyed. "It's an honor to see you again, Your Majesty."

Aros blustered gruffly. "Please. None of that, my dear. You're family now. I hate all that posturing and bowing, anyway." He pulled a chair out next to him for her. "Come, child, have a seat. You shouldn't be standing in your condition. We have to take care of that baby."

Kiara glanced at Nykyrian to see how he was dealing with his newfound family. As usual, she couldn't tell.

Without a word, she moved toward his father and the chair Aros held for her. Nykyrian's mother and aunt exchanged worried frowns and each kept looking at him nervously while he seated himself in a chair next to hers.

He was so tense, though she suspected she was the only one present who knew that. And it was only because of the time they'd spent together that she'd finally learned to read him . . . a little, anyway. It still didn't mean she could read his thoughts or identify the source of his unease.

He could be angry or hurt . . .

Or even both.

"We will no doubt have beautiful grandchildren, wouldn't you say, Carie?" the emperor asked, pushing Kiara's seat up to the table.

Cairistiona nodded. "They will be the envy of everyone."

Nykyrian shifted uncomfortably beside her. Kiara placed her hand over the one he held in his lap. He looked up at her with something that appeared to be pride.

They remained quiet while their meals were brought in and placed before them.

Nykyrian held Kiara's soothing hand while berating himself for coming along on this stupid expedition. He didn't know these people, and he wasn't really sure he even wanted to.

Just ask them to protect Kiara, then get to Caillen and the others.

Why was that so hard?

Because they left you when you needed them most. Why should that change now? That, and he'd never asked anyone for anything. Ever.

The oddest part was that he'd ached for this moment most of his life. A brief chance meeting where he could talk to his mother, have her look at him with love or maybe even pride, have her accept him.

Now that they were finally together, Nykyrian didn't know what to do with it.

"I know this must be hard for you," his father said after the servers had left them alone again. "I had no idea you were alive. If I had even suspected, I would have torn the galaxy apart looking for you."

That comment made him seethe as bitter memories scorched him. How ironic that his father had no more memory of him than his twin brother had. "We actually have met before. Twice."

His father scowled at the disclosure. "Really? When?"

"The first time when I was in The League Academy. I was the 'wretched bastard' you ordered to be strip-searched and then jailed when Jullien misplaced his ring in his own gym bag."

Kiara dropped her cutlery as she looked up at the emperor, who had no idea of the horror Nykyrian's dry, steady tone hid.

To his credit, Aros looked ashamed, but still . . .

She wanted to attack him for what had been done to Nykyrian over that act of cruelty. She could only imagine how much worse it had to be for Nykyrian to sit here and not strike him.

The emperor sputtered. "I-I had no idea . . . Why didn't you say anything?"

Nykyrian kept his tone level and his gaze straight ahead, away from his father. "When I tried to speak to you, you told me to shut up as you had no interest in anything a thief had to say. You said it was your son who'd been wronged and that I, a worthless low-bred pleb, wasn't worthy to even look at you . . . so I didn't."

The pain on his father's face was tangible. But Kiara knew it was nothing compared to the agony of Nykyrian's memory of a little boy standing so close to the father who'd abandoned him and being turned away so harshly. The fact that Nykyrian omitted the part of the story he'd shared with her about his two days in jail made her wonder what other nightmares he kept to himself.

She wished she could take every bit of his pain away.

Aros lowered his head. "I am so sorry, Nykyrian. I had no idea. I should have recognized you."

Nykyrian shrugged. "Not really. The bruises from my interrogation prior to your arrival distorted my face, and my hair had been shaved off as punishment."

Kiara felt sick at those emotionless words.

"Did we ever meet?" Cairistiona asked, her voice quivering.

Nykyrian shook his head. "I only saw you from a distance a handful of times when you came to pick up Jullien."

Tylie scowled. "Did Jullien not realize you were in school with him?"

"You'd have to ask my brother that question."

But Nykyrian had known . . . and that alone brought a lump to Kiara's throat. That he'd been so close to his family all that time and not been able to talk to them must have been sheer torture for him.

Just how hurt had he been when his cousin put him on that shuttle that he hadn't even attempted to contact any of his family?

Aros cleared his throat. "Were you listed on the roll under your name?"

"No, sir."

"Then what name did you go by?"

Nykyrian took a sip of his wine before he responded. "Hybrid Andarion."

His father gaped. "I don't understand . . ."

This time the bitter resentment was thick in his voice. "I couldn't very well go by Nykyrian eton Anatole, as it's a felony to pretend to be royalty."

His father's mouth tightened. "You *are* royalty."

"Had I tried to contact you, Majesty, and claimed to be your long-lost son, your administration would have had me jailed without even investigating the veracity of my claim, and having already gone to jail for something I didn't do, I had no desire to repeat the experience."

His mother swallowed. "And I know why you didn't bother coming to us. I swear, I shall see my mother punished for this. What she did to you was criminal."

Aros sighed. "I shudder to ask about the second time we met."

"I was on your League security detail when you attended the bicentennial council meeting on Ritadaria fifteen years ago."

His face blanched. "I do remember you . . . You were that young kid who saved me when that protestor came at me. I only remember because you looked so incredibly young to be on so important an assignment."

Nykyrian inclined his head. "You tried to have me removed."

Aros wiped a trembling hand over his face. "And they refused, telling me that you were the best they had in spite of your age. Which you proved when one of The League assassins caught the protestor but didn't disarm him. You snatched me away right before his shot would have landed between my eyes. And then, wounded, you took him down and had him cuffed before anyone else could reach us."

"The shot barely grazed me. They didn't even take me off duty over it."

Aros looked as ill as Kiara felt. "Did I even say thank you for it?"

"You were too shaken up by the attack."

"You were shot."

"It was my job, Majesty, and it was neither the first time nor the last."

Aros wiped his mouth with his napkin. He was visibly shaken by Nykyrian's disclosures—and he hadn't even heard the worst of them. "How arrogant am I? Here I came expecting you to fall down in gratitude at having been found by your mother. That you would embrace us and be grateful. But we have wronged . . . no, *I* have wronged you so greatly. Words cannot express the depth of my sorrow or regret."

Nykyrian wanted to throw those words at him—indeed, they even sounded rehearsed. He wanted to slash at his father the way he had slashed at him. But what was the purpose? It was the past.

Nothing could undo what had been done.

His father's eyes were shiny with unshed tears. "Had Carie not stumbled upon you today, would you have ever sought us out?"

"No, sir," he answered honestly. There would have been no need since he'd believed his mother wanted nothing to do with him.

And his earlier encounters with his father hadn't been any better. The only thing his parents could have given him that he couldn't have on his own was League amnesty, and that was something he couldn't care less about. So there had been no reason to seek them out.

Not to mention he'd been rejected enough where they were concerned. The thought of one more rejection would have overridden any stupid notion he had of trying to contact them.

Aros rose slowly to his feet. "I shouldn't have encroached tonight. Forgive me. I'll leave you in peace."

Kiara waited for Nykyrian to stop his father from leaving, but he made no move whatsoever. Unwilling to let this go, she stood. "Majesty?"

"What are you doing, Kiara?"

She put her hand on Nykyrian's shoulder and looked

down at him. "He's your father, Nykyrian, and he's making an effort. I can tell you from my own experience that even when you love your parents, there are times when you want to absolutely kill them. What happened to all of you was tragic—I know some of the horrors you have yet to share with them. But you have a chance to build a relationship from here on out. People make mistakes, but they shouldn't be slapped when they're trying to correct them. If they didn't love you, they wouldn't be here tonight."

She looked at Aros. "And believe me, Nykyrian wouldn't be here, either. You've no idea how hardened your son is—and with very good cause. But he's a *good* man. Stubborn to a fault, but decent and good to the marrow of his bones. All of you have a rare chance to rectify the past and move forward. Please don't let your anger and hurt rob you of that."

Nykyrian stared at the tiny hand on his shoulder. A few months ago, he'd have shoved that touch away and cursed her for it. But tonight he listened to her words.

And he remembered Thia.

No one had told him about her, and in his daughter's mind, he was just as guilty of abandoning her. For all he knew, Thia harbored the same feelings of rejection and isolation. The same feelings of hatred for him.

That revelation gave him pause.

How could he blame his parents for the same thing he'd done to his own child?

Yes, his father had fucked him over. Royally, to use a bad pun. But it had been done in ignorance and while his father thought he was protecting the one son he had.

Kiara was right. This was a rare opportunity, and though his feelings were mixed, he had a wife and two children to think about.

For them, he wouldn't be selfish.

Rising to his feet, he offered his hand to his father. "Why don't we forget the past and just start with this moment and go forward?"

Aros took his hand and covered it with his own. "I regret the lost years I should have had with you. I can tell you are a man worthy of the title."

Nykyrian snorted. "Not really." He looked over at Kiara. "But for my wife, I wouldn't even be human. She's the only part of me that's decent."

Kiara felt the heat rush over her cheeks at his praise.

Aros gave her a stately bow. "You are a wise and very kind woman. I can see Nykyrian has done well for himself."

She smiled as Nykyrian held her chair for her. "You only say that because you haven't run up against *my* stubborn streak."

"And you should be eternally grateful for that." Nykyrian returned to his seat.

Aros laughed as he sat down.

Now that the hostility seemed to be cleared and she wasn't afraid to leave Nykyrian alone with his parents, she leaned over to ask him where the restroom was.

"I'll show you."

Kiara blushed at the stares she collected. The only thing she hated about being pregnant was the multitudinous bathroom breaks. "Just tell me where it is and I can find it on my own."

He shook his head. "It's too crowded here. Too many exits. I don't think you should go out there alone."

Kiara's face felt so hot, she feared it would explode. "Nykyrian, please. I'm a big girl and it's a public place. People go alone to the bathroom all the time. I promise you, I don't need you standing guard outside the ladies' room. I'll be right back."

She could tell by the tense line of his jaw that he wanted to argue some more.

His mother leaned forward. "There are many dignitaries here and our guards are just outside. She'll be fine."

He released his tight grip on her wrist. "Don't be long. It's next to the bar, right behind the end of the counter."

Kiara patted his arm affectionately. "Thank you, Captain Worry. I promise you won't even have time to miss me."

Excusing herself from his parents, she made her way out the door. It didn't take her long to find her way through the dining room and to the restroom so that she could attend to her needs.

As soon as she was done, she left the bathroom and headed back. She waved at the maitre d' as he passed by her, leading another set of guests.

She quickened her steps, not wanting to leave Nykyrian alone too long with his parents. This wasn't easy on him and the last thing she wanted was for him to think she'd abandoned him, too.

"Kiara?"

She stopped, wondering who'd called her name as she skimmed the diners. Turning around, her breath caught the instant she recognized Jullien seated at a table with another man. Why wasn't he in their room with his parents?

Then again, given his past with Nykyrian, she was grateful he wasn't. No doubt that would have resulted in all-out bloodshed. And with that thought in mind, she didn't want to be around him, either.

Ignoring him, she headed back.

Jullien caught her arm and pulled her to a stop. "I

didn't expect to see you again so soon." He took her hand and placed a wet kiss over her knuckles.

Kiara stifled her shudder along with the urge to wipe her hand off on her dress.

His smile was warm enough, but she wondered at the coldness behind his eyes. "I realize you must be here with someone. But could you please take a moment to say hello to my friend? He's a huge fan of yours and he's dying for a chance to meet you."

She tried to pull away, but his hand tightened around hers. "I promised not to—"

"It'll only take a moment," he begged with those eerie eyes. "Please?"

Reminding herself that even if he was a heartless prick, he was her brother-in-law and a royal prince, she nodded her head.

Jullien led her back to his table where a blond man was waiting. "This is the woman I was telling you about."

The man stood and slowly turned to face Kiara. Her heart hammered in fear.

"You!" she gasped, recognizing him as the man who'd glared at them that day in the bay of her flat.

Aksel Bredeh.

He pressed a small blaster into her stomach. "Act like you're happy to see me or the chef will have fresh human entrails to serve the hybrid. Smile," he suggested.

Kiara wanted to spit in his face, scratch out his eyes, anything other than go along with him. But what choice did she have? She had no doubt that he would kill her if she so much as twitched.

Nykyrian will save me. Of that she had no doubt.

And one day, she would learn to listen when Nykyrian cautioned her not to do something—even if it was something as innocuous as going to the bathroom alone.

Aksel inclined his head to Jullien. "I owe you, old friend." He nudged her with the gun. "Walk slowly to the outside door."

CHAPTER 29

Nykyrian looked up from his food expecting to see Kiara entering. Instead it was the frightened maitre d'.

"Commander . . . your wife just left with a friend of Prince Jullien's. I don't think she went willingly . . . she appeared afraid of the man who was escorting her."

Cold, bitter rage gripped Nykyrian's soul and he tightened his hands into fists.

He heard his mother's gasp of fright and his father's curse. But that was all he heard before he concentrated on the raw anger pulsing through his body. He drew strength from it, because he knew he was going to kill someone over this.

His every move a study in predatorial intensity, he got up and left his parents. Hooking his coat into the loops to keep it out of the way when he reached for his weapons, he strode through the room with only one thought in mind.

Kiara.

He left the restaurant and headed for the nearby landing bay.

Nothing. Not a sign of her anywhere. She and her abductor had vanished into the night. Which left him with only one target now.

Jullien.

With that single thought burning in his mind, he made his way back through the restaurant to the area where his parents had the bastard cornered.

Jullien stood between them, whining. "I don't know what you're talking about. I haven't seen her. You must be mistaken."

Blind rage clouded his vision, but he knew better than to show it. Disregarding his parents, he grabbed Jullien by his dinner jacket and hurled him across the nearest table. Serving ware shattered and scattered, the icy tinkling sound mimicking the coldness consuming him.

Nemesis was awake, and demanded to be appeased.

Guards appeared out of nowhere to attack him as diners screamed and dove for cover. Whirling on them, Nykyrian caught the first one with a hard fist to the man's jaw that lifted him off his feet and sent him straight to the ground. The other went to shoot him. He flung a knife, catching the guard in his hand, then threw another knife into his shoulder.

The next three came at him simultaneously. He caught one by the arm and twisted so that the guard shot his companion and not him. He broke the guard's arm and used the blaster to knock the last one unconscious.

Draining the charge, he tossed the blaster down, then ruthlessly pulled Jullien off the floor by his neck. He pinned him to the wall and held him fast.

"Where is she?"

Jullien tried to claw Nykyrian's hand from his throat.

He tightened his grip as every part of him screamed out to kill the weasel where he squirmed. "Your life hinges on how fast you answer me, you bastard!"

He looked at his parents to see if they would interfere. They just stared at him as if he were an animal.

So be it. Kiara was all that mattered to him. To hell with anything else.

Nykyrian clicked his blaster setting to kill and held it under Jullien's chin. "Answer me, or the next sound you hear will be your brains hitting the wall behind you."

Sweat covered Jullien's pudgy jowls. "Aksel has her. I don't know where he's taking her."

Shock at Jullien's unexpected answer was the only thing that saved his life. Numb, Nykyrian released him.

He fell to the floor coughing and wheezing.

The room seemed to tilt as he took a step back to regroup.

Aksel has her. Those words echoed in his mind like a stinging nightmare.

His father reached out to touch him. Nykyrian moved away with a snarl. He glared at his father with all the hatred he had scorching his soul.

"She's the only reason I came here tonight. If something happens to her, I want you to know I'm coming back for Jullien, and when I finish with him, there won't be enough left to flush."

"Nykyrian . . ."

He ignored his mother's plea. She meant nothing to him. No one did except for a tiny dancer who was now depending on him for her life.

He would not let her down.

Nykyrian pushed the bell at Jayne's house. His hand was shaking and it was getting harder to hold it together.

Emotions are your enemies. They would weaken him.

Yet it was hard when all he wanted to do was scream and beat on Aksel until he had satisfaction. The pain of losing Kiara, of knowing what could be done to her—it was more than he could bear.

He truly understood Syn now. If something happened to her because of him . . .

I'd rather be dead.

As bad as losing Syn had hurt, it was nothing compared to this.

Jayne opened the door, then stood back, her mouth falling open as she saw him and his ragged breathing.

Nykyrian disregarded her shock, no longer caring who saw how much Kiara meant to him. Jayne let him into her house and pushed him toward the kitchen table. Dazed, he sat down in the first chair he reached.

Nothing seemed real. It was all like a terrifying nightmare.

"Aksel has Kiara."

Darling and Caillen stood up in front of the couch where they'd been sitting.

Caillen moved to join him in the kitchen. "How the hell did that happen?"

"It doesn't matter. We have to get to her." He looked at Caillen. "Did you find out anything more about Syn?"

"He's with my sisters, but I don't know where."

Nykyrian nodded, wishing Syn were there to help plan this damned thing. His emotions were too tangled. He couldn't think straight.

All he could think of was Kiara.

He ran his hands over his face as he pushed his raging emotions down. "What are you two doing here so early, anyway?"

"We got some bad news earlier."

Just what the fuck he needed. "And . . ."

The bell sounded again.

Jayne opened the door and for the second time that

night, Nykyrian's world spun. Driana stood outside, supporting Thia by one arm. The side of Driana's face was swollen and red, but it was nothing compared to his daughter's.

"That would be it," Caillen said under his breath. "She called on the link I had an hour ago, trying to reach you."

Driana stumbled toward him. "He's gone crazy." Her eyes were wild as tears streamed down her face.

Nykyrian shot out of his chair and crossed the room to see if his daughter was still alive. Every fear imaginable tore through him as he carefully lifted her in his arms and carried her to the couch.

Thia was covered in even more bruises than her mother. She turned her head toward him, but couldn't open her eyes for the injuries.

Nykyrian cursed.

"I didn't think he'd stop beating her," Driana broke off into heavy sobs. "I tried to protect her . . ."

Gingerly, Nykyrian touched his daughter's damaged cheek. He was going to kill Aksel tonight—tear him limb from limb and take pleasure in every scream of pain he wrung out of the bastard's worthless hide.

"It's all right," he whispered to Thia. "No one's ever going to hurt you again. I promise."

Hadrian, Jayne's husband, came out of the back of the house to tend to Thia. "I'll take care of her. I already have a doctor coming."

Nykyrian was immobilized by the turbulent state of his emotions. As much as he had hated in the past, nothing had ever prepared him for this burning ache in his soul that begged for appeasement.

Reluctantly, he stepped back from the couch. "Where's Aksel?"

"He's gone to his base on Oksana. He thinks he's safe there."

"And Kiara?"

"She's with him."

Nykyrian's lip curled into a snarl. He motioned for Darling, Jayne, and Caillen to come with him. They would get Hauk, and before the end of the night, he would put an end to Aksel, one way or another.

Kiara strained against the manacles holding her hands above her head against the wall. She had to get free.

She met Aksel's gaze from where he sat across the room with two of his men, gambling to see who would be the first to rape her. A knowing smiled curved his lips before he doubled his bet.

She looked away from them. Her heart pounded as she struggled against the chains. There had to be some way to get out of this.

Aksel looked up once more from his card game and again leered at her, seeming to delight in the way she fought helplessly against her manacles.

Kiara shivered. She prayed for release, but she also prayed for Nykyrian not to come near this place to save her. One too many times, Aksel had told her what he wanted to do to her husband.

If Aksel captured Nykyrian, he would torture him to death. Slowly and with relish.

Kiara couldn't understand such an intolerable hatred, and after being with Aksel, she was sure she would never ask him to find out why. The man was totally bended.

The door behind Aksel opened.

Kiara looked up to see Driana entering, her face red and swollen. Driana met her gaze and Kiara saw the sympathy in the blonde woman's eyes.

"Aksel, I need to speak with you. Alone."

Aksel curled his lip. "Can't you see we're in the middle of a game here?"

Driana moved forward with determined steps and upturned the table. She leveled a rifle at Aksel's head. "Tell them to leave."

Aksel's twisted laughter filled the room. "Sure. Boys, if you'll excuse us, my wife," he sneered the title, "would like to say a few words to me."

The two soldiers walked from the room, their own laughter trailing behind them as they said something in a language Kiara couldn't understand.

Aksel leaned back in his chair, arms crossed over his chest as he watched his wife, his confidence all too apparent. "What is it you want, dumpling?" Despite the endearment, Kiara didn't miss the raw hatred and threat in his voice.

"No one hurts my baby and lives," Driana snarled. "I'm going to kill you, you *giakon*." She clicked back the hammer on the rifle.

Aksel moved so fast, Kiara barely saw his arms uncoil from his chest before he had the gun out of Driana's hands. "You stupid *harita*." He jabbed the stock into her stomach so hard, it knocked her straight to the ground.

Kiara cringed in reflex.

Driana slumped to the floor, clutching her middle as she cried out in pain.

He pulled Driana up by the hair. "Where's Thia?"

Driana glared at him and, even from her distance across the room, Kiara recognized the hatred burning in the blue eyes. "I gave her to her father."

Aksel's chest pulsated with his deep, angry breaths as he looked up at Kiara.

"The hybrid?" he screeched.

Kiara winced at the tone, unable to believe a man could make it.

Driana smirked at him. "Yes. He was a better man and lover at seventeen than you'll ever be."

Aksel lifted the stock up and brought it down across Driana's back with a dull, heavy thud.

She screamed, collapsing to the floor.

Kiara buried her head in her arms and tried to block out the sound of the blows that followed in rapid succession.

Finally, Driana's screams stopped completely.

Kiara raised her head and saw Driana lying on the floor in a pool of blood. Her stomach twisted. For a moment, she thought she'd be sick.

Aksel walked toward her like a prowling lorina. He tossed the blood-covered rifle onto the overturned table.

His eyes were a stormy gray as he raked his gaze over her body and curled his lips as if the sight of her disgusted him. "Did Nykyrian ever tell you how they train assassins for The League?"

He was insane. She stared at him in disbelief, unable to comprehend his friendly tone after what he'd just done to his own wife.

Aksel reached out a cold hand and touched her cheek. "They take you for three months and keep you completely isolated." He disregarded her attempts to pull away. "You're sent into holo-rooms where they play your worst fears over and over again until you no longer fear anything."

His fingers traced the line of her chin. Kiara shivered, wishing she could do something other than stand before him in helpless expectation.

Having no other recourse, she spit at him.

A smile curved his lips at her reaction. He wiped his cheek, his eyes never wavering from hers.

As if she hadn't done a thing, he continued talking in that eerie, dead voice. "They only feed you raw meat and while you eat it, they play tapes of dying victims begging for their lives."

He held his hand out in front of her face.

She took a step back, the wall blocking her retreat.

"With this hand, I could rip your throat out." He snatched her closer to him and placed his hand over her neck. She waited for him to demonstrate his point.

But he didn't.

Instead, his cold voice droned on. "The hybrid could tear out your heart with *his* bare hands. Does that excite you?"

"You sicken me."

Aksel gave her a twisted smile, his hand stroking her cheek. "Did Nykyrian tell you he killed two instructors before he finished training? He did, you know." His hand fell away and he turned her to face him, his hands resting on her hips. "He was always better at killing, but I was the one who enjoyed it the most."

His laughter rang out, chilling Kiara.

"Nykyrian would sit for hours after a mission, staring into space, feeling *guilty*," he sneered the word like it was the worst thing imaginable. "I was a true warrior. I went out afterwards, celebrating my glory." His hands tightened around her waist.

She bit her lip, wanting some way to strike out at him.

"So why did *my* father brag about his half-breed foundling?" Aksel snarled, his face a mask of contorted rage. "It wasn't my kills he talked about with pride. It was always Nykyrian's. Always Nykyrian's!"

Kiara cried out as his hands bit into her flesh.

Aksel shoved her back against the wall with a solid thud that knocked her breath from her. He leaned his body against hers and she could feel his desire bulging against her stomach. Sweat beaded on her body as she feared his next move.

He ripped the top of her dress open.

She screamed, struggling against him in desperation.

"I should take you now," he said in a ragged whisper, running his hand over the top of her bra, oblivious to her cringing. "But I won't. That wouldn't be any fun." He stepped back and smiled at her. "When the hybrid comes for you, I have a special place for him to watch me rape you. Then you can watch me cut off pieces of his body until there's nothing left but his ear, which I shall gladly give to you as a token to remember him by."

"You're insane!" Kiara kicked out at him with her legs.

He slapped them aside. "I've never known an assassin who wasn't." With an evil laugh, he strolled casually out of the room.

Sobs racked her body. She pulled against her chains, but all she succeeded in doing was tearing the flesh off her wrists. There had to be some way she could escape. Some way she could warn Nykyrian.

Because if she didn't, they were both going to die, and it would be all her fault.

CHAPTER 30

Nykyrian and Caillen sat in the council room of The Sentella's base, reviewing data about Oksana. Hauk paced the floor behind them, his boots clicking an eerie beat against the porcelain floor that ate at his tolerance. Jayne and Darling sat across the room, listening to him and Caillen argue battle plans.

He clenched his teeth in frustration as he stared at the statistic sheets laying in front of him. A frontal assault would end in complete annihilation, and a covert attack was almost as risky. Aksel's men knew each other well enough to spot a stranger immediately.

At this rate, they'd never get Kiara out alive.

Caillen leaned back in his chair, a smile spreading across his face as he drummed his fingers against the table. "You know, I've been making deliveries to Netan Raananah. If I were to fake a shipment to him, I could smuggle you guys into Aksel's base."

Nykyrian frowned. "How could you get us through the scanners?"

Caillen tilted his chair back on two legs and put his hands behind his head, that cocky grin Nykyrian despised breaking across his face. "You're going to regret every nasty thing you've ever said about my ship. The *Malia* is equipped with special jammers no system in existence can pick up on. They'll have to do a personal inspection to verify my cargo." He laughed. "Remember, guys, I am a *third*-generation smuggler."

Hauk snorted. "Yeah, well, once we're in, they're not going to just let us sail right back out. The *Malia* is too fragile and slow to outrun a fighter."

Caillen rubbed his jaw as he thought about Hauk's words. "Her cargo hold will carry two fighters, plus passengers."

Nykyrian nodded in agreement. This was the first plan they'd come up with that stood even the breath of a chance. "That's it, then."

Darling cocked his eyebrow at Nykyrian. "Aren't you forgetting something? How do we get out once we're in there?"

Nykyrian studied Darling's face. A million thoughts passed through his mind. But it all came down to one fact.

"Simple. It's me they want. You and Caillen will stay on board the *Malia* and monitor Aksel's men and the base's corridors. Hauk will grab Kiara, get her inside his fighter and take her to safety. Jayne will be waiting to cover them once they're out of Oksana's orbit."

Hauk cocked one curious brow. "And what about you?"

"I'm bait. I'll fly out in an opposite direction with my fighter. The bulk of Aksel's troops will follow me." Nykyrian narrowed his eyes at Hauk. "You will not engage any fighter at any time. You will keep your engines full-throttle. Let Jayne take care of whatever follows you."

He looked back at Caillen. "You and Darling need to rig additional power to the *Malia* to make sure she can tel-ass as fast as you can pilot her. She's too big to dogfight."

He tossed the printouts to Darling. "Aksel will probably be holding Kiara in his office. I'll need a dummy bomb. Can you do it within the hour?"

"Is my hair red?"

Nykyrian stood. "Then we prepare."

Jayne, Caillen, and Darling left. Hauk stayed behind with a face that reminded him of Syn's doom-and-gloom attitude. Disregarding him, Nykyrian pulled his Nemesis gear from the closet.

"You're not planning on coming back, are you?"

Nykyrian paused. With a deep sigh, he pulled his boots out of the closet and set them on the floor. "I'm good, but no one's good enough to survive the number of fighters that'll be after me."

Hauk tapped his fingers against the tabletop in a pulsing rhythm that set his teeth on edge. "Why not send Kiara back in the *Malia* and let me fly out with you to fight?"

Nykyrian unbuttoned his shirt. "The *Malia* might get caught. I trust Darling and Caillen to make their way safely home. I *need* you to see to it that Kiara makes it back to her father intact."

"I'd rather keep you alive."

"Kiara is my life," Nykyrian whispered. He sat down in his chair and placed his head in his hands.

This was the only way that made sense. If he were dead, Kiara would be free, he would be free. Strangely, he felt no remorse, somehow it felt right.

He looked at the ring on his smallest finger, the ring he'd bought right before he went to see Kiara the first time after her father had shot him when she'd been dancing on Gouran. The ring he'd intended to give her as a wedding band, but hadn't been able to do it. The rows of red and black diamonds, surrounded by a gold band, glinted in the dim light.

He pulled the ring off and handed it to Hauk. "I want you to give this to Kiara."

Hauk studied it, then looked at him with a severe frown. "This is a wedding ring."

"I know. We were married according to Andarion custom a few months ago."

Hauk cursed foully.

Nykyrian ignored him. "I'm depending on you to make sure she's recognized as my widow. I know I'm asking the impossible, but she carries my child and I want her to have what's rightfully theirs."

He hesitated with the last bit, but it had to be said. "If I don't get the chance, tell her I love her, that I've always loved her and that I couldn't have been more thrilled about the baby. I just wish I could be with her when it's born."

Hauk gnashed his fangs. "I can't do this."

Nykyrian cleared his throat of the lump. "We've had too many missions together for you to go soft on me now."

Hauk looked away. "You always planned to come back from those missions."

He scoffed. "Not really. This is the first time in my life I actually want to return alive. Pretty damned ironic, isn't it?"

Hauk fastened the ring inside his pocket. "What do you want me to tell Syn?"

Nykyrian smirked, jerking his boots off. "Ask him where the hell he was when I needed him most."

Hauk's eyes widened incredulously.

Sighing, he shook his head. "I'm only kidding. If you said that, he'd start drinking again. Since he was the driving force behind The Sentella, I leave it for him to run. He's better at that shit than I am, anyway." He stood and reached for his clothes. "Also tell him that I leave my lorinas to him."

Hauk laughed. "He might dig up your body just to shoot you for that."

Nykyrian paused at the thought. He just hoped Aksel left enough of him *to* bury.

CHAPTER 31

Caillen sat at the controls of the *Malia*, waiting for clearance to enter Aksel's base. He smiled at the six crates of damson alcohol Nykyrian had graciously donated to add realism to the scam.

Man, Syn would shit himself to see that wasted . . .

The orange light on his control panel flashed, warning him the probe scanners were on. Pushing in his sequence, he smiled as the jammers hummed on.

"Take that, you *swixtas*." He laughed.

"*Malia* cleared," the controller's voice echoed. "Dock in bay eight."

Caillen complied. He loved his job. There was nothing like extreme danger to get the blood pumping and the brain juices flowing.

Several soldiers stood by, waiting to board his ship. Caillen shook his head, and double-checked the settings on his control panel.

He walked past where Nykyrian and the rest were hidden, wasting time. The longer the guards had to wait, the more anxious they'd become. It was a childish ploy, but it always served to unnerve sentries.

With a silent salute to his father's picture that hung by the door—his good luck charm—Caillen slowly lowered the ramp. He opened the hatch and stared down the barrel of a laser rifle.

"Problem?" he asked calmly.

The helmeted soldier cocked his head. "We're expecting Quiakides."

Caillen burst into mocking laughter. "Is that you, Marek?"

The soldier shifted nervously before pulling his helmet off. "Yeah."

He shoved the barrel away from his face and sauntered back inside his ship. The other soldiers filed on board and set about searching his cargo. "Buy a clue. What would I be doing with Quiakides? Hasn't anyone bothered to tell you we don't get along?"

"You run missions for him."

Caillen gave him a droll stare. "Duh. I'd run missions for the devil as long as he pays me on time."

"That's why we're searching you."

He rolled his eyes. "Like Quiakides can't afford a better mode of transportation than this dilapidated junk heap. Forget a clue, buy a brain."

Marek glanced around the ship. "Where's Kasen?"

Caillen shrugged. "Off with Shahara."

There was no missing his disappointed expression.

The other soldiers returned, shaking their heads. "He's clean."

Marek nodded. "You looking for Netan?"

"Yeah, where is he?"

"He's with Aksel." Marek replaced his helmet. "I'll tell him you're here."

Caillen took a deep breath, grateful the ruse had worked. "Do it. I don't have a lot of patience. If he doesn't get here quick, I'm leaving."

Marek motioned his group of soldiers off the ship.

"Hey," Caillen mischievously called down the ramp

after him. "I hope you don't mind, but I'm going to lock my systems down while I wait. I just can't trust you mercenary sons of bitches. You guys are a rotten group."

He saw Marek stiffen, but he didn't say a word in reply.

Caillen smiled in self-satisfaction. He locked the hatch, then ran to free the group from their hiding panels in the walls.

Darling moved to the front to monitor communications.

"You'll have to rush," Caillen said to Nykyrian, who checked his blaster's charge level. "If Netan stays on board too long, they'll get suspicious."

Nykyrian nodded, his stomach knotting. He had to succeed. There was no alternative.

They took positions on opposite sides of the hatch, ready to pounce.

Their wait was short. Netan must have really been in the mood to get flagged, as it was, he ended up unnaturally unconscious.

Caillen opened the hatch just enough for Nykyrian and Hauk to squeeze through.

With practiced ease, they made their way out of the bay and down the hallway. Darling instructed their path via a headset and map inside the *Malia*.

Nykyrian knew he could rely on his friends to get Kiara to safety. They wouldn't let him down.

"Two more corridors, then Aksel's office is on your left," Darling instructed.

Hauk moved.

"Wait." Darling warned.

Nykyrian's heart skipped a beat.

"One being coming down the hall up ahead. There's a door behind Nyk—use it."

Nykyrian led the way into the dark room.

"I hate this shit," Hauk hissed.

He ignored him.

After a few seconds, Darling's voice returned. "Clear all the way. Move."

He opened the door and went out first. They made their way to Aksel's office as quickly as possible.

He tried the door's security code, but it wouldn't budge. "Damn."

"What?" Hauk asked, scanning the hallway.

"Aksel must have changed codes."

Stifling his temper, Nykyrian quickly rewired the lock and raised the door.

He saw Kiara first. Her jubilant face looked up at him with adoring eyes that cut through to his soul. He ran across the room and jerked the chains out of their hook in the ceiling. Relief coursed through him as he picked the locks and freed her wrists from the metal cuffs.

His eyes hardened as he noticed the tear in her dress. "Did he hurt you?"

"No." She held him close. "He was waiting for you."

Nykyrian kissed her, his arms tight around her waist while he thanked God she was safe. She trembled in his arms like a frightened child and he vowed once more to see Aksel pay for this with his life.

Hauk came up behind him. "Come on, we don't have time."

Nykyrian moved away from her. Hauk was right.

"Where's Aksel?" Nykyrian asked her.

"I don't know. He left a few minutes ago."

Hauk cleared his throat and pulled at Nykyrian's shoulder. "You need to see this."

Nykyrian turned around, then went numb. For the first time, he noticed Driana lying on the floor. He crossed the room to stand over her body.

"She's dead," Hauk confirmed, stooping to feel for her pulse.

He looked back at Kiara in confusion over the grisly sight. "What happened?"

She covered her trembling lips with her hand. "She tried to kill Aksel, and he beat her to death."

Wanting to comfort her, he moved back to her and held her close for a few heartbeats, knowing this would be the last time they ever touched. "You're safe now, *shona*. But we have to hurry."

Handing Kiara over to Hauk's arms, he adjusted his link. "Darling, report."

"You're clear the whole way back."

He nodded to Hauk. "Get her home."

Hauk hesitated. He gave Nykyrian a look that told him how reluctant Hauk was to leave him to his own defenses. "Walk with peace," Hauk said quietly before dragging Kiara out of the room behind him.

Nykyrian thought over the old League phrase. He finally understood how an assassin could walk in peace.

With a sigh, he welcomed the peaceful slumber of death.

He gave them a good headstart before he left the room. Hauk would take care of Kiara.

This was the only solution.

"Walk with peace," he repeated and opened the door. He ran down the hallway back towards the bay.

"Nyk, to the right!" Darling's voice shouted.

Nykyrian whirled, his hand drawing his blaster. Too late. The shot ripped through his shoulder with a painful sear. Returning the fire, he watched the soldier crumple.

Alarms blared and flashed all around him.

Nykyrian ran full speed, trying to get to his ship

before the area was sealed off. The blast shield to the bay rumbled as it came down.

Falling into a roll, Nykyrian barely made it under the heavy steel before the huge door slammed shut with a loud crash.

Unfortunately, he stopped rolling right at Aksel's feet.

"Still predictable," Aksel sneered, clicking back the release of his blaster as he looked at Nykyrian disgustedly. "I knew one day your sense of valor and fair play would be your death."

Nykyrian rose slowly to his feet.

"Kiara's on board and safe," Darling said in his ear. "Detonation in four . . . three . . ."

Aksel leveled his blaster at Nykyrian's head. "You're so disappointing."

The blaster and dummy charge fired simultaneously.

Nykyrian dodged the blaster's shot, then rushed Aksel.

Catching Aksel about the waist, they tumbled to the ground. Aksel brought his legs up and kicked Nykyrian back, then threw himself on top of Nykyrian at the same moment Hauk launched his fighter.

Nykyrian took advantage of the distraction and landed a solid fist into Aksel's jaw. With a curse, Aksel reeled backward.

He extended the blades in his boots and kicked at Aksel, who rolled away. They went at each other with all the years of hatred manifesting in and empowering them. Slashing, punching, they gave it everything they had.

"They're scrambling fighters," Darling warned in his ear.

Nykyrian cursed. He had to get to his fighter and provide cover or they were doomed.

Aksel caught him a slice to his shoulder. Whirling around, Nykyrian returned it with a side wound. Then he kicked him back and bolted to the *Malia*.

As quickly as he could, he climbed up the small manhole underneath the craft.

"Shields up!" Caillen called.

Nykyrian lay on the steel floor, his shoulder throbbing.

Forcing the pain from his mind, he knew he had to launch before Aksel's men reached Kiara.

Within seconds, he was inside the *Arcana*, his engines roaring. He launched and flew off in the opposite direction from Hauk.

Darling updated his report. "Fighters are changing course and heading straight for you, Nyk. Three remain after Hauk. It looks clear for us, we're out of here."

Nykyrian checked his monitors. He knew Jayne could handle three fighters with little trouble, but his scanners glowed almost solid white from the amount of ships trailing him.

"Surrender." Aksel's voice snarled through his link.

Nykyrian slowed his speed so that they could catch him—the longer they fought him, the more chance Hauk would have to get Kiara to safety.

This was what he'd always wanted. A warrior's death. To go out in a blazing battle. No begging. No compromising. He would die like a man in a single moment of truth.

He'd come into this world alone and that was exactly how he was going to leave it.

Let the dance begin.

"You want me, brother? Come get some."

Unlike his, Aksel's voice betrayed his fury. "You're outnumbered fifty ships to one."

"Wow, you finally learned to count after all these years. Amazing, truly. Dad would be so proud of you."

"Shut up!"

"Why? Irritating you is so much fun." Nykyrian goaded him intentionally, knowing Aksel would break away from the squadron and engage him one on one.

"Talk about predictable," Nykyrian whispered as Aksel's fighter broke formation and dropped in behind him.

He turned his ship around and prepared for the fight. Kiara would be safe by now. Jayne should be running behind them.

By the time he was dead, she'd be home safe with her father. An icy, calm lucidity descended on him as he accepted the inevitable.

Aksel shot first.

Nykyrian barely had time to dodge the blast of color that skidded past his ship into the darkness of space. Three more shots were fired in rapid succession. Space fights were always interesting to watch. It seemed like there should be some sound. But there wasn't.

All he heard were the sounds in his cockpit and the beating of his own heart. He gripped his throttle tighter, the leather of his gloves creaking ominously.

The other fighters were moving in fast. He had to destroy Aksel first, only then would Kiara truly be safe from the psycho-bastard.

He rolled and tried to come up behind him, but Aksel was smarter than that. He banked and cut, flying out of range.

"Come back here, you wanker . . ." Nykyrian headed after him.

Aksel was headed for his troops.

"C'mon, baby," he whispered to his ship. "Don't let me down after all we've been through."

He opened the throttle and let her burn after Aksel. A dozen shots came at him. He did his best to roll through them, but one caught the side of his ship.

Cursing, he heard Aksel laughing over his link.

"We've got you now, hybrid! Prepare to die."

Nykyrian's blood ran cold as he saw his opening. It was an old trick he hadn't used in awhile, but as he'd told Kiara in her flat, always do the unexpected.

He gunned his engines, heading straight for the cluster where Aksel was. His men panicked and scattered.

Taking the opening, Nykyrian fired his ion canon.

In one brief flash of orange light, Aksel's ship disintegrated. His brother's scream was cut short as he breathed his last.

Nykyrian leaned his head back in satisfaction as he pulled his hand away from his trigger.

Mission accomplished. All that was left now was the dying.

Kiara turned in Hauk's lap as she tried to see what was behind them. She was desperate to see anything of Nykyrian. "We have to go back. We can't leave Nykyrian out there."

Hauk shook his head as he stayed on course. "My orders are to get you to safety."

She wanted to scream in frustration. "Don't you care?"

His hand jerked on the throttle, and the ship listed sideways in response. "I care more than you can imagine, but I also made a promise to him, and I'd open a vein before I'd break it." With another angry jerk, he righted their craft.

Kiara sat back, her tears scalding her cheeks. "He's out there alone," she whispered, feeling sick to her stomach.

"Jayne's gone back for him. He'll be all right."

Kiara heard the doubt underlying his words. She prayed as hard as she could. Nykyrian had to come back, he had to. The thought of him dying . . .

It wouldn't end like this. It couldn't.

She blinked in semi-relief as Gouran finally came into view.

Hauk set his links to pick up her father's frequency. It took several agonizing heartbeats before she heard her father's voice.

"President Zamir, I have your daughter Kiara, but I need a squadron of fighters. One of our pilots is in danger. If I send you the coordinates, will you assist us?"

Silence greeted the request.

Kiara's anger built to a dizzying height. "Father, if you love me at all, you will do as he asks."

"Kiara—"

"Daddy, please," she begged. A sob cut short her words, but she forced her tears aside. "Please don't do this. I finally understand why you've held on to me so close all these years. Why you locked yourself in your room at night with Mom's pictures and couldn't be disturbed. I can't lose him, Daddy. It'll kill me. Please don't make me bury him like we did Mom."

"Baby, don't cry. Please . . ." The anguish in his voice made her tears fall even harder. He cleared his throat. "I'll have a full squadron launched as soon as we can rally them."

In unison, Hauk and Kiara breathed a sigh of relief.

"Thank you, Daddy."

Hauk programmed the information into the computer. As they neared Gouran's bay, they were passed by a squadron of fighters on their way out to help Nykyrian.

Keifer met them in the hangar after they docked.

As soon as she could deplane, Kiara threw herself into his arms, grateful for his support.

Hauk jumped down from his ship and approached her father in steady, predatorial strides. "Sir, I request another ship to join your troops. I haven't the fuel to return in mine."

Her father glanced at her, his arms tightening around her shoulders. To her relief, he nodded. "There are three ships fully fueled on the other side of yours."

Hauk gave a curt nod before heading off to them.

"Hauk?" Kiara ran after him.

He paused and waited until she caught up to him. Her lips trembled as she stared at his Andarion eyes. There was only one thing she wanted, one thing left to wish for. "Bring Nykyrian back to me."

He looked past her shoulder to where her father stood. Reaching into his pocket, he pulled out a wedding ring and handed it to her. "Nykyrian wanted me to give you this."

Kiara bit back her tears as she stared at the beautiful ring Hauk dropped into her palm.

"He also wanted me to tell you that he loves you."

Her tears broke into a soul-wrenching sob. "Please save him."

"That's my plan, princess." Hauk darted to the nearest fighter.

Kiara slid the cold ring onto her third finger, her fears and worries choking her. The ring was a perfect fit.

Clenching her fist, she turned around and joined her father, wishing she were a little girl again and he could make everything alright just by kissing her hurt and holding her close, but to her deepest regret, those days were long past.

The only one who could kiss away her pain now was Nykyrian.

"Let me take you home," her father said quietly, draping his arm over her shoulders.

Kiara shook her head. "I have to know what's going on. Take me to the control room."

Despite a skeptical look, he did as she asked.

Silently, Kiara sat in a console chair, listening to the pilots' voices as they engaged Aksel's men.

Hauk thought he would never get to the battle. In a weird way, he was right. By the time he met up with the squadron, the battle was over.

His heart thundered as he surveyed the ships, looking for Nykyrian's.

Flicking open the channel to ask Jayne about Nykyrian's fate, he finally spied the *Arcana*. Four Gourish fighters surrounded the disabled craft.

"Nykyrian?" His heart lodged painfully in his throat.

". . . Fine . . . hurt . . ."

Frowning, Hauk surveyed the damage done to Nykyrian's ship. Sparks popped, only to be extinguished in the vacuum of space. From what he could see, it appeared that only one engine was functioning. And only barely.

He had no idea how Nykyrian could land the ship in its current condition.

"Do you need a tractor beam to help you land?"

"No . . . ship . . . destroy . . ."

Hauk could barely understand the broken garble. He let out a fierce curse, remembering the ship couldn't be pulled in. If they tried, it would self-destruct.

One of the Gourish fighters almost hit the *Arcana* as it listed to one side. Hauk clenched his teeth as reality crashed down on him.

Nykyrian wasn't going to make it back.

* * *

Nykyrian remained silent. His communications system was malfunctioning and he could only catch snatches of conversations from the pilots around him. He couldn't believe he was still alive.

After he'd killed Aksel, the rest of Aksel's men had blasted a dozen or more holes in his ship.

A strange catharsis had formed in his mind after the battle and, somehow, all his past sins ceased to bother him.

He stared at his control panel, which was lit up with every warning system on board. It was a miracle he even had enough directionals left to fly with.

He thought about Kiara and their baby. If he could have one wish, it would be to see his baby born, to hold Kiara one last time. He sighed, a knot forming in his chest. From the beginning, he'd known some things were not his to have.

Unfortunately, she was one of them.

Gouran loomed before him.

He rubbed his hand down his injured arm. Blood soaked his uniform, but it no longer seemed to ache—the deep cuts had severed his nerves.

Nykyrian stared at Gouran, wondering if Keifer would order him detonated before he neared the bay. Most governments would. It was standard practice to prevent damage to valuable bays.

Sighing, he leaned his head back on the seat as his eye burned. His ears buzzed from the radio's static, but even so, he could swear he heard the tender, dulcet tone of Kiara's voice calling his name.

His escorts, Hauk and Jayne, dropped away to allow him to land.

He headed into the bay, his hands automatically running through the landing procedure. Flipping switches and pulling gears, he couldn't get the fighter to slow down at all. A chill ran over him as he entered the hangar at full speed.

In one last effort to save his life, he pulled the ejection switch over his head. The force of the seat's propulsion shot him up, but not fast enough for him to clear the rear stabilizer. The impact sent him into blackness.

Kiara came to her feet with a scream, her mind unable to believe what her eyes registered.

Nykyrian's ship tore a hole through the bay's outer wall. Red and gold flames licked the craft and the length of the bay's floor and walls. Explosions erupted all over. Fire units descended to extinguish the blaze.

"I knew I should have detonated that ship," her father growled beside her.

Horrified, Kiara gaped at him, then ran from the room. Her feet carried her into the heat of the bay, and she shook from the emotions tearing at her. The scorching blaze stung her nose with its pungent odor and made her eyes water. She coughed, searching the wreckage with desperate eyes. Pieces of Nykyrian's ship were scattered everywhere.

For a moment, she thought she would collapse.

There was nothing left whole.

Nothing.

Kiara fell to her knees, gripping the edge of the wall until her hand was numb. Pain racked her soul and she wanted to die. This couldn't be real. It wasn't supposed to end this way.

Her gaze drifted over the scattered pieces, the firebots, the flames, down the bay to the opening until she saw . . .

Kiara blinked. It couldn't be.

A glimmer of hope sprouted as she saw Nykyrian lying at the opening of the bay in a black lump. Finding strength from an unknown source, she ran to him.

"Please be alive," she gasped, standing over his body that was covered in blood.

Kiara sank to her knees by his side, afraid to touch him. He lay on his back, perfectly still. His helmet was cracked and blistered.

She reached a trembling hand out to touch the gaping wound on his side. Nykyrian's chest didn't appear to be moving at all. There was so much blood. Her lips twitched as panicked terror engulfed her.

Hauk suddenly appeared and knelt on the opposite side of his body. He didn't look at her while he unfastened the lines securing Nykyrian's helmet to his uniform.

When he removed it, her world tilted.

"No," she cried, seeing the bluish tinge to Nykyrian's skin. She grasped his cold hand, which had somehow come free of its glove, to her breast and wiped the blood from Nykyrian's icy cheek.

A medical unit surrounded them, forcing Kiara away. In a daze, she staggered back, her mind too overwhelmed by grief and pain to think.

Hauk began shouting, but his words were unintelligible to her, as was everything happening around her. A fog clouded her hearing, her sight, and for a moment she wondered if this was what death felt like.

Suddenly, her father was there, holding her.

For some reason, her tears stopped and a strange lucidity invaded her grief as she watched the medics rip open Nykyrian's uniform and attach a series of machines to him. It was like she was watching players in a show moving to a script that she didn't know the ending to.

None of it seemed real.

Kiara looked at her father. "You should call his parents and tell them," she said in a hollow voice. "Emperor Aros and Princess Cairistiona. Please tell them. I-I don't think I can."

By the look on her father's face, Kiara knew he thought she'd gone mad. Maybe she had.

Only someone insane could be this calm while their world was shattered.

"Please call them," she said again. "I have to go with him." Her heart splintering into tiny pieces, she entered the medical unit and went with them to the hospital.

CHAPTER 32

Kiara sat in the waiting room of the hospital, staring out the window. Nykyrian had been in surgery for over six hours and as each new second ticked by, she felt her hopes diminish with it.

Thia lay asleep in her lap, tears still nestled in her closed lashes. Telling the girl about her mother's death, and about the father she'd only met once, had been one of the hardest things she'd ever done.

She sighed wearily, looking around the room. Jayne sat across from her, along with Caillen and Darling. Hauk just paced the hallway, saying nothing.

Nykyrian's parents were huddled with her father at the other end of the room. They were a somber group, and she couldn't help but wonder what Nykyrian would say if he could see them like this.

She held her left hand up before her, letting the dawning rays of the sun play across the red and black stones. She would give up everything she owned and ever aspired to if she could have Nykyrian back with her. She didn't even care if he were crippled, just as long as she had *him*.

Kiara held Thia close as a balm against her grief and smoothed the ruffled blonde curls off her cheeks. She hoped her baby shared his half-sister's blonde hair and green eyes.

The doors opened at the end of the waiting room.

She looked up expecting to see the doctor, shocked to find Syn entering the waiting room with a gorgeous redheaded woman. Tall and excruciatingly thin, the woman still looked lethal and cold as she surveyed them all with an intentness Nykyrian would envy.

Caillen rose to his feet and stopped the redhead before she reached her. Syn came straight to Kiara and knelt at her feet.

"How are you doing?" Concern was etched into his face as he gave her hand a comforting squeeze.

Grateful for his consideration, she patted his hand. "I've been a lot better."

"I'm sorry. I should have been here. I could've stopped him."

Kiara touched his cheek with a gentle caress. She understood that Syn ached as much as she did. "You know better, Syn. Nykyrian's far too stubborn to have listened to you. I have a feeling if you'd been here, you'd by lying in the operating room next to his."

Syn nodded, his lips in a tense line. "I guess you're right." He took a seat beside her.

She watched the woman who had the carriage of a dancer. "Who's she?"

"Shahara Dagan."

Her eyes widened in surprise. "The bounty hunter who was out to kill you and Nykyrian?"

He leaned his head back against the wall. "It's a long story."

After a few minutes, Shahara came to sit on the other side of Syn. She didn't say a word. She only took his hand into hers and held it in a way that made Kiara long to feel Nykyrian's.

They were forced to wait another hour before a doctor finally came forward. He stopped at Hauk, who pointed him back to Kiara.

She watched the doctor move toward her with cold apprehension, her heart pounding in fear at what he might say.

Syn held her hand.

"Mistress Quiakides?"

Kiara nodded, unable to speak past the lump blocking her throat.

"He's out of surgery, but he's still got a long fight ahead of him. There was a lot of damage done." His somber expression tore at her. "In all honesty, I don't know how he lived until now. I've never seen anyone survive surgery with the type of injuries he sustained. But it's a good sign that he's determined to live."

With every word, Kiara's throat tightened more.

"If you like, you may stay in his room," the doctor said quietly. "It might increase his chance of survival if someone he's close to stays with him."

"Can he hear me?"

"I doubt he can understand you, but he'll know you're there."

Jayne woke up Thia, who yawned and blinked at them as she tried to understand what was happening. "I'll take her home to stay with my children. When he's better, I'll bring her back."

Kiara offered her a shaky smile, grateful for the kindness.

"Kiara, I'll go with you," Syn said from beside her.

Patting Syn's hand, Kiara stood and followed the doctor, Syn by her side.

Hauk relayed the doctor's words to the rest of the waiting group.

The doctor opened the door to Nykyrian's room.

Kiara went weak in her knees as she saw him. Nykyrian lay on the bed with wires and tubes linking his body to several machines. He looked so pale.

But at least he was still alive.

"We had to wire his nervous system back together," the doctor said, pulling a chair out for her. "There's a good chance he'll be paralyzed if he wakes." The doctor cleared his throat. "If he makes it through the day, he should have a good chance for recovery."

Syn pulled him outside to give her a moment alone and to speak with the doctor.

Hearing the door close behind them, she made her way to the bed.

"Nykyrian," she whispered, her tears falling down her cheeks. "Don't leave me." She touched the spot on his cold skin where her tears fell. "I won't forgive you if you leave me alone."

She stared at his beautiful face, which was swollen and red where they had fused skin back together over his injuries.

Gingerly, she ran her fingers over his finely arched brows, wishing he would open his eyes and look at her. At the moment, she would even be grateful for one of his fierce snarls.

The door opened and Syn and Hauk came in. Reluctantly, Kiara released Nykyrian's hand and sat in the chair by the bed to wait and pray for improvement.

The week passed slowly as Kiara waited for a sign of recovery. Everyone had urged her at different times to leave the room for a little while and sleep in a decent bed, or eat a hot meal, but she wouldn't, couldn't, do it.

Nykyrian needed her and she wasn't about to abandon him.

On the eighth day, she dozed fretfully in her chair.

A soft moan woke her.

Kiara jolted up, her heart pounding. She looked over to Nykyrian, who stared at her with open eyes. Thrilled to see him awake, she rushed to his side.

"Baby? How do you feel?"

He swallowed and grimaced. "Like I just fought Hauk on his worst day and lost," he rasped. He tried to smile for her, but couldn't quite make it.

Kiara didn't mind. At the moment, she thought she could fly. Biting her lip, she stared at the gorgeous green eyes she'd feared she would never see again.

"I'll get the doctor." She kissed his cheek before dashing from the room.

Once outside, she hurriedly spread the news to his friends and family, seeking the doctor as fast as she could.

When she returned to her husband, his parents hovered over him with well-wishes and love. Warmth rushed over her at the sight.

The doctor shooed them all out.

With one last smile at him, Kiara followed his parents out of the room. Everyone chattered enthusiastically while they waited to hear the doctor's final verdict.

An hour later, the doctor left the room with a wide smile. Her heart pounded with hope.

"He'll be fine," the doctor said, stopping before her. "In fact, he should be able to walk normally after a few therapy sessions. He's a very lucky man."

No, I'm a lucky woman. She was weak with relief as her father drew her into his arms and held her tightly.

There was a God and he loved her!

Smiling, Kiara grabbed Cairistiona's hand and squeezed it before she went in to see Nykyrian again.

The pain on his face was excruciating for her to see. She walked over to him and placed her hand on his cheek. "You need anything?"

His gaze burned into hers. "Just you."

She took his hand into hers so that he could see her wedding band. "I'll always be here for you, baby."

EPILOGUE

Kiara watched Nykyrian wrestle on the floor with Thia, her heart light at the way he "helped" Thia with her homework. Somehow their lessons always ended up in play.

He was such a good father and a wonderful husband. Truly, she couldn't ask for better.

Sunlight poured brightly through the doors of the palace's library. Six months had passed since Nykyrian had left the hospital, and during that time, they'd moved from his solitary house nestled among the stars to live with Nykyrian's father, where he claimed she and Thia would be safe from anyone out to cause them harm.

The biggest benefit of his parents reinstating him as a royal prince and heir was that The League could no longer hunt him.

Total amnesty.

His mother and aunt had also deposed their mother on Andaria, and because of Jullien's cruelty and actions, he'd been removed from the line of succession. Neither was happy about that fact, but if they took any actions against Nykyrian or his mother or aunt, they'd be imprisoned for it.

Or executed. With Nykyrian's skills, there was always that possibility.

Now he and his daughter laughed as they rolled around on the floor. Thia shrieked, then ran away, the lorinas following her as she sprinted up the stairs.

A wide smile curved Kiara's lips as she met Nykyrian's gaze. "You must have tickled her."

Nykyrian laughed. Grabbing his cane, he pulled himself slowly to his feet. He still walked with a pronounced limp, but he was alive and well.

That was all that mattered to her.

"Are you glad Thia's with us?" he asked, pulling her into his arms.

Kiara grunted as her rounded belly collided with his firm, muscular body. She was two weeks overdue. "At the moment, I wish our son would join us."

Nykyrian's dimples flashed.

She touched the deep indentations, hoping their baby had a set as well. "Yes, I'm happy Thia's here. She told me yesterday she's glad she has a brother this time, but for the next one she wants a sister."

One corner of his mouth lifted. "I'm willing to accommodate her."

She gave him a wicked once-over. "Me, too. At least as long as I don't have to raise them without *you*."

His arms tightened around her. "I'm retired. I swear I'll never take another mission again."

Kiara gave him a doubting stare. "Not even if Syn comes in and begs you?"

He kissed her lightly on the lips. "Not even Syn can tempt me. I love you, *mu shona*, and I will never again leave you. Not for anything."

She started to speak and then gasped.

He pulled back. "Are you all right?"

Biting her lip, she nodded. "I think Adron wants to join us now."

* * *

Nykyrian paced the floor even though his leg shot pain through him. He couldn't stand this. Kiara had gone into complications during the birth and he'd been rushed out of the room to wait.

What was taking so long?

His parents were here, along with Syn, Shahara, Caillen, Darling, Hauk, Jayne, and Kiara's father.

Thia came up to him slowly. She was still intimidated by him at times. An encouraging smile curved her lips. "It'll be all right . . . Dad."

His heart clenched as she finally called him by something other than his name.

Dad . . .

It was a good sound and he couldn't believe he actually had a family.

Returning her smile, he pulled her against him and kissed her forehead. "I love you, Thia."

She squeezed him tight. "I love you, too."

Those words warmed him as he held her close. But the fear was so hard to deal with. He couldn't stand the thought of losing Kiara now.

If she lives through this, I'll never touch her again . . .

"Highness?"

He turned at the sound of the doctor's voice. Everyone came to their feet as dread hung heavy in the air.

The man smiled wide. "Your son and wife are doing fine. Would you like to see them now?"

Was he an idiot? What kind of stupid question was that? "Of course."

His father came forward. "We'll give you two a few minutes alone before we bombard her."

He inclined his head in gratitude before he followed the doctor down the hallway to Kiara's room. Relief tore through him as he realized how much he hated not having complete control over everything.

But as the doctor opened the door and he saw his wife and child, all thoughts scattered. Kiara looked exhausted, but stunningly beautiful, as she looked down at the tiny baby in her arms.

Love and joy ripped through him with such sharpness that it actually brought tears to his eyes.

Kiara met his gaze and the smile on her face slammed into him. "Hi."

"Hi." He made his way over to her, wishing he could run. Uncertain, he reached out to pull the blanket back so that he could stare at the smallest being he'd ever seen.

His son.

Nykyrian couldn't believe it. After all the lives he'd taken . . .

He didn't deserve this. That baby was too perfect and too beautiful to have come from something like him. His hand shook as the baby made a gurgling sound.

Kiara watched Nykyrian closely, wondering what thoughts were in his head. "Meet your son, Nykyrian." She held him out toward him.

Nykyrian stepped back as if afraid. "I don't think I should."

She arched a brow until she realized something. "You've never been around a baby, have you?"

He shook his head. "I didn't know they were that small."

She laughed. "He won't be for long." Reaching out, she pulled him toward her. "You won't hurt him."

Nykyrian swallowed as she put the baby in his arms. It was the most surreal moment of his life. He was a father . . .

While he'd grown used to the title with Thia, it wasn't quite the same as looking down at this tiny infant, and it made him ache that he hadn't been there when his daughter had been born.

He'd missed her entire childhood and he hated that fact. But he would never miss a second of Adron's. He met Kiara's gaze. "Thank you."

"For what?"

"For giving me a life worth living. I know I'm not worth it, and that I don't deserve it, but I swear to the gods I finally believe in that I will spend every moment I have left making you happy and trying to be worthy of you."

Kiara's eyes filled with tears. "Nykyrian, you are worth *everything* to me. And you always will be."

And when she pulled his lips to hers and kissed him, for the first time in his life, he truly understood love. It wasn't just an intangible emotion, it was when his own happiness was found by making her happy. It wasn't something found in a grandiose gesture. It was found in the simplest form.

A single smile that made a cold-blooded assassin weak in the knees.

Read on for an excerpt from Sherrilyn Kenyon's next book

BORN OF FIRE

Coming soon from St. Martin's Paperbacks

"Don't move," a smooth, lilting feminine voice ordered.

Syn arched one brow. It wasn't every day someone got the drop on him, especially a woman who had a voice that leant itself to seduction.

"Or what?" He wished he could catch a glimpse of whomever had outsmarted him. She had to be something, because this *never* happened to him.

She clicked off the safety release of her blaster.

Syn wasn't prone to panic, and having people level a weapon at him was pretty commonplace, but he didn't usually face unseen attackers.

Especially not in his home.

"Are you an assassin or tracer?" he asked.

"Free-tracer."

Free-tracers, unlike assassins, had a conscience, as a rule. And since he was still breathing and not dead, it told him she was going after his living contract which gave him a lot of latitude in dealing with her.

"Good." He snatched her blaster from her hands.

A blast of red sizzled up toward his ceiling, searing a long black streak across the white paint. He cursed at the mark. He'd fought too long and too hard to drag himself out of the streets and have a nice home for someone to come in and start destroying it.

"No one messes up my place." He grabbed a small, silken wrist and jerked the woman into his view. Shock jolted him as he stared into the face of a startled angel. Damn, she was beautiful.

In that instant of hesitation, she drove her knee straight into his groin.

Pure agony spread through him. Gasping, he doubled over with a sharp curse.

Shahara pulled the reserve blaster from her boot and leveled it at C.I. Syn: Rapist, Murderer, Traitor, and Filch. He was huge and powerful. She'd have to watch him closely if she were to succeed. Keeping her eyes on him, she bent her knees to retrieve the other two blasters from the floor.

The man in front of her was not the usual type she was used to dealing with. Not only was he more refined, but something proud and primal emanated from every molecule of his body. Only one word could define it.

Sexy.

And she was far from immune to it.

Unlike the other class three and four felons she'd traced, this one possessed an air of sophistication. When he spoke, it wasn't in a gruff ignorant street dialect, it was with a fluid, baritone voice that resonated deep from within him. His cadence and syntax were that of an educated man or an aristocrat, not a lowly filch.

With a deep breath, he recovered himself from her kick—something she'd never seen a man do so quickly before. He moved away from her with the lithe powerful grace of a predator.

Granted, he was still limping, but there was an unmistakable fluidity.

That was it. That was what she sensed from him. He

had a raw animal magnetism. He moved like a caged panther—sleek, rippling, deadly.

Vicious.

And he moved like lightning. Before she realized what was happening, he had her completely unarmed. She kicked him back. He spun and shoved her into the wall.

Shahara used the rebound to propel herself at him and caught him a stiff blow to his jaw. Grunting, he grabbed her. She flipped up and kicked him back.

Syn cursed at her skill. She was incredible when it came to fighting. And every time he tried to pin her, she escaped. He hissed as she caught him another blow to the gut.

Kill her!

But he had a bad suspicion about her identity and if she was whom he thought . . .

Better to have her beat on him than the alternative. Out of her sleeves, two knives appeared. She moved at him, slashing. He put his arm up to block her attack. Their forearms collided, then she swiped his arm with the blade. It sliced straight through his flesh.

"Son of a . . ."

She stomped his foot. "Surrender, convict. I don't have to take you in alive."

He glared down at her as he tried to pin her again and failed. "Then you better get ready to kill me, 'cause that's the only way I'm going in."

Shahara head-butted him, then scissor-kicked his chest. In a fluid roll, she scooped her blaster up from the floor and angled it at him.

He finally froze.

"Cute attack," she sneered, waving him back into the bedroom with the barrel of her weapon. This time she knew to keep a good distance between them.

His eyes blazing obsidian fire, he obeyed in a manner that told her he didn't often cooperate with orders.

No, she could tell by the arrogant, taunting smile that this man was a leader or a loner.

Never a follower.

"Not half as cute as yours." He rubbed his groin meaningfully.

She shrugged at his sarcasm. "He who waits, loses."

The fierce scowl Syn gave her told her he didn't like the old Gondarion proverb at all.

Disregarding the look, she tossed him a pair of cuffs. They landed at his booted feet with a soft jingle. "Put those on quick or I'll blast you straight to hell."

He picked the cuffs up in his fist as if they disgusted him. His black gaze hardened and she swore she could actually smell the danger that radiated from every pore of his body.

She tensed her finger over the trigger, expecting him to toss the cuffs in her face. It wouldn't be the first time a convict had reacted that way and she had a few more tricks to unleash if he chose that action.

A loud whistle blared in the room behind her. Startled, she snapped around to make sure someone wasn't coming in to help him. Before she could focus on what the noise was, Syn's hands closed around hers.

How had he moved that fast? He should still be on the other side of the room.

Her heart racing, she struggled for her weapon, kicking and punching at him with all the fury coursing through her body. If he got her blaster away, he'd kill her for sure.

His grip tightened around her hand, numbing her fingers until she could barely feel the roughened grip of her blaster. She tried to head-butt him, but he moved too fast.

To her horror, the blaster dropped to the floor with a heavy thud.

Cursing, she reverted to her strict training and punched at his throat.

Syn caught her hand in his before she could make contact with his windpipe. Wrenching her arm painfully behind her back, he picked her up and tossed her over his shoulder.

Shahara cursed as she struggled. In spite of her best efforts and blows, he knelt down, retrieved the blasters from the floor, then tossed her on his bed.

The soft, lump-free mattress startled her for the briefest moment before true panic consumed her. He stood a few feet away from the bed, gazing down at her with dark, lust-filled eyes.

Her vision dimmed. Snarling, she dove for him with only one goal—to escape with her life and body intact.

Syn switched his blaster setting from kill to stun and shot her in the shoulder before she could reach him.

A soft gasp left her lips. Her eyes widened as she clutched at her shoulder, then she crumpled to the floor.

A twinge of guilt annoyed him. He'd been stunned enough times to know she'd have a vicious headache when she woke up.

But what other choice did he have? She seemed to be a determined little *cozu*.

Shaking his head in bitter amusement, he knelt beside her to check her pulse. Satisfied he hadn't hurt her, he took a good look at her peaceful features. Damned if she wasn't the most attractive woman he'd ever thrown onto his bed.

The Future Is Coming.

THE LEAGUE IS HERE

Surrender to a brave new world of trained assassins and lethal lovers, when danger rules the night, passions are on fire, and those who dare to defy The League walk on thin ice…

Read all of The League novels by #1 bestselling author SHERRILYN KENYON

BORN OF NIGHT

BORN OF FIRE

BORN OF ICE

Hungry for a Midnight Snack?

Sign up for Sherrilyn Kenyon's **Free Short Story**

...and sink your teeth into a brand-new tale

from the world of the Dark-Hunters...

WINTER BORN

Bad Moon Rising

The War Is On and Time Is Running Out...

Fang Kattalakis isn't just a wolf. He is the brother of two of the most powerful members of the Omegrion: the ruling council that enforces the laws of the Were-Hunters. When war erupts among the lycanthropes, sides must be chosen and enemies must become allies. But when the woman Fang loves is accused of betrayal, he must break the law of his people to save her.

SherrilynKenyon.com

**They are Darkness. They are Shadows.
They are the Rulers of the Night.**

They Are The Dark-Hunters.®

**Don't miss a single title
from the world of the Dark-Hunters!**

Fantasy Lover

Night Pleasures

Night Embrace

Dance with the Devil

Kiss of the Night

Night Play

Seize the Night

Sins of the Night

Dark Side of the Moon

Devil May Cry

The Dream-Hunter

Upon the Midnight Clear

Dream Chaser

One Silent Night

Acheron

Dream Warrior

Bad Moon Rising